A

HAUNTING
in the
ARCTIC

C.J. Cooke is an internationally bestselling, Edgar- and ITW-nominated gothic novelist. She is the author of *The Lighthouse Witches*, which is currently being developed for screen by The Picture Company for StudioCanal. Her books have been critically acclaimed for their atmospheric use of place and historical research, and have been published in 23 languages. Born in Belfast, C.J. has a PhD in Literature and teaches Creative Writing at the University of Glasgow, where she also researches creative writing interventions for mental health. She lives by a river with her husband, four children, and two dogs.

Keep in touch with C.J.:

www.cjcookeauthor.com
@cjcooke_author
@CJessCooke
/CJCookeBooks

Also by C.J. Cooke

The Guardian Angel's Journal
The Boy Who Could See Demons
I Know My Name
The Blame Game
The Nesting
The Lighthouse Witches
The Ghost Woods

A
HAUNTING
in the
ARCTIC

C. J. COOKE

HarperCollins*Publishers*

HarperCollins*Publishers* Ltd
1 London Bridge Street,
London SE1 9GF

www.harpercollins.co.uk

HarperCollins*Publishers*
Macken House,
39/40 Mayor Street Upper,
Dublin 1
D01 C9W8

First published by HarperCollins*Publishers* 2023
1

A catalogue record for this book is available from the British Library

ISBN: 978-0-00-851595-9 (HB)
ISBN: 978-0-00-851596-6 (TPB)

This novel is entirely a work of fiction.
The names, characters and incidents portrayed in it are
the work of the author's imagination. Any resemblance to
actual persons, living or dead, events or localities is
entirely coincidental.

Typeset in Sabon by Palimpsest Book Production Limited, Falkirk, Stirlingshire

Printed and bound in the UK using 100% Renewable Electricity by CPI Group (UK) Ltd

MIX
Paper | Supporting
responsible forestry
FSC™ C007454

This book is produced from independently certified FSC™ paper
to ensure responsible forest management.

For more information visit: www.harpercollins.co.uk/green

for all who live with
the many hauntings
of trauma

The man was covered in seaweed, gnarled fronds covering him like garlands. He was fully clothed and curled up by his bed, but his face had been gnawed to the bone, and the bloodied scratches on the wood of the door matched his missing fingernails.

The two coastguard officers shared a long look.

They circled the body slowly before crouching to inspect what had become of his legs. Beneath the torn fabric of his trousers they could see that the flesh had swollen and black-ened. The mottled bare feet had split in two, no sign of the toenails, his toes lengthened to flaps of meat that had fused strangely together in a clean bisection. Like grotesque fish tails.

Dental records would confirm that he was Dr Diego Almeyda, a twenty-eight-year-old postdoc from Argentina. He had spent his last months collecting ice samples with fifteen colleagues on board the *Ormen*, a barque-rigged steam whaling ship from the late 1800s, repurposed as a research ship. Contact from the research team ceased a week ago, and the

1

Ormen had drifted almost a thousand kilometres from its base in Svalbard until the Russian coastguard pulled up alongside it. Cups of coffee paused on a table in the cabin, slices of burnt bread in the toaster. Bloodstains on the floor. Bullet holes puncturing the sails.

Pirates, perhaps.

But the man's death was harder to explain. The door was locked from the inside. His face and feet were mutilated. He was the sole occupant of the ghost ship, the bodies of the other researchers unrecovered.

These were the only facts.

They found pictures under the mattress, penned by Almeyda – presumably – in a frenzy.

All depicted the same scene: a figure on the upper deck of the ship.

They were a series of images, as though for a flipbook, and when organised they seemed to form a coherent spool of movement: each hastily drawn sketch portrayed a figure of a woman who grew gradually closer to the wreck, her face always turned away, until the last image. That sketch filled the page, a macabre spectacle of a woman with seaweed for hair and white, sightless eyes.

And the chilling words on that last image, devoured now by flame:

She is on board

PART ONE

the selkie wife

Nicky

I

May 1901
Dundee, Scotland

Nicky woke to gold morning light effervescing in the eaves of her parents' house. It was May, but in this small room winter lingered, the old fireplace unused on account of the coal stains that had ruined the stair carpet.

She pressed her feet on the floorboards, heat from the downstairs fire held in the wood slowly creeping into her bones. The mirrored door of the Georgian wardrobe threw back the white fangs of her nightdress collar, two dark curtains of her unpinned hair framing her face. Recently, her temples had begun to shimmer with strands of grey. She was only twenty-seven, and at forty-nine her mother Mhairi still had a vivid red crown, even when she removed her hairpieces. But they said grey hair was the flower of worry, and she had spent the last twenty months in two halves – her body here in Dundee, installed in her parents' house like a child, and her mind with Allan in the Transvaal, fighting the Boers.

She frightened herself by struggling to recall the exact line of his jaw, the texture of his palms, his smell. Her own husband. So far, marriage had not been as she expected.

But then, she had not expected a war.

She washed quickly by the sink, fastened her corset, slipped her petticoat and dress over her head. Then she pinned up her hair, clipping two long ringlets that had come from her sister's head just above her ears. Her own hair was poker-straight; not even the hottest iron produced a lasting curl.

It was Monday – the day Allan's letters arrived at their house on Faulkner Street. The postman came at nine, which was yet two hours away, but on Mondays she took the chance to spend the day there, beating the rugs and airing the rooms. It had been her mother's idea for her to move back into her parents' home while Allan was dispatched – a woman living alone was *indecent*, whether wedded or not – but she had surprised herself by how indignant she felt at this requirement. Wasn't war indecent? And yet. There was certainly nothing wrong with her childhood home – Larkbrae was one of the finest homes in Dundee, sitting proud above the Tay – but she felt she had moved backwards in time, into her old life.

The main reason she went, aside from collecting mail, was to feel the embrace of her marital home, and all its promise: a future with Allan.

From the floors below, a voice sailed through the shadowy hall. 'Wheesht, now. I've got you!'

She rushed downstairs to find her father, stooped over, his shirt and waistcoat unbuttoned, revealing his vest. Something was clasped between his palms, his strong arms held at right angles as he addressed whatever he held. His hands were covered in soot. Then, sensing her there, he looked up and tilted his chin. 'Open the door.'

She turned and unlocked the storm doors, watching as he inched past, two small wings poking through the gaps in his hands. He had caught a bird, and from the soot marks on his forearms and vest she gathered it had fallen down the chimney.

'Steady, now,' he said, stepping out on to the porch with

6

his arms outstretched. He lifted his top hand away to reveal a sparrow crouching in his palm. A second later, it shot off towards the trees.

Her father clapped his hands together as he looked after it, and she watched him carefully, unnerved. George Abney wasn't a man to care about small things, and never a man inclined to save a creature that had fallen into the grate. He looked like he'd not slept all night, still in yesterday's shirt and waistcoat, his eyes shadowy and the grey hair at the sides of his head ruffled.

'Are you well, Father?' she asked.

He kept his pale eyes on the garden ahead, searching after the bird. 'Yes,' he said. 'I think I am. I think I am.' He turned to her. 'Have you time for a word?'

She raised her eyebrows, certain now that something was amiss. Her father never sought her out, never asked to speak to her. They were too similar, her mother always said. Each as headstrong as the other, long grudges held.

'Is something the matter?' she asked, following him slowly along the hall to his office at the other end. He didn't answer, but she noticed he walked as though carrying an unseen stone on his back, weary from wrestling all night with the cares of his mind. Except her father never worried, never struggled. George ran one of the oldest and most successful whaling companies in Scotland, and he did so by being bullish and fierce, and sometimes cruel. Whaling was as perilous as it was necessary, for without blubber the streets and the factories would lie dark. A venture of blood and bone to sequester light.

Though George never ventured out on the ships, he had his own tempests to weather, such as the loss of three ships in as many years, and all his profits with them. The newspapers had taken pleasure in printing their speculations about the finances of Abney & Sons Whale Fishing Company, with hints that the crew of George's only remaining ship, the *Ormen*, were set to down tools in protest at their conditions.

Inside George's office, the heavy curtains were still drawn from the night before, walnut panelling and bookcases cocooning them. A lamp on his desk set an amber glow across his face, and when he closed the door she saw he was troubled, a crease deepening in his forehead.

'I want to apologise,' he said, moving to his desk.

'For what?'

'I did something a few days ago that I deeply regret,' he said, looking down at something. A letter. 'But today, I shall put it right.'

She frowned, wondering if she had missed a conversation. 'Put *what* right?'

He pulled out the desk chair and sank into it as though the metal inside him had splintered. Should she call Cat, her sister, or her mother? Was he having a heart attack? There was a glass of water on the table next to the sofa; she passed it to him, watching nervously as he raised it to his mouth with a trembling hand. Then she pulled up another chair and sat close.

'Papa?'

She didn't know what else to say. She couldn't bring herself to touch him. They'd not touched in years. She knew he loved her in that deeply unacknowledged way that their family seemed to love each other, and she was suddenly moved by the thought that he might die.

'The company is folding,' he said, dabbing his mouth with a handkerchief. 'I've not told your mother. You're not to say a word.'

The words landed like stones. *The company?* He couldn't mean the family business.

'I won't tell a soul,' she said, staggered now by the realisation that she was the first to receive this terrible news. He hadn't told her mother. Of course not. It would devastate her if it were true.

'We may need to sell this house,' he said, nudging papers across the desktop with his fingertips, a general tabling his battle strategy. 'I've written to Uncle Jim.'

'For what reason?'

'To see if he would help us move to Toronto.'

'Toronto?'

She'd suspected things with the company were tricky, especially after the last ship sank in the Arctic. Many said that Dundee was going the way of Aberdeen, whaling no longer profitable. The lost ships weren't being replaced.

But this was something else. Her father wasn't one to panic. He was never *afraid*.

'You need to be careful,' he said, coughing hoarsely into his fist. 'I'm going to put things right. But I need you to keep out of sight for a while.'

She reeled. Out of *whose* sight, exactly? How would the collapse of the company put her in danger?

'Papa,' she said again, touching his arm. 'What things? Why do I need to keep out of sight?'

He held her in a long look, his eyes softening. 'You used to sing as a child. You had such a beautiful voice. My little songbird. Why did you stop?'

She searched his face, her thoughts cartwheeling.

'You had such a lovely voice,' he said, his voice a whisper, and she felt his hand against her cheek. He hadn't touched her when Morag died. Not even at the graveside, when she fell to her knees.

He turned away and waved a hand, his voice hard again. 'Go on, now. We'll talk more later.'

She felt panicked, the strangeness of the situation forming

9

a hard knot in her throat. 'What is it you're going to put right?' she asked as he made for the window, throwing open the curtains. A spear of light thrusting through the room.

'Go on,' he said again, and she knew he would say no more.

Outside, she saw a bird in the branches of the old willow tree that poured down to the path. A sparrow, she thought, its wings still clotted with soot.

II

Nicky's marital home on Faulkner Street was a brisk twenty-minute walk followed by a five-mile tram ride from her parents' house on Douglas Terrace. She took the road that ran alongside the River Tay to hear the slap of the waves against the shoreline buffer and the call of the gulls. This part of the city was quiet, without the sound of traffic or industry, and without the cacophony of accents that swirled in the heart of Dundee. Russian, American, Indian, Polish – Dundee was a global city, now, nicknamed 'Juteopolis' for the boom in the jute trade. It was good for many – sixty jute mills providing jobs for fifty thousand. The poverty that had beaten down generations beginning to ease.

She turned the strange encounter with her father over in her mind, unstitching his words from the fabric of memory as though she might find a hidden chamber inside their echo, a secret meaning.

I need you to keep out of sight.

None of it made sense. Even if the company was going to fold – a catastrophic event – she could find no reason that it should put her at risk. And for her father to share this news with her first, before her mother, or her brother . . . Perhaps there was something more insidious at work. Her father's mind unravelling. Yes, that was it. George Abney never said sorry. He refuted, recompensed, or sought revenge. But, as a rule, he did not apologise.

She cut through Dawson Park to the tram stop just beyond the entrance. Ten minutes later, she was sitting on the top deck, admiring the elevated view of the water as they moved along Dalgleish Road. She thought of the Saturdays she and Allan would take the tram into town, always sitting on the top deck like this, high above the traffic. Often it was too busy to find a seat together. The seat now in front of her was empty, and she imagined Allan sitting there, reaching a hand behind him to clasp hers.

Letting her know he was there.

The city was thick with smoke and loud as cannonfire, the earthy smell of jute filling her nostrils. Her mother hated it, refused to go into town when the whale ships set sail for Greenland. There were always crowds at the quayside, waving and throwing oranges on the deck for good luck. Everyone knew most of the sailors were blind drunk for the departure, and not because they were happy to be leaving – some of them wouldn't return, and they knew it. Disease, drownings, and starvation characterised many a whaling voyage. Even now, when the ships were double-hulled and steam-powered, the journey was no less perilous.

But often, there was excitement.

She had been with her father the day one of his ships, the *Ormen*, returned from Greenland. It was usual for them to return with a haul of walruses, penguins, and Arctic foxes, but this time they came home with polar bears – and they were still alive. One of the bears managed to break free and roamed the docks, roaring like thunder. She had never seen such chaos. The crowd dispersed like a blown dandelion clock. Some of the shipowners jumped into the Tay, tuxedos and all, black hats dotting the surface of the water. Her father had pulled her on to a side street, but at the last moment she turned back – and locked eyes with the bear.

It was so much larger than she could have imagined, bigger than the lions she'd seen at the circus. Fur the colour of whipped butter, eyes like lumps of coal. It was the paws that startled her – plate-sized, with curled black claws that could spill her guts with a single swipe. For the first time, she faced the reality of her own death. It chilled her, the nothingness she saw spiralling ahead. An instinct that superseded every Sunday School lesson and Bible reading she'd ever heard.

That night, and for many after, she had lain in bed, digging her nails into her arm, reassuring herself that she was still alive.

Faulkner Street was a row of narrow terraced houses – like sardines, her mother sniffed – on the east side of the city, close enough for Allan to walk to work. He was a clerk at Camperdown Mill, a job he hated but did out of duty. He had set his sights on becoming a professional footballer, having earned a cabinet full of trophies in his youth, but an accident with an ambulance had left him lame and put paid to his ambitions.

She reached the house at lunchtime, pausing in the narrow hallway to close her eyes and take in the smell that clutched so many memories. Arriving here on the eve of their wedding day, heavy snow on the rooftops, the whole house freezing cold. Making love in the bed upstairs beneath the blankets, the wooden bedframe banging against the wall and Mrs McGregor on the other side banging back, telling them to shut up. Listening to Allan, naked and drunk, as he played Chopin on the old upright piano by the fire.

Nicky scooped up the pile of letters on the doormat and sifted quickly through, then again to be sure. Bills, a greeting card from her friend Milly, who was working as a governess in London. Nothing from Allan.

13

She pressed a fist against her mouth, determined not to cry. It didn't mean anything bad, it didn't. Many Mondays passed without a new letter to pore over, to scrape away the worry that congealed over her heart afresh each day. Allan's squadron had probably been reassigned, or the Transvaal postal service had been held up. It didn't mean he was dead.

It was just past nine, dust motes dancing in the morning light. She looked over the red velvet armchairs in the bay window, the bronze Axminster rug that weighed more than a man, and which she had to hoist up in the yard outside, using a winch to clean. The warm, dry day was perfect for it, she knew that, but her heart felt like a weight was pressing down on it.

She headed upstairs to the silent bedroom at the front of the house, the windows there looking on to the row of terraces opposite. She straightened the made bed, then gave in to the urge to fling open the oak armoire. There, Allan's shirts hung in a row, the sleeves flat. And a single blue dress, half the length of the shirt.

Dominique

I

I'm lost.

I take out my torchlight and shine it on the spiky basalt pinnacle thrusting out of the ground, about thirty feet tall. Is it the same one I passed by before? I'm not sure. The thing is, there are lots of spiky pinnacles around here, because Iceland is made almost entirely of volcanic rock. I lost internet connection miles back, so I'm having to rely on the map I drew to direct me.

I turn all the way around, my torchlight bouncing off the heavy mist that's rolling in from the sea. It's like I'm wrapped in mist, the landscape around me blotted out entirely. My watch says it's two minutes after midnight. I should probably set up camp, regain my strength. A sob lodges in my throat. I'm completely disoriented. I have no phone signal, no internet signal out here. I'm hours from civilisation. Nothing but lava fields and crags, towering cliffs looming over me, shadowed against the night sky.

I press on, stumbling forward into the mist. I'm fighting the urge to sink to my knees and fall asleep. Maybe I should stop being so stubborn and just call it a night.

No, I'll keep going. Just another half hour and then I'll stop.

I'm headed to Skúmaskot, an old shark fishing village on the northern tip of Iceland, twenty-five miles away from the Arctic Circle. No one has lived in Skúmaskot for over forty years, the old school, a small church, and all the old fishing huts and turf houses lying empty. The reason I'm aiming to explore the *Ormen*, a shipwreck that has been beached there since 1973. If I wake up in the morning and find I was right next to the ship all along, I'll be livid.

It's definitely the wrong time of year to be this far north, and definitely not smart to be trekking somewhere so remote. The weather is ferocious, winds that rip my coat from my shoulders and ice that seals the rocks and encases the cliffs. But the timing is crucial – the Icelandic government have decided that the ship is a hazard to wildlife, and in four weeks' time they are going to drag the *Ormen* out to sea and let her sink. Something about wanting to create an artificial reef and protect local wildlife from the chemicals that might seep out of the structure.

The *Ormen* isn't your typical shipwreck – she's partly grounded, partly in the tide. And she has quite a history, stretching all the way back to the nineteenth century. First, she was a whaling ship, built in Dundee and sent out to Greenland every summer to be filled with blubber; then she was refitted as a research ship for scientists collecting sea ice off Svalbard.

There should be scores of explorers heading to see her before she drowns, but the *Ormen* isn't typical in that aspect, either. She's ridiculously remote, hanging off the very tip of Iceland, touching the Arctic Circle. Nothing but snow, volcanos, and the occasional polar bear that has crossed the sea ice from Greenland.

I'm out here in the middle of nowhere because I want to document the wreck before they destroy her. I want to phoenix that bitch, give her a chance to roar into a second life before they smash her into matchsticks.

First, I have to find her. And that is proving harder than expected.

Iceland is like the set of a science fiction movie: sawtooth mountains crowned with clouds, glaciers clotting the valleys, snarls of steam rising here and there from hot springs like the breath of a slumbering monster. Now that darkness has set in and the weather has turned savage, it feels a little as though the monster is wakening, the ground shifting beneath my feet and the coastline disappearing behind fog. There are no roads this far north, no trails, just lava fields, which are treacherously uneven, especially now I can't see where I'm going. I thought if I kept the ocean in my sight, I would eventually arrive at Skúmaskot.

The hail dies down, a gibbous moon bright as a new coin. I'm in a deep valley, snow-capped mountains rearing up at either side. A few minutes later, a gorge to my right reveals a glimpse of ocean, the moon transforming it to hammered metal. I head towards the gorge, stepping gingerly across ice-encrusted rock and beneath a thundering waterfall towards the coastline.

Icy mist peels off the waterfall in billowing sheets, but I keep to the course and hit sand for the first time since I started walking. It's an exciting moment, and when I turn to the left I can make out an inlet. A bay.

Skúmaskot.

I start running, squinting into the gloom. I can make out the outline of a roof, then another. A row of buildings, no lights. My heart is racing. I don't want to be wrong. I've passed loads of abandoned buildings, strange houses in the middle of nowhere. Always empty. If it *is* Skúmaskot, the *Ormen* should be just past the rocky outcrop next to the mouth of the inlet.

My legs are burning from the walk, but I clamber up the rocks that jut out into the tide, and it's then that I see her.

Oh my God. She's right there. The *Ormen.*

I throw off my backpack and stagger towards her, down the side of the rocks on to the beach. I start to cry, huge, gulping sobs of relief that I'm finally here. She is so much bigger and more majestic than I could have imagined. Most abandoned structures are woefully forlorn and sad, but the *Ormen* is still intact, still partially floating, craggy volcanic rock clutching the bow as though the manmade and natural entities are fusing together. The *Ormen* was barque-rigged, meaning that she went to sea with a full sail plan across three masts, but these have long since been broken. The remains of the rig are visible, three tall prongs marking where the masts used to be. Holy shit, she is a *goddess*.

The tide is in, and I dodge away as it pounds the beach in mountainous squalls. Iceland is famous for 'sneaker' waves which can suddenly spring from the relative safety of the tide, pouncing on unsuspecting walkers and dragging them far out to sea where strong currents prevent them from swimming to shore. One of the first things I'll do is map the times of the tide and mark a boundary line with stones.

There's a ladder still in situ, probably placed by other explorers to allow easy access to the deck. I run my torchlight up the metal strakes. I scan the ladder carefully for any sign of barbed wire or anti-trespass paint. I've been bitten by that before.

At the top of the ladder, I grip on to the bolts holding it against the hull and throw a leg over the side. The deck is slippery with ice and debris, so I slide my feet forward, pausing to stare up at the main mast ahead. It would have been one hundred and ten feet tall back in the day, a crow's nest at the top. Even at around forty feet it towers above, bowline and topmast hooks glinting in the moonlight like instruments of torture.

The sensation of stepping on deck is unreal, like entering another realm. I've made it. I am *here*.

II

I pause on the deck. The *Ormen* feels alive, as though she's been waiting for me. The wind whips my hair into my face, and suddenly all the time I've spent looking for her doesn't matter. I was exhausted just moments before, but now I'm energised, my heart clanging with excitement.

I take a deep breath and look around, taking in every detail of the ship. The *Ormen* seems to have a life of her own, her wooden planks creaking and groaning as they shift with the tide. The wind howls through the rigging, creating a haunting melody that echoes across the desolate landscape. For the longest time, I've felt a strange pull towards her, as though she's been calling out to me, inviting me to explore her secrets. And now I'm here, the restlessness has ceased. I can't wait to start documenting her history.

I pull out my camera and start clicking away, capturing every inch of the ship. The darkness is thick as treacle and the deck is covered in snow, but I find gnarly bits of plastic and fishing tackle poking through, adjusting my flash to capture it. I snap shots of an old oil can, a coil of rusted chains, and a rickety crow's nest hanging precariously from the damaged mainsail. I wonder how many men risked their lives climbing to that crow's nest. The *Ormen* must have seen it all.

Opposite the top of the ladder propped against the hull is a long cabin, clearly not part of the original ship. It's an addition from the 1960s for the research team. It looks as if a caravan has been dropped on the top deck. I use my knife to prise off the board that has been nailed to the cabin door.

Inside the cabin, a wild stench hits me – vegetal, with a definite undertone of public toilet. I draw my headlight across an upturned Formica table, smashed-up chairs, hardback books splayed on the floor like dead moths.

I step carefully through the mess, tracking my torchlight slowly across the ground to check for rotten flooring, and snares. Traps are everywhere in places like this – sprung jaws to take a grown man's leg off, wooden planks embedded with vertical nails, a thin-bladed wire fixed neck-high. Poison and asbestos are the most insidious, and the rifest.

The floor seems OK, and no sign of any snares, thank God – usually finding one means there are a lot more hidden in places you'd never suspect, and it takes ages to root them out.

Most of the cabin windows have been broken, but I have a solution for that. Perspex is a great insulator and keeps flies and scavengers out, so I have sheets of it in my backpack. The cabin is about four metres by three, and I'm amazed it's structurally sound. Clearly it has been visited by many explorers before. There are a couple of rugs on the floor, a dining table, and a sofa made up of old crates tied together with rope, pillows laid across them as seat pads.

My torchlight settles on a hatch in the floor, roughly in the centre of the room. I slip my fingers through the metal loop of a handle, pulling gently to test it. The hatch is stiff, but I feel it give a little each time I pull. I get down on my knees to get a better grip, and to shine my torchlight down into the crack. I don't want to open it to a blast of toxic gas. Easy does it.

Gradually, it lifts. I shine my torch into the darkness below, noticing the rush of cold air and the stale, mineral smell on the back of it, and the black stairs that lead down on to another deck.

The stairs are mossy, so I descend backwards, gripping the edges of the steps. The lower deck is long with doors leading off to cabins. Most of this level would have been used to store whale blubber when the ship was first built, which blows my mind. The deck looks extremely sturdy – muscular, even – but I have to be careful: the floor could give way at any second.

I hug the walls, moving past old metal electrical boxes and toppled furniture, keen to see what lies behind the doors.

I count eleven rooms and six cupboards, though most are clogged with debris. Five small cabins contain metal bunkbeds, and my torchlight picks up some personal effects. Amongst these are – presumably from the 1970s, preserved in time – an Adidas trainer, a hardback book swollen with mould. These were the researchers' bedrooms, I'm guessing. There are traces of other explorers, too. The fifth cabin is the only cabin with a porthole window, though for some reason it's covered up with strips of plyboard taped to the wall. Perhaps the window was broken, and someone was trying to insulate it.

Back in the pitch-black corridor of the lower deck, I turn in a slow circle to draw my torchlight across the ceiling, then the walls. All seemingly intact, though cobwebbed and grimy, which is to be expected. I'm surprised at how level the floor is, though the ship moves slightly, the waves at the back nudging it every so often. The *Ormen* has sat here for over four decades, I remind myself, so it's unlikely to come loose now. Possible, but unlikely.

At the other end of the lower deck is another door, my torch bouncing off a rusty doorknob.

As I move towards it my torchlight finds the detail in the

wood, the ornate moulding, and the grooves in the handle. I place my hand on it, twisting, but the door doesn't budge. It's locked tight. The door is probably swollen from damp – not uncommon.

I try the next door, a small door down a step in a corner that must lead to a cupboard. But as soon as I put my hand on the handle, everything goes silent. It's like a switch has flipped – the roaring of the sea outside and the howl of the wind stops dead, completely *gone*, until all I can hear is my breath.

I let go with a start. And then I wrap my hand around it again and the same thing happens, all the sound around me vanishing, like I'm in a vacuum. My heart is thudding like a gavel. Suddenly, a terrible urge sweeps over me to press a knife against my flesh.

I let go and take a step back, then another, my eyes fixed on the door handle, panting. What the hell *was* that?

My torchlight flicks off, plunging me into darkness. Outside, the sea is lashing the back end of the ship, wind screaming through the broken windows of the cabin. I'm jittery, my nerves getting the better of me. I should get out of here and set up camp. I'll return in the morning when it's light.

III

I'm exhausted from walking, but I struggle to get to sleep. Something is scratching at the back of my mind, like a cat clawing at the front door, begging to come in. I think of the way I felt when I put my hand on the doorknob, how everything went silent. How I had a sudden urge to lift a knife and cut myself.

A voice in my head starts up. *You're a bad person, Dom. You've done terrible things. You need to be punished.*

I press my hands against my ears until it hurts, banging them until the voice stops.

I'm finally beginning to drift off when I hear a noise outside – someone is singing. A woman. No words, just a humming sound.

The same five notes on repeat.

Not loud, but clear, as though the wind is carrying it directly to my ear.

I lie very still, listening, certain I'm dreaming. The singing grows louder, and so I reach out and unzip my tent, crawling outside into the frosty heath. The wind is savage, trying to claw off my hat. I hold on to it with both hands as I scan the beach, then the cliffs behind. No woman, and the singing has stopped.

I creep back inside the tent, tugging the zip down. As I'm

locking it in place, another sound pulses through the walls of my tent. Not singing this time – a drumming sound. It grows louder, like feet pounding the sand. A crowd of people or animals are running towards me, getting closer.

My heart pounds in my throat.

The sound is thunderous. Just as I'm about to climb out of my tent and run, I hear a whinny.

Horses.

By the time I manage to emerge a second time, the horses have galloped into the distance, night swallowing them up.

Nicky

I

May 1901
Dundee, Scotland

Nicky closed the door of the house behind her and headed for the mill where Allan had worked before setting sail for the Transvaal. Last year she'd done the exact same thing as she had this morning – arrived home to collect the mail, only to find that no letter from Allan arrived. Later, she'd learned that he had sent a letter to the mill for Mr Campbell, his boss and an old family friend, and his letter for Nicky had been delivered along with it in error. Perhaps the same had happened this time, Nicky thought, optimistically. Even if it had not, the noise and bustle of the mill served as a welcome distraction. Since Allan had left, she often spent the afternoon there, helping Mr Campbell with the accounts, and sometimes assisting the children with the vats.

She headed off on foot, glad of the sunlight that was swelling along the pavement, bright sheets of laundry flapping along the back lane. Along the way, she penned her own letter to Allan in her mind – she would tell him about her father, ask him for his opinion on the matter. At the beginning of the war Allan's letters had started with characteristic honesty, as he'd sworn to when he signed up – *Brutal heat out here, my love. Very lonely. Thinking of you in that pink corset* . . .

26

But last November, General Kitchener introduced his scorched-earth policy, instructing British and Scottish troops to burn down homes and sometimes whole towns, the inhabitants moved into concentration camps, in a bid to flush out Boer rebels.

Allan was caught up in a terrible moral dilemma. He had written to Nicky in anguish about the conditions of the camps, the horrific burning of family homes. It had echoes of the Highland clearances fifty years before. Allan's father was just a boy when his family croft was burned to the ground; he still suffered nightmares, a lifelong dependency on alcohol. And now he was forced to do the same to the Afrikaners, the descendants of Dutch settlers who were fighting to keep their land, just as his own ancestors had done in Scotland.

She cut through Ellis Park towards the outskirts of the tenement blocks, passing through the heavy gates alongside men and women who were commencing the afternoon shift. A few glanced at her, and she lowered her hat over her eyes – she knew she stood out here in her fine clothes.

Gradually, Allan's letters had fallen silent on the Kitchener matter, and she understood from his tone that the troops had been ordered not to talk about what was happening, to keep it silent.

Until then, her fear had lingered over the possibility of Allan being wounded in battle. What if he was shot, lost a limb, returned home with half his face missing? And of course, she had considered the terror of widowhood. The grief at losing Morag was a darkness she had never imagined possible. Losing Allan would be a step deeper into that nightmare.

That he was now pitted between robbing innocent wives and children of their homes, placing them in ill-equipped camps wherein half the children died, or doing the duty he had sworn to his country, was a tragedy she had not anticipated.

II

In the jute mill, the children's voices were a salve. They were called half-timers, because they worked half the day and went to school for the other half, thirty hours a week for three shillings and ninepence. She knew one boy, Angus, had been scalded across his chest and neck, the skin there raised up and lurid in colour a year later. Another girl, Cora, had lost a finger in the carding machine, though she was lucky not to have died. Not one of the children complained.

'Hey, Nicky,' a voice called as she entered the jute mill. It was Lewis, the nine-year-old Allan had asked her to keep an eye on, having lost both parents in a matter of weeks.

'Hello, Lewis,' she called, pressing a kerchief to her mouth as she walked across the floor. The grease of the jute hung densely in the air, cloying in the throat.

'I've got a new joke for you,' Lewis said, sweeping dust from beneath a machine.

'Go on, then,' she said, crouching down to his level.

He cocked his head and swung the jute brush under an arm. 'Why was six afraid of seven?'

'I don't know.'

'Because seven eight nine!'

She grinned and shook off her coat. 'Very clever.'

He beamed. 'Here's another one. What kind of streets do ghosts haunt?'

'Dark ones?'

'Nah, they haunt *dead ends*!'

She watched him laugh and nudge the younger child who had joined him, keen to hear the joke. 'Come on, now, that's funny.'

'Have we a new half-timer today?' she asked, studying the face of the boy beside Lewis. She didn't recognise him. He couldn't be more than five.

'This is John,' Lewis said. 'Say hello, John.'

John looked at her warily, too shy to say hello. She bent down to him, noticing the tatty jute sack he wore, and the shoes that were clearly too big for him. Adult shoes.

'Hello, John. I'm Nicky. Do you know what you're supposed to be doing?'

'I'm showing him the ropes,' Lewis said. 'He's living wi' us now. His ma died last month an' his da's gone to work in Glasgow.'

Nicky took that in. 'Do you have any brothers or sisters, John?'

'A sister,' the boy said uneasily. 'She's called Nancy. She's eight weeks old.'

'We're looking after her as well,' Lewis piped up.

The other women were busy with the machines, so she took John to the oil room.

'These are the oil vats,' she said, pointing at the row of barrels at the back of the room. 'You have to take the rough jute and soak it, like this.'

She used the tongs to gather up a bundle of jute and lowered it into the briny, amber-coloured oil, showing the boy how it gradually softened into a kind of loose rope.

'The whale oil makes it pliable, you see? That's how we can make sacks and cloth.'

John's eyes were like puddles, taking it all in. A year ago, she had been as mesmerised, having never stepped foot inside a mill before. Allan had showed her the process, which he had learned from the women who worked under him. Now, John bent down and copied her, his tiny face lighting up when the jute became supple and limp as cooked spaghetti. She didn't ask how he felt about losing his mother, or how things were at his new home. It might stir up sadness, and he needed to be strong to survive in a place like this.

She headed upstairs to Allan's old office, shared with Mr Campbell.

'How's your eyesight?' Mr Campbell asked when she closed the door to his office.

'Good, I think. Why?'

He removed his glasses and rubbed them on his shirt. 'These aren't strong enough for me.'

She took them from him and glanced through, the pen on the table swelling beneath the lenses to three times its size. 'Jings, they're like binoculars.'

'I've been here since four this morning. I've checked these figures three times now and we're still six pounds short.'

On his desk sat a wooden file drawer of payment cards, a yard long. Fourteen thousand workers. She pulled up a chair and looked over the notebook where the names of their workers were written with wages owed.

'Is that a five or a three?' she asked, noticing a number in one of the columns.

He squinted. 'I'm not sure. It's Ginny's handwriting. She wasn't well yesterday.'

Nicky scanned the rest of the columns until her vision doubled, circling the digits that were vaguely written.

'Has the postman delivered the mail today?' she asked.

'It's over there,' Mr Campbell said, nodding at a pile on the table next to her. She sifted through the letters, her heart swelling with hope.

But nothing from Allan.

III

She spent the afternoon there, writing a letter to Allan that Mr Campbell promised to send with the next day's post. She told him about her father, about Lewis and how she had helped Mr Campbell. She told him about her sister, Cat, who had celebrated her fifteenth birthday last month and was learning to ride the bicycle her father had bought her.

And as always, she finished the letter with a joke, keen to ensure she brought some levity into his day.

Why is Satan riding a mouse like one and the same thing? Because it is synonymous!

It was still light when she set off for home.

She left several minutes before the end of the evening shift to avoid the rush of workers pouring through the front doors. But despite the crowds chatting and thronging around her, she spotted a man glancing at her, fifty yards to her right, standing in a doorway. He didn't carry a jute sack with his lunch and flask like the others, and whereas the other workers headed quickly for the gates, he had hung back, a look of recognition skidding across his face when she glanced at him.

She quickened her pace, blending into a larger group of women who she knew took the same route as she did until the tram stop.

'Hullo, hen,' one of the women called to her. Mrs Manning,

a woman in her sixties whose great-grandchildren worked alongside her in the mill.

'Evening,' Nicky said. Then, leaning closer, 'Did you have a visit from the inspector today?'

'Inspector?' Mrs Manning said, glancing up. 'No, I don't think so. At least, I hope not. Fourteen carding machines are on their last legs. I'm bringing Hamish in tomorrow to see if he can fix them.'

The man wasn't an inspector, then. He was short and stockily built, his eyes hidden by a brown cap pulled down over his forehead. She was troubled by the way he'd lifted his chin to search her out, the lift of his shoulders when he saw her.

Her father's words rang in her ears.

Stay out of sight.

When she looked again, he was lost amongst the crowd.

The top deck of the tram was full, the bottom standing room only. Two American men were sitting side by side opposite her, chatting, one of them with a lemur perched on his shoulder eating a banana. Further down the bus, someone was singing 'The Bonnie Banks of Loch Lomond'. She noticed a woman looking at her and glanced away, pulling her own hat further down over her eyes. Heat travelled up her cheeks, and her heart fluttered. For the first time since Allan left, she felt vulnerable, exposed. She scanned the metallic flick of the River Tay, searching out her parents' house. Not long now.

She got off at Dawson Park and took the path that led by the pond and the water fountains. In the distance, she could see the docks, the tall masts of the *Ormen* combing the sky, men moving back and forth along the pier with supplies. It looked as though this year's voyage to the Arctic was happening as planned. She breathed easier – if the *Ormen* was setting sail, surely everything was fine with the company? Her father was losing his mind.

She would take her mother aside and discreetly speak to her about the matter, tell her what he said.

As she passed by the tall sycamore tree she'd climbed as a child, something flickered in the corner of her vision. Footsteps sounded behind, and when she glanced back she caught sight of a man striding quickly behind her, swinging his arms, his brown cap pulled low over his eyes.

She quickened her pace, spying the gates just ahead that led to the main road. Her palms were clammy, and her heart raced. Who was he?

The footsteps grew louder. She turned to confront the man, but he was already upon her, a scowl on his face as his eyes locked on her. She opened her mouth to scream, but just then he slammed his fist into the side of her skull, knocking her wordlessly to the ground.

Dominique

I

December 2023
Skúmaskot, Iceland

I'm sitting on a rock on the beach, singing. I don't sing words, but the song I sing means revenge. I don't know how or why. I can feel the vibrations of the melody in my throat, the knowledge that each note unleashes retribution filling me with joy.

I look down at my body. I'm naked to the waist, but I don't feel the cold. And instead of legs, I have a long, black tail, like a seal, fading at my waist to pasty human skin.

When I wake, I feel pummelled. What the hell does all of that *mean?* Subconscious body dysmorphia? A hidden desire to sing?

It'll be the door handle I touched last night, the horrible feelings that were stirred up. The voice in my head hisses, but I put on my coat and go outside before the words get too loud.

My mood lifts when I set eyes on the scene outside. The *Ormen* is lit up by sharp morning sunlight, her long bow buried deep in an outcrop of pitch-black rock, white tide lashing the stern. If you can imagine those big oil paintings by the Romantics you find in the National Gallery – the

35

Ormen looks just like that. Like something coming into harbour instead of a wreck.

A word drifts into my head and comes to roost: *Lovecraftian*. That's what the shipwreck looks like, the precise adjective I'd use to describe its macabre, strange, and slightly monstrous grandeur, sitting on the black sand like something conjured from the depths of the ocean. I don't think I've ever read anything by H.P. Lovecraft, but that word has unfurled in my mind without my bidding.

The rocky outcrop at the mouth of a horseshoe-shaped bay is Skúmaskot, and I can see a row of rooftops on the other side of the water, mushroomed by thick snow. The bay is dotted with small islands – or skerries – of lava rock, all thickened with snow. The stretch of beach runs as far as the eye can see, and behind me rises a dormant volcano silkened by snow, the bend of a phoenix's head rising from white ashes. To my right, three razor-sharp rocks needle up out of the sand, several headlands running along the coast.

Lovecraftian indeed.

There are no trees, which is strange. I heard the Vikings had pretty much used up all of Iceland's forests, but it lends this place a breathtaking sterility – a black-and-white desert. My wanderings have taught me that 'dead space' is a misnomer – nothing is ever really dead. If anything, abandoned places are strikingly fertile, blooming with mould and vermin. The ruins I have visited are all saturated with all the typical signs of neglect – rot, shit, asbestos, hanging cables, collapsing walls, dead things all but consumed by the riot of new life that tends to explode into derelict spaces. Wildlife, weeds.

Go to any museum and you'll find fragments presented in glass boxes, cleaned up and pristine, as though it's the actual past, distilled in its purest form. Ruins and abandoned places – they make you work to find their secrets.

The ecosystem of decay is rarely aesthetically pleasing, but barren? Never.

It's still bright, but the air is bracingly cold, sunlight sending the virgin snow alive with gold sparkles.

I scan the cliffs at the back of the bay and the fields beyond. The rock formations are impressive – hundreds of basalt columns, some of them four storeys tall and occasionally running horizontal. There are caves here, too, but I only step inside to shield myself from the wind when it grows fierce.

I find a pathway that leads all the way to the top of the cliff, and there, right on the side of the volcano, I see movement. A white flash of fur, the flick of a bushy tail against the rocks drawing my eye. Two pointed ears. It's an Arctic fox.

Holding my breath, I stay absolutely still, elated to have seen it. I'm about thirty feet away, close enough to see the gold of its eyes. I remember hearing that regions like this were teaming with such creatures, but if you spot them it means they are probably struggling to survive. The flicker of joy I feel at spotting the fox quickly turns to worry. If Arctic foxes are struggling, there's not much hope for humans. Still, it seems healthy enough, poking its nose in the snow, and when it plucks up the small body of a rodent in its jaws I can't resist taking my camera out of my pocket for a photograph.

As I do, I slip on a rock, disturbing the silence with a loud crunch. The fox snaps its head up, its eyes meeting mine. But it doesn't dart off. I lift my camera and begin filming, crouching down and moving slowly, very slowly, towards it.

I'm curious how close I can get. Maybe it has never seen a human before. I manage to get within touching distance before it jerks its head up and zips off across the heath, vanishing into the snow.

Something flicks in the corner of my eye, at the place where the fox has just looked up at me.

A figure, facing the ocean. A woman.

I step back in shock, then look again, focusing on the spot. This time the beach is empty. I blink. I saw someone, right by the ship, standing on the sand.

But I can't have. There's no one there.

I scan the beach and squint at the tide in case the figure appears again. It's strange – I can't recall why or how I thought it was a woman standing there. Perhaps a feminine outline, but I can't envisage the figure. I must be tired, or paranoid. My excitement at finding the *Ormen* last night is already wearing thin, all the shit that spirals around my brain starting to kick up again.

And there's no movement now, other than the crashing waves and the wind ruffling the heath.

II

I head towards the spot where I saw the woman, a little nervous. How odd that I thought I saw someone. Maybe it's an effect of the light against the water, or a shadow. A lacy tide nudges at a patch of fresh snow, and long fronds of seaweed streak the black sand like strands of hair. No footprints.

I'm completely alone out here, thank God. I don't like being around other people. No phone signal, no data – just the sea exhaling up the sand, and the birds calling in the sky above. True wilderness.

In the daylight, the extent of the *Ormen*'s damage becomes apparent. At the mouth of the bay, I find parts of her strewn in the icy water: sections of the mainsail roll against rocks like tree logs, lumps of metal and several wooden tubs lie scattered about. Rusted hooks, striking in their size.

At the starboard side I notice that the black rocks holding her in place have pierced the hull, a gash about four foot wide visible from the ground. It's too high up for the tide to get in, and it's facing away from the sea, but even so – I'll need to check it out to see if she's at risk of sinking, or splitting off from the bow. The metal girders running vertically up the sides have warped, strakes of wood splitting at the chine. Waves beat heavily against the stern, and I can see that the whole bow section sways a little, as though the rocks and waves are creating pressure on the mid-section. One day, maybe even while I'm here, her whole frontage will break off.

That would be so epic, but also sad. And very, very dangerous.

Using the cracks in the hull as footholds, I climb up the side of the *Ormen* to take a closer look at the hole in the bow. Long icicles skewer down like fangs, the splintered wood slimy with seaweed. Through the gap, I see crates and barrels strewn everywhere, their contents long since spilled out and lost to the sea.

It's a thrill to climb up the ladder to the upper deck. Mercifully, it hasn't succumbed to rot. Much of the old ship remains – the masts are broken, yes, but they're enormous, thrusting up high above. Remnants of sails and rope hang down.

I explore the upper deck, filming everything. Later, I'll upload the footage for my followers. I created a social media account for this place, named *The Whale Ship*. It's got a few hundred followers so far. I'm not tech-savvy, but I noticed other explorers were filming their explorations and garnering quite a number of views for people who want an armchair adventure of abandoned places. So, I've done the same, and I've even brought an internet satellite terminal and solar batteries.

I find the ship's wheel under a sheet of old tarp. It's about four foot wide and all the spokes and handles still intact, and I can't help but yell 'Arrgh, me hearties!' I take a selfie of my best pirate grin, too – it'll make a good reel. Then I stand at the stern looking down at the waves and the beach below. It's foggy, now, the morning sun already retreating behind dramatic white clouds, but I can see all along the coastline from here, a long run of black rock punctuated by caves. The land above is spring heathland, like the bay, coated with snow.

The heathland must be where the horses came from last night, but there's no sign of them, no movement at all. Just me and the fox, out of sight. Watching me.

In the daylight, the cabin appears at once larger and more disappointing than last night. By disappointing, I mean that the amount of work it's going to take me to clean it up is considerable. There are a ton of books scattered about the place, a toppled bookcase indicating the source. Mounds of seaweed amongst fishing tackle. I pull a sheet of tarp from a corner and find a kitchenette, a fairly new kettle there. So there have been others visiting this place. Good – it's likely they'll have left their gear behind, stuff they didn't want to carry on the journey back. I see other new-ish items – a throw blanket, cushions. Home comforts. Not too mouldy, either. A desalination tank. My heart leaps at that. Fresh drinking water. Better than my little water purifier. If I can get that tank working, I'll be made.

As I move the junk that has piled up in the cabin I notice stains on the floor, dark spatters, like oil. Definitely not water. Underneath the toppled bookcase I find a big stain, about three feet wide. It has a rusty hue at the edges.

I start searching them out, using my torchlight to help, even though it's still light. The garish brightness of the torch pulls stains out from every corner, which isn't unusual for an abandoned structure. But I take note of the ones that are rust-coloured – they appear up the sides of the wooden posts in the cabin, and on the stairs through the hatch.

I think they're bloodstains. The pattern of dots around some of the larger ones is familiar. Bile rises up my throat, but the voice jumps into my head: *Every surface touched by humans is a crime scene. Every. Surface.*

The *Ormen* was a whaling ship for decades, and the mariners would have butchered their catch on board before

41

storing it in barrels inside the hold. Still, it became a research ship in the mid-twentieth century, and I can't imagine they'd leave stains everywhere . . . Maybe they were hard to get out of the wood, so they just covered them up.

I decide to do the same, arranging the furniture and rugs to cover up the bigger marks.

I'll be warmer if I stay in the cabin, so I make myself a quick tub of noodles before pulling on my gloves and getting to work. I decide to store rubbish in one of the cabins on the lower deck, staying well clear of the one at the end with the weird handle. I'll check it out eventually, but for now I need to stay focused on making the wreck a little more comfortable. I set up my phone to film myself cleaning. It gives me a sense of purpose. It helps to distract me from the voice.

As I clear the cabin of debris, I notice signs of previous visits. There are marks on the floor, odd stains here and there. I find more books, some published in the last ten years, and some from the 1970s. I find a long row of nicks in a wooden post by the cabin door, made by a knife. Dozens of them, about a centimetre apart.

Some of the nicks are fresh, the wood beneath the cut quite pale and new. I finger them, wondering what they mean. Maybe someone was counting off the days. Two hundred and eleven of them. That's quite a long time to spend on a ship-wreck. I'm impressed.

And suddenly the sun disappears. It doesn't so much set than *flee*, a thin light withdrawn abruptly just after two o'clock. I've forgotten to set out my solar batteries to soak up the light. I have standard batteries in my torch, but I'll need to be more organised from tomorrow. I can't rely on these for ever.

I move my tent to the springy heathland beyond the beach, intent on sleeping out here until I see if I can clean up the wreck and make it a liveable space, but the wind grows fierce, whipping the groundsheet from my hands and scattering the poles. I don't have much choice after that – the combination of impenetrable darkness and ferocious gales make it impossible to gather the dispersed components of my kit, so I jog to the wreck and clamber back up the ladder, heading inside.

The upper cabin has too many broken windows to be habitable; I head down through the hatch to the lower deck, where the howling wind doesn't reach. The air is dry, not as cold. I avoid the room at the end of the corridor, the one with the creepy handle, and find a cabin that doesn't smell too bad.

I clear the rubbish out and set up my tent, minus a few poles. It's still cold, but I light a candle and make myself a coffee, the double insulation of the wooden cabin and the tent warming me up pretty quickly.

It's quite cosy in here; I sit for a few hours just listening to the ship, thinking about the voices that have passed through here, now silenced. The feet that have walked these floors. The waves pound the stern, causing the room to sway a little. But it's soothing to me now.

I've been lulled into a false sense of security. At first, I think the creaking sound is just the ship offering up her complaints, but something on the back of my neck prickles and I freeze, listening hard. A rhythmic sound. Footsteps sounding across the floor above me.

Someone is crossing the floor of the cabin.

Quickly I blow out my candle, as if I can really expect to hide from intruders. They'll definitely have torches. They may even have knives.

Creak. Creak.

I hold my breath until I feel I might pass out, listening hard and trying to work out what to do. Oh God. I can't lock the door, and there isn't anything in the room I can use to block the doorway. Carefully, I unzip my tent and crawl out, feeling around the room for my knife. My fingers touch it and I clutch it to me with trembling hands.

A beam of light shines down the stairs, brightening the corridor. My heart hurls itself against my ribcage, again and again.

'Where is she?' a voice says.

Nicky

I

May 1901
10 miles off the coast of Orkney, Scotland

Nicky woke to bloodcurdling screams, the sound so horrifying it set her teeth on edge. A second later, she realised the screams were coming from her.

Pain burned in her foot, excruciating, blinding agony. She opened her eyes and saw that she was in thick darkness, a strange room permeated with the earthy tang of dung. Whimpering, she reached down and realised that a barrel had tipped over on to her ankle, crushing it and pinning her down, a thick metal shard penetrating the skin just beneath the ankle knuckle to the sole of her shoe.

She assumed she had started to hallucinate, for in the darkness came the cluck of hens, a shuffle of hooves. Briny water slapped against her face and filled her mouth, her dress soaked through. Beyond that, the noxious stench of fish. A lamb's bleat.

Where *was* she?

A sharp stinging started up in the side of her face. Her mind tipped with memories: Allan's shirts in the wardrobe. The dress hanging next to them, haunting her. The man in the grounds of the mill. He'd been watching her. The footsteps in the park, and the man's face close to hers. An explosion of pain.

That was the last thing she remembered.

The floor tilted sharply, the barrel shifting just enough to one side for her to wiggle her foot from beneath its weight. The nail tore deeper through muscle, and with a shriek she gave one last pull, freeing herself from it.

She lay back, gasping from the hot, shocking pain of it, until she could gather the strength to reach down and touch the wound. With trembling fingers, she felt the warm pulse of blood, a sharp ridge of bone making her cry out. Her right foot had been crushed, a long, thick nail gouging the inside curve open to the ankle.

How on earth had she got here? The animals and the seawater suggested she was in the hold of a ship, where they kept the livestock for long journeys. The man in the park must have put her here. Her mind raced to fit the pieces together. Was he here, somewhere in the dark?

A sudden bolt of fear set her in motion. Pressing the palms of her hands into the wet floor, she shuffled painfully backwards in the direction of the sounds that trickled into her ear amidst the slap of water against the barrels and the guttural groan of the hull.

By the time she reached where she thought the door must be, she was beginning to black out from the pain, the edges of her vision flickering. She could make out shouting, and a bar of gold light seeping from a gap in the wood. A door. She lifted a hand over her head and grasped for the handle. A metal bolt met her fingers, but it was locked from the outside. She tried to knock, pounding weakly against the wood.

Finally, it creaked open, and she fell back, amber light from an oil lamp flashing in her eyes.

'Good Christ! What we got here, then?'

'Royle! Anderson! Fetch the captain!'

A set of hands lifted her, but as they attempted to set her upright her foot touched the ground, shooting a clean bolt of pain up through her body. She howled in pain and the dark corridor around her liquefied to vapour.

II

A small cabin lit by an oil lamp.

A man tying a surgeon's apron about his waist, watching her carefully.

On a table, a neat row of sharp tools, brown medicine bottles, a folded white handkerchief.

'Do you know your name?'

The man was Scottish, but his accent was Doric.

'Nicky.' Her voice was a rasp. 'My name is Nicky Duthie.'

'Do you know where you are?'

'I . . . I think I'm on a ship.'

'I'm Dr O'Regan,' he said. He stood over her, the lower half of his face carpeted with a brown beard, the top of his head bald and shining in the oil lamp. 'How did you come to be on board, Nicky?'

'I don't know,' she groaned, shocked by the intensity of the pain that radiated up her leg. 'Someone attacked me. A man. He followed me and attacked me in Dawson Park. I woke up in the hold.'

He studied her face, reaching with his fingertips to touch the left temple. It felt like he'd burned her, a white-hot blaze of pain streaking up to her skull.

'Your nose is not broken,' he said. 'But you've taken quite a blow to the face.'

The room tilted, the door flinging open.

'Are we at sea?' she said, her stomach lurching.

'Can you see out of your left eye?'

'I . . . I think so. Have you a looking glass?'

He handed her one, and she gasped when she saw the state of her face – her eyelid swollen shut, livid blue and purple, the eye bloodshot and her nose swollen to twice its size.

It was difficult to organise her words, her foot pulsing with what felt like molten iron through her veins. She was drenched, strands of her hair stuck to her cheek with sweat. The faint scent of something industrial rose from her lips. Chloroform. Not only had the man slugged her, but he had seen to it that she remained unconscious, likely so he could dump her in the hold of the ship. Her stomach turned over and she felt the urge to vomit, leaning towards the bucket on the floor.

'You need to rest,' the surgeon said, his voice far away. 'I'll have one of the hands set up a bed. And I'll inform Captain Willingham that we have a stowaway.'

A stowaway? Something in his tone made her skin turn to ice. Still, she recognised the name of the ship's captain.

'Am I aboard the *Ormen*?' she asked. Her father's ship.

Dr O'Regan studied her, his mouth in a straight line. 'You recognise it?'

'I recognise the captain's name. May I speak with him?'

'Not until I've finished attending to your foot,' Dr O'Regan said. She watched as he soaked a clean linen in alcohol, then lifted it with tweezers and dabbed the open wound. She jack-knifed forward. The pain was electric, monstrous.

'A barrel did this?' Dr O'Regan asked.

'Yes,' she gasped. 'I woke up in the hold. It must have fallen over.'

'It will need to be stitched. You said you were attacked?'

'I was w-walking through a park . . . A man p-punched me. He might be yet on board . . .'

'And you were unconscious when we set sail?'

'I m . . . must have been. I don't know. I don't remember anything.'

'I'll give you something for the pain,' he said, lifting a small black bottle from a shelf. 'You take one of these with a glass of water every three to four hours.'

The label read *TABLOID: Lead with Opium*. A familiar bottle. When Morag died, Nicky's mother produced several such bottles from the bathroom cupboard and told her to take the contents as often as she needed.

The black pill tasted like rust. A moment later she felt something sweep across her like a fine mist, the room tilting again.

'I don't have any ether,' Dr O'Regan said, lifting a needle and thread. 'So I'll need you to be brave. Do you want some whisky?'

She gave a weak nod. The pill had made her feel nauseous but had done little to staunch the pain that shot up her leg, fierce and incessant, as though a tiger was mauling her.

Dr O'Regan unstoppered a tall bottle and poured her a glass, pressing a hand to her back to help her upright. Just then the door opened and a man stepped inside, nodding at the surgeon. Nicky recognised him, though their only encounter had been a decade before – he was Captain Willingham. He wore a white shirt and tatty waistcoat, a rust-coloured quiff and a silver beard whiskering a haggard face. He was thinner since she saw him last, his hands wormy with veins. He regarded her with a liquid, uncertain gaze.

'Captain Willingham,' the surgeon said. Then, nodding at her: 'We have ourselves a stowaway.'

'So it would seem,' the captain said, and it struck her that he didn't seem very surprised to see her. 'You have acquired an injury.'

'Pronged her foot on one of the barrels,' Dr O'Regan said. 'Said she doesn't know how she came to be on board. Says her father owns this ship.'

'Is that so?'

'We met once before,' Nicky told him weakly. 'At the docks.'

'Nicky Duthie,' he said, nodding. 'George Abney's daughter.'

It wasn't a question. He had recognised her as soon as he laid eyes on her. And he knew her married name. And her nickname.

'What day is it?'

'Tuesday, madam.'

'How far are we from Dundee?'

'We departed yesterday.'

'Can you turn back?'

'We're on course for the Davis Strait,' he said. 'We'll not be headed back to Dundee until October.'

She sat upright, the shock of this news overriding the terrible pain in her foot. 'Sir, you must turn back! I'm not a stowaway, I was brought here against my will . . .'

'You must be still,' Dr O'Regan protested, his hands on her shoulders. All at once, the room lurched, several bottles dropping from their place in the cabinet and rolling along the floor. The ship listed, the sound of a wave thrashing the deck overhead.

'We're in the middle of a storm,' the captain said. 'We must maintain our course if we're to keep to schedule.'

'There's a whaling station in Iceland,' she said, her mind racing. 'Skúmaskot. I've heard my father mention it. Ten days from Dundee. We could arrange a transfer. I could wait however long it might take for a ship to take me home. Please. *Please.*'

She started to cry, hot, bitter tears pouring down her face. The two men shared a look.

'Let me see what I can do,' Captain Willingham said at last.

Dominique

I

December 2023
Skúmaskot, Iceland

The intruders make their way down the stairs to the lower deck. Three of them, two men and a woman, dreadlocks threaded with purple velvet hanging to her waist. A voice in my head shouts at me to *run, RUN!* But my body doesn't respond. My limbs defy my instincts, locked in a crouching position, gripping the knife.

I couldn't scream even if I wanted to. My throat is wrenching itself into a tight knot. I feel doomed. Why did I risk it? Why was I so certain I'd be alone?

Images flood my mind, the sound of gunshots.

You're a terrible person, Dom.

It isn't long before a torchlight comes to rest on me like a white sword.

'Oh,' a man says. 'Hello, there.'

He sounds faintly Scottish.

'No,' I manage to say, which is an odd response, even to my ears, but I'm so terrified that I seem incapable of anything more sophisticated. One by one, they line up in front of me, the two men and the woman, their torchlights fixed on me. I am shaking so badly that the knife tumbles from my hands, useless, and I start to cry. I fold inward, my arms reaching over my head, awaiting the blows.

But they don't come.

'Hey,' another voice says. An American accent. The other man. 'Stand up, for God's sake.'

'Leo,' the woman says. 'Take it easy. Remember the plan, OK?'

I can only tremble on the ground like a newborn lamb. They discuss me for a moment as if I'm not there, and I catch snippets of what sounds like the plan to kill me.

Are you sure about this?

I think she's faking it. Seriously.

We have to.

'She's breathing super-fast,' the woman says then, turning back to me. She's also American, or maybe Canadian, I can't tell the difference. My mind is cartwheeling, folding inward, the fear of what they're going to do to me like a white-hot iron plunging into my brain.

Someone sets a solar lantern on the ground, flooding the room with diffuse light. Their faces press through the gloom. The woman is Black, early thirties, her eyes filled with wariness. The man next to her is Asian-American, the one she calls Leo. Leo chews gum and looks at me like I'm something he picked off his shoe. The other man is white, Scottish, somewhere in his fifties, his ears sticking out from beneath a pink beanie. He has a tuft of silver hair protruding from both of them. He tells Leo not to touch me.

'Samara,' he says to the woman. This is her name. I make myself remember it in case this knowledge comes in useful. In case it might save me.

He crouches down in front of me. I hear the *click* of his knees, and for some reason it makes me feel safe enough to look up.

'No one is going to hurt you,' he says. I catch myself noting the kindness in his eyes. *No,* I tell myself. *Don't be deceived.* He holds out his left hand. 'Please.'

I stare at him. Then, despite the voices in my head urging me not to, I put my hand in his. Do I really have a choice?

'Come with me,' he says.

II

Somehow I've ended up in the main cabin on the upper deck, sitting on a chair while the intruders set about trying to block up the windows. I try to remind myself that they're technically not intruders – I don't own this place, even though I was here first – but this very much feels like an intrusion, and they know it. If I could, I'd run out of here and not stop until I reach a town.

I'm holding a cup of tea. I can't remember anyone giving this to me, but it feels hot in my hands. I sip it, realising a moment too late that it could contain drugs. If it does, I don't taste anything other than sugar, and a splash of milk.

Leo is wiry and super strong, hefting two-by-fours across the cabin and fixing them in place with a hammer and nail. He gives off an angry air, and I try not to make eye contact. Every time he lifts the hammer I expect him to stride across the room and bludgeon me with it. Samara finds an old oil can, about the size of a bucket, and slices the top off with a sharp blade. I flinch. Are they going to douse me with it, set me on fire?

I eye the door of the cabin leading to the deck of the ship, and the ladder. Maybe I can try to escape. I remind myself that they aren't exactly holding me hostage, but my fear is aflame with questions. And besides, my legs still won't work, everything disconnected from my brain. I just want to hide, to fold myself back into the darkness.

When they all finish bustling around, setting a row of old chairs around the oil can, I find I'm angry. It's a startling kind of anger. I hate them, all three of them. I wanted to be here, to witness the sinking of the shipwreck. Alone. And now that dream is over.

Leo puts some of the old books inside the oil can, then strikes a match and sets it alight. The man in the pink beanie hangs a solar lantern from a hook in the ceiling, and the darkness lifts.

I keep my eyes on the ground as they sit down, forming a semicircle around me and the oil-can fire. I'm still shaking, the tea spilling out of the plastic cup on to my lap.

'What's your name?' Pink Beanie man asks.

I keep my eyes down. 'Why?'

'That's an unusual name,' he says with a grin. 'Why.' He waits for me to correct him. 'My name is Jens.'

I shrug. 'I don't care.'

'And this is Leo, and Samara,' he continues. 'Your tea is cold. Would you like a fresh one?'

I don't answer.

After a few moments he gets up, and I hear him in the corner of the room, boiling a kettle and stirring. He returns with two cups this time, handing one to me and one to Samara, and it's only when I see her look of surprise that I realise he has handed us actual porcelain teacups.

'God, Jens,' Samara says with a laugh. 'Where the hell did you get these?'

He looks pleased with himself. 'Trade secret.'

I allow myself to sip the tea. It tastes warm and sweet, the steam curling up from my cup an undeniable comfort in a place as cold as this. It gives me courage to speak up.

'Look,' I say, to no one in particular. 'I was here first.'

I make eye contact with Jens.

'OK,' he says, before glancing at the other two. 'Can you tell us what your plan is? I mean, why you're here?'

'I imagine I'm here for the same reason you are,' I mumble. 'The wreck is being sunk at the end of the month. I want to document her.'

'Really?' Leo says, leaning forward. 'Document the wreck?'

Samara catches my eye.

'Can you tell us more about that?' she says. 'As in, *how* you plan to document the *Ormen*?'

I feel my throat tighten again.

'I've brought some cameras, a drone,' I say, pushing the words past my teeth. They seem interested. Flames lick the kindling in the oil can, pulling warmth into the room. 'I thought I could get some followers, maybe some paying subscribers. I felt it was a shame that they'll just, you know, destroy this whole ship after all she's seen.'

'Cool,' Samara says, though I have a feeling she doesn't believe me.

'I've got some followers already,' I say. 'Over a hundred on TikTok.'

'TikTok?' Leo says, lifting his eyebrows.

I shrug. 'Yeah?'

He shares a look with the others. What's wrong with TikTok?

'You know the *Ormen* was a whaling ship, right?' Jens asks after a few moments.

I nod. 'Yes?'

'Late eighteen-hundreds,' Jens adds. 'Then a research ship.'

'Do you know why they killed whales?' Leo asks me, lifting another piece of wood and placing it in the fire can. 'Why they built an entire industry out of it?'

'Not exactly past tense, is it?' Samara interjects, folding her legs up beneath her. 'They still kill whales, right?'

'Yeah, but for different reasons,' Leo says. 'And they're starting to ban it now.'

'About time,' Samara says drily.

'For their blubber,' Jens says, answering Leo's question. 'Whale oil was used for light. Streets, houses, trains.'

'Also for whalebone,' Leo says, his sharp eyes lit up by the flames. 'The nineteenth-century version of plastic. Everything that is now made of plastic was probably once made from whalebone – brushes, chopping boards, fishing nets.'

'I knew they made corsets from it,' I say, drinking more of my tea. I feel myself relax a little, though the voice in my head tells me this is all part of the game. They want me to lower my guard. It could be ritualistic, the killing. The tea laced with drugs so they can take me apart slowly.

'They made *everything* from it,' Leo tells me. 'They used every single part of the whale. Zero waste. A gruesome industry, yes. But you know, much more eco-friendly than plastic.'

The room falls silent again. I'm not sure why he's telling me all this.

'We'd like to make you an offer,' Jens says.

I look up, puzzled. 'What offer?'

'We get that you were on board the *Ormen* first,' Samara says. 'But we'd like to document the ship, too. We can team up, if you like. This doesn't have to be . . . you know, awkward.'

I feel my shoulders lower. She seems nice. I look down at my tea, and as though reading my mind, Jens says, 'It's not poisoned, I promise.'

I give a nervous laugh.

'You think you can tell us your name?' Jens says.

Against my better judgement, I say, 'Dominique.'

He glances at the others, and I look down at my hand, thinking of the way he took it before.

How, for a moment, the feeling of another person's skin against mine was the most beautiful thing in the world.

III

I wake the next morning in my tent in the cabin on the lower deck, though it takes me a few seconds to remember where the hell I am. It all comes back in a startling rush – the wreck, the torchlight pouring down into the darkness, the three strangers. For a moment I wonder if I actually dreamed it all, and when I climb out of my tent and pull on my coat I peer into the corridor, half expecting to find that I'm alone after all.

But then I see a green glow along the wet floor, and when I step into the corridor I see a lime-green tent in the cabin next to mine.

They're here. And despite all the fireside chat last night, I feel anxious.

I head up to the main cabin, eager to get outside and feel wind on my face. My thoughts are scrambled. Sure, the *Ormen* doesn't get a lot of visitors, on account of how remote she is. But this is a big moment for her, the end of an era. She's probably one of the last whaling ships on the planet.

Will more people come? What will I do if there's a crowd of us?

Maybe teaming up with these strangers isn't such a bad idea. A considerable percentage of explorers are heavily into drugs. I don't suspect this trio are junkies, however, given the level of fitness, organisation, and clear mindedness required to explore a place like this. There's also a nerd factor, that I fall into, and most explorers of that ilk are anti-drugs, hard-core activists of one kind or another, too dedicated to their cause for drugs. Environmentalists, vegans, anti-establishment, anarchists, religious fanatics. A small percentile of athletes who combine exploration with long-distance running and parkour.

Outside, the sun is low but strong, a scrim of silvery light illuminating the cliffs and the bay behind us. The snow is still thick, and I can imagine it'll only get thicker as we plunge to the bottom of the year. I look up at the masts thrusting up from the deck and remember again why I came. I felt a pull to her, to tell her story. This abandoned place is special. People are afraid to come here, and I can understand why. But the other side of the tracks, the margins of transgression – I feel at home, here.

Not exactly at home, perhaps. But I feel safe. It has become familiar, this life. A routine.

I watch the mists swirl across the bay of Skúmaskot, thickening and thinning, a kind of dance. It's astonishing how they change the landscape, revealing and obscuring, like an eraser. The row of derelict buildings along the bay – that's where I'll head today.

'Good morning,' a voice says behind me. I turn sharply, spotting the pink beanie, the kind blue eyes in a haggard face.

'Hello,' I say. 'Jens.'

He pushes his hands deep in his pockets and looks out at the view. The gradients of the hills press through the mist in shadowy arcs, and a low wind whistles through the sand.

'This is quite a place,' he says. 'A shark fishing village.'

'It used to be,' I say. 'It's been sat like this since the nineteen seventies.'

'I wonder why it didn't become a raving tourist hotspot,' Jens says. It takes me a moment to decipher that he's joking.

'Right?' I say. 'So scenic. So much to do.'

'It *is* scenic,' he says. 'Though maybe not for anyone who likes vitamin D. Do you explore a lot?'

'A little,' I say. 'What about you?'

He shrugs. 'A little.'

I watch him from the corner of my eye, reading him. There's something familiar about him, the shape of his nose, a little hooked, and the deep lines of his long face. His skin is weathered and pocked – the face of an explorer. We don't tend to look after ourselves very well. No time for SPF and moisturiser. Sometimes it'll leave you with broken bones that never heal right.

It's as I'm thinking this that I notice he only has one hand. His right sleeve is rolled up a little, revealing a muscular forearm with a small anchor tattoo, the skin gnarled at the stump where his wrist should be.

'Is there a problem?' he says, catching me staring, and I flinch, embarrassed.

'Sorry. I didn't mean to be rude.'

'Lost it in a fight,' he says, holding it up.

'God.'

'Just kidding. Osteosarcoma. Had it removed when I was eight.'

I'm not sure which story to believe. 'Is that a type of cancer?'

'I barely remember it. And it was so long ago I just got used to it.'

He nods in the direction of the cabin. 'Come inside,' he says, 'I'll make us all some breakfast.'

'Jens?' He turns to face me, and I hesitate.

'I was just wondering . . .' I say, worried I'll sound stupid. 'Did you see anyone else down on the beach yesterday?'

62

His eyebrows knit together, and he glances towards the beach. 'No. There's no one around for miles.'

'Well, except for us,' I say. He stands closer to me, scanning the coastline. The waves are thunderous and brilliant, thumping down on the sand, a fizzing sound like fireworks when they roll back.

'What did they look like?'

'I'm sure it was a woman. I think she was only wearing a dress.'

'A dress?'

'I think so.'

His eyes settle on me. 'Maybe you saw a ghost?'

'I don't believe in ghosts.'

He's amused at this. 'Perhaps you saw a mermaid, then.'

'A mermaid?' I think back to my dream. The long tail stretching out in front. The sound of a woman's voice, singing.

'You'll have heard Iceland's folktales about mermaids?' he says.

I haven't. Like, not at all. 'Not really.'

He takes a step back towards the side of the hull that overlooks Skúmaskot. The bay is bustling this morning, the sea pushing in so fast that the ice hasn't solidified all the way across. The water is deep navy, boiling around the skerries in the middle of the bay. Jens points at one of them, a tessellated formation of basalt rock, like those hexagonal structures at the Giant's Causeway in Northern Ireland.

'That's a mermaid stone,' he says. 'Can you see the shape?'

I squint at it. 'It looks like a chair, or a throne. Is that what you mean?'

'The curve around the front of the stone is said to be created by the mermaid's long tail when she sits on the throne. It means a mermaid has lived here.'

'Nice,' I say, though I give a shiver, my mind turning to the way the wind sounded like singing last night.

'No,' he says. 'Not nice.'

'Why isn't it nice?'

He turns his eyes to me. 'Icelandic mermaids are not the sort you see in the movies. They want to punish both the living and the dead.'

I raise my eyebrows. It seems fitting that a place like this would subvert the nicer mythical tropes into something macabre. Or Lovecraftian.

Inside the main cabin, Leo is up and stacking old bits of cardboard and wood into the oil can to build a fire. The flame grows quickly, and I stand next to it, rubbing my hands against the warmth.

Leo doesn't acknowledge me. That's fine. As long as he builds fires like this every morning, I think I can handle it.

At the kitchenette, Jens sets up a gas-cooker and makes a fry-up, replete with mushrooms. The smell almost makes me cry. The whole breakfast comes from dehydrated packs much more sophisticated and expensive than mine – Jens is clearly an experienced explorer, not cutting out too many home comforts. His pink beanie tells me he's not a macho kind of guy either. He's likeable, but still – I feel cautious.

Samara joins us soon after, smiling when she sees me at the fire with my plate of food.

'God, that looks good,' she says. Then, to Jens: 'We have eggs this time?'

'We have eggs,' he replies with a proud smile.

'Score!' she says, high-fiving him.

I want to ask how long they've been exploring together. It seems they have a bit of a routine going, with Leo stacking the fire and Jens cooking meals and making tea with his delicate porcelain cups.

I listen more than I talk, gauging all the while how much I can trust these folk. My instinct tells me they're fine, but I force myself to keep my guard up. I'm the outlier here, and I remember the whispers I heard last night, when they were coming down the hatch into the lower deck. *Where is she?*

They knew I was here.

How, though? With a shiver, I think about the feeling I had yesterday, when I saw the fox. That I was being watched. Maybe they saw me on the deck and decided to work out what to do before coming on board. Yes, that was it. They'd seen me before the sun went down. It must have been disappointing, hiking for countless miles to stake out the wreck, only to find someone else had got there first. Maybe that's why Leo radiates such angry vibes. He doesn't like me at all.

I'm working up the courage to ask them what their dynamic is. Are they a throuple? It seems naive to ask – of course they are. As far as I can see, they all slept in separate cabins last night, but that doesn't necessarily mean anything. Sometimes explorers team up for bigger, more dangerous explorations, which is possibly the case here.

Samara is a sound engineer, which makes sense – she strikes me as someone who works remotely and sporadically, on her own terms. A professional, not a lame-ass wanderer, which is the type drawn to sites that are easier to get to: inner-city urbex sites you can reach by bus. Old schoolyards, crumbling mansions. As we eat, I ask her about her favourite exploration, the one that's stayed with her, and she tells me about a place in France, an abandoned farmhouse in a medieval town. All the rooms were still furnished, probably a hundred years after the owners left. A bar of soap sitting on the bathroom sink.

A pot on the stove, houseplants withering in their pots. A little girl's bedroom, dolls and handmade teddies on the bed. And a low whispering that she couldn't trace to anything.

'Weren't you scared?' I ask. We're sitting in the messy cabin, ignoring the junk around us. The fire is burning high in the oil can. It's all very wholesome.

Samara sips her cup of tea and sighs wistfully. 'No. I hear it a lot, actually. A kind of whispering. Sometimes I've heard voices.'

I watch her carefully. Does she believe in the afterlife? 'But . . . not ghosts?'

She takes a pause, choosing her words carefully. 'It's a revenant,' she says finally. 'Not a "ghost", not the way we think of ghosts. More like breath on a windowpane or lip marks on a cup. Sound leaves a trace. The human ear usually can't hear it. Like, if you sit completely still you might pick up the odd floorboard moaning, or the wind, maybe the birds nearby. But the mic picks up traces. There's a spectral ambiance I always manage to find, even just for a moment. Like an echo.'

'Wow,' I say. 'That sounds . . . spiritual.'

'It's scientifically proven,' she says. 'Traces of the past hang in the air around us. Millions of them, still suspended. Like time is a glass and we kind of smear it a bit as we pass through it.'

She tells me that Leo is part Korean, born in Chiacgo. He's a parkour expert, incredibly strong. His talent will enable him to get some cool footage out here, she says. He's not visibly ripped, his arms covered up by a long-sleeved jersey shirt, and he's quite short, about five foot five. He is sharp, his keen black eyes seeming to look right through me, and I can tell he doesn't suffer fools.

'Is that a bloodstain?' Samara says, pausing halfway across the cabin to survey a mark on the floor.

It is – the rug has shifted. 'There are a lot of those marks,' I say. 'Gross, right?'

'It does look like old blood,' Jens says, crouching down to touch it. 'Or shit.'

'Shit doesn't stain wood like that,' Leo says.

Jens raises his eyebrows at him, amused. 'Do we want to know how you've acquired this insight, Leo?'

'No,' Leo deadpans. 'Here's another one.' He points at a splodge on the wall by the cabin door, an icky hand-sized splash surrounded by tear-shaped droplets.

'Places like this always have a history,' Jens observes, trying to steady the mood. 'That's why we're here, right?'

Samara looks stricken.

'Could be worse,' Jens tells her. 'Could be dead bodies lying around.'

IV

We spend our daylight hours hefting the rest of the junk from the cabin into the hold, making it homely.

'What's behind this door?' Leo calls from the far end of the deck.

'I think it's the captain's cabin,' I tell him. 'I've not been able to open it.'

Leo tries the handle, pushing against the wood of the door with his shoulder. 'Man, it really is jammed.'

'Maybe it's jammed for a reason,' Samara says, and Leo frowns at her.

I tell them about the hole I found in the hull, that maybe it is causing a vacuum to seal the door tight. Samara tries the door next to it instead, the one that freaked me out when I first touched it. I haven't tried again since. I don't mention the weird thing that happened with the handle when my fingers came in contact with it. Instead, I watch her, waiting for her to remark on the sound fading or something similarly strange.

'Huh,' she says.

'Something wrong?' I ask.

'Locked,' she says, trying the door next to it, which opens.

'What's in there?' I ask, cautious.

'About a foot of dust,' she says. 'A storeroom, by the look of it.'

I glance in after her – just as she says, it's a storeroom with some old boxes. Nothing sinister. Even so, I won't risk touching the door handle. Not yet.

Samara finds tins of food down in the bowels of the ship. The last explorer who stayed here must have travelled to Skúmaskot in a four-wheel drive packed with luxuries. There's a bin and a toaster, for God's sake. The real find is an old desalination tank, providing fresh water. Often explorers leave behind things they brought to make their stay more comfortable, but we really struck gold here.

I wonder if the nicks in the wooden post are to do with food rations.

Leo finds an old generator in the cabin he's claimed as his bedroom, which brings a moment of excitement. Sadly, it's broken.

When I check the solar battery packs this morning, I discover they aren't charging enough for all my gear. It's minus five at night and one or two degrees during the day. Yes, we have four hours of daylight, like I told Samara, but the quality of light changes all the time: sometimes it's bright and brilliant, the sun like a torch behind a brocade of cloud. But a moment later a mist will rise, hemming in the bay like we're on a desert island. And then it'll burn away, leaving the sky crisp and clear as a bright coin, the ocean like liquid mercury.

But it's not enough for the solar chargers which provide my – or should I say *our* – electricity: they're the only way we can charge the cameras and internet terminal, which the others are keen to use, too. The batteries *are* soaking up enough sunlight to power the kettle, electric hob, the laptops, and our cameras, but the internet satellite terminal requires much more battery than I'd calculated, especially for uploads. We'll have to be judicious about how we use the charge, is what I'm saying.

On our walk around the deck today, we also find that the lower deck of the shipwreck has been blocked up by a thick sheet of metal that was soldered to the hatch opening, maybe to stop tourists from climbing down there and getting trapped inside. But Samara manages to prise some of the metal off the sides, creating a hole about the width of a football to shine her torch through.

'I think I see a wine cellar,' she says. 'And there are barrels down here. Do you think they're left over from the whaling era?'

'Let me see,' Leo says, and before any of us can blink, Leo has squirrelled down the hole in the floor and dropped to the deck below.

'Leo,' Samara calls after him. 'How're you going to get back up?'

'Are you serious?' he asks, and she doesn't respond.

We attach my camera to an extendable grip and lower it down into the hole to film him. It's flooded, so Leo wades up to his knees in filthy black water that seems much deeper at the stern, odd bits of rubbish floating on the surface – pieces of wood and metal from where the ship had hit the rocks, dead fish, old fishing nets, and endless coils of rope. We can make out a row of old barrels at the shallow end, too.

'How piratey is that?' Samara says, flashing her torch over the barrels. 'Do you think they have gunpowder inside?'

'Hardly,' Jens says. 'The *Ormen* was never used as a battleship.'

There's a sudden knocking sound as Leo tries to hack one of them open with an axe. He manages to get the lid off, and we all hold our breath as he looks inside.

'Oh my God!' he screams.

'What is it?' Jens yells back.

'There's a dead body in here!'

'Shit, get out of there, Leo!' Samara shrieks, and he starts laughing. Samara's face changes as she realises he's pulling her leg.

'You bastard,' she says.

'It's empty,' he says. 'God, what a stench.'

'What's over there?' Samara asks, poking her head through the hatch and shining her torch into a corner. A large object sits covered up, ominous in its shape – a head and shoulders, I think. Leo sloshes through the filthy water towards it and pulls off the sheet of tarpaulin. It's a metal storage unit with cans of food dated until next year, which proves my point that recent explorers have stayed here.

'We got wine, folks!' Leo shouts, holding up two black bottles.

Leo stuffs some of the wine and food cans down his sweater and climbs back up through the hatch. Samara takes out a can opener on a keychain and sets about opening a can.

'I wouldn't risk it,' I say, watching Samara dip her finger into the juice of one without a label.

'I'll be the poison tester,' she says, sucking her finger. We all watch in silent trepidation as she tastes, gasping when her body goes into violent spasms.

'Jesus,' Leo shouts.

'Ha!' Samara says, pointing at him, and he rolls his eyes.

'Definitely poisonous,' she says, sitting cross-legged on the floor of the lower deck.

'What is it?' I ask.

'Peach slices. I'll make peach cake, I think.'

I figure she's kidding, but she bakes an actual peach cake on the fire bucket using ingredients we find inside cans and old sacks – flour, peaches, flax seeds, sugar, and oil. It smells incredible. We dust down an old bottle of red wine and drink

71

it out of our aluminium cups huddled around the fire. Jens puts candles all around the cabin to create ambiance.

In the main cabin, I sit on the makeshift sofa by the fire, looking over the work we've done, and these new faces that were strangers just days ago. You would *never* think that this place is the same grimy shithole I walked into on my first night here. No, it's not spotless – there are still blooms of black mould on the walls and bloodstains on the floor – but with my Perspex windows nailed in place, all the rubbish cleared out and candles glittering along the window frames, it feels almost homely.

Just before midnight I head downstairs into the lower deck where Leo has left a few more bottles of wine from the hold. I bring one up to the main cabin, and as I'm making my way back to the hatch, I hear Samara, Leo, and Jens talking to each other in low voices. An instinct makes me pause on the stair and listen for a moment.

'How can you be so sure it'll work this time?'

It's Leo's voice. He sounds urgent, frustrated. I freeze, wondering what he means.

Jens says something I can't fully hear, but the second part I hear clear as a bell.

I'll work on her.

'Not like we have much of a choice,' Samara says, with a sigh of resignation.

It sounds like they're making a plan, and so I make my way through the hatch, curious if they'll fill me in.

'More red, anyone?' I say, holding up the bottle. Leo glances at me before turning back to Samara.

'Great!' Jens says.

I wait for someone to loop me into their conversation, but they don't. Leo suddenly won't make eye contact, and Samara shifts the conversation to music. I try to read the mood. Something hangs in the air, heavy as a sword.

Jens holds my gaze for a few seconds, and there's a message there – a warning. But I can't read it.

I'll work on her. That's what he said.

Did he mean he would work on *me*?

Nicky

I

When Nicky came to, the room around her swayed, the musky scent of wood and lantern oil hanging in the air. For a moment she fancied she was at home in Faulkner Street, with Allan in bed next to her. She reached out a hand and felt hard wood. When she opened her eyes, she saw she was in a cabin on a slim hard bed, the whole room lilting a little as though it sat on springs.

'Ah, welcome back,' a voice said, and she lifted her head to see a man standing next to her, a white apron daubed in old blood. Dr O'Regan, she remembered, and with a dizzying rush the realisation came that she was on the *Ormen*. Her foot had been bandaged, though it hummed with white-hot pain.

'Reid will help you to your quarters,' Dr O'Regan told her. A blonde-haired boy of about fifteen stood warily in the doorway, his inky eyes shifting across the room. Dr O'Regan pressed a palm against the small of her back to help her upright before handing her a cane made of whalebone.

One arm across the boy's slim shoulders, the other leaning on the cane, she hobbled out of the captain's cabin, back along the narrow deck to a small cabin at the opposite end of the deck.

It was no bigger than a cupboard, the ceiling barely high enough for Reid to straighten to his full height. A straw mattress and blankets on wooden crates wedged into a corner. A stained ceramic bedpan sat on the floor, a gnarly sea chest adjacent to it with a Bible on top. A brass oil lamp swayed from a hook on the ceiling. No window.

'This is a bonnie cabin,' Reid said, helping her sit down on the mattress. 'At least you won't be bothered by any snoring.'

She nodded but couldn't return his smile. She reminded herself that she couldn't expect much more. It was temporary. And the thought of sleep was sublime.

'Do you share with many others?' she asked the boy.

'Six of us sleep in steerage,' he said.

She winced. 'Is it uncomfortable?'

'It's all right,' he said. 'If I ever make it to second mate, I'll get to sleep in a room like this one.'

'I hope you do,' she said weakly, sitting on the bed, and watched as he reddened.

'I'll bring you food in the morning,' he said, turning to the door. 'I can't promise it'll be what you're used to.'

'Thank you,' she said.

She listened to his footsteps as he headed to the kitchen. Inside the sea chest, she found some clothes – woollen socks, a fisherman's jumper, trousers. Her dress was still wet, and so she slipped it off and pulled on the dry clothes, before lying down on the bed and covering herself with the blanket.

The waves outside beat against the hull, the noise of the men above ringing in her ears. She thought of Allan in the Transvaal, waiting in line for the mail delivery. Her father and mother and Cat would be worried. They'd wonder why she hadn't returned from the mill. She imagined the police rallying to her mother's shrill voice, a foot kicking in the door of her house on Faulkner Street.

She felt panic rise in her chest, the whole room beginning to spin. It felt like she might go mad, the thought of how much everyone at home would be worrying about her, believing her to be dead.

Strange, she thought, that the man in the park did not steal any of her jewellery. The fine gold chain she wore at her neck would have been easy to rip off and pawn, as would the gold wedding band on her finger. She touched it now, holding the metal between finger and thumb as though it might transport her to him.

Their wedding had been exhausting, a stiff, rote affair organised largely by her mother, Mhairi, and her new mother-in-law, Alison. The friction between the two women spilled over into almost every corner of the arrangements; Mhairi had wanted Nicky to wear her grandmother's wedding dress, which Mhairi had worn for her own wedding day. Alison, however, protested loudly, claiming that it was unfair for Nicky to wear both her grandmother's wedding ring *and* her wedding dress, and that she should instead wear the dress that Alison's mother had made for her almost thirty years before. Nicky worked hard to broker a truce between both women, offering to wear Alison's old-fashioned, oversized dress – a potato sack with a throttling collar – and invite all six of Allan's sisters to be bridesmaids, as well as her own younger sister, Cat. Three hundred guests were invited, the majority of whom Nicky had never met.

On the morning of the wedding, Mirrin, one of Allan's sisters, and Cat accused each other of taking the other's bonnet, and soon Mhairi and Alison had chosen sides. The bonnets were torn and lopsided, both girls wearing hand marks on their cheeks from where they'd slapped each other. Alison stormed off, refusing to participate in the ceremony. Just as the organ sounded, Nicky took her father's arm to be given away and her mother hissed into her ear – *If you go through with this, hell mend you!* – and so she took Allan's hand in marriage with her mother's glare burning a hole in her back, Alison's footsteps ringing down the chapel foyer, and an occasional sob rising from the bridesmaids.

That night, the heavens opened, the cobbled streets of their neighbourhood soon awash with water. Allan dutifully carried her over the threshold and upstairs to the bedroom.

'Give me your ring,' he said, when she started to undress.

She frowned. 'Why?'

He was lying on the bed, naked to the waist. His eyes full of kindness. 'Your ring, madam.'

She was down to her slip – new, not borrowed – when she removed her wedding ring and handed it to him.

He looked it over, then squinted at the inscription. 'Fourth of June 1832.' He looked up with a furrowed brow. 'Did we time travel?'

She sighed and sat down next to him. She had tried so, so hard to appease both her mother and her mother-in-law, but she had liked the idea of wearing a ring that had belonged to her grandmother, a stern woman who believed strongly in not sparing children the rod.

'It doesn't fit, either,' she said. 'I'll need to get it resized.'

He put the ring in his pocket, then.

'What are you doing?' she asked.

'How about we put your grandmother's ring in a box, and we put this one on your finger.' Removing his hand from his pocket, he opened his palm to reveal another gold wedding band, bright and shining. Brand new.

She gasped and took it from him, looking it over in the light. An eighteen-carat gold wedding band, with an inscription: *12 April 1895.*

'It's beautiful,' she said, slipping it on her finger. The fit was perfect.

He stood up, lacing his fingers through hers. 'I'm sorry the wedding was a nightmare,' he said, kissing her neck.

'Your mother told me that weddings are for other people,' she said, removing her hairpin. 'I didn't think she meant it quite so literally.'

'I suppose a single day isn't too much to ask,' he said, lifting her slip over her head.

'What do you mean?' she said, and he paused, their faces close. His eyes were tender, softening as he looked down at her.

'I mean, the wedding was one day,' he said. 'But we've got the rest of time together. If you'll have me.'

She smiled. 'I will.'

II

As the *Ormen* passed by the Orkney archipelago, the ocean stretched out, an infinite sheet of metal, no land in sight. At night, the shrieking wind and pounding waves were so loud she wondered if the ship was sinking. When the pills wore off and the wound in her foot flared again, she wished more than once that it would.

She imagined Allan's worry, the torment of it. How anguished he'd be. To think she had been worried just two days ago, when his letter didn't arrive. She had had to distract herself at the mill, and that was possibly why she was here . . . How did the man know she would be there? Or was it a random attack? She remembered how he'd searched her out, his eyes meeting hers through the crowd. Who was he? A disgruntled colleague, someone who had a bone to pick with Allan?

No – it was something to do with her father. He had told her to lie low. But he had also said that the company was folding, and yet the *Ormen* had set sail as planned. Why, then, had the surgeon known her name?

When she ventured out of her cabin and up onto the deck, she spoke to the crew, asking questions about their tasks, before steering the conversation to her attack to try to probe them for answers. The tactic had mixed results – some of the men, such as Ellis and Arnott, made lewd comments that embarrassed and confused her, and so she left them alone. The men made no bones about singing bawdy songs and telling crude jokes in her presence, occasionally using their genitals to demonstrate a punchline. They seemed equally fine about pissing and shitting in front of her, lowering themselves a little down the bow and using the end of a shared tow rope for cleaning. She would have confined herself to the small cabin, but it made her seasickness intolerable, and the wind on the upper deck soothed her injured foot.

Never in her life had she been exposed to such scurrilous behaviour. There were no washing facilities, no practice of even rudimentary hygiene, or manners. She had imagined sailors to have a loose tongue, but on deck, the men's language was incendiary. It had almost moved her to insist that they curb their tongue, but then she had heard the men discuss money, the lack of food in their homes, a child they'd had to leave behind with consumption, and their coarse language ceased to matter. Consumption, she knew, was fatal, especially so when a family hadn't the means to pay a good doctor. The conversations she overheard taught her that their wages were paltry, and often not paid at all, if a voyage made slim gains. Their wives and children had gone hungry, had died, as a result.

She thought of her father bitterly. How often he had boasted of his profits from the company. How he had complained about his 'sea dogs', the men that were working twenty hours a day in the most horrendous conditions, and spoken openly about trimming their provisions to the bare bones.

There were twenty men on board, including Dr O'Regan and Captain Willingham. Reid and Anderson were the youngest crewmembers, smooth-faced boys whose voices had barely dropped. Reid's uncle, Daverley, served as boatswain.

Then there were the boatsteers, McIntyre and Gray, both Dundee men around her father's age, perhaps younger – she well knew the ravages of poverty ground the young old before their time. The harpooners were Ellis and McKenzie, who also served as the Spektioneer. Skentelbery was the ship's cook, Royle and Arnott served as seamen, Lovejoy was the first mate, Wolfarth the second, Stroud and Martin were landsmen, Collins and Goodall were coopers, Harrow was the skeeman, and Cowie served as a carpenter.

She etched all their names on her mind, filing away tidbits of information in case it linked any of them to her attacker.

One of the mariners had to have known. Someone had to have arranged it with the man in the park. She had watched the crew carefully to work out if she might recognise one of them, and when she didn't, she studied their interactions, and their relationships, for the man in the park couldn't have been working alone. The park was some distance from the docks, so it would have taken more than one man to get her on board the ship, and even then it could not have been done without witnesses.

She noticed that both Royle and Gray frequently rested their eyes on her, and when she looked back neither of them looked away. She wondered if they had worked alongside the man, perhaps, or if her memory served her poorly. No – the man who had attacked her had a bent nose, and his build was different than any of the crew. Daverley and his nephew were quite close, she could see, with Daverley acting protectively towards him, helping him when he trapped his hand in the rigging, and when Lovejoy screamed in the boy's face she saw Daverley consoling him afterwards.

As they sailed towards the Arctic, the ship's hierarchy became clearer – the captain was hapless when it came to ordering the men, preferring instead to leave such duties to his first mate, Lovejoy, a stout, pale-eyed man with a mouthful of broken teeth and greasy black hair that moved with lice. He was the only man to address her as Miss Abney, and she hadn't had the nerve to tell him that her maiden name had been abandoned almost six years hence.

Witnessing the ship's hierarchy in operation made her realise that they were far away from the authorities, or indeed from anyone who might protect her from being violated, or killed. The captain was perpetually busy, and the surgeon was disinterested. A few days into her ordeal, she approached Ellis, a short, stocky man with a thick ginger beard, and asked him how far they were from Iceland.

'Why?' he said. 'Not thinking of leaving us, are you?'

She was suddenly wary of how close he was leaning in to her. In the corners of her vision she saw Lovejoy watching, and ahead of them, Cowie and Royle had turned to her. Her foot shrieked with pain.

'Thank you,' she said, not wanting to stay on deck any longer.

Back in her cabin she swallowed several pills quickly, sinking into her bed as the room around her faded.

She woke to the sound of 'Land ho!' and footsteps pounding the deck outside.

When she opened her eyes, she saw a familiar face above her, groaning and grunting. It was Ellis, and he was naked, thrusting inside her, a hand pinning her wrists above her head. She gave a scream, but immediately he clamped a hand over her mouth.

'Quiet!' he hissed.

She began to tremble, the effect of the drugs sharply tapering. Ellis got up then and wiped his mouth. He sat on the side of the bed, belching as he pulled on his shirt.

'You beast,' she whispered, pulling the blankets around her.

A moment later, the door burst open. Lovejoy stood in the door with a face like thunder.

'You!' he shouted, lunging at Ellis and dragging him out of the room by his collar.

Dominique

I

December 2023
Skúmaskot, Iceland

I dream terrible things. I see myself on the mermaid rock in the bay, my throat burning with a mystical song. It's not a song of delight, but one of darkness – each note that leaves my mouth is like a curse sent out into the world. A long black tail flicks at the end of the rock instead of legs, settling into the groove in the rock.

I wake up with a headache, the rasp of the ocean outside making me fear for a moment that the wreck has cut loose and is being pulled out to sea. That would be a first.

I find my lantern and turn it on, sending the tent aglow, my little blue cocoon inside the cabin. The images in my mind swirl, grainy and sickening. I remind myself that I'm safe, that this is my tent, my sleeping bag, my water bottle, my gloves. I take a long, deep breath, then let it out.

I have no idea what is going on with my brain right now. Jens told me about the mermaid stone, and maybe it has freaked me out. Or maybe it's the darkness, and the strangeness of the ship. Sleeping on board has taken some getting used to. I've set up my tent in the cabin, both for the double insulation factor and the familiarity. But still, the creaking and the groaning of the hull is pretty loud at night, as is the ocean. Those waves are fierce.

'Score!' I hear Samara shout upstairs.

I head up to see what the excitement is about. Leo has lit the fire, and I see him busily carving the top off another similar oil can, presumably to create an additional source of heat. Samara is sitting on the floor pulling the contents out of her backpack. I see a laptop and a microphone beside her, and she looks over a pair of earphones with an expression of glee.

'This is the best day of my life,' she says.

'What do you mean?' I ask, wary. She's pulling out her kit like she's never seen it before.

'Did you forget you packed those, Samara?' Jens says from behind me.

'What?' she says, looking up. 'Oh. Yeah. Yes, I did. *So* much stuff I forgot I brought it.'

'Is this your recording equipment?' I ask, picking up a shiny black box with a mic attached.

'Yes,' she says, happily, looking it over.

I watch her carefully, unsettled by her behaviour. *Is the equipment stolen?* I wonder silently. She's looking at it like she's never seen it before.

I don't say anything to her about what I overheard last night. She is wrapped up in the gear she forgot about, murmuring to herself about the things she will record. It reminds me to check the battery packs, and try again to set up the internet terminal.

'What have you got?' she asks Jens, and I turn to see that he's holding what looks like a model airplane.

'A drone, by the looks of it,' Leo says.

'A drone,' Jens repeats.

'Can you sort one out for me, too?' Leo asks me. I watch as he unzips his rucksack near the cabin door, unsure of how to answer. Is he accusing me of theft? He pulls out a laptop and a small camera with a headstrap.

'A headcam,' he announces, putting it on and fiddling with the buttons. 'That'll do, I guess.' He angles his face to me and grins, that same jaw-splitting grimace. 'It's just like Christmas. Thanks, Santa!'

'Leo,' Samara says, a warning in her tone. She flicks her eyes at me warily.

Santa? I don't understand Leo's sense of humour, or even when he's being serious. He heads outside, and a few moments later I see him racing across the sand, breaking into a series of backflips and twirls like a gymnast.

'Parkour helps him deal with it,' Samara tells me when she sees me watching.

'Deal with what?' I ask.

She hesitates. 'The isolation,' she says finally. I can't help but feel she was going to say something else.

'What's the deal with the three of you?' I ask carefully. 'Are you all in a relationship?'

She pauses before breaking into a loud laugh, her head thrown back.

'No,' she says. Then, pulling a face of disgust. 'God, no. We're . . . colleagues.'

'Colleagues,' I say. 'For this trip, or . . . ?'

She shrugs, her face darkening again. 'For the foreseeable.'

The weather this morning is foggy and cold, which is to be expected in December in Iceland, but when it feels like knives acress my skin I can't help but wish this site was further south, or closer to civilisation. While the sky is light and the snow isn't falling, I decide to go for a walk along the beach towards the caves, filming content: the shipwreck from a distance is an incredible image, and as the light goes it looks black and white, no filter needed. The rocks are packed with birds and nests, black birds with long red beaks. They squeal above the cliffs, circling and diving. I watch for a long time, growing strangely emotional. The sight of them struggling to survive out here in such a savage environment makes me sad, and yet the sign of life is moving. Maybe the cold is starting to get to me.

I search the horizon for the horses I heard the other night, but there's no sign of them.

II

It's dark when I return to the *Ormen*.

There's a mood in the cabin when I enter, as though I've interrupted a conversation, or an argument. Leo is fixing another two-by-four on one of the cabin windows, hammering aggressively, as though trying to channel his anger. I feel myself tensing – all the good feeling I was starting to have about the three of them begins to fade. Maybe I need to leave. Maybe I should grab my gear and leave right now. There's no reason to stay on the ship. I could camp outside, build my own goddamn fire.

But I remember I wanted to film the ship, to explore the cabins. There might be things I find here that tell her story.

I hang my coat up, then finger the long row of cuts in the wooden post. 'Did you see these?' I ask Samara when she looks up.

She stares, so I tell her what they are, how I counted them.

'I think they're marks someone made to tally the number of days they stayed here.'

'Two hundred and eleven, right?' Leo says in a flat voice.

'You counted them?' I ask.

He looks up as he positions the last piece of wood against the window frame.

'Obviously.'

I'm trying my hardest to set up the internet terminal, but it won't connect. I move to a different spot close to the bookcase, re-plugging the cable into my laptop. The others are quiet, just the sound of the fire crackling in the background, and the waves beyond. I feel like I might cry – if I don't manage to connect to the internet, the project is ruined.

I watch the screen of my laptop, praying silently as the terminal lights up. My webpage stutters before connecting to TikTok.

'Yes!' I shout, punching the air with my fists.

'What?' Samara says, approaching with a smile.

'We're online,' I tell her, clapping my hands to my mouth in excitement. 'I got it working.'

'Really?' Leo says, sceptical. 'How far will the signal reach?'

'It won't extend much beyond the ship,' I say, clicking through to the project TikTok account. 'But we can film outside and upload to the project social media accounts. I'll show you.'

I show him the TikTok account for the project. It's the first time I've been on it for a few days and I notice my followers have gone up. 'I have four hundred followers now,' I say, showing her the tally on the top of the screen.

'Wow,' Samara says, taking the seat next to me. 'People are interested?'

'Of course they're interested,' I say.

I have this dream, albeit a recent one, that this exploration will make it possible to continue exploring. Urban exploration isn't a hobby – it's a lifestyle. Of the urban explorers I've met, I don't know a single one who has a career, or a demanding job, because to be able to drop everything at a moment's notice and spend a month in an abandoned mall in China, or trawl a Nazi bunker in eastern Germany, you have to work zero-hour contracts.

'My goal is for the project to hit ten thousand followers,' I tell Samara. 'We have more chance of going viral then. And hopefully we'll all end up with more subscriptions on our individual channels.'

I turn to Jens and Leo. 'We have one chance of telling the story of the *Ormen* before she gets destroyed,' I tell them. 'And if we're going to do it properly, we need to rethink how we document her story. How we structure the narrative.'

I want to say that filming endless amounts of stuff and then hoping it'll all coalesce into something interesting is too slapdash and time-consuming, but I hold back.

But then, the webpage glitches, before crashing altogether. I reboot the terminal, my heart in my mouth. It says there's a problem and refuses to open the page. Why is nothing working? I try not to show my frustration, or my fear that the terminal is dead.

'We need to film the *Ormen*, obviously,' Samara says, sitting down at the dining table. 'But we need to tell the story of Skúmaskot, too. Like, I had no idea there would be so many buildings here.'

'Wasn't this place a shark fishing village?' Leo says, taking the seat opposite her.

'Up until the turn of the twentieth century,' I say. Samara pulls out the seat next to her and I take it, setting my laptop in front of me. Finally, it logs back on.

'They ate sharks here, right?' Leo says.

Samara nods. 'It wasn't like they could grow crops. Way too cold, especially back then. Fishing was the only way they could stay alive.'

'So why did they leave?' I ask.

Samara pulls my laptop towards her and types into a Google search bar. *Why did the villagers leave Skúmaskot?*

She finds a Wikipedia page. 'It says the trade for fishing

Greenland sharks died out when the demand for shark oil decreased,' Samara says, scrolling. 'Which makes sense, right?'

'Skúmaskot is cursed,' Leo says darkly. We look over at him and he shrugs. 'That's what I heard.'

'So, folklore, in other words,' Samara sums up.

I glance at Jens, recalling what he said about mermaids. 'You heard about a local legend, didn't you?' I ask him.

He glances from me to Samara. 'Not really local. It was a folktale related to Iceland. Icelandic folklore is savage.'

'I guess it would have to be,' Leo says.

'Why's that?' Samara asks.

'You've got to be tough, living out here,' Leo says. 'Especially in the olden days. Brutal winters. Can't raise kids to be soft and then expect them to cope.'

'My mother taught me an Icelandic lullaby,' Jens says.

'Your mom?' Samara says. 'She was from here?'

'Not this region,' Jens says. 'But yes, she was born in Iceland. She moved to Orkney as a child, which is where I was born.'

'What's the lullaby?' Leo asks.

'The translation is something like this: "Sleep tight, be kind, and do no wrong, lest mermaids wound you with their song, prayers and penance do not postpone, lest they trap you by their stone."'

The air in the room feels charged.

'Fuck, that's weird,' Leo says, breaking the silence.

'"Lest mermaids wound you,"' Samara repeats in a low voice. 'Am I missing something? I thought mermaids were pretty and shit.'

'In Iceland they're savage,' Jens says.

'What's the last part about?' Leo asks. 'The stone?'

'Is that something to do with the mermaid's chair out on the bay?' I ask, and Jens nods. He tells the others: 'A mermaid's stone is where she sits and sings, and all those who haven't

91

repented are chained to the stone for the rest of time. And actually, the first part – "Sleep tight"?'

'Yeah?' I say.

'It means death, not sleep as we know it. It's a warning to the dead not to be wicked.'

'Shit,' I say.

'So the throne is hell, basically,' Leo says.

'The entrance to Valhalla,' Jens agrees.

'Great,' Samara adds. 'Not only is there no Wi-Fi here, but it's right next to hell.'

'All of this is good,' Leo says, drumming his fingers on the table.

'Really?' Samara says. 'How is it good, exactly?'

'Well, we're here to make content, aren't we?' he says. 'To tell the story of the whaling ship, and of Skúmaskot.'

'You're right. There's so much more here than I expected,' Samara says with a sigh.

'In what way?' I ask.

'I mean, the history, and that lullaby . . . I went out first thing this morning to record some sound. It usually takes days, weeks, even, to pick up the kind of tonal textures of a place that tell its story. But this place . . .' She shakes her head. 'As soon as I put my headphones on, I could hear so many different registers. It's like poetry.'

Leo gives an amused laugh. Maybe he's thinking the same thing as I did when I first heard it – that all Samara's evangelising about sound is a bit woo woo.

From her pocket, Samara produces her spiffed-up audio recorder and sets it on the table, then bends down to her backpack and fetches a small round speaker and a cable. She plugs one into the other, then presses a button. The room is suddenly filled with what sounds like the ocean moving up the beach, but beneath it is a rhythmic popping sound that's hard to place.

'It sounds like . . . fireworks?' Leo says.

'Is it stones?' Jens says. 'You were standing on the beach and the sound is the waves hitting stones?'

Samara shakes her head. 'I used a hydrophone mic in the bay. This is what it sounds like underwater.'

'Wow,' Leo says. 'I thought underwater would sound a lot more . . . wet.'

We all hold our breath, listening hard. Slowly, I can hear that the rushing sound isn't like the ocean at all – it's almost synthetic, the bassy pulse of a rave.

'You're sure you recorded that here?' Leo asks, and she nods.

'I told you,' she says. 'Sound tells a story different from the one you can see.'

'Maybe we're approaching this all wrong,' Leo says. He chews the inside of his cheek, thinking.

'Do you mean, we shouldn't film it?' Jens says.

Leo shakes his head. 'No, I mean . . .' he pauses. 'Maybe we need to approach this differently. If it's for social media, I mean.'

'Differently?' Samara asks him, her eyes narrowing.'

He shrugs. 'Like, give all these followers a reason to really tune in. A contest.'

'A contest?' I say, and he nods.

'Yeah. With teams.'

I think back to last night, when I heard Jens say *I'll work on her*. I feel my cheeks burn a little. 'There's a lot to uncover about the shark fishing industry here,' I say. 'Why the villagers *really* abandoned this place, and why people are still scared of it.'

'We should explore the houses here,' Samara says. 'Along the bay.'

I boot up my laptop and start writing a list. 'And we'll do a story on the shark fishing era of Skúmaskot,' I say.

'What about wildlife?' Samara says. 'Sharks?'

'You planning to go scuba diving?' Leo says with a laugh.

'We might see them from one of the cliffs?' Samara says. 'Loads of bird nests there.'

'I'd like to do some parkour episodes, too,' Leo says.

'You could do some tutorials,' I say, nodding at Leo.

'I'll stick with the trails,' he says, shooting me down, and I feel my cheeks burn.

'Jens,' Samara says. 'What do you think?'

'I could explore the geography,' he says. 'Take my drone camera and film as much as I can. Some really old rocks around here.'

'I think a contest will work,' Leo says. 'We form two teams. One team will gather information on the whaling ship era, and the other will try to find information on the research ship era. And Dom, we tell everyone following your project TikTok feed that they get to judge which team wins.'

'Imma warn y'all right now,' Samara says, before I can answer. 'I am *crazy* competitive.'

'Oh yeah?' Leo says, cocking his head. 'I'm an ESTP.'

'What's an ESTP?' Jens asks, side-tracked.

'It's the Myers Briggs personality test,' Leo says. 'ESTP stands for extraverted, sensing . . .'

'. . . thinking and perceiving,' Samara finishes, nodding at Leo. 'Also known as the Dynamo. Yeah, I'm also an ESTP, thank you.'

'Oh my God,' Leo says, high-fiving her. 'Two ESTPs on one ship. That's like finding two nuclear bombs inside a shoebox.'

'I think I saw a book about Myers Briggs on the floor earlier,' I say.

'It's probably been used as firewood,' Jens says, almost too quickly, folding his arms.

'I'd say you're an ENTP,' Leo tells me.

'Definitely,' Samara says.

'What's an ENTP?' I ask.

'You're a Visionary,' Samara says, throwing me a wink. 'You're a creative, an innovator. Da Vinci was an ENTP. I read about it.'

I smile, the tension in my shoulders fading a little.

'Folks, this is riveting,' Jens says. 'But can we get back to the topic at hand?'

'Yeah,' Samara says. 'Sorry, Jens. The contest.'

'The *Ormen* has two main stories, right?' Leo says. 'The era when she served as a whaling ship, circa 1890 to the late 1950s. And then her research ship era, circa 1960s until 1973.'

I feel the hairs on the back of my neck prickle. This is changing the whole scope of the project. He's dominating, taking over. And I feel like there's a reason for it.

'So what's the criteria for winning?' Samara asks.

Leo holds up his phone. 'We let the followers vote. And the winner gets to . . . open the door to the captain's cabin!' he says.

'Wait . . .' I say.

Jens cuts in. 'The captain's cabin is sealed shut. Hardly much of a prize, is it?'

'We'll cut it down. It'll be dramatic,' Leo says.

Jens still doesn't look convinced. 'We're going to get into teams and find stuff out about the ship. How do we do that, exactly?'

'We're explorers, aren't we?' Leo says. 'So, we explore the ship. The ship *is* the story. There will be clues, relics we've not found yet. We've found stuff already . . .'

'And we search online,' I say. 'We all have laptops, don't we?'

'We do, thanks to you,' Leo says with a smile. Again, I have no idea what he means, but he still unnerves me too much to ask. So, I smile nervously back and he winks.

'So,' Jens says. 'Who's doing the era when the *Ormen* was used as a whaling ship?'

'I will,' Samara says, raising a hand.

'I'll join you,' Leo tells Samara. They fist-bump and look at me and Jens.

'And you two will do the research era,' Leo says.

'We get four hours of daylight,' I say, 'so we'll have to plan everything to find inside those hours.'

'Four hours,' Samara repeats with a sigh. 'What a shame they couldn't decide to destroy the wreck during the summer.'

'Maybe we could time travel,' Leo says. 'Ask the wreck very nicely to land somewhere like California. Or the Maldives.'

'Leo,' Samara says, irritated at his sarcasm.

'Hey, did you know what Skúmaskot translates as?' Leo asks me.

I shake my head. 'I didn't think to translate it.'

'A dark and sinister corner,' Leo says, triumphant. 'Isn't that just so fucking perfect?'

'Godless,' Jens adds. 'That's what this place is.'

'I would say it's more Lovecraftian,' I offer.

'What did you say?' Samara asks after a beat.

'Lovecraftian,' I say. 'You know, after the style of the writer, H.P. Lovecraft.' Samara's eyebrows raise, and she glances at Leo.

Suddenly, Leo claps his hands together and gives what sounds like a shout of joy.

'Lovecraftian!' he shouts, his arms pumped high above his head. 'Did you guys hear that?'

'I don't understand,' I tell Samara, but I can see she has a look of excitement on her face. She glances at Jens, who reads her look before turning away.

Leo leaps up and runs to the top of the room. Then, by the post with all the nicks in it, he crouches down, fingering the line of cuts. I stare, wondering what the hell he's doing. Near the middle, he taps one of the cuts and says, 'Aha!'

He straightens, then takes his seat by the fire again, like he's just won a prize. He lifts his glass and salutes Jens. 'You were right, my friend.'

'I'm sorry, right about what?' I say, turning from Leo to Jens.

'It's nothing,' Jens says, but I watch Leo closely, the way he turns and glances at the post lined with cuts. He walks up to Samara and high-fives her.

'Different this time,' he says to Jens. '*Different.*'

'Did you make those marks?' I ask.

He takes a drink before answering. 'No,' he says. 'Of course not.'

But the lie is written all over his face, and when I look over at Jens and Samara, I see their faces hold the same look.

A knowingness. Like they've just achieved something.

What is it they're not telling me?

Nicky

I

May 1901
Skúmaskot, Iceland

Nicky curled up in the bed, her legs pulled tight to her chest, her wounded foot beginning to bleed afresh through the bandages. The shock of waking to find Ellis raping her seized her like a cage of thickest iron bound tight against her skin. She felt like she'd pitched from one nightmare into a deeper one, a horror beyond words. A thousand needles scratched against her skin, the air turned to smoke, too heavy to breathe. She could hear Lovejoy roaring at Ellis on the deck outside, Ellis squealing like a stuffed pig. *Not yet*, Lovejoy was shouting. *You weren't supposed to yet.*

Dragging the chest across the small room, she pressed it tight against the door, then sank down, barricading it with her weight. On the upper deck, the rig creaked and the anchor clanked, suggesting they were pulling into port. *Iceland*, she thought, suddenly. *The whaling station.*

This would all soon be over. A dark memory.

It was dawn when the ship finally stopped, a heavy rocking toppling the blanket from her bed as the ship moved close to the shore, the engine shuddering to a halt. The deep moan of

98

the ship pulling into port, the high-pitched whine of the pulley lowering a rowboat, the gurgle of the bilges emptying.

She waited until the footsteps faded, the men's voices dying down, before getting to her feet. Her head felt like spun cotton. Although the bleeding had stopped, her foot felt hot and frightfully painful. She would seek help at the whaling station. She would crawl, if she had to, and have them send a telegram to her father. She would find the courage to tell them about Ellis's shameful, cruel assault. Two brutal attacks from two different men in just over a week, her foot destroyed and her strength depleted from appalling food and sleepless nights. She would leave this ship as a different person altogether.

As she moved the chest away from the door and pulled it open, Allan's face was vivid in her mind, telling her to be strong. That she would see him again. That the horrors of the last week would someday be nothing, absolutely nothing.

II

Wrapping herself in a blanket, she stepped out on to the deck, steadying herself with a hand on the wall as she moved up the steps and through the hatch to the upper deck. The sky was vivid gold, a new dawn gilding the hills in the distance. She felt tears of relief pricking her eyes. Iceland had always struck her as a strange place, a mythical land of fire and ice in the distant north, but she had never been gladder to see it.

She glanced across the deck for any sign of Ellis, or the captain, but they were nowhere to be seen. The ship had not pulled into a port as she'd thought, but was docked about half a mile from the Icelandic coastline. She saw a black sand beach ahead, the land behind rising into the steep apex of a volcano. A little to the right was a large bay filled with boats, houses on either side. No sign of another ship yet, but she could wait for one. Even if it took months, she would get off here and wait.

'Forgive me for asking,' a voice said. 'But are you all right?'

The boatswain, Daverley, stood next to her, running a loop of rope into a coil. He had seen that she was crying, and she tried to swipe the tears from her cheeks.

'I'm getting off at Skúmaskot,' she said. 'At the whaling station. When do you expect we'll pull into port?'

He cocked an eyebrow. 'The whaling station?'

She nodded. 'I expect to arrange a transfer. My father will pay, so money isn't a problem . . .'

'There's no whaling station at Skúmaskot,' he said.

'There is,' she said, her voice growing louder. 'I heard my father talk about it. They built it a couple of years ago . . .'

'They *did*,' Daverley said. 'But then the villagers burned it down.'

'What?' she gasped.

He nodded, searching out the remains of the station.

She looked back at the land beyond the boat in alarm. Cowie and Royle stepped out of the rowing boat and tethered it to a boulder.

'Where are they going, then?' she asked in disbelief.

'They're collecting fresh water,' Daverley said. 'The villagers are no longer keen on whaling ships, though, so they'll need to be quick.'

Just then, she heard shouts from the bay. Cowie and Royle were hefting barrels on to the small rowing boat, and behind them a group of men were racing up the pier. They began to throw rocks at them, then at the ship, though the stones landed far off the hull. Their anger was visible, even from a distance.

At the stern, she could see Lovejoy gesturing at the sails.

'Bo'sun!' Lovejoy called, and Daverley raised his arm in reply.

'Aye, sir,' Daverley called. Then, to Nicky: 'Excuse me.'

The crowd of angry Icelanders had swollen on the shoreline, a shower of stones landing in the water near the rowing boat and the ship. One of the rocks struck Arnott, who slumped over the oars, and another hit one of the *Ormen*'s sails, landing on the deck.

'Bastards!' Lovejoy roared, picking up the stone and flinging it back. It landed not thirty feet into the navy sea between them.

The *Ormen*'s engines roared into life, and as the crew winched up the rowboat the sails unfurled, fattening quickly with wind, driving the ship forward.

As they pulled away from Skúmaskot she watched, horrified, as a line of men formed on the beach, gesticulating and shouting. There was a structure on the far edge of the bay, the blackened wood suggesting that it had been subjected to a fire. In a moment, it was less a structure than a blotch in the distance, a dark stain erasing what chance she'd had to escape.

III

'Captain? A word, if you please.'

She found Captain Willingham in his cabin, seated at a broad mahogany desk, his pipe sending an earthy spiral of smoke into the air.

'What ails you, woman?' he sighed when she stormed in, her despair having transformed to simmering fury.

'You told me that I would be able to depart at the whaling station,' she said, tears in her eyes. 'Why, then, are we sailing away from Skúmaskot?'

'The whaling station was destroyed,' he said, pausing to cough into his fist. 'The villagers claimed that whalers were wrecking their industry. So they set fire to the station.'

'Two years ago,' she said forcefully. 'Two years! You *knew* there was no chance I could leave.'

He lifted his eyes to her in a liquid gaze. 'I'm afraid we need to negotiate some new terms. Please, have a seat.'

She was shaking all over as she took the seat in front of his desk. 'Negotiate? No, Captain. Turn this boat around immediately and return me to Skúmaskot.'

'You saw what they did to our man, Arnott,' the captain said. 'He's unconscious. May never wake up. They'll do the same to you.'

'I'll take my chances,' she said.

The door swung open; Lovejoy entered, a broad grin forming on his face when he saw her. 'The Icelanders are a fearsome lot, aren't they?'

She wanted to burst into a scream. 'I care *not* if the Icelanders are fierce,' she said, trying to control the urge to cry. 'Captain, you well know who my father is. One of your men raped me in my bed in the night. My father will have you and your crew hanged when he learns of it.'

They were words of anger, but a moment after she said them she saw that they had not struck the fear she had anticipated.

Lovejoy stood next to the captain, the two men sharing a glance. 'That's as may be,' Lovejoy said at last. 'When your father learns of it. Maybe we'd be best just throwing you overboard.'

'You would not,' she said in a low voice.

'You'll have heard about your father's finances being in a bit of disarray,' Captain Willingham said.

Her father's face came to her mind. The awkward, flushed look on his face. *Lie low.* 'And what of it?' she said.

'What of it?' Lovejoy parroted with a mock-casual shrug. Then again, 'What of it?' Stepping towards her, he repeated it over and over again, each time in a different tone and with exaggerated hand gestures, as though the statement was a conversation, a journey through ignorance and injustice leading all the way to raw fury. She saw it in the men's faces as he ambled around the room: *this* was where the nature of her entrapment lay. *The men were angry at her father.* Captain Willingham, Lovejoy . . . she had found herself in the crossfire of a dispute – about their wages, perhaps, or the precarity of their work. The conditions of the ship . . . Suddenly, she understood that the potential reasons for why these men wanted to take revenge on her father were vast.

She found her anger dissipating, then, as she glimpsed the terrible reason for her internment here on the ship. She was a prisoner. There would be no court, no law above the men who stood leering in front of her. She was theirs to do with as they pleased. Her anger vanished, and in its place, she felt terror.

'Please,' she whispered, feeling fearful. 'I just want to go home . . .'

Lovejoy positioned himself against a wall, a hand on his chest, his face pulled into a thoughtful expression. It struck her that he was in control, here, and he knew it.

'Have you heard the tale of the selkie wife?' he asked after a moment.

She shook her head, swallowing hard.

Lovejoy pursed his lips and whistled. 'Oh, it's a good 'un. And there's a moral to the tale, if you'll listen closely.'

Bile curdled in her stomach as Lovejoy prepared himself to share the tale, removing his cap and setting it on her lap, designating her temporary keeper. Then he licked his palms with a long tongue before running them across the greasy sides of his hair. He positioned himself in front of the fire, like a circus master poised to call in the lions.

'Once,' he said, gesticulating with his hand, 'when the whaling first began, folk of a certain island realised that their ships could not withstand the wild tempests that lashed the shore. They became skilled at building stronger ships, and sharpening both their harpoons and their aim, but when a hundred men drowned at sea in their efforts to feed the town, a clever woman decided to visit the sea gods and ask what could be done.

'The sea god appeared to her and told her, "Be ye a Selkie Wife, and the seas will be calm." The clever woman felt confused. "A Selkie Wife?" asked she. "I am wife to my husband, that is all."

'The sea god explained that if she were to accompany her husband on his next voyage as wife to both him and the sea god, one night in the husband's bed, another in that of the sea god's, the men would be spared, and their hunt would feed their town for a season. The clever woman agreed, understanding that, in order to share the bed of the sea god, she would be changed for a time, part fish, in order to survive the depths, returning at dawn both to her former self and to her husband's bed.

'As promised, the hunt yielded more flesh and blubber than ever before, and the people lived long and prosperous.'

Lovejoy fell silent, frozen in a pose with his hands held high, as though he had concluded the performance of a stage play for children, awaiting a round of applause. Nicky felt the room tilt, her stomach in a tight knot. She was panting loudly from fear, now, unable to hide it.

'As you'll no doubt have noticed,' Lovejoy said, approaching her slowly, his gaze darkening. 'We're missing a selkie wife on the *Ormen*. And I'm sure the tale has illustrated how much we need one.'

'Please,' she said, her eyes dropping to his feet. 'I have a husband. My family will be worried . . .'

'You have more than one husband now, selkie,' Lovejoy said, as though she had won a prize. 'You have a whole ship of husbands.'

'Captain,' she said, pleading. 'Surely your honour forbids you from . . .'

Just then, Lovejoy bent towards her, leaning his hands on the arms of the chair and drawing himself close until his nose touched hers.

'A selkie wife does not speak,' he said. Then, straightening sharply, he struck her hard across the face. He caught the bruised part of her cheekbone that still ached from where the man in the park struck her. The room spun, and she gave a loud cry of pain.

Drawing a trembling hand to the smarting cheek, she looked in horror at Captain Willingham. Was he going to allow this? She watched, her stomach dropping, as something skidded across his face. A wariness.

'You will be fed while you are on board,' he said, a slight apology in his tone. 'And Reid will assist you with obtaining fresh water for bathing and drinking.'

She broke down then, the reality of what lay ahead pulling her apart, bone by bone. *Yes*, she thought. *He will allow this. He is party to it.*

'You may say "Aye, Captain",' he said, a little louder.

Her father's eyes flashed in her mind. The bird trapped in his palms. Its sooted wings.

She took a breath, the words like burning coals in her throat.

'Aye, Captain.'

IV

That night, when the pain in Nicky's foot grew so intense that she wanted to howl for hours, she found the bottle of pills that Dr O'Regan had given her. The effects were quick – a soft mist seemed to bloom in the cabin, distancing the pain as though it was a memory of an injury, something she could only recall with her mind.

She took off the shirt and heavy fishermen trousers and replaced them with her dress. It felt warm, and she was less exposed than she had been in the shirt and trousers. Then, too woozy to stand up any longer, she lay back in the bed, tugging at the gauze around her foot. It felt too tight, so she unwrapped it entirely, staring hazily at the wound just beneath her ankle, on the instep. Dr O'Regan had stitched it roughly, leaving huge gaps between each stitch, so she could see the bone beneath.

Except, when she looked again, it appeared that her ankle bone had darkened, the wet white sliver between the folds of raw skin now dark grey. She moved closer to the lamp, arching over it. She could feel no pain, now, and it was likely the drugs making her wound appear different. But even so . . . she stared down, noticing that her toes seemed different, too. They were still bruised and swollen, but they were folding in towards each other, the skin shimmering.

Like the pelt of a seal, growing beneath her skin.

Dominique

I

December 2023
Skúmaskot, Iceland

I think I've managed to fix the internet terminal, but it is *very* temperamental. We stand in front of the shipwreck and film each team – me and Jens, then Leo and Samara – explaining how we're going to research the two different eras of the ship and then present our findings, and they get to judge which of the two research projects is the winner. Jens throws a bit of a curveball while we're filming, offering two voters a thousand pounds each.

When Leo stops filming I confront Jens, alarmed at what he's promising.

'We don't have that kind of budget,' I say. 'We don't have *any* budget.'

Jens holds up his hands. 'I never asked you to contribute to it. I'll pay for it, OK?'

'Like, how will you choose which voters to give the money to?' Samara asks.

'At random,' Jens says with a shrug. 'We'll set up a poll for everyone to vote on the research teams. The voting will be anonymous, but we'll set up a place for everyone who voted to tag themselves. And then we can run it through a random selection app and give the prizes to the winners.' Fair enough. It's his money, I suppose.

We've also made a plan to help us cope with the lack of sunlight. Every morning, we get up at eight, make coffee, and exercise. The exercise part is important to help us cope with the cold and the dark, which Samara says will drive us mad if we don't learn to adjust. Jens likes to run up and down the beach, I guess because the snow isn't as bad there, and Samara does press-ups against the rocks that Leo uses for his parkour. He does it over the top of the *Ormen*, which is amazing. We film it three or four times and people love it.

Our follower count is skyrocketing now. I think most of them have followed just for Leo's stunts. And it turns out that Samara is great in front of the camera, much better than me, though she'd argue otherwise. She's funny and warm, whereas I'm awkward and come across a bit unfriendly, a bit cold. It's a shock to the system, because I don't see myself as unfriendly and cold. Maybe it takes practice. In the meantime I'm fine to take a step back and let her talk to the followers.

At nine, we begin preparing firewood, or bashing doors, as I call it – we're using the old doors of the ship for firewood, but they're a bugger to break up. Yesterday, Samara made us film her doing it and she was *fabulous*. She should have been a TV host or something, because her personality comes right through the lens. Samara has that rare mix of dorky and intelligent and smooth. Few people can make breaking an old door apart look dignified and even funny, but she manages it.

At ten, more coffee, then it's research until three, when it's properly dark. After that, we have personal time until seven, and then we meet up in the main cabin for dinner.

The fire bucket has made a huge difference to our camaraderie; in the evenings, we all sit around the fire with a bottle of wine and talk, and it has helped us bond as a team. We've even filmed some of that and uploaded it to *The Whale Ship* TikTok and it went down well.

The next day, while the sun gasps out a few rays of thin light, I suggest that we do some livestreaming while we have the battery power.

Jens films me climbing down the ladder of the *Ormen* to update our followers on the research progress.

'Hi folks, how are you all this morning? Here in Skúmaskot it's bloody freezing, but gorgeous. We've not had much of Iceland's famous wind lately, just a lot of fog, which is wrapping us all in a big blanket. Anyway, vote Team Research Era! Jens and I have learned that Skúmaskot was not just a fishing village, but a *shark* fishing village, back in the eighteen and nineteen hundreds, and for reasons we don't quite know, everyone up and left at the turn of the twentieth century. So, tune in later on when we'll be uploading all our fabulous content!'

Jens signals to me a thumbs up and logs off.

'How many viewers?' I ask.

'Eighty-five,' he says, and I frown. 'It's actually not bad, considering the time of day and how short that snippet was. We've had a lot of new followers on *The Whale Ship* TikTok.'

'How many?' I ask, pulling out my own phone to check.

'Four hundred new ones overnight,' Jens says. 'And some new subscribers on the Patreon.'

Thank God, I think.

'That's amazing,' Samara says, high-fiving Leo. Then, catching the look of confusion on my face: 'Leo uploaded some parkour footage, didn't you see it?'

'I'm just seeing it now,' I say, flicking through six new videos. They are brilliant. I was a bit worried that the snow would prevent Leo from doing anything parkour-ish but he's got cool footage leaping across the rocks at the top of the *Ormen*, cutting between Samara's camera and a headcam.

The sun is already low and a heavy fog blots out what remains of the light. The water in the bay isn't frozen over completely, but there are sections along the beach that are frozen solid, so Samara shows us where she drilled a hole about an inch in diameter to record the sound. She crouches down, holding a pebble in one hand and a microphone in the other. Then she plugs a set of headphones into her recorder and hands them to me.

'Listen,' she says, holding up the pebble and angling the recorder at the hole. And then she drops the pebble down. It makes the most incredible sound, not what I expected at all. Like lightsabres, with the whip-crack of lightning.

'It's the reverberations of the stone off the ice,' she says. 'Pretty neat, huh?'

She lets Jens listen in, then Leo, and we all have the same reaction.

'Told you,' Samara says, smiling. 'The sounds of the dead.'

'Like anything is dead there,' Leo says, teasing. 'It's ice, for God's sake.'

'This is *dead* ice,' Samara says. 'Look it up. It's ice that isn't moving.'

We watch as she throws another pebble down, the same strange echoes calling back through the earphones. I give a shiver this time, realising a moment later how Samara's explanation has affected me. *The sounds of the dead.*

'Speaking of sound,' Leo says then. 'I could have sworn I heard someone singing last night.'

Samara cocks her head. 'Singing?'

'Outside,' Leo says. 'A woman's voice.' They glance at me. 'Wasn't you, was it, Dom? Singing us all a lullaby.'

I feel an icy chill up my spine, recalling my first night here.

Those rising five notes, clear as a bell. 'Of course not,' I say, keeping my eyes on the ground.

'I'm going to set up a Spotify link for the sound documentary,' Samara says, changing the topic.

I tell her it's a great idea. I had no idea that sound could do so much. But I'm fast becoming a convert, what with the ideas that Samara is bringing to the project. She explained what a field recording can offer in capturing a sense of place, how everywhere is porous and filled with echoes.

II

We decide to explore the abandoned village of Skúmaskot on the other side of the bay. It takes us almost an hour to walk there. It's not actually that far, maybe a half-mile loop, but the snow is deeper on the far side than it is on the beach, nudging right up to the shore. Fresh virgin white that comes up to our waists, huge chunks of ice floating in the bay.

It isn't completely frozen, though, as the sea cuts rivulets through, so we can't skate across. We have to climb up the side of the volcano to find a pathway, and even there we're forced to zigzag up and down the valley to avoid the geothermal steam pumping out of the earth.

When we finally make it to the village on the other side, we discover that there are about thirty buildings, not just the ten that I had counted from the other side of the bay. The older buildings are traditional *torfbæir*, turf houses, constructed out of flat stones and turf, with grassy A-frame rooftops that are doused with snow – more like igloos than turf houses. Leo is able to climb up there and film the old turf beneath the snow.

Snow has clogged the doorways, though we could enter some of the tin huts that were still standing. They're empty, save some bits of turf. We manage to pull some of it out and carry it back to the ship for the fire.

*   *   *

114

The next morning it's foggy and the air inside my cabin is so cold it stings my face. Leo lights the fire bucket and Samara makes hot tomato soup for breakfast, dishing it into our plastic bowls. I don't question it. It's a relief to hold something warm in my hands, and the flames that begin to lick the sides of the oil can feel so good that I think for a moment about the fire gods worshipped by ancient tribes. I would worship this oil can, and this soup, simply because they bring respite from the biting cold.

We eat in silence, too cold to speak. But after a few moments, Jens gets up and says he's going outside for a walk.

'Are you off to do some filming?' I ask.

He shakes his head, not making eye contact. 'Just a walk. Got to stay fit.'

'If you're not taking your drone,' Samara says, 'could I borrow it? Just for a little bit?'

Jens raises his eyebrows, and I wait for him to say no.

'I was going to film more of Leo's stunts,' Samara explains. 'But I kind of thought it might be cool to alternate between the headcam and the drone this time.'

'Sure,' Jens says. 'Do you know how to use it?'

Samara nods. 'I think so. I'll look after it, I promise.'

He takes out the controller and sits down next to her, giving her the low-down on how to manoeuvre it.

'How about I film from the ship?' I say. I'm feeling warmer, now, and outside the fog is beginning to lift. 'We can cut between the three shots. Get some wide shots to create more perspective.'

'Sounds great,' Leo says.

Samara and Leo head off towards the rocks at the far end of the beach. It's still light, though just barely. I'm glad I suggested filming from the stern of the *Ormen* – the waves are spectacular, rising up to the deck like charging horses before spreading across the black sand as a fine white lace, and the trio of lava rocks sticking out of the sand look epic against the purpling sky. They look like guardians, watching over the ship. A dramatic canvas for a dramatic scene, in other words.

I wait while Leo stretches his calves and Samara sends the drone further up the bay, capturing landscape footage before he starts.

I set my coffee mug on the ground and begin filming; my thinking is that I will capture more than I need and edit accordingly.

When I press 'record', I notice a third figure on the beach, about ten feet away from Leo. A woman, judging from the slight curve at the waist and the long hair.

I stare and squint, determined not to lose sight of her. It's *her*, the woman I saw the first day. I open my mouth to call out, then decide to keep filming.

Leo has stopped stretching, his hands on his hips, his face turned to her. Samara turns back, too, clutching the controller and the drone. I watch with intensity. They're talking to this woman. I give a small laugh. Thank God. I'd thought I was seeing things before.

She's not wearing a hat or coat, though, and it's freezing. I can see her dark hair and what looks like a pale jumpsuit or dress. I lower the camera quickly, wondering if I should go and help. But then Leo turns to me and waves, like he's inviting me to come and join them. Maybe the woman needs help.

I head across the deck quickly and climb down the ladder, my mind racing. Who is she, and how long has she been out here? How has she managed to survive these temperatures without proper clothing?

By the time I climb down the ladder, the woman is no

longer there. Leo and Samara are walking back towards me, chatting. The woman is gone.

'Did you get it?' Leo says when I reach them.

'Oh my God, tell me you got that backflip off the big rock,' Samara says to me. 'I think I messed up with the drone. It was incredible, wasn't it?'

I open my mouth but realise I'm too confused to answer.

'You OK?' Samara asks. 'You look like you saw a ghost.'

I give a nervous laugh, and their faces fall. 'Who were you talking to?' I ask.

'Who?' Samara says.

I tell them both what I'd seen, just minutes before – a woman standing between them. They looked like they were all chatting. I thought maybe she needed help. She wasn't dressed like the rest of us, all wrapped up in puffer coats and woolly hats. She was wearing a long, pale dress, no hat.

Leo and Samara turn back to stare at the spot on the beach with the rocks.

'When?' Samara says. 'Where is she?'

I feel awkward, and I see Leo's gaze hardening.

'But you got the footage, right?' he asks.

'She was literally right here,' I say, 'where you both were standing by the rocks.' I pull out my phone to show him.

I rewind the footage right to the beginning. Leo and Samara appear on the screen but there's nothing of the woman. I try again, then zoom in.

'Where?' Leo asks.

I can feel myself growing flustered. Samara and Leo are sharing looks while I rewind the footage. Where the hell is it?

'I really did see someone,' I say. 'It looked like you were all talking. I have no idea why it didn't film . . .'

Leo's expression darkens. 'Are you fucking with me?' he says.

I snap my head up. 'No, I'm not.'

I feel so confused, I keep rewinding the footage, as though the woman will appear again. Why isn't she there? I saw her on the screen. I *know* I filmed her.

Samara puts a hand on his shoulder to reassure him. 'How about we go back and I'll get it from the ship?' she says.

Leo looks up. 'The light will be gone soon. We can do it tomorrow.'

'I must have been mistaken,' I say quietly, my cheeks burning. Leo throws me a look of disgust before turning and heading to the *Ormen*.

Inside, I feel embarrassed all over again. Jens is back from his walk and is making a coffee.

'Hey,' he says. 'You get the footage?'

'No, we fucking didn't,' Leo says, and storms off to his cabin.

'I think I'll go for a walk,' I say.

'You want company?' Jens asks.

I still feel too embarrassed. 'I'll be fine,' I say. 'I'm just heading along the beach.'

The truth is, I have a small torch in my pocket, and I am heading back along the beach specifically to check out the big rocks where I saw the woman next to Leo and Samara.

I don't know what I'm looking for, exactly. But I know I saw something. I suspect I'll find that the rocks are angled in a way that creates a shadow, and even though it's getting dark I have this urge to see it up close and piece together the puzzle.

The sea is roaring and hissing, the powerful waves punching down on the sand. I try to keep clear of the tide in case I get dragged out by a rogue wave – I know the drill – so it takes a while until I can step up on to the rocks and check them out.

Up close, they are exactly as they appeared from the *Ormen*, only bigger and rougher, no sign of shadow casting or hidden contours.

I understand a little more now why Leo was disappointed that I didn't capture his backflip; they're huge – one fall and he'd have broken his neck.

I walk back to the ship, defeated and angry at myself. Leo hates me now, I'm pretty sure of it.

I brought my motion sensor module, which attaches to the camera and forces it to turn towards movement; I usually use it when there are predators about.

Now, I set up my camera on a tripod and position it at the window of the main cabin that overlooks the beach. The sensor is super sensitive, and it makes the camera record the first ten seconds of whatever it picks up. I think I've done this for myself more than anything else.

'What's that for?' Samara asks when she sees what I'm doing.

'To film the horses,' I say. 'I saw them the other night, galloping across the beach.'

'Really?' she says. 'I've not seen any.'

The truth is more sinister than horses.

I need to prove to myself that I saw what I saw.

Nicky

I

May 1901
90 miles north of Skúmaskot, Iceland

The storm struck as the *Ormen* crossed the Arctic Circle.

Waves tall as houses reared up at the bow, pummelling the deck so hard the crew feared the ship would capsize. Water thundered down the stairs, flooding both decks. Hens carried into cabins, all the lambs plucked from the hold, tumbled like wet cloths.

Nicky was an open wound, the burning agony of her foot slamming through her bones. She followed the men up to the top deck where the scene of white-crowned squalls greeted her, a forest with teeth, watery oaks swaying in the gale. The wind flung anything that wasn't tethered down.

'Get back downstairs!' Lovejoy roared at her, but she decided she needed to see the tempest. She was freezing cold, wearing only a dress. But if she was going to die, she wanted to see the sky again.

And the storm – it was a divine punishment, the beautiful and terrible end of the world, as though the *Ormen* was crossing the River Styx and taking them all to hell through a valley of monstrous waves. Nicky managed to tether herself to the rig as the nightmare unfolded in front of her – the hands frantically hauling the sails, two of them torn and jagged above, the hold officer and harpooners heaving buckets of water from the deck while the surgeon and steward hefted an injured crewmate from the ground and hauled him to the surgery. She saw blood and vomit pooling on the deck, only to be washed clean by a wave that came punching down, ripping one of the crew from the rig and carrying him far off to sea.

The ship made a sound like a bear growling, listing for a moment at a terrifying angle, sure to plunge into the deep. Stanchions, davits, kegs, and a try-pot all showering down from the deck into the ocean. The sound of screaming beneath the deafening roar of waves, a man's voice calling out the Lord's Prayer.

Nicky felt herself being hurled upside down against the rig, the power of the water flipping her like a rag. Her head collided with something hard, and everything fell into silence.

Olav

September 1902
Skúmaskot, Iceland

He was known as a belligerent drunk and for leaving dark marks on his wife's face on market day, when invariably takings were slim. The villagers of Skúmaskot had long memories and held longer grudges, and so he was the first in a long line of horse breeders to struggle to feed his children.

The night Olav saw the creature, however, he was feeling rather at peace with the world, and with his lot in life. His horses were healthy, the yield of new foals larger than last year's. Forty-eight foals, thirty of them already sold at market. Money had been tight for years but now he felt he could breathe a little easier. He could afford to clothe his children and fix the holes in the walls of their small home. His son, Gunnar, had been asking for a pet dog. He would buy a pet dog.

He decided that Skúmaskot in September was the most beautiful place in the world. The evening was warm, and he had drunk mead at the home of his friend Ragnar before heading off home via the beach. He liked to check on the horses, make sure none of the wilder ones had broken free from the field. More than once he had found the two copper

122

ones racing along the beach. His father had punished such horses with a whip, but he prided himself on taking a gentler hand. Besides, an injured horse sold for less at market.

The midnight sun was often torturous, especially when the children were young, but tonight he greeted the tide with resolve and contentment, the soft blush of the sun and the downy heather lifting his heart.

And then he saw her.

Before him, the shape of a woman, lying on a rock. He squinted, puzzled. Her arms were raised up over her head, her face buried into the sand. He could see that she was naked to the waist, a streak of pale wet skin catching the light.

He staggered towards her. She had likely gone for a swim. Perhaps she had fainted, or drowned. Either way, he was aroused.

Standing over her, he felt his jaw drop. Where he expected to find two slender legs was a thick black tail, like a seal, a set of flippers deep in the sand. When he recovered, he reached down and grabbed one of her arms, pulling her roughly over. Two black eyes flung open, the mouth pulled back in a snarl. He caught sight of the teeth, sharp as a shark's, the grey gums, before stumbling backwards with a shout.

He found himself on all fours, shaken to the core. He looked up, expecting to see her sitting upright, primed to attack. That face. A demonic, inhuman face. And the tail . . .

But she was gone. He jumped again in fright, scanning the beach on either side. No sign. No marks on the sand. He rose to his feet, only to stumble backwards with confusion. She had been right there. He had seen her. He had seen *it*.

Olav was not the same after that. How could he be? He had touched the creature. He felt possessed. He drank every night and used his fists on his wife, and when Ragnar intervened he took a swing at him, too. He was losing his mind.

He visited the oldest woman in Skúmaskot, Katla, who was said to be a white witch.

Tell me, he asked her. *Am I cursed? I touched it.*

She looked him over with her pale sharp eyes, and nodded. *Yes. She cursed you. As she will curse others. Beware.*

Some years later, he saw her again. In the field with the horses. A moment, and there she was again. In his home, by the hearth. In place of his wife in his bed.

He found himself holding a knife in one hand and his foot with the other. It made sense, the impulse. Somewhere in the darkness, someone was singing. He should make his feet like flippers in order to swim to her swiftly. The song told him this plan.

His wife saw the blood and locked her children's doors, then her own, leaving him to it.

At the shore, he dropped to his hands and knees, crawling. He had cut his feet to the bone, blood and muscle trailing in the sand behind him. His feet split between the second and third toes.

He saw her head bobbing above the water, and lunged into the cool waves. Her black eyes, watching him. The dark water, swallowing him whole.

Dominique

I

December 2023
Skúmaskot, Iceland

I am in Skúmaskot, but something is different.

It is summertime, but I recognise the volcano and the beach, and the three rocks at the far end. No snow, gleaming fields, green as malachite, a leathery sea against the black sand. The bay is brimming with boats, the row of turf houses bright with lights and noise. People move busily through the fields behind the volcano. Several of the fields contain horses. Dozens of Icelandic horses with their distinctive shaggy coats and stocky build. I see a child riding one of them, a boy of about ten, a man walking behind. They are moving the horses to a gated entrance overlooking the bay.

I know without any doubt that the man and boy can't see me. I feel filled with rage, absolutely burning with it. As the man opens the gate I start to sing, each note of the melody carrying my craving for revenge into the wind. None of the people hear me, but the horses do. The one carrying the boy rears up, blonde mane flying, a loud whinny drawing the man's attention. He races to help the boy, who has fallen off, but as he does so the rest of the horses bolt towards the gate. They have been spooked by my song, sent into a wild stampede. The gate is unlocked, and so they run loose down the fields.

As the man helps the boy to his feet, he spots me, just for a moment. Wide-eyed terror skids across his face as he sees me, a shape in the mist. I feel suddenly conscious of myself, and how I appear to him – I wear a long, ragged dress, seaweed fronds braided through my hair, and my feet – no tail this time – are bare. I bare my teeth at him, revealing my black gums and my pointed teeth, sharp as a pike's.

And I don't stop singing, not even when the horses plunge off the side of the cliff, down, down on to the rocks below.

I wake with a gasp, the walls of the cabin filled with shadows, reminding me where I am. My sleeping bag feels damp, and for a moment I think I've pissed myself. No – it's sweat. I am absolutely soaking with sweat, my heart pounding.

What is *wrong* with me? Why am I having such crazy dreams?

I get up and fetch my flask, sipping the cool water slowly. Outside, the rush of the sea is rhythmic, a kind of *wash-wash* on repeat, and I focus on it.

It felt more than a dream. That's what is freaking me out here. It felt like a vision.

I head upstairs and make a pot of coffee, then decide to crack open my pancake mix and make an apology breakfast for the others. I feel vulnerable, in need of company, which is bizarre. I feel scared.

'Wow, smells amazing,' Samara says when she surfaces through the hatch a half-hour later.

'Come and sit down,' I tell her, and she's followed soon after by Jens and Leo.

'I wanted to apologise,' I tell Leo. 'I honestly didn't mean to fudge the recording.'

He shrugs. 'That's OK. I probably overreacted. I'm a bit of a hothead, in case you hadn't noticed.'

I feel a weight slide off my shoulders. 'And Jens,' I tell him. 'I snapped at you the other day, about the contest money. Sorry.'

He gives a small smile. 'Hey, no problem.'

'Speaking of,' Leo says. 'How's the research?'

I sigh. 'I've barely started. I got excited when one of the links on the Wikipedia page took me to a paper published by someone who had carried out research into Arctic Sea ice in 1973. They mentioned the ship and referred to it as "a former whaler, named the *Ormen*".'

'That's encouraging,' Samara says. 'It must have brought up some websites? Or research papers?'

'I found some links to academic papers on Google Scholar,' I say, 'but they all cost a fortune to purchase. Like, twenty-five quid per download.'

'I can split it, if you want?' Jens says, and I nod, grateful.

After breakfast, Jens and I venture down into the hold. We take solar lanterns and set them up on the stairs while we wade through the disgusting, ice-cold water. It's my first time down here and I hide how unnerved I am, how anxious, and I don't know why. I mean, of course it's dangerous – the decks above could suddenly give way and collapse on top of us, or there could be toxins down here that Leo didn't encounter, or we could get stuck and die of hypothermia . . . Take your pick. But my anxiety is placed elsewhere. It's the feel of this place. It holds something, a feeling. Of course, I say none of this to Jens because he'll think I'm crazy.

I concentrate instead on sorting through the personal effects that I find there, some of them in barrels and containers, spared from the water. So many books, a mixture of novels and academic texts about Arctic Sea ice and geology.

127

One of the books has a message written inside – *para Diego de tu Abuela, Navidad 1970.*

'Look,' I call to Jens. 'You think this belonged to someone on board the ship?'

He wades over to me, shining his torch down on the inscription. 'For Diego from your grandmother, Christmas 1970.' He wipes his face and squints down again. 'We should google it and see what comes up.'

'Not much to go on,' I say. 'Not even a surname.'

'I should show you what I found about the research era,' he says, turning and flashing his light at the hatch. 'About the ghost ship.'

'Wait, what?' I ask, reeling. 'What ghost ship?'

He turns back to me and furrows his brow. 'You don't know about the ghost ship?'

II

'You must have read somewhere online that the crew went missing?' Jens says.

'The ship was abandoned,' I say. 'It drifted over the Barents Sea . . .'

'Yes, but they never found the crew. They literally vanished.' He takes a breath. 'Except for one man. The coastguard found him.'

'That's not what I read,' I say. 'I read that no one was on board. That the crew got off the ship and instead of spending money dismantling an old ship, they just let it drift across the ocean.'

'What you read was whitewash,' Jens says.

'Whitewash?'

He nods. 'It was a cover up. I'll show you.'

I follow him through the hatch to the lower deck, where we head into our respective cabins to get dried and changed. A few minutes later, he knocks on my door.

'Am I OK to come into your room?'

'Sure,' I say, though the only space is inside my tent. He steps inside and sits down on the floor beside me, his iPad on his lap. 'Show me what you found. About the ghost ship.'

It isn't a news article that he finds, but a 2012 scholarly article making a case for unmanned vessel technology.

The highlighted line says: '. . . and the 1890 barque-rigged steam hybrid known as the *Ormen*, found floating in the Barents Sea in 1973, the crew completely vanished and never located . . .'

I look at him, astonished. 'Can we find some more on this? Like, how and why, and so on?'

'Already done it,' he says, clicking on a tiny column in the *New York Times*.

Missing Crew Still Not Found, August 31st, 1973

A research team based off the coast of Svalbard is still missing after the coastguard located their vessel adrift and unmanned in the Barents Sea. Families are working with authorities in the High Arctic to provide information about letters sent home and details of the crew's last moments.

'Shit,' I say, reading it over again. 'I thought the crew just left the ship. Surely they found out what happened?'

He shows me his search history, a long scrolling list of websites. 'I've not found anything that suggests that,' he says. 'It all seems pretty ominous, right?'

I start to shake, still cold after wading through the icy water in the hold.

'Are you all right?' Jens asks.

'I keep having dreams,' I say.

'What kind of dreams?'

I rub my forehead, which has started to throb. 'Nothing.'

'Don't dismiss it,' he says. 'Tell me.'

I sigh. 'Just crazy nightmares. Like mermaids with these hideous faces. I dreamed about Skúmaskot. About horses . . .'

'Horses?' he asks.

'I saw them diving off a cliff, because I possessed them.' My throat tightens with a knot, squeezing my voice into a sob. 'Oh God,' I say, clasping my hands to my mouth. 'Sorry. I'm emotional because I'm not sleeping properly.'

'I'll give you some sleeping pills,' he says. 'And make sure you go outside when the sun is up. Icelandic winters are not for the faint of heart.'

I nod and say I will, but when he leaves, I zip up my tent and curl up in my sleeping bag. And of course, I dream – about an empty ship, floating on a vast ocean. Blood trickling from a wall on to the floor below, and a bird pecking at a faceless corpse.

III

I don't know how long I sleep, but I wake to laughter. It's a pleasant sound, bringing me out of my dreams with relief.

Upstairs, the others are in the main cabin, the oil cans burning brightly. They're all a little drunk.

'Come and have a seat, Dominique,' Leo says. His voice is slurred, but there isn't the usual nastiness buried in his tone. I take a seat opposite. He hands me a bottle of wine, but as I go to take it, he pulls it back.

'First, you have to tell us something.'

I glance nervously at Samara and Jens. 'OK.'

'What is it you want with us?' Leo says.

I try to get the joke. 'What do I want with you?'

'Yeah, like – when's it all going to stop?'

I blink, waiting for the punchline. 'I don't get you, Leo.'

This makes Jens laughs, which in turn sparks Samara's laughter, but they both sound forced. 'No one gets Leo but Leo.'

'I want a hot shower,' I tell him, 'clean clothes, and a glass for my wine. And a steak.'

'Medium rare?' Jens asks.

'Exactly.'

'That isn't what I asked,' Leo says, his smile fading. The sharpness in his eyes is back. 'I asked what do you want *with us.*'

'Come on, Leo,' Samara says, tapping his leg. 'Play nice.'

'I'm fucking done playing this game,' he snaps.

'What do you want with *me?*' I ask, playfully. 'I was here first, remember?'

He lifts his eyes to mine, a snarl forming on his face. 'You don't want to know,' he says, and I flinch. Leo's moods are like storm clouds passing through the ship. He makes me want to shrink into myself.

'Well, I would like you to pass the wine,' Samara says to me, deflecting Leo's surliness with a light tone.

I try to steady my hand in order to pour myself a tumbler before handing it to her. The fire is soothing, and the wooden boards that Leo pinned to the windows are holding up. I allow myself to breathe deeply, grateful for food and warmth.

'Seriously, though,' Samara says thoughtfully. 'If I could have anything, I think I'd have one day with Lenny.'

'Lenny?' I ask.

'My dog,' she says. 'I found him while I was at college in a box behind a dumpster. He lived until he was thirteen, and then he died.'

'You'd ask for just one more day?' Leo says. 'Why not a lifetime? Or like, forever?'

She nods, her eyes moistening. 'Forever, then. Forever *and* a day.'

'My old home,' Jens says then. 'That's what I'd ask for.'

Leo bristles. 'Who is it we're asking this stuff for, exactly?'

'The one I shared with my wife,' Jens continues, ignoring him.

I stare at him, shocked. I hadn't figured Jens was married.

'Your wife?' Leo asks, a surprised laugh in his voice, as though he's thinking the same thing as me. 'God, Jens. You have a *wife?* Since when?'

'She's dead,' Jens replies in a flat voice. 'Our house was by the river. She used to sit in the side garden looking out, sun in her face. Beautiful row of terraced houses, that whole block. I turned up a few years ago, hoping to remember her. Maybe lay a bouquet at her favourite spot. They turned the whole block into an indoor trampoline park.'

'God,' Samara says, disgusted.

'That's rough,' Leo says.

'I'm sorry,' I tell him, thinking of how sad his eyes are.

'Eilidh,' he says, his face aglow as he stares at the fire. 'That was her name.'

'Eilidh,' I repeat.

'Do you think I'll ever see her again?' he asks. It takes me a moment to realise he's asking me.

'I don't know,' I say, stumbling over my words. 'I mean, I hope so, right?'

'But if it was up to you,' he says, turning to face me. 'What would you say?'

What would *I say*? 'I'd say, absolutely,' I tell him, and his face lights up. 'Absolutely, you'd see her again. And Samara would be with her dog. And Leo would be with . . . whoever or whatever Leo wants to be with.'

'Lucas,' he says hoarsely.

'With Lucas,' I say, raising my glass. Samara does the same, and we repeat their names.

With Lucas. With Lenny. With Eilidh.

But I don't add my own. That space in my mind is a blank, and it puzzles me.

Why isn't there someone, or something there? I can feel there is.

But I can't remember their name.

Nicky

I

May 1901
20 miles north-west of Skúmaskot, Iceland

Clouds.

A blue sky.

The sound of someone vomiting.

She came to on her back by the try-pot, which had somehow been flung back on to the deck, though now upside down. Next to her was the body of a dead lamb, and one of the men. Collins, she recalled, from his black neckerchief. Daverley approached with Captain Willingham, their faces drawn as they lowered to inspect Collins. His head was turned and his eyes stared ahead, fixed on her, his right arm reaching out.

'Where's Ellis?' Daverley asked Reid, who shivered next to him, soaked to the bone but otherwise spared. He shook his head, and the captain grimaced. Two men gone. And the storm wasn't finished with them.

'You best get downstairs to your cabin,' Daverley told her. He pointed grimly to a dark line on the horizon. 'There are more of those waves coming, bigger than before. Go to your cabin and lock the door.'

He said it with enough urgency to persuade her to obey. She nodded, then made her way quickly down the stairs to

135

the deck, which sat in three inches of water. A brown hen floated past, seemingly content to brood on the water, and in a corner a cow ate from a burst bag of oats. Outside the captain's room was a row of sandbags, preventing water from entering. If the maps got wet, they were done for.

She went into her room and made to shut the door, but just then a hand slapped on the wood, stopping it. Lovejoy stood there, that horrible, grimacing grin on his face, close enough for her to see the black holes in his teeth.

'What are you doing?' she said. Then, braver: 'Why aren't you up on the deck helping with everyone else?'

'Ellis is dead,' he said, looking her up and down. 'You must be happy.'

The pills made her reactions slow and sluggish, so as he reached out to touch her cheek, she found she could do no more than freeze to the spot, her eyes on his.

'*My* selkie wife,' he said, stretching a smile across his black teeth.

II

The first night, he stayed with her a while, after. The length of him on the small bed, insisting that she lie with her arm across his round chest, his filthy hand gripping hers. She felt drenched in shame. In guilt. In disgust. She felt like the most integral part of her had been scooped out. She felt like she wanted to fold inwards, in, in, never to return. She was in two places at once. On that hideous bed and elsewhere, floating, screaming, both at the same time.

Lovejoy talked as though nothing had happened, as though they had always been confidants, and not strangers, she held hostage to his dark desires. He told her about his childhood. About his sons, Ben, Arthur and Philip. Scoundrels, he said, picking his teeth. In and out of prison, one of them locked up now for good. Murder. Another child in the Highlands from a relationship in his youth. His own years in prison, and the beatings he meted there.

She began to hum. It was half intentional, a bidding of her body to close out the very fact of him, his gravelly voice, the rasp and wheeze of his chest under her ear. The stubborn thud of his heartbeat.

'What's that you're singing, selkie?' he asked.

She didn't answer, not verbally. Hymns she had sung in church and school, lullabies her mother had sung to her as a child . . . they spilled out from her now, soft, wordless. An involuntary response to what had happened. To what he had done.

He grew angry when she didn't respond, tightening his grip on her arm and making threats, then pushing her off him and storming angrily out of the cabin.

In the darkness, she curled the bedclothes around her aching body. The melodies continued in her head, seeping from her memories, until sleep rescued her with its wild and dreamless silence.

Dominique

I

December 2023
Skúmaskot, Iceland

The weather becomes what Jens calls 'wolf weather', meaning that the elements want to eat us.

It reaches minus nineteen, the kind of cold that threatens to peel off your skin, or turn your digits into charcoal from frostbite. Sometimes the dark is that velvety midnight blackness, and around lunchtime it fades to a moth-light, owlish and ethereal, softening the lines of the hills in the distance and the zigzag of the turf houses on the other side of the bay. The desalination tank provides water for fresh drinking water and technically washing, but we've all avoided washing in case it runs dry. It's so cold that we all live in our outdoor gear pretty much all the time now, except for the evenings, when Leo gets the fires going.

We have five oil-can fires, dotted around the main cabin and two in the corridor in the lower deck. It's a workout, keeping them all lit. It's a fire hazard, quite literally, and I have dreams about the ship burning down with us inside it. We prop them up with old metal hooks from the upper deck, otherwise the wind finds a way inside and knocks them over.

I had the same experience as I did earlier in the week.

139

I went downstairs to use the bathroom – a pot that we throw into the sea, nothing glamorous – and when I was coming back up the stairs into the main cabin I heard whispering. Leo, mostly; Samara saying something back in sombre tones. When I popped my head up through the hatch, the whispering stopped, but I heard it.

We're trapped, remember?

Leo's voice this time.

I pretended I hadn't heard anything when I emerged, covertly reading the room to deduce if anyone was going to fill me in. But of course, they didn't, and I've been trying to work out what he might have meant.

I have no idea. If he means they're trapped by the weather, I think it's an exaggeration – the snow is still heavy and the winds are savage, but trapped? Not exactly.

I've put the whole thing down to eccentricity. He's a weird guy. I'm going to keep out of his way until the project is done.

The next day, there is no proper sunlight, and we start talking to our battery packs, willing them to charge, urging them on like small children. The project social media accounts are glitchy too. My phone takes ages to connect. It's got to be the internet terminal, but it's a pain – we're relying on follower engagement to get word out there about what we're doing.

'Guys, guess what I found?!'

Samara's voice sounds from the cabin, and I rush back upstairs.

'What is it?' Leo is asking, and we approach her as she sits on the sofa with her iPad.

'Has anyone got a camera with battery life?' she says, glancing up at us. 'You need to film this.'

'I do,' Jens says, and he pulls out his camera.

Samara is beaming, and I see on the screen of her iPad that

she has what looks like a document. She looks into Jens' camera.

'So I managed to hack into an academic research journal that has legit *thousands* of old newspapers and articles and photographs from the whaling era. Anyway, I did some searching and found some scholarly papers that mention the *Ormen*, and I've got some info for you all.'

Leo claps his hands together, then glances at Jens and me with a shrug as if to say, *Sorry, losers.*

Samara high-fives Leo, then holds up her iPad. 'So there's quite a bit to get through, but already I've found out that the *Ormen*, this very ship we're standing on, was built in Dundee in 1890. It was owned by a number of companies right up until the 1960s, but it was a big deal when it was first built because of its auxiliary steam engine. It says here, "In a time when whaling ships were powered mostly by wind and muscle, and subsequently ended up becoming crushed by pack ice, a ship that had the capacity to power its way through an ice-choked Arctic was regarded as a state-of-the-art vessel, and the solution to the single most perilous challenge faced by one of society's most important industries."'

She looks up and pulls a *wowzers* face. 'The ship was named *Ormen* – the Norwegian word for serpent – because of her ability to wind through icy paths as easily as a snake. Her first owner was the Abney & Sons Whale Fishing Company, George Abney, and he ran it from 1890 until 1901.'

She pulls another face at the camera, darker this time, then turns back to her iPad. 'There are some footnotes and links here to numerous newspaper reports of the *Ormen*'s voyages in the Arctic. I've actually got a list of the first crew who sailed here. The *Ormen*'s crew were regarded as heroes of Dundee, so they all got a full mention in the newspapers.' She pauses before looking up at us. 'Should I read their names out?'

Jens nods. 'Go for it.'

'OK. So we have twenty crew members. Captain Jonathon Willingham, Dr Edward O'Regan, followed by P. Arnott, T. Collins, E. Cowie, J. Daverley, Y. Ellis, A. Goodall, G. Harrow, F. R. Gray, D. Lovejoy, F. Martin, N. McIntyre, B. McKenzie, S. Royle, L. Skentelbery, T. Stroud, V. Wolfarth, and two unnamed ship hands.'

She looks up. 'Ship hands?'

'Deckhands,' Jens says. 'Cabin boys. Usually in their teens.'

She nods. 'So, most of these men made ten journeys to the Arctic between 1891 and 1901. Probably some of them died on the voyages too, though. They spent up to nine months on board and then had three months at home with their families.'

We all fall silent, our excitement eclipsed by the dawning meaning of what Samara has discovered. After a moment, Leo says, 'Hearing their names like that is so powerful.'

Samara nods, her smile replaced by a thoughtfulness. 'It makes me remember they were real people. And up to nine months at sea in the Arctic. We're only here for a few weeks. *And* we have solar chargers and shit.'

Jens stops filming and gives a thumbs up.

'Thanks,' Samara says, the buzz a little flattened. Her smile returns when she looks at her iPad. 'Honestly, guys, there is *so much* stuff here, just in this one article. The contest is *over*, I'm serious. Take me to the captain's cabin, that door is *mine*.'

I give Jens an 'Oh yeah?' look. 'I'm hacking that academic website,' I tell Samara, half-joking. 'I see your boring crew list and raise you a shit ton of info on the research era.'

'You're on,' she says, fist-bumping me.

II

This afternoon, Jens announced he was going for a walk. He left at three and it's now gone eight o'clock. It's pitch-black outside, and it feels like moving through treacle, a viscous kind of dark, so we've been taking it in turns to stand on the deck to keep an eye out for him. Leo spots his headlamp in the distance and races out to greet him.

Jens looks pale when he comes into the cabin, a wide, liquid gaze and his shoulders rounded.

'What happened?' Samara says when he staggers into the cabin.

Leo gives us worried looks. 'I think he's dehydrated.'

Jens' eyes fall to my water bottle on the coffee table, and I hand it to him, reading his gaze as desperate thirst.

'Where've you been?' Samara asks. Then, 'You didn't take a water bottle with you?'

Jens drinks deeply, wiping his mouth roughly on his sleeve. He steps forward, but stumbles, and Leo catches him.

'Whoa there. Come and sit down.'

Leo and I support his weight as he sinks down on to the couch. The three of us trade *oh shit* glances. What the hell is wrong with him?

We all take our seats near him, waiting for him to say what happened. He doesn't seem to be injured, no blood or bumps, just badly chapped lips and a wind-whipped face. It's treacherous weather, minus twenty. He's bloody stupid for going out in it.

Samara grows impatient. 'Jens, whatever it is, spit it out.'

'I was out walking,' he says, his voice hoarse.

'We kind of know that,' Leo says. 'You were gone a long time.'

'I was exploring the caves.'

My mind flies to the rocks that run all the way from the volcano into the distance. We've scoped out the area enough to know that there are four main entrances to the cave, but the one he seems to be referring to – the largest of the four entrances – isn't that far away.

'That took you five hours?' I say.

'I got lost,' he says, gasping. 'I just kept moving in circles.'

He swallows hard and draws a hand to his mouth, like he's going to be sick.

'For God's sake, Jens,' Samara said. '*What?*'

'Bones,' he pants. 'Skeletons. In the cave.'

'Oh my God,' Samara says. 'Are you kidding?'

Jens lifts his eyes to her. He looks haunted. 'I wish I was.'

'What kind of bones?' Leo asks.

'Horses,' Jens says. I thought of the horses I heard the first night I arrived. 'And markings on the cave wall,' he says. 'It looked . . . Satanic.'

'Jesus,' Leo says. Then: 'Is it weird that I want to see?'

'Did you film it?' I ask, and Jens shakes his head.

Samara shrugs. 'Well, we're here to explore. Let's explore.'

We get dressed quickly, throw on our coats and hats. Outside, the wind is wild, the sea slamming the ship so hard that we almost fall off the ladder. I grip the sides tightly and try not to look down as I feel for the rungs with my feet.

We walk across the beach, the black sand glistening with frost, sand snakes rippling towards us.

Jens leads us to the cave, a black maw in the belly of the cliffs. At the entrance, I feel a raw, primal fear in my gut, and I want to grab Leo and Samara and ask them whether they trust him. If we should let him fly his drone in there and show us the horses on a screen. But I know what the answer will be – we've already walked some distance and Jens has told us that he's reluctant to fly his drone in caves. Too much risk of damage.

'What if it's anthrax?' I call after the others.

Jens turns, and I notice he glances at Leo and Samara to check their reaction. 'It isn't anthrax.'

'I'm not sure I want to see it, actually,' Samara says, frowning.

We all trade looks, weighing up if we should leave the skeletons alone.

We follow Jens inside the cave. The mouth is like the entrance to a French cathedral, an arched opening of those basalt columns I admired the day after I arrived. Absolutely stunning, especially where the snow sits on top of the shorter columns like white caps in perfect hexagons. The ocean doesn't reach inside the cave – we check the tide to be sure – but it is very damp, the poor light eroding our sense of depth.

'It goes all the way back,' Jens says, turning on his head-lamp, though the beam melts into the distance. 'The length of the headland and then some. There's probably a network of caves throughout this whole section of the coastline.'

'All right, let's not freak ourselves out,' Leo says. 'We've all seen some scary shit in our time, right?'

I do wonder why Jens didn't film it before. Not even on his phone. But maybe he was too freaked out. Jens is always so bloody straight-faced and stoic that I feel more unnerved by the fact that Jens is unnerved, of all people. Nothing seems to rattle him, but this has.

Samara and I flick on our hand torches and draw the beams of light over the damp cave walls. The rock pattern that I saw on the entrance continues inside, concealed in some places by moss and the calcium deposits that spiral down like fangs from the ceiling. The cave narrows as we press on, and I feel conscious of my heart, which is starting to gallop.

I pull out my phone and begin to film, doing a three-sixty turn to capture the mouth of the cave and the beach beyond. My light falls on Leo and Samara behind me, wrapped up in thick winter coats and hats and face masks, emerging from the snow and mist into the darkness of the cave like astronauts stepping out of the fog of a spaceship to explore a distant planet.

'So right now, Jens is taking us to see something he discovered in this cave.' My voice sounds reedy with fear as I do the commentary. 'Not sure if you can see, but the roof is about thirty foot above me here, and the width about fifteen feet. It smells disgusting. I think there are bats up above, or something flitting. Leo, are there bats in Iceland?'

'No,' he says, shining his torch up to the cave roof, though the light is blunted by mist. 'I mean, they might have been artificially introduced as a foreign species, but they're not native here. And I dare say it's too cold this far north for them to survive.'

A loud rustling sound overhead makes us all stop in our tracks.

'It's just birds,' Samara calls back.

'Or cave people,' Leo says. 'A vampirish human-mole hybrid species that survives by eating urban explorers.'

'Leo!' Samara snaps. 'Shut the fuck up!'

Just then, I spot something at the mouth of the cave behind us.

I glance back and see a figure standing there in silhouette.

The woman. I give a shout, a loud 'oh!', as though I've stubbed my toe. Samara asks me if I'm all right and I stand like a deer in headlights staring at the mouth of the cave, frightened out of my wits. I had swung my phone around to film it, but in that moment the figure is gone, melted into the white glare of moon on the cave entrance.

'Did anyone see that?' I say.

'See what?' Leo says. 'You saw something behind us?'

I turn back to check, the hairs on my arms standing on end. 'I . . . I think so.'

Samara and Leo exchange looks, and I swallow hard, reminding myself of when I saw the woman standing next to Leo when he was doing parkour. The ghost, ghost, ghost, I think, trying to imprint the word into my mind, the possibility of it. The only thing worse than a ghost, after all, is madness allowed to gallop unchecked.

I close my mouth, relieved that the conversation has moved on while I composed myself.

My hands are trembling as I lower my phone and stop the recording, then hit rewind to see if I've managed to film the figure. I haven't. Of course. Every time I see her, the others don't. It's unbearable.

'How far in do we have to go?' I ask, my voice catching.

Jens turns and glances back at us. All three of us are hesitant now. 'Just a little further,' he says.

We walk further, the width of the cave expanding and the pattern of the rock changing. Leo stops and holds up a hand.

'Guys.'

He bends down and lifts something slowly.

'What is it?' I ask.

Leo doesn't answer, but as I turn my camera and zoom in, he raises something in his hand. I see a round thing at the top of the object, a kind of knob.

'It's a femur,' Leo says.

'Holy shit,' Samara says. 'Put it down.'

He sets it back down, then takes out his torch and directs the beam at it. I film it all. The femur is too big for a human, which is a relief.

'A horse bone,' Jens says.

'Is this what you saw before?' Samara asks, and he shakes his head. 'I think the first skeleton was just by that stalactite,' he says, sweeping his torchlight over a four-foot mineral dagger hanging from the cave roof. The roof is lowering here, which is starting to make me freak out. What if it collapses? What if we can't get out?

'Here,' I call out, stopping by the stalactite. I can see a shadow on the ground, a large rock, I think. But then Leo's torchlight reveals a pleated pattern, and I realise it's not a rock. It's ribs.

'Oh God,' Leo says, jumping back. He crouches down, covering his mouth. 'You're right. I think that's a horse. There's a mane attached to the skull. Look.'

He lifts a small stone to scrape away some of the dirt. The long shape of a skull appears, thick bunches of what look like coarse jute visible in the earth.

Jens walks on ahead, then stops and waves back to us. 'Another one here.'

'God, do we have to?' Samara says.

I press on, silently filming, until I reach Jens. At either side of me are more and more bones, far more than I'd expected. Images flash in my mind. The dream. The boy on the horse, the man leading them and the rest of the herd to the entrance of the field. The song, and the horses bolting to the edge of the cliff.

III

Outside, the wind has grown fierce, whipping up the sand in frightening black columns that spiral around us like a thousand crows.

We head back to the *Ormen*. Inside, Leo makes us all cups of tea while Jens sets about lighting the fire to warm us up. Samara is pacing and murmuring to herself, saying over and over how she can't, she can't.

'Dom?' Leo says. 'Dominique?'

'Yeah?'

'I've asked you four times if you want milk in your tea.'

'Uh, no. Thanks.'

In my mind, I keep seeing the horses falling over the cliff, that terribly whinny.

A part of me feels angry at Jens. What did we gain by encountering the horses for ourselves, other than being scared witless?

Unless he wanted to make a point. Unless he wanted *me* to see them. I told him that I'd heard horses the first night I was here. And I'd told him about my dream.

No, I tell myself. It isn't like he planted the bones. He's as shocked as the rest of us. But that feeling returns, the one that rested inside me when I arrived here – caution. An instinct to be guarded around him. Around all of them. Though maybe it's too late for that.

Samara finally sits down close to the fire. Jens throws a blanket across her shoulders and Leo passes her a cup of tea, then crouches down in front of her.

'You want to talk about it?' Leo asks her with uncharacteristic tenderness.

She wipes a tear from her cheek. 'I can't,' she says, her voice shaking. 'I can't go through with this. I can't.'

'Can't go through with what?' I ask her. 'The contest?'

She doesn't answer. Leo is rubbing her hands, urging her in soft whispers as she shakes her head. 'A night's sleep and you'll feel a lot better,' he says, glancing at me.

'No, no,' Samara says. 'It's never been as bad as this. You said it would work but it's worse this time. I want to . . .'

'You know we can't, Sam,' Leo says. 'Let's just stick to the plan, OK?'

I feel a prickle on the back of my neck. The plan?

Just then Samara stands up and marches across the cabin towards the door.

'Samara, come *on*,' Leo calls loudly after her, holding up his hands. 'It's Armageddon out there. The wind will fuck you up.'

Samara yanks her coat off the hook and spins around. 'It doesn't matter how long ago it was,' she shouts, her voice shrill. 'You were wrong, Jens. This isn't working. I can't go through with this!'

Leo is trying to calm her, taking her hands again and telling her to repeat a mantra, but she pulls away.

'Can't go through with what?' I ask, because there's a horrible feeling in my stomach, and a strange sense of déjà vu. Samara looks up at me, her face full of fear. I turn to Leo and repeat it. 'Can't go through with what?'

Leo ignores me. 'If you want to bail, we can do that,' he tells Samara. 'OK?'

Samara is nodding and wiping her eyes, but she's unravelling.

'This is all too crazy,' she says. 'Too, too much. I mean, what does it mean?' She looks up at Jens. 'I can deal with the research thing, I can, really. And the laptops and the wine . . . but I cannot deal with this . . . *mindfuck*.'

Her eyes travel to mine, and I do a double-take at the look on her face when she sees me. She looks terrified of me. *Why of me?*

'Samara,' I say. 'It's OK.'

I reach out to touch her arm, but she pulls away.

'Don't fucking touch me,' she hisses. '*Witch*.'

I reel. She called me a witch?

'You did this,' she says. 'You killed them!'

I stare at her, horrified. Why is she saying this? She's distressed, I can see that, and the room is charged with emotion. Outside, the wind howls, a loud, high-pitched shriek that bangs against the cabin. One of the Perspex windows blows in, and Jens rushes to catch the sheet as it drifts across the room towards the fire bucket.

'Somebody help?' Jens calls from the blown-in window. I rush to help pin the Perspex sheet into place, but the wind is too strong. Finally, Leo picks up a sheet of wood and leans in against the gaping space, and the cabin falls into silence.

'Come on,' Leo tells Samara. 'A good night's sleep will help, OK?'

Jens looks at me but says nothing. I feel completely alone. I feel sick. The look on Samara's face when I touched her . . . it was pure terror.

I head down to my cabin and close the door. There's a mark on the floorboard near the door that looks like another bloodstain. I feel my skin crawl.

151

There's malice in the persisting midnight, a cruelty. I know this makes no sense. I sound paranoid, out of my mind. But that doesn't make it any less real to me. And Samara is right.

I *am* a bad person. If I could change the things I've done, I would.

But I can't. I can't.

PART TWO

the mermaid stone

Nicky

I

A month had passed since Nicky woke up in the stinking hold of the *Ormen*. Her injured foot did not heal but seemed to grow infected, though Dr O'Regan swore it was not. The infection was spreading up her leg, a dark bruise. He claimed he could not see it, but the evidence was there, and so she kept it bandaged.

The sea disappeared beneath a vast mosaic of ice. Thick slabs thudded against the ship, and Nicky feared they would breach the hold. The knocking of them, the blinding whiteness as far as the eye could see – she wondered how any boat could sail through such dense matter. But they did.

The weather calmed after the storm that took Collins, Ellis, and the lambs. The crew buried Collins at sea, despite misgivings. According to Daverley and several others, a sea burial resulted in a vexed and vengeful spirit, one that might haunt the ship. They had no choice but to lower him into his watery grave, a stitch at the nose to keep the soul inside the shroud. Ellis' body was never recovered. Captain Willingham asked Nicky if she would write a letter to his wife, capturing Ellis' labours on board before he died.

She wondered if she'd heard him correctly. Ellis had raped her, and now he was asking her to redeem him in writing? 'I will do no such thing,' she said.

'You write that Ellis was a good whaleman,' Captain Willingham said, lacing his fingers together. 'An elegant rendering of his part in the capture of whales and such like.'

She cocked an eyebrow. 'How about I write it, and you turn the ship around and take me back to Dundee.'

Captain Willingham produced a jar of sweets from a secret store. Pear drops, Highland toffees, and apple sours. 'That's the best I can do,' he said.

In the end, she agreed.

They faced other problems, including the destruction of the sails. The mariners replaced and repaired where they could, but the ship would have to rely on its steam engines to power through heavy ice.

One by one, the mariners started making their way to her cabin. Gray, a young man of nineteen who walked with a limp; Wolfarth, who never spoke a word to her; McKenzie, who told her secrets about his wife; Stroud, who sometimes cried. They arrived at her door with sheepish looks, forewarned about her tendency to sing strange songs. She kept her eyes on the door as they grunted above her, melodies that Allan had played on their old piano in Faulkner Street spilling from her lips. Often the men begged her to stop, but she didn't, not even when threats were made. Some of the men resorted to filling their ears with bits of rag.

The captain's wedding ring glinted in the amber lamplight, an apology folded in his silences. She spied the man behind the title, a quivering thing, buckled by too many years at sea. His command was sloppy, his words liquefied. He smelled of rum and shame.

And still she sang.

She came to expect a knock on her door at dawn each morning, the captain's early morning visit, his silent apologies diminishing like arpeggios. She learned quickly that the key to survival – while she still believed in it – was to ram the fear that threatened to consume her right down into a tight box of hell deep in her heart, to lock it shut with a fake smile stretched across her face like a rictus.

There was a palpable dynamic at the heart of her role as selkie wife that cut through the fear. The men grew jealous of each other, and their jealousy spurred a bizarre protectiveness over her that she understood was no more than a sense of proprietorship. McIntyre in particular was a nasty and prolific drinker, given to picking fights with the younger men, such as Royle and Wolfarth. Her body was a territory, just like the ship, and each of them wanted to stake a claim.

She understood it was only this jealousy and proprietorship that spared her from violence. Lovejoy seemed to be the man in charge when it came to who ventured to her cabin; even McIntyre deferred to him. She considered it bitterly ironic that a man named Lovejoy was so utterly incapable of love and an antidote to joy. Some of the men were sympathetic, asking about the injury to her foot and the bruises on her face. The bruises had faded, but her foot had not healed, or rather it had healed with chimerical effect; like a limb trans-figured by flame is often useless long after the bleeding has stopped, perhaps withered, so her foot was not the way it had been. It was no longer human. The grey pelt she had spied forming beneath the skin had continued up her ankle, fading at the calf. She asked Dr O'Regan for fresh bandages, applying them herself so he would not see.

But it was only a matter of time. And Allan – what would he think? How could she ever return to him like this?

II

She thought of the day she went into labour, how her mother had wanted her to give birth in Larkbrae but the plans fell apart when it progressed too quickly.

'What should I do?' Allan said when she woke him with a yell. She had felt the pains earlier in the night but thought nothing of it. She wasn't due for another month, and her mother told her to expect the last weeks to be painful. 'The body prepares itself for labour by faking it,' she said.

But by the time she realised that this wasn't fakery, her waters had broken.

'Get Dr McGill,' she said through heavy breaths, and so Allan pulled on his trousers and raced off to the doctor's home two miles away.

The relief of pain during childbirth was considered sacrilegious, and therefore forbidden, on account of the Old Testament pronouncement, *in sorrow shalt thou bring forth children*. Even Dr McGill, who had delivered her and her sister, held fast to this rule, worried that she and the child might be cursed if he disobeyed.

Allan occupied himself in a stupor, following the list of chores Nicky's mother had provided – light the fire, open the windows, boil towels and blankets. Ready the crib, and the cabbage leaves, and the leeches. He completed his tasks and took to holding Nicky's hand and dabbing her forehead as she screamed.

'You're doing well,' he whispered by her head. 'You're a champion, Nicky. A champion.'

She felt as though her back was breaking, the child presenting with its spine against hers. Dr McGill resorted at last to forceps, a fearsome contraption that drew a gasp of concern from Allan.

'Surely that will only hurt the bairn?' he asked.

'Better an injury than a corpse,' Dr McGill grunted. 'Or two corpses.' He threw a meaningful look at Allan, who turned pale. He gripped Nicky's hand and nodded at Dr McGill, who inserted the mechanism between Nicky's legs.

A moment of tugging, then a shrill cry. The baby covered in chalky vernix, placed on Nicky's belly. Its cone-shaped head, bruised and misshaped from the forceps. The placenta removed, and the leeches placed on her cervix to stem the bleeding.

She remembered the impossibly small fingernails, the lines on the palms. The delicate feet, identical to Allan's.

The bird-like mouth, searching for milk. And against all odds, alive.

III

The pristine shores of Greenland pricked the horizon, towering jags, crisp as broken glass, mantled by feathery haar. The air glittered. Absinthe-green patches peeked up through the ice slabs on the surface of the ocean, and glassy lozenges bobbed against the hull, thick and solid as concrete. The combination of colours was striking – alabaster white against cornflower blue and polished silver.

A small pod of grampus grew curious of the ship one morning, their slick black bodies ploughing the sea. Longer and darker than dolphins, they huffed in a single file like a sea serpent weaving the waves. Dolphins travelled in pods of thirty, sometimes more. They liked to race the ship, the younger mariners tapping the side of the hull to encourage them. She spotted sea eagles flying overhead, their wingspan longer than a man. And on the sheet ice, walruses with fangs the length of her forearm barked at them, while smaller seals darted through the blue water.

She woke one morning to the blare of bagpipes. Harrow, the second mate and one of the oldest of the crew, liked to stand on the poop deck on slower days playing Scottish tunes, waving a Saltire and taking requests. In between tunes he'd announce that the bagpipes were weapons of war, hailing from the Battle of Culloden when Scottish pipers roused their

160

troops against the redcoats, and banned thereafter by the British.

'Aye, we know,' McIntyre shouted back.

'We're Scottish too, you dunderhead,' Gray shouted, flinging a becket at him.

Harrow was undeterred. 'The Highland Clearances began with the silencing of the national instrument. When we play the pipes, we echo the voices of our ancestors, lads! We defy our oppressors!'

'We're in the Arctic, you nugget,' Lovejoy bellowed back. 'The only oppression here is the lack of whisky.'

Harrow asked Nicky what she'd like to hear, and she hesitated. She wasn't keen to join in with the men's play, certainly not in any way that might indicate her consent to being held captive like she was. And the bagpipes had marked almost every occasion of her life – her wedding ceremony and every Burns night her father employed a piper to address the haggis. The last thing she wanted to hear was a tune that might disturb a sacred memory.

After a while, she suggested 'The Parting Glass', a song she had never heard on the pipes.

Harrow gave a bow and played it with feeling. The call of the pipes amidst the loneliness of the polar expanses brought the men to contemplative silence. 'Play "Scotland the Brave"!' Lovejoy shouted after a while, and the plaintive mood that had settled across the ship was broken by a rousing melody.

The first whale they caught was a bowhead whale, female, forty feet long. It had seemed enormous in the water, almost the length of the boat. Nicky had heard the men shouting and headed up to the top deck. About thirty feet from the side of the boat she could see the line of a leviathan cutting through the waves. McIntyre and Gray were already lining up the harpoon cannon, but Lovejoy called out to them, ordering them to hold fire.

'We've not dunked a man,' he roared. He whistled at Cowie, then nodded at Reid. 'Chuck him in, lads.'

Reid looked startled as the two men laid hands upon him, before heaving him over the side and into the dark water below.

'I'm not a strong swimmer!' Reid shouted from below. 'It's . . . it's too cold!'

Daverley stood on the side of the rig glancing down, stricken at the sight of Reid thrashing in the dark water below. He pulled off his boots and hat before jumping feet first into the water near Reid, who was paddling frantically at the water with his hands.

'Why on earth did you do that?' Nicky asked Cowie as she watched Daverley drag Reid to the anchor rope, pulling them both up on deck again.

'Bad luck to start fishing without dunking a member of the crew,' Cowie said.

As the boat turned towards the whale, she saw another, smaller fish in the water next to it – a calf. She waved up to McIntyre, calling out for him to stop, but just then the harpoon shot out from the cannon with a force that she felt right through her feet up to her neck. Instantly, the dark water reddened, bubbles of it rising and turning the side of an iceberg pink.

The calf didn't swim away, didn't make a sound, but Nicky imagined the helplessness of it as it watched its mother bloat with air from the harpoon, floating to the surface like a hot air balloon. 'The red flag's flying!' Cowie shouted, as the water around it began to spew with blood.

The men hauled the whale alongside the hull for flensing, the tail held fast by a fluke-chain and the fins fixed with a fin-chain. Wolfarth fastened a blubber hook to a second fin-chain and pronged it on the upper lip, the lower jaw hanging open, the fringed baleen riffling in its enormous mouth like a lace curtain. Lastly, Arnott threaded a chain through the blow-hole to stop the weight of the beast's body tearing it free.

Wolfarth, Royle and McKenzie set to the carcass with long-handled axes, with Lovejoy overseeing the process of stripping the flanks and hacking at the blubber that lay like a hot mattress underneath. From a distance, it looked like they were stripping a tree of its bark. She made herself look at the parts of it that were mammal, the navy eye buried in bloated eyelids. The air around it steamed with the heat of its body releasing into the cool air.

The men were tiring and drenched in blood. Reid and Anderson's job was to fetch fresh buckets of seawater to rinse the deck, while Stroud, Arnott and Daverley stacked and hefted barrels filled with blubber into the bowels of the ship.

'Five and forty more!' Stroud shouted, meaning that the last piece of blubber had been swung inboard.

And then the boiling of the blubber in the try-works, the brick ovens abaft the forehatch containing try-pots, two enormous cauldrons, where oil was removed from the blubber for storing in casks. Feeling the heat beating from the ovens, Nicky moved closer to warm herself, one eye on the calf moving in the white foam ruffling at the ship's side. To the distant east, she had spotted three black fins, though they slipped away as quickly as they reappeared, each time in a new position, as though they had sped up underwater.

'Orcas,' Daverley told her, appearing by her side, wrapping a length of rope between his palm and elbow. 'They'll come for the calf. Put it out of its misery.'

'Why didn't you just kill the calf, then?' she said. 'If it's going to be killed anyway?'

163

'Not my call. Captain's orders.'

She felt her feet grow wet and looked down to see that a tide of blood had swept across from the butchered whale while she was searching out its calf, drenching her feet and soaking the bandages.

Daverley was still there, making a serving with string and a mallet as he glanced over the side. Usually he was high up the ratlines, checking the ropes for frays, or slathering foul-smelling tar across the rig. She sensed he wanted to speak to her. Next to him, behind a row of barrels, was a rusted metal cage, too large for fish. A length of heavy chain was attached to the top, and inside she could see long spikes angling down.

'What is that?' she asked. She'd never seen it on board before.

He turned and glanced at it. 'It's a brig,' he said.

She searched her mind for the term. A brig was a whaler jail for rowdy crew, but it was usually a small cabin in the ship with a set of chains and a padlocked door.

'We use the ship's brig for storing meat,' he said. 'So the cage takes its place.'

She frowned at the spikes, long as her finger. 'What's the chain for?'

'If any of the men break captain's rules, they're put in the cage, and then the cage is thrown in the water and dragged behind.'

'That's barbaric.'

'Nothing warm and cosy on a whaling ship, as I'm sure you've found.'

'I suppose you'll be visiting my cabin next,' she snapped, kicking the blood off her feet.

'I will not,' he said quietly, his eyes still on the water below. 'And neither will Reid.'

She felt relieved. The sound of footsteps had started to

make her heart race with fear. She had come to associate the sound with the first sign of a man outside her cabin door.

'But you're content with what your crewmates are doing? Taking a woman prisoner?'

'Prisoner?' Daverley looked puzzled. 'You're getting paid, aren't you?'

She laughed bitterly. 'Paid? You call that vile slop "payment"?'

'Why did you come, then?' he said. 'I mean, why come on board if you don't like it?'

She was shocked. He thought she was a prostitute. That she was here by agreement. Her stomach dropped as she thought of Ellis, and the lewd comments the others had made. Lovejoy's tale of the selkie wife. Surely the men had all known that she was taken, plucked off the street because of her father's company? That she was collateral?

'I was kidnapped,' she said. 'I'm not here because I want to be.'

He narrowed his eyes, processing her meaning. Wolfarth and Anderson were nearby, sweeping blood off the deck.

'Did you know about it?' she pressed, stepping closer to Daverley. 'I mean, it must have been planned. Did the captain call a meeting with the crew? Why was I attacked like that?'

He lowered his eyes to the ground. 'Whatever the situation is, I want no part of it. I work, I get my wages, and I go home to my wife.'

'Is that what the others think?' she said, feeling sick. 'That I'm . . . a common prostitute?'

He lifted his eyes to her, and his look told her that they did. 'I don't care about your line of work,' he said simply. 'A woman's bad luck on a ship.'

'Rubbish,' she said. 'And in any case, I didn't choose to be here. So I can't exactly bring bad luck.' She watched him look over at Reid, who gave him a wave.

Daverley tied the end of the rope in a knot, then slipped the hoop of it over his shoulder. 'He's my sister's boy. She passed this last Christmas.'

She heard the catch in his voice. 'I'm sorry.'

'I got him this job. He's almost sixteen. He needs to make his own living, now.'

Her own sister floated to her mind, Cat's slim form at her usual spot in the round window on the landing at Larkbrae, holding her beloved dogs. A lump formed in Nicky's throat. How could she tell Allan about what had happened? How would he look at her, knowing how many men had violated her?

'My father owns this ship,' she said. 'George Abney.'

He nodded. 'I know.'

'You honestly believe the daughter of George Abney is a common prostitute?'

Daverley crouched down to set a dozen grommets in a bucket.

'What did you hear?' she pressed, gritting her teeth.

'It's not my place to say.'

'I swear on my life,' she said, a catch in her voice. 'I was kidnapped. A man attacked me in Dawson Park. My husband will be worrying about me.'

A flicker of something passed across his face, and she tried to recall what she had said to spark it.

'Please,' she said. 'Tell me what you know.'

'What does it matter?' he said hastily. 'The captain has said you're here for the remainder of the voyage. That's all I know. Happy?'

Just then, a voice called 'Daverley!' and she saw Lovejoy stomping across the deck, his face twisted in a scowl. Nicky shrank into herself, lowering her eyes, but not before she saw the way Lovejoy looked from her to Daverley.

'You two have something to chat about?'

'We weren't chatting,' Daverley said.

'Not what it looked like to me,' Lovejoy said, raking his eyes over Daverley. 'If you're not interested in swyving you'll stay well clear, aye?'

'Aye, sir,' Daverley muttered.

Lovejoy squared up to her, his eyes tracing the claret stain on her bandaged foot.

'Downstairs,' he said. 'Now.'

As she moved towards the stairs, she risked a glance at Daverley, who flicked his eyes at her. Something had shifted during their conversation, she had felt it. Perhaps he believed her. Or perhaps he was no better than the other men. Even the most grandfatherly of the crew, like Harrow and McKenzie, the ones who had been tender with her, eventually found their desires overwhelming their decency. Harrow often offered the crook of his arm to help her when she struggled to limp across the upper deck, and McKenzie had been nothing but courteous and even sympathetic whenever she came across him. Even so, they arrived at her cabin, shame-eyed, only to leave with a flushed radiance that they'd somehow found beneath her skirts.

She would ask Daverley again. He knew something. She would persist until she found out the truth.

In her cabin, Lovejoy undid his belt in haste. She could read him now, the rush to take her emerging from the exchange he had witnessed between her and Daverley. She feared Lovejoy, but she well knew how pathetic he was, how much he needed to feel he owned her. The kind of man who would beat a cow for not producing the amount of milk he desired. Usually he ordered her to strip naked, but this time he threw her skirts over her head and thudded into her, blaring out like a stuck pig a handful of seconds later.

167

Afterwards, she limped down to Dr O'Regan's cabin to have her bandage replaced before the blood from the culled whale infected her wound.

She lay down on the bed, wincing as he took off the old dressing and dabbed the wound with a clean linen soaked in alcohol. In the mirror opposite, she could see it – her foot was no longer human, but the fin of a cetacean, dark and slick as ink, bringing fresh revulsion every time she looked at it. If Dr O'Regan saw it too, he said nothing, but then he wasn't interested in her foot. He looked at her with heavy eyes, and before she could move from the bed, he had slipped his hand down her top.

'It's been so long,' he whispered, cupping her breast. 'So long.'

Sigrún

March 1914
Skúmaskot, Iceland

The old woman looked over the bodies of the dead horses with a heaviness in her heart. Yes, the loss of so many horses would affect the family purse. But the way that they had stampeded off the cliff was greater cause for concern. And her grandson, Kristjan, had told her a strange tale of a hideous creature singing by the field. A face like a fox, a tail like a seal.

It was a devil, she knew that. A devil that had driven the horses mad, sending them over the edge of the cliff to their deaths. There was only one way to treat such a thing.

By night, Sigrún instructed her son, Stefan, to burn the bodies of the horses. He was not to shave the luscious manes to sell them. Everything was to be burned, right down to the bone. The flames licked the walls of the cliffs, birds screaming and wheeling above.

When the job was done, Sigrún drew blood from the arms of Stefan and his children, until they grew faint. Smelling salts brought them around. They had a job to be done before the blood grew too cold.

She took them deep inside the cave.

'Here,' she told them, handing them brushes made of horse-hair wrapped around sticks. 'I want you to dip these into the pots and paint what I show you.'

On the walls of the cave and on the bones, they drew patterns, lines upon lines. Cages designed to trap the devils that lay inside the bodies, and perhaps the very bones. Then, they painted themselves, and the archway of their homes. And in the hearth, Stefan chiselled another cage to prevent a demon from coming down the chimney.

Kristjan had once laughed when she told him about such things. But now, she watched as he painted himself in earnest, terrified by the thought of the creature who had bared such sharp teeth at him clawing her way inside him.

Wearing his skin.

Dominique

I

December 2023
Skúmaskot, Iceland

Samara is afraid of me, and I have no idea why. I try to tell myself that we were all freaked out by the bones in the cave, and exhausted from the walk back through the storm. But the way she looked at me . . . I hardly sleep, but instead sit in my tent in the darkness, contemplating whether it's time to go.

This has all got too much.

My head is bouncing as I head up to the main cabin. I had my heart set on telling the story of the *Ormen*, but I did *not* count on doing it with three strangers, one of whom hates me and another who is inexplicably afraid of me.

Outside, it's a bright day. Freezing, yes, but postcard-pretty – a clear blue sky, fresh snow twinkling over the heath, a layer of ice making the sand shimmer like a slab of black opal. The savage wind of the night before has relented, softening to a gentle ripple across the ocean.

Upstairs in the main cabin, I find Leo has made a generous breakfast – pancakes with agave and chocolate sauce, coffee, orange juice, scrambled eggs from powder, and – God knows how – banana muffins. Samara is dark-eyed, a blanket wrapped around her shoulders, but she looks heartened by the food.

I don't want to upset her, so I take a seat near the oil can. 'Hey,' she says. 'Dominique.'

I look up. She smiles. No sign of the fear she showed before. 'I want to show you something.'

I sit at the table opposite her and she swivels her laptop around to show me, pointing at the screen. 'I couldn't sleep,' she says, 'so I thought I'd try and find out more about the horses and the cave.'

Jens comes up through the hatch then, and she waves for the others to come over.

'These don't exactly look like photographs of horses,' Leo says, setting a plate of food on the table.

'They're of the *Ormen*,' she says. 'I couldn't find anything about the horses and that cave, but I came across these.'

I notice the word '*Ormen*' in old lettering. Two of the images are from 1899, and three were taken in 1901.

Jens starts filming her, holding the iPad with the photos on the screen. 'Tell us what you found, Samara,' he says, zooming in on the photographs.

She turns her laptop to him. 'Well, if I show you the two from 1899, they're really cool, but they're clearly press images of the ship leaving the docks in Dundee.' The image on her screen is of the *Ormen*, taken from a distance. It looks majestic, the sails unfurled and masts standing tall, a large crowd watching on at the docks as the ship departs for the Arctic.

Samara swipes to the other photographs. 'These three are kind of slice-of-life shots, taken on board during the 1901 voyage.'

Jens zooms in on an image of the upper deck. A teenage boy wearing a neckerchief and flat cap is standing near the ship's wheel, a fag in his mouth. He is holding a huge albatross upside down by the feet, its head falling limply on the ground. The boy's head is raised as though responding to a shout. On the rig behind him, a man is in the process of painting the ropes, and there are figures moving in the background, too, blurred by movement.

'Who is that?' Leo asks, leaning in closer. He taps the screen with his finger at a figure almost out of the frame, their face blurred but turned to the camera.

Samara moves closer to it, studying it. 'I dunno. Why? You recognise them?'

Leo looks now, and I see Jens falter, not sure whether to keep filming. He decides to stick with it.

'It looks like a woman,' Jens says.

'Well, that's unlikely,' Samara says, bringing up another browser. 'I found this academic book. It says the crews from Dundee were always men.'

'Looks like a skirt,' Leo says, tracing the outline of something that fans out at the very edge of the photograph, and he's right – the image is faint, but it does look like a long, billowing skirt. 'And the figure has long hair, too. There's the shoulder, and you see a flick of something that looks like hair.'

'Jesus, Leo,' Samara says, impressed. 'Talk about the eyes of a hawk. I've never seen that before.'

Jens says nothing, making sure to film the three of us in conversation.

'You really think it's a woman?' Samara says to no one in particular. I take another look, trying to see the image from another angle. The cabin is dimly lit by candles, but Samara toggles the brightness until the contrast is just right. The outline of the skirt appears, then a slim waist and shoulders. It's a feminine silhouette.

Something twists inside me, a sudden fear. I think of the figure I saw on the beach. The woman.

'Are you OK?' Jens says.

I nod. 'Yeah. Fine. I think it is a woman.'

173

'Just because it looks like a woman doesn't mean it's a woman,' Leo says.

'I very much doubt that a whaler in 1901 is going to be wearing a corset and skirt,' Samara says.

Leo shrugs. 'I'm just saying.'

'Could be one of the mariner's wives,' Samara says with a frown. 'I read that the US whaling industry allowed wives to go with their husbands sometimes. Kids, too. But this book is pretty clear about how things were in Dundee . . .'

'We could search through the academic research site you found?' Leo says. 'Find out more about what she's doing there?'

Samara nods, and I feel queasy. There is something about the woman in the photograph that feels familiar, and an icy shiver shoots down my spine.

She looks like the woman on the beach.

II

Jens and I step up our search of the missing research crew in 1973, though we're kind of limited – he's convinced that a lot of print media is still to be digitised, and we'd have better luck in a library with old print archives and microfilm. Nonetheless, I come across a blog that contains photographs of the *Ormen* from 1973, when it was carrying researchers studying glacial ice. For a while I forget the creepiness of the ghost ship, the fact that all the researchers vanished – poof! – into thin air, and pore over photographs from the period. It's cool to compare the two eras, with Samara's photographs from 1901 and the ones we've found from seventy years later. The ship looks much the same, but there are vivid differences in what the people are wearing and how the ship is laid out.

The four of us sit around the dining table and check out the blog, and sure enough, there are a ton of photos there, some with names of the scientists – I search hard for Diego's surname but he isn't mentioned. It is interesting to see the way the crew were dressed, and the cabin that we are all sitting in laid out as a research lab, long tables with maps and microscopes.

'Some of that stuff must still be on here,' Leo says, writing down an inventory of things we've identified in the photographs. 'I guess some of it would have got washed off during storms.'

'Not the bloodstains,' Samara says.

'And scavengers,' Leo says. 'I mean, we can't be the only ones who came on board.'

'We know we aren't,' Samara says. 'The desalination tank was definitely put on board after 1973 . . .'

'Yeah, but I bet anyone who came to explore didn't take souvenirs,' Jens says. 'I bet most of it is all here. If we search all the rooms and the crawlspaces we'll find it.'

'And the shoreline,' Leo says. 'I think we might want to trawl along the bay a little more in case we find anything.'

The conversation spins off towards the contest again. I noticed on our TikTok that people had started talking about which team they were going to vote for. It sparks up conversation, and I tell Samara and Leo that I'm going to win.

But then Samara falls silent. She is staring at something on her laptop, another browser page full of old-fashioned newspapers.

'Guys, look at this,' she says.

'What are we looking at?' Leo says, and Samara zooms in on a newspaper headline.

DAUGHTER OF ABNEY & SONS STILL MISSING, REWARD OFFERED

3 October 1901

The oldest daughter of George Abney, owner of the troubled Abney & Sons Whale Fishing Company, remains absent, her whereabouts unknown. Abney's daughter, Nicky Duthie, was last seen leaving the Camperdown Works jute mill in Dundee on the evening of 6th May this year, and has not been seen since. Abney & Co was the subject of much controversy in the Spring, due to sunken ships and creditors seeking reimbursement. The saga continues, however, in the form of Mr Abney's recent death, and the hasty sale of the business by his widow, Mhairi Abney, without consulting Abney's business partners. Notably, the company's single remaining vessel, the *Ormen*, is due back in Dundee later this month, when the crew will learn of the company's new ownership.

A reward of £80 is offered for information on the whereabouts of Mrs Duthie. Anyone with relevant information should contact Chief Constable James Michie at Dundee City Police.

'That's sad,' Leo says. 'But – sorry if this is harsh – what does that have to do with the *Ormen*?'

'Well, this is when the *Ormen* changed hands,' Samara says. 'It doesn't say who the new owner is, but it seems weird that it was sold under such tragic circumstances. The daughter missing, the owner dead, the owner's wife forced to sell the *Ormen* off before it even got back from the Arctic.'

'Was she found?' Jens says. 'The daughter?'

Samara clicks on the search bar and types 'Nicky Duthie', but the search yields only a single newspaper article, which is the one she showed us. She tries again, typing 'Nicky Abney', but nothing comes up.

I feel a prickle along my spine when I see the woman's name typed out like that, as though each letter is stirring something.

III

I am on the *Ormen*, but she isn't a wreck. She is out to sea, frothy waves bobbing up the sides, white sails unfurled in a splendid grid. Absolutely glorious. But I see myself in the reflection of the water. I am that hideous woman again, my face fixed in a gruesome smile. Black gums, fox teeth, sharp as daggers. My hair braided with seaweed.

I stand on the deck and sing my song of revenge. I want to hurt everyone on the ship. I want them to suffer.

I wake up, gasping for breath.

Switching on my lantern, I unzip my tent slightly to let in fresh air. Upstairs, floorboards creak like someone is moving around. Probably just one of the others, getting a drink of water from the desalination tank.

I lie curled up in my sleeping bag for a while, heart thumping in my throat, hating myself. Why did I dream again? Why am I dreaming such horrible, sickening things?

A scratching sound starts up, and I grow worried in case it's rats, or something bigger, like the Arctic fox I spotted. I pick up my box of matches and a wad of scrunched-up paper spiked on the end of a biro. I figure I'll make a flaming torch if it is the fox, to try and scare it off.

Upstairs in the main cabin, the scratching grows louder.

No fox that I can see, and no rats. Someone is crouched by the door, and I freeze, certain we have an intruder. I point my torch in the direction of the sound and see Leo's head. Thank God. It's only Leo. What the hell is he doing?

'Leo?' I call out.

Leo doesn't answer. I'm worried he's going to freeze to death. He's crouched down on the ground, stripped down to his boxer shorts, and kind of hunched over, one of his arms moving back and forth in a really weird way.

I approach him slowly, recognising instantly that his behaviour is super odd. He's clearly sleepwalking, and I've heard that you shouldn't wake someone too abruptly when they're in that state. But what the hell is causing the scratching noise? It has an odd rhythm. Sometimes slow, like someone dragging nails down a chalkboard, and then quick, like he's hacking something. All the hairs on the backs of my arms stand on end.

I take a step to the side and spy something glinting in the safety light. A knife. I freeze, more certain now that I've worked out what's happening here.

He's cutting himself.

My eyes scan the floor for blood. He shifts to the side and I step back quickly, hiding behind the bookcase. I'm worried in case he sees me. He doesn't, but he moves the table, and I notice that he has written something – or carved something – into the surface. He sits back on his heels as though to look over what he has done, before returning to it.

I don't know what to do. I'm wary of waking him, but I also feel unnerved by what he's doing.

Just as I'm considering a way to wake him gently, there's a noise on the lower deck. A moment later, Samara's head pops above the hatch.

'Will you *please* shut the fuck up?' she says, and Leo gives a loud shout, like he's burned himself. The knife flings out of his hand and lands somewhere by the door, and he falls back, flat on his arse. Samara laughs. She mustn't have clocked that he was sleepwalking, and she hasn't seen him scratching the table with the blade.

'Leo,' she says testily, and I watch as Leo comes to. He blinks and glances around, clearly not sure why he's in the cabin.

'What's going on?' Samara asks, stepping up to help him to his feet.

'Nothing,' Leo mutters hazily. He's so out of it that he doesn't even see me. I watch as he staggers towards the hatch and down the stairs, my heart cartwheeling.

What is it about this place that makes everyone do weird things in their sleep?

IV

I sleep in after that, exhausted from finding Leo upstairs and ruminating about it afterwards.

At eleven, I head upstairs for breakfast and find Samara, Jens and Leo up there, sitting at the table. They all turn to me when I appear.

'Hello,' I say, suspicious.

'Good morning,' Samara says, her fingers laced on the table. 'Did you run out of paper or something?'

'What?'

She points at the surface of the table. I look down at it and see scratch marks that Leo made while he was sleep-walking. When I look closer, I realise they aren't random scratches. He has written something. A kind of broken, half-remembered poem:

> When once   its men
>   a wife ne'er again
> the sea   hearts to grieve
> and sailors to their would
> So upon her knees
> prayed Lír calm the seas
> Lír heard changed this night
>   my queen til first light

these seas   cause thee strife
if you'll become my

It is difficult to read, some of the chipboard splintered, but it's clearly a poem of some sort.

'What is it?' I ask Leo. 'Some kind of nursery rhyme?'

'You tell us,' Leo says, a hard edge to his voice.

I do a double take. 'What?'

'Shame it's unfinished,' Samara says. 'Calm the seas. My queen . . . something about making a deal with Lír? Who's Lír?'

'I think he's the sea god in Celtic mythology,' Leo says.

'"and sailors to their . . . would . . ." weave?' Samara tried.

'It's an AA BB rhyme scheme,' Jens offers, tracing the carved words with his fingertips. 'Grieve leave sheathe . . .'

'Maybe *you* wrote it, Jens?' Samara says.

Jens cocks his head and smiles, but says nothing.

'Dom can tell us,' Leo says.

I shrug, feeling the charge in the room. 'I have no idea.'

'Well, someone wrote it,' Samara says.

'Jens said you've been having nightmares,' Leo says, his eyes fixed on me.

I bristle, turning to Jens. 'That was shared in confidence.'

'When it impacts the rest of us, it's important that we share,' Leo says.

'OK,' I say, trying to swallow back my irritation. 'I *have* been having nightmares. But that doesn't automatically mean that I carved up the dining table.'

'Who did, then?' Samara said.

I nod at Leo. 'You did.'

He gives an amused laugh. 'Are you serious?' Then, when he realises I am serious: 'When am I supposed to have done this?'

'Last night,' I said. 'I came upstairs to see what the scratching was. You were sleepwalking. I didn't want to disturb you.' I look at Samara. 'I saw you come upstairs. Didn't you see me?'

She shook her head. 'No. I saw Leo, but there was no one else there.'

'How can you not have seen me?' I say, my voice growing louder. 'I was right there.'

'It was dark,' she says.

With a sigh, Leo reaches out to touch the carvings. 'So, no one knows who carved a poem into the dining table.'

'I think it's just sleepwalk-ramblings,' I say.

He shakes his head. 'It's a proper poem. Look at that rhyme scheme. I'll bet you a burger it's an authentic folktale.'

'What's the last line?' Jens says. 'If you'll become my . . .'

'. . . selkie wife,' I say. Everyone looks at me, and I raise a hand to my mouth. Where did *that* come from?

'Selkie wife?' Leo says. 'That fits.'

'I thought you said you didn't write it,' Samara says.

I feel lightheaded. I said 'selkie wife' before I had even thought of it, as though my mouth spoke of its own accord.

'"Wife" does rhyme with "strife",' Jens says.

'Do you know the rest?' Leo asks, but my heart is clamouring, and I've broken out in a cold sweat. Where did those words come from? Why did I say that?

Why do I know the words to Leo's goddamn poem?

'Let's google it,' Leo says, and right as he types the words 'selkie wife' on his laptop I get up and walk out of the cabin.

I go for a long walk across the beach towards the headland, until my calves are on fire and my lungs are working harder than my brain. Even so, I feel embarrassed, blamed for something I didn't do. This isn't just about who wrote the poem,

183

or why. I feel that old injustices from my past are being poked and prodded, and it hurts.

I'm freaked out. I'm afraid to even think about the poem, because the more I circulate the words in my head the more the blanks seem to come bubbling up from the depth of my brain.

All the secrets I've managed to keep hidden inside are being stirred by this trip. I sit down on a rock, pull the knife out of my trouser pocket, and cut a fresh line into my stomach.

It feels good for all of two seconds.

I should have known that Jens would follow me. The minute I spot him – about twenty feet away to my left, his head cocked – I hate myself more than I hate him right then.

'Does that do it for you?' I shout. 'Creeping around after people?'

He doesn't answer, but walks slowly towards me. As he gets closer I can see he's looking at me warily, as though I'm holding a grenade. I pull my jumper quickly down over my bare flesh, but my coat is unzipped and I'm still holding the knife, which has a little blood on it.

'You want to talk about it?' he asks.

'About what?'

His face softens. 'The fact that you're self-harming.'

'I don't see it as a problem.'

He looks out to sea. 'Why do you do it?'

'It makes me feel better.'

'Feel better about what?'

I look away. Images flash in my head. A man's face, frozen in a snarl. My fists pounding against a locked door. I feel my throat tighten, and the urge to cut myself rises up again, ferocious.

'Dominique?'

I snap back into the present, trembling. Jens is standing over me still, looking at me with concern.

'It's the dreams, isn't it?' he says. 'You dreamed about horses, and then we found them. Is that what you feel guilty about?'

A sob rises up in my throat. I nod.

'What about the poem. Did you dream that, too?'

I get to my feet and start to run, the icy wind beating against my face. I can hear him calling after me but I have to run, as though all the whispering memories inside my skin can be left behind.

As though they'll someday stop hissing in my blood.

Nicky

I

July 1901
Karsut Fjord, Greenland

Days on the *Ormen* were spent in extremes – either the men would be bored and agitated, their chores finished by lunchtime and the sea around them scrolling like an endless blank canvas, or they'd spy a whale, and the hunt would occupy them from dawn until dusk, or sometimes until the next morning, leaving them drained and bloodied. The ship's harpoon was mechanised, sparing the men the ordeal of hunting by hand, using boats and old-fashioned, javelin-style harpoons. In years gone by, a whale took days to die, with the men having to stay out all night on their small boats in freezing conditions, waiting for the beast to give in. Now, the whole ship rocked as the harpoon cannon thrust out, spiking out of the leviathan and filling it with air so it would float to the surface. Even then, the task of flensing the blubber and carting it off in barrels to the hold was backbreaking.

The provisions from Dundee were dwindling, the meals supplied from the sea around them. She had never eaten seal or whale before, but now it made up almost every meal, the sight of albatross turning on a spit by the ship's wheel a constant sight. Royle and McKenzie took to climbing the rig with pistols, then sling and stones, shooting the birds for supper.

Nicky spotted young Reid writing at a table in the galley one evening, and sat down next to him. The men that stayed clear of her cabin were relatively safe, in her eyes, and Reid was always pleasant to her.

'Would you have any paper I could use?' she asked. 'I'd like to write to my husband.'

Reid nodded. 'I have a notebook. I'll tear out some sheets for you.'

'A notebook?' she said. 'You mean a logbook?'

Reid reddened again. 'Nah. That's Wolfarth's job. I like to write.'

'You send letters home?' she said, and he shook his head. 'I write for myself, mostly. Silly little songs. Sea shanties for the men when the hunting's not happening.'

She straightened, surprised. There hadn't been the slightest hint of culture since she'd been aboard. 'I'd like to read them,' she said. Reid lifted his eyebrows, and she worried she'd offended him. 'I mean, only if you don't mind.'

He beamed, a small nod. 'I'd be honoured.'

'You would?'

He dropped his eyes to his boots, but he couldn't wipe the smile off his face. 'No one has ever wanted to read them. I mean, the men sing the shanties when they're bored, but I don't tell them it was me who wrote them.'

She smiled. 'I'll look forward to it.'

II

She chatted with Reid most days after that, in the quieter periods when he could steal away for a short while to write. She made sure to stay out of Lovejoy's sight, and it brought a small comfort to build a friendship with one of the crew. He was her sister's age, and although he had left school at twelve his writing skills were good.

'Did you always want to be a whaler?' she asked one afternoon, when he had helped the men haul a thirty-foot sperm whale on to the boat. He was spent from the effort, and agitated by the animal's death. Reid struck her as a sensitive lad, unsuited to this life.

He shrugged. 'Didn't think much about it. I need to earn money. It's this or the mill. And my cousin died in the mill, so I prefer this. Especially since I don't get seasick. My da says I've got good sea legs.'

'When did you start writing?' she asked.

'I can't remember,' he said, scratching his chin. 'I've always liked a good story. *Macbeth* is my favourite.'

'That's a play,' she said.

'Aye, but it's still a story.'

'Have you ever seen it staged?'

He scoffed. 'What, at the theatre? Naw. No money for things like that. Do you read Rabbie Burns?'

She nodded. 'Of course. "Wee, sleekit, cowrin—"'

Reid clapped his hands together in delight, finishing her sentence. '"—tim'rous beastie, O, what a panic's in thy breastie." That's one of my favourites. I've memorised loads of his poems.'

'We were forced to memorise them at school,' she said. 'I suppose it took the joy out of them a little.'

'Oh, I love him. Could read him all day. No books on a whale ship though. That's got me writing, actually, more than I do at home.'

'That's understandable.'

'I think I'd like to write a song,' Reid told her. 'For the men to sing.' He looked at her meaningfully. 'Could you help me?'

She nodded. 'Of course.'

They wrote several shanties together, he offering the themes and the opening lines and she helping him swap words to make the rhyme and rhythm stronger. He wrote shanties mostly to make tasks easier, such as hauling the bowline and flensing a whale, which the men could sing while performing their duties.

It lifted the men's spirits to try and learn a new song when the days stretched out. Wolfarth played Reid's tunes by ear on his fiddle and memorised the words, before leading any willing crew members in a singsong. Even Lovejoy joined in, his face lighting up as he clapped and sang along.

She watched the men carefully as they sang, tankards and spirits high, many of them still drunk from the night before. She wondered if whaling didn't breed men like this, debase them – men who might have exercised dignity and morals in some other form of employment, but out here, forced to slaughter such majestic beasts of the ocean, they became, stroke by stroke, little more than animals.

It wasn't just work that made monsters of men, but guilt. That, after all, was something she understood only too well.

She thought of the small shoes she first bought Morag, the red leather laces she taught her to tie. She liked to play hopscotch in the garden, a handful of sticks laid out to mark the boxes. Every trip to the park became a search for treasure in the form of the perfect hopscotch stick – straight, not too thick, a foot in length. A game that involved song was her favourite thing in the world.

Daffodils, baby birds.

She once found a robin's blue eggs and begged for a dress in the same colour.

When Morag died, Nicky's mother advised her to get rid of it all – every toy and shoe, and especially the dresses.

But the blue one, the silk dress the colour of robin's eggs – she kept it to remind her. To remind her of what she had done.

Dominique

I

December 2023
Skúmaskot, Iceland

I'm on the upper deck watching the snow swirl down, melting as soon as it hits the tide. The ship moans and burps, the waves sucking at the debris on the sand. It snowed heavily last night, all the green patches of heath filled in with a blanket of blinding white snow. We've been filming it all morning, the snow. This is nothing like the kind of snow I've seen before. There are these weird ice formations all over the ship that look exactly like a crown of silvery hair with a centre parting, as though there's a body emerging from the hull. The more regular kind of snow has mushroomed along the masts and the gunwale, and we have to push it off the roof of the cabin with kitchen utensils in case the weight of it brings the whole thing crashing down.

I hear the cabin door open and shut, Samara pulling on her green beanie as she approaches.

'Hey,' I say.

'Hey.' She stands next to me, her arms folded across her. 'Can we take a walk this morning? Just you and me?'

I feel something inside me tighten. 'Sure.'

We climb down the ladder and walk along the beach, away from the buildings across the bay.

The beach is kind of grizzly today, a ton of seaweed dumped on top of the sand and snow. We reach the turning point of the bay, where the turf houses line the shore. There's one in particular I like, the house with a red door. The rest are in darker colours – blue, grey, black. The snow has covered them all, but the red peers through like a heart in the midst of so much white.

She sees me looking. 'That's your house,' she says.

I look at her, puzzled. 'My house?'

She looks away, and I see it again – the look on her face that says she's hiding something.

'Look, Samara,' I say. 'I wanted to ask you . . .'

Our voices eclipse. '. . . wanted to ask you . . .'

She stops, and we both laugh. Mine is a nervous, brittle laugh. I think of when she called me a witch. The way she feared me.

'You go first,' I say.

She stops, eyes fixed on the bay, biting her lip. 'Jens told me,' she says carefully. 'About your self-harming.'

I feel my cheeks burn, the sting of shame rising up in me. 'OK.'

'You want to talk about it?'

I shake my head.

'We can't support each other if we don't know what's really going on,' she says. When I don't answer, she places a hand on my upper arm.

'I'm your friend,' she says gently. 'I know you've been alone . . .'

'It's a release thing,' I say. 'When I'm stressed.'

She nods. I suck my teeth, reluctant to say more. But she's waiting for it.

'And usually I'm fine. But sometimes I have . . . thoughts. And it gets too much. Cutting makes it feel better.'

'Thoughts of what?'

I pause for a long time, and she waits, patient.

'I think I was attacked,' I say.

'Attacked?' she says. 'When? By who?'

I feel my skin crawl and my throat tighten.

'They . . .' I say, but I can't finish the sentence. The memory is there, but it's too murky to put into words. It's a scream that runs right through me.

'*They?*' she says. 'There was more than one?'

I can't speak, can't even nod. My whole body has gone rigid, as though I'm turning to stone. I squeeze my eyes shut. I can't bear the images. I can't bear them.

She touches my arm. 'Oh God, Dom. I'm so sorry.'

I try and slow my breathing, remember to take it from my diaphragm, but it's useless. My head is light, and I can feel myself trying to dissociate. Like an internal mist blanking everything out, including my sense of self.

'Do you want to talk about it?' she says.

I shake my head, and she steps back, as though she's pushed me too far. 'It's not that I have a problem with telling you what happened,' I explain slowly. 'It's just that . . . I don't have the words for it. That's why I cut myself.'

She nods, and I can see she's trying to understand, even though she doesn't. No one ever does.

'I mean I literally don't have the words,' I say. 'Maybe you'll get it, being into sounds and everything. It's like, some things that happen to a person are so awful that they exist outside language. Am I making sense?'

I turn to her, noticing her eyes have softened. 'You're making complete sense,' she says with a smile.

We stand in silence, looking out over the bay. But it's not an awkward silence, and I've stopped shaking. I feel a weight has lifted inside me, just a little.

'Thank you for telling me,' she says finally. 'Anytime you want to talk, I'm here.'

'You're welcome,' I say, on autopilot and regretting the words as soon as they're out. But then, this is my point – words are meaningless. They're used up and second hand and they never, ever capture the truth of an experience. They're just a keyhole. Never the full picture.

'Next time you feel the urge to cut,' she says. 'Come and talk to me instead.'

I nod, relieved, because this means she isn't going home. And suddenly it strikes me – I've spent so much time and energy convincing myself that I'm fine being alone.

But I don't want to be alone anymore.

II

'Samara, tell us what you found.'

Samara sits at the dining table, her face lit up in a smile. She looks very pleased with herself; we all are. I'm filming her, not live, but I'll edit and upload tomorrow morning. My battery is at 19 per cent and I'm silently praying that it doesn't run out, because we will never be able to capture the sheer excitement vibrating off all of us right now.

She throws a massive, all-teeth smile at the camera, beaming with excitement. She's not even told the rest of us everything that she found, and now I see why – it translates better on camera if she's kept it to herself.

'OK, first some backstory,' she says. 'I've been having some crazy dreams since coming to the *Ormen*, but I'm thinking now that maybe there's something more than my imagination to these dreams. I dreamed that I heard someone singing, right here on the shipwreck, right? And in the dream I was searching for them.'

She pauses for dramatic effect, and my palms begin to feel clammy.

'I went into this little crawlspace on the lower deck,' she says, 'and I saw some floorboards that were out of place, with something poking up underneath. So, the next day, I thought I'd check out the lower deck, right? Just to see if there was an actual crawlspace like the one in my dream. And there was.'

'Oh my God,' Leo says. 'Tell me you didn't find that box there.'

She holds a finger to her lips, and I want to be sick. 'So, right where the floorboards were all out of place in the dream, I found – guess what?'

'You found floorboards,' Jens says.

'And something poking up from underneath,' Samara says, gesturing at the box.

'Holy shit,' Jens says.

'It was the muse calling,' Leo says.

'Yeah, seriously,' Samara says. 'I'd lifted some of the floorboards, and I saw something was underneath, covered in dust. And it was this.'

I start to shake, and the image in the viewfinder begins to wobble. I want to scream at them all to run, to leave the tin box and run, but instead I do my best to keep completely still, panning slowly to the tin box on the table next to her. It's the size of a shoe box, still filmed with dust and cobwebs, the corners crumbly with rust.

She lifts out a bundle of old papers, dusty and fragile, and lays them across the table.

'Oh my God,' Jens says.

'Are you fucking kidding me?' Leo says, clapping his hands together.

'There are some old maps,' Samara says, holding up a folded map.

'Get the date,' Leo says, pointing at some writing at the bottom of the cover. It says 1885.

'They're super delicate, so I don't really want to unfold them. There's a gorgeous vintage cigarette box here too. It's so pretty, I want to keep it.' She lifts it up and I zoom in on the design. The box is dotted with weevil holes. The inks are faded, but I can make out a British flag on the front, old-style lettering that reads 'Redford's Navy Cut'. Samara lifts the flap gently, revealing eight cigarettes inside, in pretty good nick.

'That must be super valuable,' Leo says. 'This is why we explore, folks,' he says into the camera. 'You come across stuff like this. Not cleaned up and in a museum. Straight from the source.'

Samara and Jens hold the opposite corners and unfold it super slow across the table. It's a map of a place called Baffin Bay.

'This is where the ships sailed,' Samara says as Leo moves his camera up close. 'I looked it up online.'

'Baffin Bay?' I say. The name sounds familiar.

'Greenland,' Leo says, pointing at the name written in capitals along the map.

I draw my camera slowly across the shapes of the land while Jens holds a torchlight over the map to pick up the faded writing. I can make out some place names. *Lancaster Sound. Prince Charles Island. Clyde River.*

'And . . .' Samara says suspensefully, lifting out a small envelope.

'Holy shit,' Leo says. 'Is that a letter?'

She nods, gleeful. 'There's no stamp, and it's never been opened.' She fingers the edges of the envelope like a dark secret. It's clear that the envelope has been exposed to water, the writing faded and blurred by damp. She looks up at the camera, and we all pause. 'It seems wrong to open it, doesn't it?'

'Can you make out more of the address?' Jens asks.

She squints down at the writing. 'I can't fully make out the name. It starts with an 'E', I think? And the surname ends with a 'D'?'

'That's not even the best part, is it?' Leo says, grinning.

'Seriously?' Jens says. 'There's more?'

I watch my battery light flash, pleading with it to last. 'Maybe you should film this, too,' I tell Jens. 'Just so we have a copy.'

He nods and pulls out his own phone to film.

Samara waits until he nods, signalling that he's recording. 'I found a notebook,' she says, her smile widening, 'and I believe it is actually a mariner's diary or logbook from when the *Ormen* was a whaling ship.'

She holds up an A5-sized leatherbound notebook, weathered at the edges and the brown leather worn thin. Inside there are notes in old-fashioned cursive letters. None of us can read the writing, but we can make out several pictures inside of a ship and whales. And the year at the top of the pages is discernible – it says 1901.

'Maybe one of our followers could help decipher the writing?' Leo says.

Samara wags her finger at Leo as though he's a naughty schoolchild. 'Ah, my dear Leo. I am one step ahead, baby. One step ahead.'

She visibly prepares herself and turns to the camera. 'So as you all know, I hacked into an academic journal,' she says. 'And I found a paper from 1962 from a professor at Dundee University. He was convinced there was someone else on board the *Ormen* in 1901.'

'What does that mean?' Leo says. 'Someone else on board?'

'A stowaway,' she says. 'He said he had analysed several crew diaries, and one of them mentions a *siùrsach*, which is Scots Gaelic for "whore".'

'So you're saying . . . what?' Jens says. 'That there was a prostitute on the ship?'

'It could have been a male prostitute, right?' Leo says, but Samara shakes her head.

'*Siùrsach* is a specifically female term.'

She nods, then lays out the logbook on the table, carefully turning to a page that she's marked with a bookmark. 'As you can see, the writing is super difficult to make out. It's mostly tallies and things I don't understand. But, I did find the official crew list, with a date. This is from the beginning of May in 1901.'

I zoom in on the names of the men as Samara points to them.

'There are twenty names there,' she says. 'Remember that number, OK?'

We all watch as she turns the pages slowly to another section, which is dated 3 June 1901. At the top of the page is a tally:

tttt
tttt
tttt
tttt
l

'What does that mean?' Leo says.

'There's twenty-one people on board,' Samara says. She turns over to another page, dated 30 July.

tttt
tttt
tttt
tt / /
l

'What are the two leaning lines?' Leo asks.

'Two dead mariners,' Samara says. 'But even if you include those in the tally, there are twenty-one people.'

199

Another, dated 20 September, has the same tally. Only this time there are three dead mariners.

'That's a high percentage of deaths for one voyage, isn't it?' Samara turns to them all to ask.

It's Jens that responds. 'Aye,' he says, with a confident authority that takes me by surprise. 'But you never know what's going to happen on a whaling expedition. Especially when there's a woman.' He was staring at the notebook, but didn't say anything more.

'Well, how sure are you?' Leo asks, sceptical, breaking the silence that followed. 'I mean, this is all speculation, isn't it?'

'Thanks,' Samara says flatly. 'I worked really fucking hard to check my facts.'

'Sorry,' Leo says, pressing his hands to his face. 'It's just . . . wow. We saw that photograph of the person in the skirt, too. That was from the same time, right?'

Jens nods. 'Yes. 1901.'

Leo shakes his head. 'My mind is blown.'

'That's some incredible detective work,' Jens says, high-fiving Samara. My battery is at 8 per cent and my mind is racing. How did Samara learn the location of the box from a dream? And what about my own dreams? They've seemed so real. What if they're a form of control? What if the woman I keep seeing is possessing us? Is that what happened to Leo when he sleepwalked? I tried to shut my mind off, remind myself I'm being ridiculous. But I can still see the woman even when I close my eyes. Her long black hair, hanging like seaweed over her shoulders. Her ragged dress, the colour of dusk. Her hands by her sides, clenched in fists.

'You heard it here, folks,' Samara tells the lens as my battery flashes. 'A female stowaway was aboard this ship in 1901.'

Nicky

I

July 1901
nr Devil's Thumb, Greenland

As they pressed further north, something new appeared on the white shores of Baffin Bay.

Inuit.

Nicky was mesmerised by the men and women who appeared there, dressed in coats and boots made of deer hide, all of them healthy and happy in appearance. They greeted the ship waving and cheering, and she looked around eagerly for any sign of a ship. But they had none – their homes were tents that they erected and dismantled just as fast, moving to whichever part of the Arctic they wished to explore and hunt. They had pipes, she noticed, made of whalebone, and long rifles. As the ship drew closer to the water's edge, she saw that some of the children were fair-haired and pale-skinned. She had heard of this – whaling crew fathering children in the Arctic. And here was the evidence.

Royle and Arnott took rowing boats to the land for fresh water and returned with two young Inuit women, about sixteen years of age, long black hair to their waist. The arrangement seemed consensual, and when ardent sounds of lovemaking sounded in the cabins above, Nicky wept with relief. Perhaps the new instalments would quieten the traffic in her own cabin. All but four of the men – Daverley, the boatswain, his nephew, Reid, Anderson, and Cowie – were regular visitors to her cabin now. The men were always sheepish at first, then more brazen, expectant.

The arrival of the Inuit girls sparked fights among the men. Each day the rowing boat that ventured to the shore for water returned with freshly replenished buckets and several new Inuit girls.

On the fifth day in Baffin Bay, she heard footsteps on the deck outside a little after midnight. A knock on her door. She froze. She could hear the voices of several men, and suddenly she feared they would all come into her tiny room. They were drunk, she knew that. She was terrified of what they would do in this state.

'Open up, selkie!' Lovejoy shouted, and her heart pounded in her chest. She stared at the door handle as it shuddered in the frame against the weight of fists pounding against it. 'Open up!'

She reached forward and unlocked the door, holding her breath. Lovejoy and Wolfarth stood there, holding Reid roughly by his shirt.

'Good evening, selkie,' Lovejoy said, his pale eyes lit with excitement. 'This boy here became a man of sixteen at the stroke of midnight.'

He shoved Reid inside with a yell. 'A virgin on a whale ship's a curse on all our heads!'

Reid fell at her feet with a clatter. Lovejoy and the men behind him stood and laughed, the sound of it booming off the walls. They'd been drinking, but Reid's terror had sobered him up.

'Are you all right?' she asked, once the door was closed.

He shook his head, then slowly sat upright. She knew he

wasn't going to hurt her. He seemed more afraid of the other men, and embarrassed.

'Come and sit down,' she said, and he sat with her on the bed.

'I should never have come on this godforsaken voyage,' he said after a long silence. 'If my mam was still alive I'd be at home. But I have to earn a wage.'

She found herself putting an arm across his shoulders. 'You're earning a wage, though,' she says. 'That's good, isn't it? Once this is all over you can go home after all. And you'll have something to show for it.'

He wiped tears from his cheeks and nodded. 'I wish I could go home,' he said. 'I didn't think it would feel so long, being away.'

A lump formed in her throat. She knew exactly what he meant, and although her situation was infinitely worse than his, she knew he was tender in years. 'Everyone feels that way, the first time they leave behind everything that's familiar,' she said. 'The trick is to remember that you can get used to anything.'

He looked up, his eyes red. 'Even this?'

'Yes. And much worse.'

He took her hand, recognising that she spoke from experience. 'I'm sorry.'

She nodded and smiled.

'We caught something today,' he said after a moment. 'Do you want to see?'

She followed him out the door, along the corridor, then downstairs into the hold. A memory flashed brightly in her mind of the day she had woken in that dark space, when a barrel tipped over on her foot, a nail piercing her skin and creating the wound that was now transforming her leg entirely. She shuddered at the thought of it.

There was barely enough space in the hold now for them

to enter, rows of barrels stacked there, the air thick with the sour stench of blubber. She started at a noise – a low growl.

'Come and see him,' Reid said.

'Who?' she said.

He lifted the oil lantern and nodded at a cage in a corner. 'We caught him today, Daverley and I,' he said. 'When we rowed to land for fresh water.'

She squinted into the shadows cast by the amber light of the lantern. Something moved inside the cage, something with white fur. Too small for a polar bear. Perhaps a cub. She felt uneasy.

Reid made a tutting sound as he moved towards the cage. He lifted the lid off a barrel nearby and found some meat, then slipped a piece inside the cage. A bushy tail lifted, a glint of two red eyes.

A white fox.

'An Arctic fox,' Reid told her. 'Very hard to catch, these guys. The fur is worth a fortune back home. God blessed us.'

She looked at the fox squatting low as it chewed the whale meat, watching them anxiously.

'You won't kill it, will you?' she said.

Reid's smile faded. 'How would we skin it if we didn't kill it first? Be a bit cruel, no?'

She opened her mouth to say that maybe it would be kinder to the animal to set it free, but then she thought of Reid, and where he came from. She had seen the squalor in Dundee, and the hungry children who came to the mill, day after day.

It was cruel to kill the fox, but it was also cruel to deprive Reid of the money that would come from the sale of the fur. But as she watched the animal swallow the last of the meat, that thick, pristine fur like a cloud, her mind turned to the man who had attacked her in the park, and the conversation with her father the morning she was attacked.

An endless chain of purchase, the blood that tinged the waters around the *Ormen* a reminder that the new world of electric light and consumer goods cost murder and bloodshed in Arctic waters.

If her capture had purchased something she did not yet understand, what would her freedom cost?

II

Allan coming home from the mill, pulling off his clothes. The smell of jute under his fingernails. She prepared the bath by the fire, washed his back.

The line of his neck, the curve of skin from his ear to shoulder. His hand reaching for hers.

He left the house at dawn six days a week and returned after dark. One night, she woke to feed Morag and found he was pacing the hallway, restless. He'd been up for hours, clearly, an open ledger in the front room suggesting he was still working.

'Allan?'

He turned to her, his eyes dark.

'What's the matter?'

'My mind is wandering, is all. Go back to bed.'

They'd barely spoken for weeks, passing like ships in the night. She felt anger rise up – he had taken on extra work, by the looks of it.

'You want to work *more*,' she said. 'When you already work every hour under the sun.'

A cry sounded then, the sort that made her breasts leak milk. She turned to fetch the baby, holding her for a feed in the armchair by the window. Her breasts burned, and she felt pummelled. She lowered Morag into the crib, but she screamed again, her face scrunched up and her legs drawn to her stomach.

A thumping started on the walls: Mr Baird, telling them to quiet the baby.

Nicky pounded the wall. 'Be quiet, yourself!' she shouted angrily.

Morag wouldn't be consoled. Nicky plucked her up from the crib and held her upright, but the wailing continued.

'I don't know what's wrong with her,' she told Allan. 'She does this all day, every day. Feeds then cries until she's exhausted. Then wakes and repeats it all.'

Allan took the baby from her, rubbing her stomach. Slowly, she quietened. Nicky felt relieved and frustrated that she couldn't manage to console the baby.

'They lowered my wages,' he said. 'And our rent is due.'

She looked him over, realising how thin he'd become. He wasn't eating, either. So much had changed since the baby came. They were exhausted, wrung out with cares. It had been weeks since she kissed him.

He laid the baby back in her crib, the silence stretching, delicate and sweet. He made to go back to his work, but she took his hand.

'Come back to bed. You need your rest.'

He made to turn, but stopped, the touch of her hand rooting him there. She stepped forward and took his face in hers.

'I'm here,' she said.

'I'm here,' he said back. Then he followed her back into bed, wrapping his arms around her. Curling into each other in the dark.

Dominique

I

December 2023
Skúmaskot, Iceland

After Samara's discovery we've had messages from our followers. The others are over the moon. We've been getting lots of comments and likes but *messages* are a whole other level of engagement. And everyone's so excited about the discovery of the logbook and the letter.

I ask Samara about her claim that she dreamed about the location of the tin box, and she's less confident about it this time. The story a little less defined. She sees how relieved I am and laughs.

I'm even wondering now if the items are real. The tin box seems genuine enough, but the map and the cigarette box and even the logbook . . . Samara could easily have planted those to drum up a bit of theatre for our followers. If that's the case here, great. I can stomach a fraud easier than I can the idea that she legit dreamed about singing which led to her finding some genuine material from over a century ago.

It is disquieting, downright stomach-churning, the idea that nudges at me. That we're all being influenced by something here. First my dream of the horses, then finding horse bones. Then Samara saying she dreamed of singing. I'm sure I've

208

never told her anything about my own dreams about someone singing. So that's two coincidences.

I hope, I *hope* the tin box story is false.

Jens and I still haven't had much luck with our own research. The internet continues to be super glitchy, but when I can log on I decide to start looking into Skúmaskot and the reasons why the villagers left. I find a Facebook group set up for people with ties to Skúmaskot and ask to join, and in the meantime I look at old photographs posted online from the early twentieth century. There are kids standing on the pier and boats in the harbour, and there's a mention in several blogs of a school.

I get approved for the Facebook group, so I run a search for any mention of a curse. Nothing comes up. A thread from 2014 pops up:

Gunnar Einnerson: Hi there, anyone know why the villagers left Skúmaskot so abruptly?

Ella Boyce: My great-great-grandma was born in Skúmaskot in 1898. Her parents moved the family to Holmavík when she was 4, and she said it was because there was a fire. Not sure what kind but that was the story I heard.

Hildur Magnusdottir: You're right, there was a fire in Skúmaskot. Early 1900s, I believe. The villagers burned down the old whaling station pretty much as soon as it was built. Skúmaskot was historically a shark fishing village and the villagers said the whaling station would destroy their income because the whales scared off the sharks. I think that's why people left. People started fishing out of Holmavík, which had more amenities. And when that town grew, people stopped travelling to Skúmaskot.

Olaf Urwin: Retrospective BS. Skúmaskot still had a school in the 1960s.

I search the terms 'shipwreck' and '*Ormen*' and the threads are so numerous I spend an hour trawling through them all. One stands out, and I notice it has forty-five likes:

Esther Watson: My father-in-law worked for the coastguard when the wreck washed up in Skúmaskot in the Seventies. He was one of the first people on the scene to view it. And you're right, @olafurwin – there was a school there in the 1960s and the town was thriving. But after the wreck washed up, everything changed. *That's* when people left. The government wouldn't move the ship and people were freaked out. My FIL had violent nightmares for weeks. He's seen all kinds of things on the coast but the *Ormen* had a super nasty vibe. One of his workmates said he saw a woman on the beach every time he visited and he was so freaked out he asked for a transfer. Stay well clear, folks.

I pause at the mention of nightmares, and the woman. Many commenters claim that Skúmaskot was an otherwise normal, uneventful fishing village, winding down after friction between whaling companies deepened. But a few mention that the *Ormen* was the real catalyst, and not just because of the spectacle of a crumbling ghost ship close to the bay. Anyone who ventured out to see it experienced nightmares or a feeling of being watched, and some people said they saw a spectre. A woman.

I really want to believe that Skúmaskot was deserted because of infrastructure, but I find myself searching out those comments that mention a woman. It is majorly coincidental that Samara has a theory about a woman being on board the

Ormen and loads of people claim to have seen a ghostly woman on the beach here. And there's the woman I have seen here, too . . . I suppose you could argue that the female stowaway was local knowledge. Samara's research paper from the 1960s – the one that mentions the *siùrsach* – proves that someone had already theorised it decades ago, and possibly folk mythologised a ghost on the back of that rumour. I've seen this happen time and again with abandoned places. People love to make up stories, and especially when it concerns ghosts.

But on the other hand, I've seen the woman with my own eyes. I've dreamed her. The singing I've heard . . . I could swear it's a female voice. And I can feel it, the sense of malice that lingers in this place. You just get a feeling from places. Sometimes there's a sense of peace, and sometimes there's even humour. But Skúmaskot is a place of cruelty.

I can feel it as strongly as though the rocks are shouting it.

II

I'm crawling across the beach, a heavy black tail beneath my dress. It's dark, and I can see the wreck of the *Ormen* in front of me. I hate it with every fibre of my being.

I want it to burn. I open my mouth and let out a long scream. Black birds shoot out of my mouth, flying up over the shipwreck before pummelling down like darts to their death.

I wake up sobbing, clawing at my mouth. I can still taste the feathers, their texture. I could hear the cry of the birds all around me. I bolt out of my bedroom, then stagger upstairs and throw up into the sink. It's still dark.

Samara is sitting on the sofa.

'Are you OK?' she asks.

She looks upset, like she's been crying. She's wearing her pyjamas and her orange beanie, her knees drawn up to her chest.

I wipe my mouth and approach her. 'What's wrong?'

With a sigh, she takes her audio recorder from her pocket and taps the screen. She holds it to my ear and I listen. It sounds like gunshots. Just like the first recording she ever played me did, too.

'I recorded it last week,' she says. 'It's from the ice in the bay.'

'It sounds like someone's pumping rounds out of a shotgun,' I say.

She nods and taps her recorder, then holds it up to my ear again. A similar sound bleeds into my ear, the crack-sound more like a pistol this time. 'Everything I record sounds like this,' she says. 'This whole place is just filled with the sounds of gunshots.'

She plays another track and tells me it's from the turf houses. She spent two hours in one of them, not moving, just recording ambiance. For a moment I can't hear anything, but then there's a noise like the slowed-down blast of a rifle in the distance, the echo continuing for ten seconds.

'I don't understand,' I say, sitting down next to her. 'How the hell do you get gunshots from an empty turf house?'

She shrugs. 'I mean, it's sped up. But I'm freaked out. *Everything* I'm recording sounds like gunshots. It's triggering me.' She rolls her eyes. 'No pun intended.'

I stare at her. 'Why is it triggering you?'

'It's like you said,' she says, slipping the audio recorder back into her pocket. 'Some things exist outside language, right?'

'Right.'

Samara looks out the window at the ocean like liquid amethyst, a black line of horizon separating a bank of lilac clouds.

'I was shot,' she says finally. 'By a guy I'd been kind of flirting with. That's why the gunshots are freaking me out.'

I watch her as she keeps her eyes away from mine, sounding out the words.

'I'm sorry,' I say.

She nods and wipes a tear from her face. 'I've blanked out most of it. Before and after. That's the basic fact. But the sound of fireworks, poppers, any loud noise at all . . . It has always triggered me.' She turns to me, her eyes softening as she looks at me. 'It's like you said. Us explorers always have a story. It's why we come to places like this, right?'

I nod. 'Did he get put away?'

She shakes her head and looks at the ground. 'He turned the gun on himself straight after.'

'God. I'm so sorry.'

'I wasn't the only one he hurt.' She says it like she's remembering it for the first time, like something she has buried deep in a secret part has suddenly come loose.

'Is that why you were so upset about the horses?' I ask.

She bites her lip. 'I need to ask you something,' she says then. 'About your past.'

I stop. 'My past?' I say.

Just then the cabin door opens, and Leo bursts in.

'You want to see something?'

Samara wipes her eyes and throws me a look that tells me at once that she's grateful for the chance to share and that we'll not mention any of this to Leo. We get up and pull on our coats before heading out on the deck.

Leo is starboard, ocean-side, looking down over the waves.

'There's a seal,' he says. 'It's been hanging out by the boat for days. Just one. Usually they're in a bob.'

'A bob?'

'The collective for seal.'

'Where is it?' Samara asks.

Leo points at a spot in the sea, about twenty feet from us. 'There,' he says.

We stare for at least a minute, looking hard at the sea.

'Is that it?' Samara says, pointing at a white wave.

'No,' Leo says. 'I can't see it anymore. That's a shame. I was watching it for a while, too.'

Samara encourages him to fetch the cameras, and we run

back to the cabin to get them. Samara lifts the binoculars and pauses at the window of the cabin that overlooks the beach, in case she might see something. She scans the horizon, and I stand behind her, looking out at the sea.

Part of me is looking for a human head, and the outline of a shoulder.

Nicky

I

30 July 1901
Melville Bay, Davis Strait

The *Ormen* was deep in the Davis Strait, winding past islands and channels and surrounded by inky pyramids daubed with snow that knifed into a marbled sky. The ocean was still, no heaving waves, the surface blanketed by large chunks of clear ice that crowded around the helm like an insurrection. Further out, icebergs sat large as mountains, a verdigris halo in the water marking their depth. Nicky had always thought heaven would be white, and therefore serene and comforting, but the whiteness here was menacing. Everything was angled and chromatic, and as the men scrubbed the deck Nicky could make out their breaths glistening with ice fractals, a row of icicles along the ratlines like fangs.

In the crow's nest Cowie stood huddled in an overcoat, his chin buried beneath his collar. None of the men seemed to be as awe-struck as she was – they barely looked up at the staggering scenery all around. But then, the Arctic was familiar territory to them. For a quarter of the year, they walked the streets of Dundee, just like her, but the other three quarters they lived in this otherworldly place, with its hoary cathedrals and murky waters under which shadows moved quietly, and the ocean transformed itself from a wilderness of squalls to a cracked window.

The *Ormen* turned towards an ice shelf that adjoined the land, some shrubs and heathland visible beyond, and a waterfall. She thirsted after freshwater, the thought of bathing in clean water a sudden compulsion. Nicky could see what looked like fallen tree trunks on the ice shelf, but when the men gathered on the deck with their rifles, she realised they were seals.

Finding fresh candles and a bedwarmer in the galley, she retreated to her cabin and wrapped herself with the bedwarmer beneath the blankets of her small bed. Outside, gunshots rang out, one after the other, followed by shouts of joy. It went on for hours, growing more distant and the length of time between the gunshots drawing out longer and longer.

It was almost dawn when she returned to the top deck to empty her bedpan, and she found the light was as bright as it had been that evening, though the ice shelf was no longer pristine – instead, it was scrawled with garnet. The men laid out their haul on the deck, exhausted and bloodied. She counted twenty-nine walrus and more than sixty seals. Lovejoy was still on the ice, yelling at Reid and Anderson. When she looked down she saw that he was trying to bring a dead polar bear on board. It was just a cub, but even so the boys were so tired that they couldn't lift it whole.

That night, when three knocks sounded on her door, she found Lovejoy there. As usual, her stomach tightened at the sight of him, though she noticed he had combed his greasy hair in a side parting, and he was wearing a clean shirt. Also, he was holding something wrapped in a blanket.

'A gift,' he said, when he closed the door behind her. 'For a selkie wife.'

He unwrapped it, and she saw it was a skull, yellow teeth

as long as her thumbs angling down, sharp as knives. Cleansed with rubbing alcohol, Nicky realised with a jolt it was the upper half of the skull of the polar bear cub that Lovejoy had killed earlier that day.

He told her to sit on the bed. As usual, she did not speak, but did what he asked.

'A crown,' he said, placing it on her head. Lovejoy had padded the underside with cloth – a small mercy, to prevent the sharp bone digging into her head, and also to keep it in place. The skull of an adult bear would have been too large, the length of a man's forearm, and she suspected Lovejoy had killed a younger bear for exactly this purpose. There was something in his stare as he looked at her wearing the skull. A transfixed kind of murk.

'Undress,' he said in a hoarse voice.

As Lovejoy grunted above her, his face shining with sweat, he kept his eyes on the skull, as though he was fucking the bear and not her. She wondered if he cared anymore about what she was becoming. She kept her foot bandaged, hidden out of sight, but the wound was still badly infected, spreading up her leg like a second skin. A pelt. As though her body was desperately trying to heal itself, using whatever means necessary – human, or animal.

As she hummed, she imagined herself swimming underwater, the bear skull on her head as a crown. Her tail flicking through the blue, her bare breasts cupped by shells, and an icicle in her hand, long as a spear.

Sharp enough to kill.

Dominique

I

December 2023
Skúmaskot, Iceland

Jens and I discover Diego's surname.

I find it in my cabin, of all places. In the morning, as I come out of my tent I drop my torch. It rolls under the old metal electrical box, and when I search there I put my hand on a dusty old book. It's a Spanish edition of a Truman Capote novel, *Otras Voces, Otros Ámbitos*. The cover has been torn off, but inside I see that someone has written their name: *Diego Almeyda*. I remember the book I found in the hold with 'Diego' written in the front, how Jens had said we needed the surname. Here it was: Almeyda.

'Jens!' I call, and he comes running into my cabin, as though something was wrong. When he looks down at the inscription, his eyes go wide. 'Google it,' he says.

Quickly I open my laptop and connect to the internet terminal, expecting it to glitch again. But no, this time Google appears, and I type words into the search bar:

Diego Almeyda Ormen

Eventually I find a newspaper article in *Argentina News* about

219

a man from Mendoza, but it's all in Spanish. I cut and paste it all into Google Translate:

Funeral Held for Mendoza Man Found Aboard Ghost Ship

21 December 1973

Today the family of Dr Diego Almeyda, 28, laid his body to rest in his hometown of Mendoza. Dr Almeyda was found on a research ship, the *Ormen*, which was found adrift in the Barents Sea. The search continues for the rest of his colleagues.

'Holy shit,' I say, glancing at Jens to gauge his reaction. He looks every bit as shocked as I am.

'Search again,' he says. 'Different keywords.'

I try 'Diego Almeyda body found *Ormen*'. We click through twenty pages of searches but nothing seems relevant. I try 'crew of *Ormen* 1973' and nothing comes up either. It feels disappointing, like we're on the verge of a huge find for our research. A thread that, once pulled, could unravel a seriously sinister mystery. This discovery might lead us to find the whole list of people who were on board during the time they went missing, and maybe even the cause . . .

'My bet is that they were researching something shady and got on the wrong side of some nasty people,' I tell Jens. The Arctic has been contested territory for decades because the oil is worth billions. There are shedloads of military vessels and personnel, mostly Russian, dotted throughout, trying to extend their territory into the Arctic. The Russians even planted a flag on the seabed beneath the North Pole in 2007 to claim territory. Russia's Arctic territory accounts for a fifth of their economy, so it's no wonder. Some countries have been known to train whales to scope out submarines and other vessels with spy cameras and location instruments attached to their bodies. How ironic – during the whaling era, the Arctic was fought over for whale oil to light cities and factories and basically prop up mechanical production. While from the *Ormen*'s research era until the present day, the Arctic has been fought over for fossil fuels. Capitalism, in other words. The Arctic is the cradle of capitalism. So much has changed since Victorian times, and yet many things remain exactly the same.

A few days before Christmas, Leo suggests we should hold the contest vote.

'A good way to celebrate the solstice, no?' he says.

'I thought we were waiting until next week?' I say.

'People will be focused on the *Ormen* being broken up,' Samara says. 'We should do it now. A surprise for the followers.'

I'm still not convinced, but Samara's more media savvy than I am, so I decide to go along with it. I'm still super shocked by the revelation about Diego Almeyda. I can't stop looking at the marks on the floor of the main cabin. The bloodstains. The reasons for an entire crew – save one man, who was found dead – going missing on a ship are likely to be violent.

We sit down at the dining table and eat lunch while Leo sets up the internet terminal to do a livestream.

'Here we go,' Leo says, lifting his laptop on to the table. He sets his phone on a small tripod and films the four of us. We wave at the screen like a team, like four friends, though the dynamic is still charged.

'Hey everyone,' Samara says. I see the TikTok counter start to climb. Fifty-four viewers. 'We're opening the voting for our fun contest today, woo hoo! Just a recap about what we're

221

doing and what you'll be voting on. My buddies Dom, Leo, Jens and I have been researching two different eras of the shipwreck we're living on right now. Leo and I have been researching the whaling era – say hi, Leo.'

Leo presses his hands into his cheeks and makes a goblin face. 'Hi.'

'And Dom and Jens have been researching the period when the ship was used for research here in the Arctic.'

Jens and I do a thumbs up. 'Vote for us!' I say.

'We'll leave the voting open until midnight,' Samara says. 'Have a look at the footage we've posted and make your decision. Remember, the winning team gets to open the captain's cabin! And we've got a super-duper cash prize for two fabulous voters, chosen at random. Get voting!'

Leo reaches for the phone on the tripod and cuts off the recording, and we all sigh with relief. I sense that we're exhausted by this exploration, drained by excitement, apprehension, and, at times, stone-cold fear.

II

It's twenty minutes to midnight.

We're all heading to the captain's cabin, Leo guiding us down the steps and along the lower deck with a flashlight. We've gathered our solar lanterns and laid them along the corridor, but the additional light of Leo's torch is necessary both for the live, and because Samara is carrying the tin box containing the logbook, maps, and the letter. The deck is still slippery.

Samara takes her position beside the ornate door that remains sealed, and the set of chisels that Leo found in the hold, which the winners are to use to unjam the door. Despite this plan, I'm nervous that we have promised our followers something that we can't fulfil, that we won't be able to break the door down to the captain's cabin. And part of me is also nervous about what lies behind it. It could be a trap. That's not just paranoia talking. Samara said so as well. Or if not a trap, the air could hold spores.

I don't want to be a killjoy, but the climactic end of our contest might be our own end if we're not careful.

Samara's going to open the letter and attempt to read the contents outside the door, just before the countdown. I've brought the Capote novel with the missing cover and a screenshot of the guy whose signature is scrawled there. Jens has brought some old science instruments he found washed up in the bay – a microscope, some old test tubes, and, our *pièce de résistance,* a brass cylinder that turns out to be a research instrument used for icebergs, called a tiltmeter. We'd spotted it in the filthy water in the hold when we first went down there but didn't think it was anything significant. According to Google, a tiltmeter measures an iceberg's basal melting, as well as tidal motion and changes caused by tremors, so it likely would have been used during the *Ormen*'s research era.

'I wonder if it still works,' Samara says, looking it over as Jens holds it up to the light. We cleaned it up, bringing the brass to a decent shine.

'Even if it does,' Leo says, 'do any of us know how to use it?'

'We'd need an iceberg,' Jens says. 'Or a volcano.'

'We've got a volcano,' Leo says. 'I don't think it's active, though.'

'Are we ready?' Samara says, glancing at her watch, and we all nod.

Leo sets up the tripod with the camera and light fitting, then scoots back alongside us all for the livestream.

'Hey everyone,' Samara says to the camera. 'We're about to reveal the winners of our contest. You've still got ten minutes to vote, so we thought we'd reveal our very last discoveries for those of you who might be sitting on the fence.' She turns to me. 'Dominique? You want to go first?'

I nod, instantly embarrassed. Even without a visible audience I know how bad I am on screen. I hold up my Capote.

'I found a copy of a Truman Capote novel,' I say, fingering the yellowed pages gently as I hold it closer to the lens. 'It's missing a cover but you can see the title here. And I saw that the owner had written their name inside. Diego Almeyda.'

'What?' Samara says.

'Diego Almeyda,' I say again, and I see her face drop. 'I googled him and it turns out he was one of the scientists on board the *Ormen* in 1973, right when the whole crew went missing.'

Jens starts to clap. Samara looks stunned. Leo glances at her, nervous.

'Samara, you OK?' he whispers, and she looks paralysed, utterly stricken. We all trade looks for a second, wondering what to do.

'Uh, yeah,' she says finally, visibly attempting to snap out of whatever was running through her mind. She holds up the letter but seems to freeze again, her eyes wide and her mouth open.

'So we have a letter, here,' Leo says, stepping in. He takes the letter from Samara's hand and holds it up to the lens. 'This was in the tin box that Samara found, *unopened*. We reckon it's from 1901. A little warning: this isn't the moment you want to nip to the loo, folks. I'm going to open this *hundred-and-twenty-something-year-old* letter right now, and read its secrets to you all watching at home. Ready?'

I squint at the viewer counter on the screen. It looks like we're at three thousand viewers, which isn't bad at all.

Leo slips a knife under the fold of the envelope and opens it carefully. Gently, he pulls out the letter. The ink is distorted by water damage, the letters faded and blurry. Leo tries to read it but can only make out a handful of words that don't make sense.

'I think that says "mother",' Leo says hopefully, and we all look at the word he points at.

'Could be,' Jens says. 'Or perhaps "mottle"?'

Leo squints at it a while longer before giving up. 'Sorry, everyone,' he says. 'Still, a remarkable document right here. And if you look at our previous posts, you'll see Samara talking about the logbook with its incredible reveal of a stowaway! How's *that* for a discovery?'

We have a few minutes left, so Jens holds up the microscope. 'This is from the research era, obviously. It has a Leica lens and would be worth a bit, if it weren't for the bullet hole through the casing.'

I turn to him. 'Bullet hole?'

He nods. 'Pretty sure.' He turns the microscope upside down and shows us a round hole in the metal casing.

'Wow,' I say, taking that in. 'Maybe it broke and someone used it for target practice?'

Samara looks uneasy, her face dropping again. It's awkward, as this is a livestream and usually she's the frontwoman, talking non-stop and leading the dynamic. But she looks dazed.

'OK, that's thirty seconds left,' Leo says, and I silently sigh in relief. We all count down from ten, and when it hits midnight Leo shouts, 'Voting stops!'

We gather around the phone and look at the results: 46 per cent of votes are for the research era, and 54 are for the whaling era. Samara and Leo give a shout for joy and wrap their arms around each other. Jens and I share a brief look. Winning means nothing to either of us, really. If anything, I'm relieved that I'm not the one who'll be opening the door to the captain's cabin.

Leo leans his shoulder against the door, giving it a test, just in case. It doesn't budge, so we all set about using the chisels that Leo found in the hold to hack into the frame. It should feel like sacrilege, but after bashing in so many other doors for firewood, this doesn't seem any different. Still, it's a shame that the beautiful hand-carved oak will be underwater in a fortnight. I watch everyone warily, remembering the weird sensation I had that first night here. The feeling when I turned the handle. I've been dreading this.

'That's it!' Leo says then, setting down the chisel and pressing his hands flat against the wood. 'Can you feel that?'

Samara leans against it too. 'It's definitely shifted,' she says, glancing at me and Jens.

'Let me have another try,' Leo says, and we clear a space as he steps back along the corridor, then takes a run at the door and, with a roar, kicks it.

I cover my mouth as the door creaks open, only a couple of inches, the hinges refusing to yield. Samara and Leo push against it, but I back away, too nervous to approach. After a minute or so they manage to shove it open enough for Samara to slide through the gap.

'A desk has fallen against the door,' she calls back to us. 'That's why it wouldn't open.'

We hear the wail of wood against wood as she drags it back. Leo grabs the camera and heads inside. Jens turns to me.

'Feeling nervous?' he says.

I keep my sleeve to my mouth as I follow him inside.

'Here we are,' Samara is saying to the camera. 'The captain's cabin! Opened for the first time in God knows how long.'

It's a large cabin, a window blocked up, a gaping hole at the far corner visible behind a bookcase. An old wooden desk is overturned, a chair toppled beside the bookcase. Samara opens the drawers and lifts out sheaves of paper, badly stained. From the ceiling, an old brass oil lamp hangs crookedly, covered in cobwebs and dust. I help Jens right the desk. I can tell it's the original desk from the nineteenth century. The old brass handles on the drawers, the black leather writing surface. When Jens shines his light down on to the leather I can make out impressions. I think of a man writing on this desk, over a hundred years ago. As I'm leaning down, running my eyes over the still-visible imprints of writing, I think of the words that Leo carved into the dining table in the main cabin, the poem about the selkie wife and sea king. A melody slips into my mind. It fits the words. It isn't a poem.

It's a song.

And I have no idea how I know this.

'As a special thank you to our wonderful voters,' Leo tells the viewers. Only five hundred are still watching. 'I'm going to do a pretty epic parkour challenge across the bay next time we have enough light and battery to livestream. Stay tuned, folks! It'll be mega!'

III

We wake to sunlight. Actual light, a ball of pearly brightness cradled by the mountains.

'Holy shit!' I hear Samara shout, and I run out onto the deck to see her halfway up the stairs. 'Do you see that?'

'See what?' Leo calls after her, only to yell when they see the streak of light funnelling down the stairs.

We all race up to the cabin. It's eleven o'clock in the morning and technically we've all slept in, but the darkness has disrupted everyone's sleep patterns. When it's dark like this there is no day and night, only a round continuum of time.

I check the solar chargers by the window. The red digits read 78 per cent charged.

'They're at seventy-eight,' I call to Leo and Samara. 'One has charged all the way to eighty.'

'Holy *shit*!' Samara shouts again, in a different tone. 'That's amazing!'

'That's enough for the parkour,' Leo says. 'I'll do it now before the light changes.'

I start plugging the cameras into the solar chargers to give the batteries as much charge as I can.

We hear the familiar sound of Jens climbing up the ladder. 'What's all the screaming about?' he says. 'Haven't you ever seen sunlight before?'

'Not for weeks,' I say, holding up the solar chargers.

'We got enough charge for the Parkour Thank You,' Samara tells him. She bounces to the kettle. 'And I'm making coffee. Anyone want one?'

We all do. It's been a long few days without enough charge for a kettle.

Leo tells us he's going to parkour over the bay and needs us all to film. 'We'll do a drone *and* a headcam live,' he says. 'And maybe two other angles from both sides of the bay.'

Samara, Jens, and I share a look. The range of camera angles *would* be really cool, and we could edit the footage later to cut between them all. It *would* be cinematic.

Jens shrugs. 'I'm up for it.'

Leo tugs his red bobble hat down over his forehead before heading towards the cabin door. 'You better grab your cameras, folks, because I'm only doing this once.'

'Shit,' Samara says, scrambling for her camera. Leo's already out the door. I flick on the internet terminal and log in to our project TikTok account. I hit 'live' and turn the lens to my face.

'Hi friends, we've got some exciting content coming up so stay tuned. It involves Leo, it involves parkour, and it involves *ice*. Are you ready?'

'I need to get my drone,' Jens says.

'You better hurry,' Leo says, pulling the door open.

We all rush after him, stepping out into the bracing air. The wind is kicking up the sand, sending it dancing across the bay like the inside of a snow globe, and I can't help but laugh with excitement. Doing a live is stressful at the best of times, because you can't control things, and certainly not the weather. Doing a live out here is like aligning the planets, and after everything that's gone wrong for us, this combination of good light, charged cameras, and Leo's eagerness to do an epic stunt all feels like a gift. I watch the numbers climb on the screen – we're already at four hundred.

We climb down to the bottom of the ladder. Jens fetches his drone while Leo stretches on the sand, raising his calves and circling his narrow hips, then windmilling his arms. I film it all, positioning myself so that I get the shipwreck into the frame behind Leo and a good section of the beach. The black sand against the thickening snow is gorgeous. Six hundred and ninety. Seven hundred and ten. This is phenomenal. By the time I've been filming for four minutes we're at a thousand.

'Samara's going to film from the other side of the bay,' I tell the viewers. 'And in the meantime, Leo's making sure he stretches out his muscles to prevent injuries. A really important part of parkour, right, Leo?'

'Damn right,' Leo says, sinking down easily into a split. 'A warm muscle is a safe muscle.'

'I can't even touch my toes, folks,' I say into the lens. 'So don't feel bad if you too can't do the splits in minus six-degree temperatures.'

'Ready?' Leo says.

I look over at Jens. He has the drone set up and livestreaming on his own TikTok account, and I tag him into mine. Samara's green hat is visible at the bend of the bay in the distance, and I see her livestream on my phone. She's jogging and laughing into the lens, chatting away but so exhilarated I can't make her out. The closed captions can't either, nonsense sentences blinking up on the screen before her face.

I watch the view numbers, expecting them to decline, but they continue to climb until they reach 3,074. Bloody hell. Comments pop up, too, remarking on the landscape, the ship, and conversations break out – people who hadn't heard about our project beforehand are intrigued while older followers are informing them about it. *They're a group of explorers*

231

checking out the shipwreck in Iceland before it's hauled into the sea. It was an old whaling ship and apparently it's haunted. Reactions flood up the screen like bubbles, thumbs and hearts and 'wow' emojis.

I look around for Jens and spot a pink dot on the side of the volcano. His beanie. Leo has finished stretching out and signals to Samara on the other side, before turning to me. 'Tell us what you're going to do, Leo,' I say, holding my lens on him.

He points at the frozen water of the bay. 'I'm going to parkour over that to the turf houses on the other side.'

'Can you tell us a little about what parkour is?' I say.

'Parkour is a dark poetry, bitches,' Leo tells the viewers, making a peace sign and pressing his face so close to the lens that I can make out his eyelashes furred with snowflakes. He leans back and rolls his neck from side to side. 'Seriously, though, you have to move fearlessly. Parkour is moving without hesitation, like you could dodge a bullet. It's a combination of dance, gymnastics, and extreme mental resilience and determination.'

Leo clicks on his headcam. I check that the livestream is showing up on his TikTok feed before tagging it for our viewers.

'We're livestreaming from four angles,' I say into the lens. 'We're calling this *Live Parkour in Four Dimensions,* right Leo?'

'Right!'

I look over to Jens and hold up an arm, then give a thumbs up to let him know that we're good to film. I can't see his drone in the sky, so I check his livestream. Instantly I see Leo and me from above, the two of us small figures on a bed of white.

The project livestream has 4,007 viewers. I screenshot to prove it to the others. They won't believe me otherwise.

'OK, we're ready Leo,' I say, stepping back to allow him

space to get into position. Already the sunlight is fading, clouds thickening overhead.He pulls off his coat, leaving him with just a beanie, a V-vest, and gloves for warmth. And then he's off, bursting off the bank towards the bay, snow kicking up behind his heels.

We all click into action, Jens' drone lowering into view like a black cross against the white curtain of snow. I keep my camera steady, but Leo is barely visible now. On the headcam footage I can see the icy surface of the bay, and he's using the rocks and ice blocks to propel himself forward, lowering on to all fours, then spinning into a backflip. The image wheels as he somersaults, and Samara comes into view, standing on the pier. She gives a whoop as Leo dives past her towards the turf houses.

Leo makes it on the roof in two leaps, and from there he hurls himself on to the next roof, then the next, like a panther in human form. Like he's literally unafraid of falling.

I watch, open-mouthed, as he reaches the edge of the last turf house. There's a huge gap between it and the school, and for a moment I think he's going to attempt to jump it.

My heart rises into my mouth, and Samara must be thinking the same thing, because I hear her voice over the livestream: 'Don't be an idiot, Leo.'

Leo is a speck in the distance, almost blotted out completely by fog, but I see from his headcam that he's doing a handstand on the edge of the turf house, his hands planted on the lip of the roof and his legs held high in the air. Suddenly Leo springs backwards, his body wheeling through the air. I can't bring myself to look, because I know what he's doing – Leo has sprung off the roof of the turf house into a mid-air backflip and is trying to land on the roof of the school. It feels like an eternity as he spins through the air, the footage on his livestream a blur of granite sky and white ground.

I can't look.

Samara lets out a shout. Leo has landed, a little wobbly, but he rolls into it before springing up again on all fours, leaping down to the ground.

Jesus Christ. My heart can't take much more of this.

Emojis of hearts and faces bubble up across my stream. I lower my phone and squint through the blizzard. Samara steps off the pier and runs towards Leo, and I can hear her laughing. She wraps her arms around Leo and on Samara's livestream I see her and Leo's faces, wet and smiling and encrusted with snowflakes. Their exhilaration is palpable. I want to run over and join in the celebration. I want to show them that we have almost five thousand goddamn viewers tuning in from every corner of the globe right now.

But Leo's on the move again. I flick to Jens' drone feed to work out where he's going – he is headed for the bay, close to the bend. I raise my camera to film, wiping the lens with my glove to clear the moisture from the snow. I should have brought a lens cloth. In a moment it clears, and I see Leo bounding across the ice, zigzagging towards the beach. We're at five and a half thousand viewers now, my phone pulsing with notifications. It's terrific, but also draining my battery. I pause and find the 'settings' tab, then tap the button that lets me switch off the notifications. When I glance up again Samara has cut across the ice instead of looping around the bay, approaching Leo as he holds a handstand on the mermaid stone, straight and still as a lightning rod.

The light is fading fast, shadows blooming across the heath. Something stirs in the corner of my vision. A figure at the turn of the bay in the distance, about two hundred metres away.

Fear thumps in my throat, acidic.

It's the woman.

I turn my phone to film her, toggling the zoom. Desperation burns in me to catch her, to snare the proof of her existence. But she's gone, only shadows where she stood before. I zoom in frantically anyway, sweeping my camera across the whole of the bay.

A yell echoes across the plain. I turn back to Leo and squint into the murk. He's off the rocks, moving quickly towards the pier. From his movements I can tell he's running towards something. Where is Samara?

I flip across to her live feed and see it is no longer capturing the whiteness of the bay but is a dark blue, a stream of bubbles and a hand reaching forward.

'Help!' Leo shouts. 'Dom, *help!*'

Oh my God. Samara is underwater. She has fallen through the ice.

Jens' drone appears in the sky above, diving down over a large hole in the ice. I frantically check Samara's footage to work out where she is, but just then her footage cuts out, goes blank. I can't move, can't will my legs to run towards her. And then I see Leo racing across the ice, and I realise he might go underneath, too, and suddenly I'm running from the other side towards them, shouting at them to get off the ice.

I find myself kneeling by a square-shaped hole about the width of the hatch in the *Ormen*, shouting for Samara. Leo appears with a long plank of wood and lowers it into the dark water that laps up around my knees. My hands are so cold they won't work properly.

'Samara!' Leo shouts again, leaning down to the hole in the ice. He pulls off his hat and plunges his head underneath in a bid to see her but it's so dark, impenetrably dark, and it strikes me that she's been underwater for over a minute. I'm gasping and crying into the wet dark, pawing at the water in the hole in case I might somehow find Samara there.

Something pushes to the surface, the crown of a head glistening in the moonlight. It's Samara, her mouth open as she gasps and claws at me. I reach out to her, grasping her shoulders, but suddenly the ice beneath me tilts, lightning-shaped cracks streaking across the pale blue surface. Leo gives a deafening shriek, and on instinct I push myself back from the ice that crumbles into the dark water beneath, widening the hole.

Samara slides back down, despite Leo reaching for her, their hands clasping. I lunge forward, reaching down for her too. My hands hit something but I can't grasp her. Leo is screaming, 'Samara! Samara!' and I see the ice beneath his knees begin to fold, a creaking sound indicating that it's about to give way.

The noise grows louder, and I realise it's coming from behind. I turn to see Jens running towards me, pulling off his boots and hat as he moves. He jumps feet first straight into the hole, sending the icy water sloshing around Leo and me. I watch him as if in slow motion, as though I am far away, distanced from the scene in front of me.

A sense of déjà vu is creeping through me, as though I know this scene, as though I have watched it all before.

My reverie is broken by Leo shouting my name. Jens' jump has weakened the ice shelf, and I manage to grab Leo's hand right as the ground beneath us both collapses, pulling him towards me.

We cling to one another, our breaths pushing out like clouds into the darkness.

Stillness. Jens and Samara are underneath us, deep in the water. We've lost them both.

Then I feel something move beneath me, as though a hand is scratching at the ice. I feel sure I can see Jens' face staring up through the layers of ice. I move forward and plunge my

hand in the water, splashing and yelling, 'We're here! Here!'
A second later, Jens bursts up through the surface, gasping
for air, and I see he has Samara in the crook of his arm.
Somehow Leo and I manage to haul him up on to the ice
while he holds Samara, and he drags her awkwardly up, her
body weighed down by water.

'Give her CPR!' I scream at Leo, and he hesitates before
lowering, pushing air into Samara's lungs, then turning her
head to the side.

Water dribbles from her lips, her eyes staring. Leo leans
down and breathes air into her mouth, then straightens and
presses down, down, and down.

Samara gives a faint cough, and I shout out.

'Yes!' I say. 'That's it, Samara! Breathe!'

'We have to get off the ice,' Jens pants. The ice is bending
beneath our weight, water bubbling up through narrow cracks.

IV

The ice breaks a second after we lunge towards the pier, folding inward like a shattered window.

Leo and I carry Samara back to the *Ormen*, her body limp as a doll's. She is unconscious, her mouth open and the whites of her eyes showing, but she's hanging on by a thread.

Inside the cabin, Leo makes a fire hastily while I strip Samara of her wet clothes and dry her with a towel, before wrapping her with a thick blanket. Jens watches on, shivering and refusing to get changed. I think he's in shock.

'You have to take your clothes off,' I tell him. 'Jens! You'll go into shock!'

But he stands like a sentinel, watching on as I remove Samara's socks and rub her feet, finally lifting my shirt and pressing the soles against my belly for extra heat.

'We're on the ship now, Samara,' I say loudly. 'We're getting you all warmed up. Stay with us, OK? You just keep focused on my voice. We're going to get the fire going and you'll be right as rain really soon.'

I think of the woman appearing at the edge of the ice right before Samara fell. There's no denying it, now. There's no denying what she is. And every single time she appears, bad things happen. But I still can't bring myself to mention it to the others. Not now.

Oh God, the livestream is still running, my phone in my pocket. All of this has been seen. What will our followers think?

'It's my fault!' Leo groans. 'I did this! I did this! She wouldn't have stepped on the ice if I hadn't have gone on it.'

'The ice cracked,' Jens says, a statement so obvious and yet so devastating that we all nod. 'No one knows where or when ice will crack. It has nothing to do with you.'

'No!' Leo shouts, and he repeats it, beating his fists against his head. I want to stop him, but I don't. I know Leo is shouting at the situation, at the fact that we can't turn back time.

'We have to get her help,' I scream.

'How?' Jens says quietly, and Leo covers his face with his hands and breaks down into ugly sobs. I feel angry for no good reason, particularly with Leo. For crying. But mostly, I feel like I'm the one who's really to blame. I feel it so strongly, without really understanding where it comes from. The nagging, tormenting guilt.

We are at least six hours from help. Six hours on a clear day. We can't even risk venturing to the nearest town, because the snow is now falling so heavily we risk getting lost, or getting trapped.

We sit quietly, praying the fire won't go out. Praying that Samara will survive the night.

And no one is listening to our prayers.

Nicky

I

September 1901
Upernavik, Greenland

Nicky sat in the galley with Reid while he unfolded the piece of paper. His cheeks were flushed, and she saw his hands shook.

'Are you nervous?' she asked him.

'A little,' he said, lowering his eyes to the page.

'You've shared your songs with me before,' she said.

'Aye, but this one's about you,' he said shyly. 'I hope you don't mind.'

'About me?' she said, looking down at the words on the sheet of paper.

'Well, it's about the folktale, too,' he said. 'But I thought of you when I wrote it.'

She felt something turn in her stomach as she looked down at the words written on the page.

> *When once a town lost half its men*
> *a wife did swear that ne'er again*
> *the sea would cause such hearts to grieve*
> *and sailors to their wives would cleave.*
> *So by the shore, upon her knees,*

240

she prayed that Lír would calm the seas.
Lír heard and said, be changed this night –
part seal, my queen, until first light
these seas no more will cause thee strife
if you'll become my selkie wife

'It's fiction,' she said, trying to raise a smile to match his.

'But you're the selkie wife,' he said. 'That's what Lovejoy said. Only . . . Daverley said I'm not to . . .' He saw her face fall. 'I didn't mean to upset you,' he said.

'You haven't,' she said, forcing a smile on her face. 'It's just a song, isn't it? Why don't you go and teach it to the men?'

'Won't you come and listen?' he said.

She desperately wanted to say no, but she saw the look on his face, his childish eagerness to impress her. Reid looked on her as someone he could talk to, and she found herself acting towards him as though he was a younger brother. When Daverley was distracted, she kept an eye out for Reid in case he got into trouble. He was a good boy, eager to help, and he often brought her extra portions of food from the galley.

'Yes,' she said. 'I'll come and listen.'

She followed him up to the deck, bringing an extra blanket for her shoulders as Reid handed out the new sea shanty to the crew. Most of them were drunk, their limbs loose and their eyes moving across her.

'What's this, then?' Lovejoy said, lifting his eyes from the page to Reid in suspicion. 'A selkie wife?'

Some of the men threw furtive glances at her, as though they'd worked out the connection between her and the shanty for themselves.

'It's my new sea shanty,' Reid said proudly, standing before them. 'I'm going to teach you the tune.'

He sang it aloud, and the men repeated it. After several

tries they'd managed to get it, and Reid lifted his arms to conduct them. The horizon was beginning to darken, a storm coming. She waited for a call from Lovejoy or the captain to bring in the sails. But no call came; the captain was out of sight, and Lovejoy was singing loudly with the men, his arms wrapped around Wolfarth and Harrow as they danced and kicked their legs out.

The men's singing outpaced Reid's conducting, faster and faster, the lyrics beginning to run together.

And then, with a loud cheer, the song finished, and the men burst into applause. It had started to rain. Nicky shrank back under the cover of the forecastle. She saw Daverley approach then, a bucket of tar in one hand and a paintbrush in the other. Reid turned to him, beaming with pride.

'Uncle,' he said. 'What do you think of my—'

Before he could finish his sentence, Lovejoy grabbed him roughly by the collar, yanking him towards Nicky.

'If you like her that much, what say you give her a poke with your stick?' he said. 'Come on, now. Right here.'

The other men laughed, but Reid's face had flushed red with humiliation. He looked like a child, radiant with fear. Lovejoy reached forward heavily and pulled at the boy's belt, as though to strip him of his trousers. The movement prompted an instinctive reaction from Reid – with a cry, he struck Lovejoy in the face, as hard as he could.

The men fell silent. It was quite a punch, coming from such a scrawny lad. Lovejoy staggered slightly, the blow catching him on the jaw, but it would take more than that to knock him down. He straightened and cocked his head, shrugging off Royle and Gray when they stepped forward to intervene.

'That's enough,' Daverley said, his eyes settling on Reid. 'All of you, back to your stations.'

The rain fell hard, pelting the deck and bouncing upward.

The boat had started to rock, ravenous winds clapping the sails. The men glanced uneasily at each other, but no one moved.

Lovejoy turned to Reid, and then Nicky, who had risen to her feet, outraged at the way he had seized the boy. She opened her mouth to shout at him to stop, but just then he raised his eyes to her, and she shrank at the look on his face. It was the same transfixed expression that came over him when he made her wear the bear's skull, as though degradation was a drug he couldn't resist.

'He's just a lad,' Daverley said, approaching him.

'Maybe he's a eunuch,' Lovejoy sneered. Slowly he removed a knife from his pocket and held it by his side. 'We can make it so, if not.'

'Put the knife down, Lovejoy,' one of the other men called, and for a moment it seemed he'd realised he'd gone too far and would comply. He gave a great laugh, as if it was all a game, and the men laughed in echo. She saw Reid relax, his face loosening. But then Lovejoy lunged at Daverley, managing to shove him to the side. For such a stocky man he was surprisingly swift; in an instant he was holding the blade against Reid's smooth throat.

On the ground behind them, Daverley struggled to his feet. He had blood in his hair from where his head struck an iron hook hanging from the mast.

'I think we've got two lasses on board, lads,' Lovejoy hollered, holding Reid tight with his free arm.

'I'm . . . I'm not a lass,' Reid stammered, his hands clawing at Lovejoy's arm held fast across his chest. Reid's eyes fell on Nicky. She held up her hands, signalling him to stay calm. Lovejoy's knife flashed in the sunlight, and a sudden movement might result in it cutting too deep.

'Prove it,' Lovejoy said. 'Prove you're not a lass. Go on.'

He lifted the knife and pointed it at Nicky, instructing her to move towards him. 'Swyve her right here and prove yourself.'

Lovejoy nodded at the rest of the crew to join in. A chant rose up: *Swyve her! Swyve her! Swyve her!*

Reid's face had crumpled. Lovejoy pushed him towards Nicky, the knife at his back, while Cowie and Gray tugged at the hem of her skirt, trying to lift it.

'Stop it!' she shouted.

She looked at Daverley, who was on his feet behind Lovejoy, trying to gauge how to intervene without worsening the situation.

'Captain!' he shouted. 'Captain Willingham!'

Lovejoy nodded at the two men at either side of Nicky, and quickly they seized her, holding her in place. Lovejoy lowered before her, lifting the hem of her skirt on his blade.

'I'll make it easy for you,' Lovejoy told Reid.

Reid hesitated, unsure of what to do. Liquid bloomed on the deck by his feet, and Lovejoy roared with laughter.

'He's pissed himself!' he yelled to the others. 'So afraid of a woman that's he's pissed himself!'

'You've made your point,' she said angrily. 'Put the knife down.'

Lovejoy's smile faded, his eyes darkening. He moved the knife away, only to ram the wooden end into her face. She felt a hard crack against her cheek, the heat of blood rising quickly around her eye.

'You don't give orders,' he said with a growl. 'You don't speak. Got it?'

She cowered from his hand, raised again to strike her.

'You want to know how you came to be on this ship?' he said then, a cruel smile on his face.

She noticed that Reid had stepped backwards, as though he wanted to run away.

'You were attacked in a park, correct?' Lovejoy continued.

'I was,' she said, cupping her injured eye. 'What do you know of it?'

'Oh, I know plenty,' Lovejoy said. 'And I believe Master Reid knows plenty, too. Don't you, lad?'

'I had nothing to do with it,' Reid shrieked. 'I had no say in the matter!'

Somewhere behind her she heard footsteps on the stairs from the captain's cabin. Her mind raced. Why was Reid reacting like this? Had he been involved?

'I think you'll find that Master Reid here was the one who assisted in carrying you aboard,' Lovejoy said. 'While you were asleep.'

'I was *unconscious*,' she spat.

Reid trembled, his eyes brimming with tears. She looked to him, unable to hide her confusion.

'I was only doing what I was told,' Reid said, a sob in his voice. 'I didn't know . . . I didn't know . . .'

'You knew plenty, lad. And you knew exactly why we were bringing a lass on board.' Lovejoy glanced at her. 'I don't know about you, selkie, but I'd be livid if I knew I was helping out the very lad who'd bundled me aboard a whaling ship.'

She felt suddenly as though she was falling. Reid's face told her everything – that he had helped the man who had attacked her. Perhaps the man was Lovejoy, his appearance changed by the hat and clothing. Either way, Reid had placed her in the hold, where the barrel had fallen over and pierced her foot.

'Why?' she whispered. 'Why did you do that?'

Reid covered his face with his hands. Whatever he said, she didn't hear through his sobs.

Lovejoy chuckled to himself, bending to the coil of rope

by the mast. Daverley approached Reid, resting a hand on his shoulder. 'Come on, lad,' he said.

Just then, Reid gave a strangled cry of fury and charged at Lovejoy with his fists. In a single movement, Lovejoy side-stepped Reid's blow and swept his knife across, slicing Reid's left thigh. She heard Reid cry out as he staggered forward, falling on all fours.

A ruby-dark patch bloomed beneath Reid, and he fell slowly into it, like a bale of hay collapsing in parts. He made no sound, but the red puddle drew shouts from the men. His body spasmed and jerked with shock.

Nicky lunged at Reid quickly, pressing her hands against the wound to stop the bleeding. 'Call Dr O'Regan!' she shouted.

With a wounded yell, Daverley charged at Lovejoy, but in a moment Captain Willingham was there, ordering Stroud and Cowie to pull Daverley off Lovejoy. As they grabbed Daverley he swung an arm at Lovejoy, landing a heavy blow that streaked the air red.

'Get this man in the brig,' Captain Willingham yelled at Daverley. 'Back to your stations!'

But the men didn't move. They crossed themselves as Nicky leaned down close to Reid, her cheek against his, whispering the Lord's Prayer into his ear.

'Please,' he said, grasping her arm. 'Please don't let me be taken.'

'I won't,' she whispered. She felt the warmth of Reid's blood around her knees and on her arms. She clasped both hands tightly around his leg, until she felt she might squeeze the very bones. But the blood flowed from the cut like a tap, pumping vehemently through her fingers and revealing muscle through his torn trousers.

'Clear a path!' Dr O'Regan shouted, and quickly he cut

the boy's trousers to attend to his wound. 'Thomas!' he shouted. 'Keep your eyes on me, Thomas!'

But Reid had fallen still, his eyes staring up into the sky.

By the time Dr O'Regan made the first stitch, Reid was already gone.

Dominique

I

December 2023
Skúmaskot, Iceland

Samara's frighteningly limp, like a rag doll, laid out on the sofa by the fire. I wrap her up with blankets, then bring my sleeping bag upstairs to sleep on the floor next to her. She falls asleep, which I know is dangerous, but I figure she will sleep it off. She hasn't gone into shock. I think it will be OK.

I stoke the fires, making sure she stays warm. Darkness falls like a blade.

Exhaustion consumes me. I don't know how long I sleep for, maybe just a couple of minutes, because when I wake the fire is still hot. I reach out to check on Samara. She seems . . . different. Panicked, I put my hand to her cheek to make sure she is warm enough, and she is, but there is no breath against my hand when I move it to her mouth. I reach for her pulse. Nothing.

'Jens!' I scream. 'Leo!'

Leo comes racing up the stairs and I show him.

'She's not breathing,' I say, pressing both hands on her ribcage. I can feel the bones snapping with a terrible crunch. Jens is there, and he kneels beside her, taking her hand as I breathe into her mouth. Frantic, I slap her cheeks, turning her on her side and back again to breathe into her lungs. Her eyes are open and staring straight ahead, like stones. They didn't flicker in the torchlight.

'Please don't die!' I yell. '*Please!*'

Jens rests a hand on my arm and looks at me with those terrible sad eyes. 'Enough,' he says, but I don't stop slapping her until he pulls me away.

Leo is panting beside me, his hands pressed to his cheeks. 'What do we do?' he says to Jens. 'Jens, this hasn't happened before. What do we do?'

I watch, sobbing, as Leo's voice rises into a panic. 'This hasn't happened before, Jens! Where is she? What's happening?'

He grabs Jens by the upper arms and shakes him, but Jens simply holds him in a flat stare, sadness etched deeply on his features. Leo is spiralling now, screaming things that don't make sense.

'You said it would work! You said it would fucking work! What's happening? Answer me!'

Jens doesn't speak, doesn't react at all. He is so still and vacant that I wonder if he's having a heart attack. It sends Leo wild. He picks up a camera and hurls it at the wall, smashing it. Then his laptop – he throws it against the door, then picks it up and throws it out into the wind. He lunges at me, his fists bunched, but Jens reaches a hand out to stop him.

'You fucking cocksucker!' Leo screams at him, before staggering out on to the deck.

I stare at them. I know this is my fault, that I have done this, but I can't quite put my finger properly on where my feeling of guilt is stemming from. But one thought is racing through my mind, constantly flashing through on repeat; She is dead *because of me*. I plead with her not to be. I tell her I'd do anything if she came back. Anything.

II

Our batteries are all completely done. We try and try to power them, but *nothing* works. Darkness has closed in now and without light, we have no battery, and that means we can't call anyone for help.

Not that anything would help Samara now. We have covered her up with a blanket, her beloved green beanie and walking boots on the floor beside her.

It feels like the inside of my brain is coated in acid. Leo is outside right now doing parkour against the side of the boat and howling like he's lost his mind. None of us know what to do. Her body is still here, and we are all on this boat, trapped by ice and fog and dead phones.

I look at the tin box on the table, the letters and the logbook still inside. How excited and sickened Samara was by what she read there.

A woman kidnapped and held captive here on the *Ormen*. And the words of the poem, the *selkie wife*.

I pull on another coat and stand outside on the deck of the *Ormen*, watching my breath turn to ice fractals in the moonlight. Never have I been so desperate for the sun to rise, for the reassurance that the dark will pass.

Jens, Leo and I haven't talked about what we'll do now. We're shellshocked, robbed of words. I think at least two of us will have to walk to the nearest town and get help while the other stays with Samara. With the body.

I know what I saw, right before Samara fell through the ice. It can't be a coincidence.

Maybe I was wrong not to say anything to the others about the woman. About the ghost. I felt ashamed, and I worried about their reaction.

But it seems we're no longer exploring the *Ormen*.

We are being hunted.

Einar

Dawn; a hard light beating down on the bay, the dregs of a snowstorm flickering across the volcano. A crowd gathered around the scene, surveying the damage to the rocks and the fishing boats in the bay. At first, many of them thought they were under attack, the huge ship ploughing into the mouth of the bay to be taken as a hostile act. But it became clear that the ship was a wreck, a remnant, adrift and unmanned.

Einar was one of the youngest fishermen in the village, and had grown up trawling the fishing grounds with his grandfather's fleet, filling their nets with cod and sleeper sharks. He knew how to extract oil from the sharks' livers and how to salt and hang the cod on the racks. He had heard the stories of the whaling station that his grandfather burned down to protect their village and their livelihood. This, he knew, was a whaling ship, and its arrival had damaged his neighbour Gunnar's fleet of small boats. But he was excited. The village was quiet and offered little for young men and women in the way of entertainment. He couldn't wait to explore the new arrival.

The enormous masts of the ship stood tall above, the thick

252

beams of wood and the hooks striking awe in all the men who had a keen knowledge of ship-building, most of them claiming Viking heritage. This was an old ship, yes, but clearly one of the first to embrace steam. Many of their own boats still relied on wind and muscle alone.

'Stay away,' his uncle Aron told him when he attempted to climb up the hull, but Einar tugged his arm free. In a handful of moves, he was on board, his arms raised on the top deck in triumph.

Einar and his friends found the vast new arrival to be a treasure trove, teeming with strange objects. Most of them were scientific, and they found charts and maps in the main cabin that would prove useful for their fishing routes. The microscopes were taken for the local school, and they found wine, which was quickly drunk.

The wreck had crashed into the old whaling station itself, ripping off the blackened roof and sending the weakened structure into the bay. The villagers were careful not to allow the bay to become polluted, but they let the station sink. A feeling of unease rippled throughout the town. And when it became apparent that the coastguard were in no rush to remove the wreck, they grew fearful.

At midnight, his mother, Hildur, called him outside.

'Hold the ladder,' she said, propping it against the stone archway of their front door.

He watched as she painted a symbol, just as she had seen her mother do before her. A series of runes crisscrossed as a cage to trap demons.

It was as he was returning the ladder to the shed behind the croft that Einar saw a figure in the middle of the bay, by the rock they called the mermaid stone. A seat, his grandmother taught him, reserved for the creatures of the sea who passed between the realms of the living and the dead. Creatures of punishment. He was never to give any reason for the mermaids to approach him, and if he saw one, he was to look away and pass by.

But the figure was no mermaid. She was a woman and she was beautiful. A girl he had never seen before.

Quickly he swam out to her, and before long she was kissing his face, little pecks all over his skin that felt like butterflies, draping him with soft scarves. He felt alarmed when he saw drops of blood on his hands and on his trousers, but she was insistent, and he didn't want to stop.

And so he let her gnaw away his nose and lips, the scratches at his cheekbone like teasing tongues, the soft scarves she wrapped around his neck tightening until darkness took him whole.

Nicky

I

September 1901
Upernavik, Greenland

'It was the selkie wife, sir,' Lovejoy said. 'She was the one who kindled the fray.'

Nicky stood in the captain's cabin alongside Daverley, Lovejoy, and Harrow, the second mate. Daverley's arm had been bandaged, and Lovejoy wore a thick dressing across his broken nose. Daverley swayed slightly, his legs threatening to give under him. She could tell he was in shock after what had happened to his nephew.

'Is this true?' Captain Willingham asked Harrow. 'The selkie wife kindled the fray?' Harrow's eyes darted nervously at Lovejoy. She could tell that Harrow was wary of crossing him.

'Aye, sir,' Harrow said finally. 'She tricked the boy into writing a song about her. It set the men off, sir.'

'Explain what you mean by "set the men off",' Captain Willingham said.

Harrow flicked his eyes from Lovejoy to the captain. 'Well, they were all stirred up. And then a skirmish broke out . . .'

'Between who?'

'The boy, Captain. And Lovejoy.'

'What was this skirmish about, exactly?' Captain Willingham said.

'Jealousy,' Daverley said quietly.

'I beg pardon?' the captain said.

A muscle twisted in Daverley's jaw. 'I said, jealousy.'

'Who was jealous?'

'Captain Willingham, if I may,' Nicky said, her voice shaking. 'The boy, Reid, was merely trying to lead the men in singing a sea shanty. Lovejoy goaded him.'

From the corner of her eye, she saw Lovejoy turn to her, a threat in his stare.

Captain Willingham turned to Lovejoy. 'Is this true?'

Lovejoy bristled, affronted. 'I did no such thing. Ask any of the men.'

'Lovejoy tried to force Reid on me,' Nicky said. 'To make him violate me on the upper deck in front of the rest of the crew. He did it to humiliate us both.'

'She speaks the truth,' Daverley said.

Captain Willingham looked over them all, his eyes resting on Lovejoy. 'Is this true? You tried to force Reid on the lady before the eyes of the crew?'

Lovejoy cleared his throat. 'The japes may have gone too far, Captain. But you've seen for yourself the way the lady has spent time with Reid, helping him write his sea shanties and poems and what have you. I think the jealousy referred to was the boy's jealousy towards me. He made to shiv me, so I defended myself. A hand attacking a first mate, Captain! There must be order aboard a whaler.'

The captain murmured in agreement. He turned to Nicky, then Harrow. 'Can you confirm this?'

Harrow shuffled his feet. He seemed reluctant to be addressed. 'Aye, I can, Captain, but—'

'Enough,' Captain Willingham snapped. 'I've heard enough.'

He rose from his seat with an angry sigh. 'Daverley, you'll spend the night in the brig for your part in this fray. The boy will be buried at sea.'

Daverley groaned. 'Captain—'

'What would you have me do, Daverley?' the captain asked. 'Carry the boy's corpse on board with us for another quarter of a year?'

'A sea funeral's the surest way to trouble his ghost,' Daverley said under his breath.

Captain Willingham straightened at that. 'The old superstitions don't hold true. You know that.'

'Aye, they do,' Daverley said with a growl. 'And a woman aboard's the oldest of them all. No wonder the boy's dead.'

Nicky flinched. He was implying that she was responsible for Reid's death.

Captain Willingham rose slowly from his chair and glowered at Daverley. 'You will address me as "Captain" at all times.'

Daverley raised his eyes, though they were haunted. 'Aye, Captain.'

'The lady will stay in her cabin until I decide how I wish to proceed.'

Captain Willingham nodded at Harrow. 'See to it that McKenzie takes over Daverley's duties until I set him free. Off you go.'

Nicky went to her cabin, shutting the door behind her without a word. She felt numb with shock. Reid was dead. Just a boy of sixteen, dead on the deck.

The knowledge that he had helped kidnap her twisted in her gut, sharp and alarming. She reminded herself that he needed the money. It had not been personal.

And yet.

She thought of Daverley, sent to the upper deck to spend

a night in the brig out on the deck. The old cage, she thought, barely large enough for a cat. The sea was rough, and it was freezing cold. It would be a tough night for Daverley. And he'd just witnessed the murder of his nephew.

Just as she felt herself drifting off to sleep, a knock sounded at the door. She listened hard to work out who it was. Usually she could tell from the rhythm of the knocks which man stood outside her door, but it was difficult to tell.

'Who's there?' she called into the darkness.

No answer.

She held her breath. What if she just didn't answer?

Another knock, just one.

'No,' she said firmly. 'Get away from me!'

Suddenly the door exploded open, whoever stood behind ramming their foot into the wood and knocking the old lock off its hinges.

'You bitch,' Lovejoy growled, a heavy blow sending her to the floor. 'Dare you challenge me?'

She curled up in a ball as his fists rained down, and as the boot of his shoe lifted again and again she imagined herself underwater, seeing the ship as though from the depths, pulling it down, down with her.

Dominique

I

December 2023
Skúmaskot, Iceland

I wake to the sound of screaming.

I race upstairs to the main cabin to find Leo tearing the place apart. God, it's a mess. The dining table is upside down, coats and books strewn across the floor, and the sofa that Samara was lying on is now on its side.

I scan the room but I can't see the body. The blanket we covered her with is on the floor, next to the sofa.

Leo runs up to me, his gaze liquid, stunned.

'She's gone,' he says.

I stare. 'Who's gone?'

'Samara,' he says, turning to the coats on the floor. 'Her beanie and coat are gone, too. And – oh God! – her boots! Her boots are gone!'

Leo's face breaks into an exhilarated smile and he shouts for joy, clapping his hands to his face. I take a step back, frightened.

'What are you talking about?' I say.

'She's *gone*!' Leo says, gesturing towards the sofa. 'I can't find her anywhere! She's escaped!'

He breaks into a loud laugh, his eyes wide, and despite

myself I start to laugh, too. It suddenly seems hilarious, the sight of Leo searching under books, lifting cushions as though Samara has mysteriously shrunk to the size of a thimble. We've lost a dead body! What next?

Samara's coat is gone, just as Leo said, and her boots. And her phone isn't on the table, but her laptop is. I run down to her cabin to check. It's just the same as it was. A couple of books on the end of the bed, her rucksack filled with clothes and food sachets. Her tent rolled up. If she wanted to leave, surely she'd have taken her tent?

I stop at the foot of the stairs. What am I thinking? Samara is *dead*.

We all witnessed her body. I felt her cold, stiff hands, and bent her arms a little forcefully to tuck her in to make it seem like she was sleeping. I closed her eyelids with my fingers.

I gave her the kiss of life.

There was no pulse.

I must have blacked out for a while because the next thing I know I am upstairs again, and Jens is there, his face twisted in wild confusion as Leo explains the situation to him in a shrill, hysterical voice. *She's gone! She's gone!*

I watch Jens try to take it in. The empty sofa, the missing coat and shoes. We all watched Samara die and now it seems that she had been fooling us all. I feel that nervous, wild giggle rise up in me again, and I want to throw my head back and roar out a wide-jawed belly laugh. Samara simply got up, like Lazarus, put on her coat and boots, and left! Hilarious!

'There's no way she just got up and walked off the ship,' I say, pulling the door open and rushing outside. Leo and I follow, and we stand in the freezing snow scanning the bay. The wind is so wild it's as if it wants to claw off our faces.

'She'll not be far,' Jens says when we stagger back inside

and close the door against the wind. I watch him closely, the guarded way he's handling Leo's enthusiasm, his certainty that Samara is gone. He must suspect Leo has done something with her. That he's hidden the body somewhere. That he's having a full-scale breakdown.

'You think maybe she's in one of the turf houses?' Leo says, pulling on his coat.

'Where are you going?' Jens asks him.

'Where do you think I'm going?' Leo snaps back, his voice breaking. 'I'm going out to find Samara, that's what.'

Leo looks at us both in disgust. The guilt that has driven through me at Samara's death pricks me once more, and I grab my coat.

'I'll come with you,' I say.

Leo turns to me sharply. 'The fuck you will. After what you've done?'

'I want to find Samara as much as you do,' I say, a laugh of nervous disbelief in my voice. 'Please, let me come with you.'

Leo takes a step towards me, his eyes burning with hate. My mind wheels back to the night before, that terrible moment when Samara's head emerged from the square-shaped hole in the ice, her mouth gaping. Another flash: her body laid on the bank, limp and doll-like. We are all so tired and traumatised from it, and the dark is driving us crazy.

Leo lifts his fists as though he's going to pound them on my chest, or on my face, and I watch him shake, and though the anger is so great it wants to burst out of him. I don't budge. 'I'm sorry,' I say, sobbing. 'I'm so, so sorry.'

I feel something release within me as the words tumble from my lips. But Leo backs away, his face twisted in disgust. 'I know who you are,' he snarls.

This isn't the response I was expecting. 'What?'

Leo pokes a finger at me. 'I know what you did,' he shouts. 'I *know*.'

'She hasn't done anything,' Jens says. 'Let's work out a plan of action, OK?' He looks over the length of the room. 'Is Samara's laptop here?'

I nod. 'It's on the table.'

'What about her phone?'

'I have no fucking clue,' Leo says. 'What difference does it make?'

'Have you checked her cabin?'

Leo seems to right himself, visibly taking a breath and biting his cheek, thinking. Then he heads downstairs to check, and Jens shifts his eyes to mine.

'Do you think she left?' I ask, realising as soon as I've spoken how stupid the words sound aloud. 'I mean, she was . . . well, we all thought she was dead. I don't see how she was physically capable of leaving.'

Jens turns and looks out the window. 'We should go after her,' he says. I wonder if he's worried that Leo might just be telling the truth.

I wait for him to offer an alternative to the theory that her heart started beating again and yet she still just walked out of the cabin. Perhaps her body was kidnapped? But that doesn't make any sense, because there is no one around for miles, and even if they could have somehow come aboard, there would have been footprints, a wet trail of snow on the floor of the cabin, such as Jens had left just then.

My head throbs from the chaos of it all.

Leo emerges through the hatch. 'I can't find her phone.'

We all exchange glances. Leo looks like he needs to run off more angst. He moves quickly to the cabin door, and I know he is going outside to see if there is any sign of Samara.

After a few moments, Jens says, 'I'll go too.' Leo tries to

argue with him, telling him that *he'll* go, *alone*, that Jens should stay. Jens simply pulls on his coat and pink beanie and heads to the door.

He turns to me. 'Stay here,' he tells me. 'We'll be back soon.'

Nicky

I

September 1901
Upernavik, Greenland

Reid's body was kept in Dr O'Regan's surgery until it could be prepared for burial.

Daverley was held in the brig overnight, as per Captain Willingham's orders. He had pleaded to stay with his nephew's body, promising to do two nights in the brig in lieu. His request was denied, and so he asked for one of the others to stay with the body. No one had come forward.

Nicky dabbed her face with a towel, wincing when the fabric touched her lip. Blood globed on her lip, her cheekbone blooming with bruises. Her ribs ached, but it seemed that none were cracked. When Lovejoy drove his fist into her belly, she'd vomited all over him, and he fled.

After she cleaned up the pool of bile on the floor she crept out of her cabin with a blanket and made her way through the dark hallway to the surgery. Inside, she found the boy's body laid on the table where Dr O'Regan had stitched the wound in her foot. *Thomas*, she remembered. That was his given name, the name that Dr O'Regan had called him.

He was naked to the waist, his slim arms and bony shoulders luminous in the gleam of her lantern. His eyes had been closed, long black eyelashes against the delicate skin above his cheekbones, and his wound cleaned, though the bloodstain on his trousers remained.

She took his hand and found it was already hardening.

She found another bottle of pills in the apothecary cabinet and slipped one into her mouth. Then she sank down into the chair next to the boy's body, the pain dissolving slowly.

II

Morag loved horses. Nicky had been a keen rider since she was a child, and so she took Morag as often as she could to ride the ponies at her uncle Hamish's farm in Perth. The ponies were tame as house pets, following Morag around while she picked flowers in the meadow and allowing her to thread them in their manes. And on the streets of Dundee, she would stop by every carriage to greet the horses, asking her parents to lift her up so she could speak with them face to face.

It happened on a wet Tuesday night. She and Allan had ventured to Her Majesty's Theatre to see *The Notorious Mrs Ebbsmith*. It had been difficult when Morag was born, and for many months she had not wanted to leave the house out of both exhaustion and a strange fear that crept in whenever she thought of speaking to people. But now, it was their wedding anniversary, and Allan had surprised her with tickets that morning.

'You look braw, Mammy,' Morag had said from the doorway of her bedroom. She was clutching a teddy bear, her wet hair hanging in ringlets on her shoulders.

'Thank you, darling,' Nicky said, turning to view her dress from the side in the long mirror. She was wearing a forest-green velvet dress with a lace neckline, her corset pulled so tight she could barely breathe. Before Morag was born, the

266

dress was loose at the hips, but now it sat tight. She could manage it, so long as she didn't take long strides.

'Daddy and I are going to see a play,' Nicky said. 'Remember we took you to see the puppet show at Carolina Port?'

Morag screwed up her face. 'You're going to see a puppet show?'

'No, but it's *like* a puppet show. A bigger version of that. It's on a stage and there'll be lots of people there.'

Morag's little face brightened. 'I liked the puppet show. And the fireworks after. Will there be fireworks at your play?'

Nicky laughed. 'No, I'm afraid not. It's indoors.'

'So what?'

'The roof would be set on fire, darling.'

Morag's blue eyes went wide. 'That's no' good.'

Nicky fastened her pearl choker. 'You promise you'll go to bed for Mrs Mackie?'

Morag gave a woeful sigh. 'I promise.'

Nicky tugged up the skirt of her dress and knelt by Morag, dabbing her nose with the tip of her finger. 'If you can't sleep, remember what Daddy told you to do.'

'Think of horses jumping over a bale of hay and count them all.'

'Exactly.'

'Granny says I should count sheep, not horses.'

'You can count whatever you like.'

'I'll count horses then.'

Nicky leaned forward and kissed Morag on the cheek. Morag struggled to sleep in her own bedroom, plagued by dark imaginings and a curious mind that seemed to spark at night-time, just like her father. 'You be good for Mrs Mackie, won't you?'

'Yes, Mammy,' Morag said. Then: 'Can I come to the play, too?'

'Sorry, love. It's a play for adults. But if you like, I'll take you to see a play for children. Would you like that?'

Morag nodded. 'Yes, please.'

'Well, you have to promise that you'll try very, *very* hard to go to sleep.'

Morag took a deep breath and gave a solemn nod. 'I promise.'

She heard Allan answer the door to Mrs Mackie downstairs and gave Morag another last peck on the cheek. 'On you go, now.'

'Ready?' Allan said from the top of the stairs. Then, seeing her in the dress she'd not worn for years, 'Good God. Maybe we should just get a hotel room instead.'

She tutted. 'There's a good chance I wouldn't be able to get the dress back on.'

He approached and kissed the patch of exposed skin between her ear and shoulder. 'You smell like glory.'

'What on earth does glory smell like?'

'I have no idea. But I reckon it's beautiful.'

She kissed him on the lips, leaving a trace of rouge. 'Thank you.'

The theatre was resplendent and heaving with crowds, the shimmering lights and the gold balconies a welcome relief from the days she had spent at home alone with Morag. Allan clasped her hand and smiled at her; he worked so hard lately, such long days in the mill, that she had wondered if they might ever get a chance to spend time together again. And here they were, laughing at the play, holding hands, both of them dressed in their finest clothing. She never wanted the night to end.

When the play finished, Allan suggested they take a carriage home. He seemed anxious. 'We should relieve Mrs Mackie,' he said. 'She'll be tiring, no doubt.'

Nicky felt crestfallen. She had one night and one night only to be her old self, to remember what it was like to be alone with her husband.

'Perhaps we might walk home?' she said. 'Spend a little more time together?'

Allan hesitated, and she could see he was pained. But in a moment he nodded, and they took the path along the River Tay, admiring the lights on the water and the clear night sky. She felt light on her feet, and whatever had been bothering Allan had passed.

But as they turned into the main road near their home, she heard a commotion. In the dark, she could see a carriage had toppled, and the crumpled heap at the side of the road was a horse lying dead. Nearby, the driver was sitting on a wall speaking to two policemen. As they drew closer, a howl pierced the air. A woman being taken into a police carriage. The wheels grinding across the cobbles.

'They've just taken her to the hospital,' one of the men said. 'Awful scene.'

'Taken who away?' Allan asked.

The man nodded at the fallen horse, and Nicky saw one of its legs had been broken. The teeth glinting in the light of the street lantern.

'The bairn,' he said. 'Ran straight out in front of the carriage.'

Nicky felt a terrible chill race up her neck. 'What bairn?'

'A lassie. Dashed out to see a firework. Driver couldnae do nothin'.'

As the police carriage passed by, Nicky saw the figure inside was Mrs Mackie. Her eyes turned to Allan, his expression changing to horror as he realised. And when he raced after them, calling *Mrs Mackie! Mrs Mackie!* she couldn't bring herself to move. Didn't want to think of whose bairn had been struck by the horse.

269

They found Morag at the hospital, her little head wrapped in bandages. Her eyes closed, her curls shorn. Bedclothes drawn up over her broken limbs. A nurse had placed a cloth doll in her arms and encouraged them to speak softly to her.

'She might still hear you,' she said.

Allan watched blankly, his face an open grave, as Nicky took her daughter's hand in hers and pressed it gently to her lips. They whispered to her, told her bedtime stories as though she was simply lying in her bed at home, preparing for sleep. They told her they loved her.

When she had drawn her last breath, they knew, the stillness of her chest and the parting of her lips signalling that she had passed away before them. But still they whispered, as though the words might call her back, back to the ones who loved her most.

III

The day of Thomas' funeral, the crew gathered around the body. Like Collins, Thomas was wrapped in a sail and stitched tightly like a shroud, the last stitch through the nose to prevent the boy's soul from following the ship.

'All hands bury the dead, ahoy!' Lovejoy shouted.

Nicky watched from the forecastle as the men placed cannonballs into either end of the fabric, before Daverley and Royle lowered the body on a wooden slab into the ocean. Daverley looked haunted, his face dark. None of the men spoke as the shrouded body sank quickly, the grey water opening as if to accept him, before healing again, no trace left. A different kind of grave.

Three men dead in as many months. The human toll of whaling would never be measured, but in death it was felt most keenly.

She thought of what Daverley said about Thomas' soul being unable to rest if he were given a sea burial, how he might haunt the ship and seek revenge. She would have dismissed such a tale out of hand in the past, but her own secret, the wound that was somehow spreading up her leg, made her less sceptical. So she found herself turning to look behind the ship, studying the water there in case she might see Reid unfurled from the sail, angrily trying to catch them.

271

For a moment, she thought he would be justified. Perhaps, in his immortal form, the boy would have powers that would enable him to enact revenge on his killer. Lovejoy's claim of acting in self-defence was a bitter pill to swallow; even Harrow had seemed reluctant to agree. It should have been Lovejoy in the brig, not Daverley. She hadn't heard him speak a word since.

Her door was quiet for two nights afterwards, and she felt relief at the men leaving her alone but also an overwhelming guilt at the cost of her peace. And she couldn't help but feel that she had played a role in his death. Lovejoy had taunted Thomas by revealing his part in her capture; he had known that the boy would react.

Perhaps if she had not shown her dismay so nakedly, Thomas would not have lashed out the way he did. She had known, almost immediately, that Lovejoy's divulgence was not out of any wish to share the truth with her of her misfortune, but to goad the boy. To rip apart the relationship he had formed with Nicky. Lovejoy was jealous of Thomas' sea shanties, and his ability to write. He was jealous of the way he made Nicky laugh, at the way her face lit up instead of folding in disgust.

And that jealousy had cost Thomas his life.

IV

Three days after Thomas' funeral, a knock sounded on her door.

Cautiously, she opened the door just wide enough to let the amber light of the oil lantern in the hallway trickle inside. She had expected Lovejoy to be standing there, that vile grin on his face and his pale eyes running the length of her body. His fists ready to strike her if she displeased him.

Instead, she spotted the tall figure of Daverley. His shoulders were rounded and his eyes were dark. She reeled at his presence at her door, knowing what it meant.

She stepped back into her room, confused and saddened. She didn't like Daverley, but she had thought him principled. But now that Reid was gone she expected he didn't have to set an example. He was just like the others.

He closed the door behind him, the small room lit only by the candle that shivered on the sea chest next to her bed. She sat down, keeping her eyes fixed on him and her mouth closed. He remained standing, his eyes on the floor.

'Well?' she said when several moments had passed like that.

Slowly, he sank to the ground, his face twisted in pain. He drew his palms to his eyes. Around his wrist, she noticed the small bracelet made of rope that Reid had worn. *Reid,* she thought. *He's here because of Reid.*

Slowly she moved to the floor and sat next to him. After a minute she slipped an arm across his shoulders, and he moved into an embrace, letting her hold him. When she was sure he wasn't here for anything more than friendship, she sat on the bed and invited him to sit next to her. Then she lay down and held him, his arms around her, his tears dampening the sleeves of her dress.

'It's my fault,' Daverley murmured.

'It's not,' she said.

'He wouldn't have been here if it wasn't for me.'

She felt the sting of recognition at his words, a painful memory unfolding of the time she and Allan had held each other like this on the floor of the house on Faulkner Street. The devastation of their daughter's death should, perhaps, have drawn them together, but instead she found it housed Allan and her in two separate rooms, or in two different countries. She saw her daughter in Allan's face, and found herself hating that he was alive and she was not. The pain of Morag's death was a wound that drew across every inch of her heart, and she could not love while that wound was unhealed.

But of course, it was an unhealable wound.

The pain Daverley held within, she knew well. It was still there, in her own body, as real and tangible as metal. Thomas' loss would live within Daverley forever now, that much she knew. There was no use telling him otherwise.

Dominique

I

December 2023
Skúmaskot, Iceland

Jens and Leo still aren't back. It's been forty-two hours since they went after Samara.

I'm so worried, I'm beside myself. What is actually going on? Samara died, and then she didn't. Jens and Leo said they'd go and look for her in case she *had* actually walked off the ship with a brain injury and needed help, but they've not returned.

And I can't stop crying.

Are they injured somewhere, or lost? Have they all walked off the project without telling me? Jens took his backpack, but his laptop is here. So is Leo's. I don't know whether to go and look for them or stay here and keep the fire going in case they come back.

It's probably a very unwise move, but I decide to use what's left in my solar charger to attempt to call Jens.

It doesn't connect.

I try Leo, then Samara. None of the calls connect. I click on the TikTok app. They've not logged on to any of their socials. Jens' TikTok seems to have been deleted. Or maybe it's glitching again.

I do a livestream to connect with the 5,098 followers who have logged on, no doubt eager to see more of the *Ormen* or Skúmaskot or the logbook we found in the crawlspace.

'Hi everyone,' I say, giving a little wave. My throat is tightening and I'm overwhelmed by the impulse to start crying again. Oh God. *Hold it together, Dom.*

'I have some news,' I say, digging my fingernails into my palm to distract myself from the sob that wants to explode out of my throat. 'First of all, Samara is OK. I know the livestream cut off super abruptly so you were all probably really worried. So don't worry! We'll be announcing the winners of the contest very soon, and filming the dismantling of the *Ormen*, so stick around! And tell all your friends!'

I give a cheesy thumbs up, shamelessly mimicking Samara.

'I'm going to log off now,' I say. 'Because I need the battery to cook a meal. But I'll upload more footage tomorrow, I promise.'

Heart emojis stream up the screen, and I see the battery begin to flash.

I make a peace sign and give what I hope is a strong, resolute smile. 'Over and out.'

I promised I'd be honest with my followers, but I can't do it. I don't want to admit that they've all abandoned the project. That they've left.

The cabin plunges into darkness. That's it – no more battery until the sun rises, though 'rise' is inaccurate. A bright sun in the sky is a distant memory. Thinking of it now, I probably shouldn't have promised to upload tomorrow, because really, I'm at the mercy of the elements.

I reach for the wind-up torch and turn it quickly, relishing the brief reprieve from darkness when it glows faintly.

Outside, the wind sounds like someone is singing. I hold my breath, listening as the melody deepens, a sound of humming. And then it fades to a whistle, the ship rocking in the wind's hands.

I wrap myself in a thermal blanket and hold my hands to the fire bucket, an exhalation of warmth rising from embers at the bottom. I so wish Jens had stocked up the wood supply before he left. We're pretty much out of doors, so either I start pulling up floorboards or I trek to the turf houses on the other side of the bay. But I'll have to, at some point, if I want to stay warm.

The fog is thick tonight, draped over the volcano like the neck of a dragon. I think of Jens with his backpack and tent – maybe he has managed to find somewhere to pitch it, and Leo is with him. I think of the glow cast by his camping lantern, transforming the tent into a lime-green dome against the dark sky. Maybe if I climb to the top of the cliffs, I'll spot it.

The thought gives me hope.

A voice in my head tells me I'm merely looking for a sense of purpose to distract myself from the terror of being alone, but I ignore it. I can't give in to that voice.

My knife is sitting on the worktop in the kitchenette, a flicker of light from the LED safety light running across the blade. I lift it slowly and feel the whispers beneath my skin growing louder, almost shouting now. I slip the knife inside the sheath on my hip, for safety, and the voices stop. It's a relief. Usually they don't stop until I draw blood.

Instead, the cabin is quiet and I feel reassured to have my knife in place, its protection right where it needs to be. I can go outside with confidence, as long as I have my knife. I can go to the turf houses and collect fuel for the fire. I think I'll make myself some porridge. I've not yet used the sachets I brought. I figured I'd spare them for an emergency, or for a time when I felt I needed a little boost. Some people use alcohol for a boost, I use porridge.

Outside, the fog lifts, and it's so beautiful I pull out my phone and feel my heart sink when I remember that the battery is dead. It is literally like being inside a snow globe, one of the posh ones with the fir trees and foiled robins, a polar bear wearing a gold crown. I hadn't expected to be so struck by the scenery; there's been so much fog lately that I suppose I expected the same murky grimness. But tonight is heartbreakingly gorgeous, a silk of snow across the volcano and over the bay. The sky is a bruise, moonlight parting the sea with a silver causeway. It's as though a great battle has been fought between Day and Night, the darkness showing off her regalia in triumph.

There are the most beautiful textures, too, as though we've had some kind of weird wind that has combed across the snow, lifting it slightly in tessellated formations. I don't mean to go on about it – actually, I do – but it's alarming how the same piece of land can look so different according to the light.

The light is a costume. A skin.

II

It's Christmas Day.

I have spent so many Christmas Days alone that it shouldn't bother me. But I feel utterly gut-punched today. I feel utterly confused by the Samara thing. By the fact that no one has contacted me. I managed to turn my phone on for a few minutes to check my messages and the TikTok account. For about a minute it looked like the project account had vanished. Nothing on there. I panicked. Had one of the others deleted it? We all had admin control. But then it popped up again. Jens, Samara, and Leo have gone dark digitally, too. They've not messaged me, and they've not posted anything on their own accounts. None of them.

If I'm honest, I feel abandoned, which I know is terribly self-pitying and childish, but there it is. It feels like there is more to this feeling, that it has *layers*.

The project TikTok has *tons* of messages from our followers, though, checking in on us all. A few accusations from the followers that the others haven't left at all but are staging a pretend walkout to generate drama and likes. I don't blame anyone for thinking that. Mostly, though, the comments are super nice. And we've got a lot of new followers. I didn't even count them, that's how low I feel about everything. Before, it really mattered to me. Now it doesn't. I don't even care if I never explore again.

I post some old footage of me and Jens researching stuff online from 1973 before my phone dies again. It's crap footage but at least it shows us doing something.

The knocking against the hull has started up again, and maybe it's my imagination but it has a rhythm that doesn't seem to be in time with the waves. It's starting to drive me insane. I've gone outside a couple of times to see if I can move the chain that's causing the sound, but the rocks are icy and if I fall and crack my head open . . . well, it's as Jens said. No one is coming for me.

I did see the chain and it was moving for sure, but it wasn't moving in a rhythmic, knock-knock-knock way. That's the rhythm of the sound from the inside. Three knocks, and a pause. Then another three, followed by another pause.

I'm sitting here listening to it and there's nothing I can do. I can't record it, can't contact anyone. I have the overwhelming sense that someone is outside.

I can literally feel them looking at the *Ormen*. If I close my eyes I can almost see myself inside, a little silhouette framed by the cabin window. As though I can see from two angles at once.

Stop it, Dom. You're being paranoid again. You have the feeling that someone is outside because the knocking sounds like someone is at the front door. Keep it together, will you?

I keep looking outside, partly to see if one of the others has returned, or in case I see the woman. Ghosts can't knock, can they?

I keep thinking of what Samara said so poetically about sound being a revenant, a trace.

No. The knocking is from the chain. Maybe in the morning I'll try and fix the chain so that it doesn't bang into the hull. Keep focused. Christmas Day is just another day, right?

III

It's still Christmas Day and I'm drunk. I climbed down into the hold to see if I could find some vodka. It took a lot of rummaging through debris and I went over on my ankle, but I came up trumps. This bottle of vodka is absolutely gorgeous and has put a real shine on what was otherwise starting to feel like a proper pity party. Go me.

I've actually had a pretty productive Christmas. The project has almost ten thousand followers. Ten thousand! A month ago, that would have been my goal. I can't just up and leave, because I'll be ending the story before its natural conclusion of the ship being destroyed. I just have to make sure I have enough charge for when the breakers arrive. And I'll also need to think carefully about how to get close enough to film it all without getting arrested. Demolishers and breaker crews *hate* squatters. They're often briefed before going in on the possibility of environmental protestors, and sometimes they come with police. It's when they come alone that you have to be careful. They'll not even wait for you to be arrested – they'll just beat the shit out of you. And they'll know that I have no signal out here to livestream anything, so they can pretty much do what they want.

I'll need to hide. Maybe I'll leave the *Ormen* a day or two beforehand and hide out in one of the caves.

I also spent this afternoon setting up my sensor camera on

the tripod here in the main cabin, where I'm going to sleep from now on. I want to see if I'm doing something in my sleep when I have nightmares. I want to record myself and get a clearer idea if something wakes me up or triggers me, and maybe I'll figure out how to stop it.

I put on my balaclava and coat and take the camera off the tripod mount to do some filming. A little bit here and there will give me enough to make a nice reel of Christmas Day alone here on the wreck. Some of the comments on the TikTok account said I was brave. I usually disregard that kind of stuff but actually, it made me feel better. Maybe this *is* a total badass thing to do. It's not my fault that the others left. They had the freedom to stay or go and they left. Fine. I can choose to stay or to go and I'm choosing to stay.

And I feel like I'm confronting some personal stuff out here, too. I haven't told anyone about the rapes in . . . actually, I can't even remember a time that I told someone. And yet I told Samara. That took courage. Saying it aloud felt like I'd been punched in the chest. I know I'm not ready to go any further down memory lane, though. The whispers beneath my skin get too loud when I start to think of that, and I know what happens then. I'll need to cut, and I know it's not a good thing, the cutting. I don't like to cut when I'm exploring. I've become so good at stopping my memories, at blocking my mind from looking into the past at all, it barely feels like it's there for me anymore.

The sun is finally lifting into the sky, brightening the horizon with a weak dusk light. Thank God! Keep shining, sun! We're past the winter solstice now, so maybe we'll get a little more light during the day. I'm just thinking about my solar chargers. Every second of light counts.

Outside, snow is falling again. This is also a good sign – it's getting warmer, though it's still minus fourteen. I had started to worry that the temperature would continue to drop, and the fire wouldn't light. It would be game over, then. Plenty of explorers have been killed that way, especially now, with the weather being so extreme.

The deck is slushy, and I walk carefully towards the ladder, noticing the way the wind sounds like singing again. I pause and get my phone out of my pocket to record it, turning all the way around to get the top deck in a nice three-sixty spin. The singing has stopped, which is typical, so I put my phone away and head back to the ladder, and climb down to the sand.

For a moment, it feels magical. I'm sure the vodka has helped, but I feel warm inside. The tide has pushed most of the snow off the sand, and so the black beach sits like an inky margin against the perfectly white snow, cottony and untouched. I climb up to higher ground, looking out over the bay to my left and the beach to my right. I wonder if I'll see the horses again. I have heard them a few times since that first night but never seen them. I wonder if the dead horses in the cave put them off coming here.

The walk to the turf houses sobers me up and gets me into a good sweat. I had almost forgotten how much a brisk walk helps clear my head. I must remember that – even when the weather is as bad as it has been, *get outside, Dom!* You know it works.

Carrying the turf back, though – I didn't think that through. I should have brought a sledge of some sort, a sheet of metal or plastic. I carry as much as I can, then leave it on the ground outside the *Ormen* and carry up as much as I need to get the fire going.

I break up the turf and feed it to the fire, then set a lid on it with the kettle on top of that. It'll take ages for it to boil, but I've got time, and it gives me something to look forward to. The solar packs will be full of charge tomorrow, now that I've got some light, and I'll be able to upload the footage from the last few days and film some new stuff. I'm looking forward to that. And I'm looking forward to seeing how many new followers I've got, and how many have subscribed to my paid content. Yes, Dom. There is *lots* to look forward to. Really, though, I'm itching to check whether Jens and Leo have contacted me. Whether they've walked back to the nearest town and have sent me a message, letting me know they've found Samara.

That they're coming back.

Shit, the snow has got really heavy. I need to get the rest of the turf before it gets too wet. I head outside, moving too fast across the slush. I manage to throw my arms out and stop myself from falling backwards. At the ladder, I pause, sensing something nearby. It's not just the snow, or my pounding heart rate from the almost-fall.

There is someone standing right below, directly at the bottom of the ladder.

At first, I think it's one of the others. That would make sense, wouldn't it? They never left me! They went for a walk and got lost, and now they're back!

But it's not Samara, or Leo, or Jens.

It's the woman, her back turned to the ladder. Her wet shoulders glistening in the dark.

I give a shout and fall backwards with fright, and there's a loud bang from where I catch my head on the sharp corner of the raised platform of the forecastle.

I hear the knock of feet against the rung of the ladder, one after the other.

And everything goes dark.

IV

I can't tell if I'm dreaming or if I'm underwater.

I can see shapes floating around me, a huge one above. At first, I think it's a whale, but then the shape of a rudder comes into view and I know it's a ship. I am instantly filled with rage, such hatred that it seems to burn inside me. I want to scream with fury.

I start to move towards the shape, and I know what I need to do. I need to get on board that ship and kill everyone on it.

I come to. My mouth is filled with something, and it takes a moment to realise that I'm not underwater but on the top deck of the *Ormen*, lying flat on my back with my arms spread out at either side and a mouthful of snow.

I pull myself slowly upright, the back of my head throbbing from where I fell. Muddy slush is all around me. Luckily, I'm wearing my waterproofs, so I'm dry, if not very sore and annoyed at myself for getting drunk. Then I remember what caused me to fall – I saw something at the bottom of the ladder. The woman. She was standing with her back to me.

My heart racing, I look over the side, and instantly I see it – the shape of someone there. But then my eyes adjust, and I realise it's just a shadow. The moon has cast a shadow of the rocky outcrop and thrown it across the snow, and it looks very like a person standing there. Jesus Christ. *That* was why I fell?

A shadow?

At once relieved and annoyed, and still quite drunk, I head back inside the cabin, where the fire is throwing out a tremendous amount of heat. Oh, blissful heat! I pull off my hat and coat, then step out of my waterproofs. My fingers find a small amount of blood and a large lump, about the size of an egg, at the back of my head from where I fell. I must have been unconscious for at least a few minutes. I could have a concussion. But I feel OK, just sore, and suddenly ravenous.

I find one of Jens' fancy food packets on the worktop and decide to make use of it. Korean Style Beef and Rice. Oh my God – I rip open the packet and eat it cold, each mouthful the most amazing food I've ever tasted. Jens is not here to tell me otherwise, and it's technically still Christmas, for crying out loud. Forget turkey and trimmings – cold, vacuum-packed Korean Style Beef and Rice is the best goddamn Christmas dinner in existence.

The rest of the turf is still at the bottom of the ladder. So, I know I have to go out there and get it, and I'll confront whatever waits for me. If it's a ghost, I'm going to laugh in its face. I'm going to tell it to go fuck itself.

I fetch my knife and fasten the holster around my waist, slipping the knife inside.

It has stopped snowing. The wind has died down on the deck. It was singing before, but now it's so completely silent. Only the wash of the sea, but even that seems muted.

I step carefully through the slush to the side of the hull and stare down at the bottom of the ladder. I can see the turf, half-buried in the snow. No footprints. No ghost.

I gather up the turf and head back up the ladder, a shiver running up my spine. I still feel watched. Despite all my bravado, despite the knife in my sheath, I can't bring myself to turn around.

V

Research, that's the ticket.

Sorry, Samara, but you've left your laptop behind and it has 53 per cent battery life, so I'm using it to check out the academic articles you've downloaded.

I've locked the cabin door, and my knife is out on the dining table next to me. I risk a glance at the window.

She's left a screenshot open. It's of the newspaper article from 1901 about the missing girl, the daughter of the first owner of the *Ormen*.

I stare at the name. Nicky Duthie. There's a scratch starting up in the back of my mind. I click on the bottom right, where the other open browsers are minimised. One of them is the photograph we all stared at, trying to work out if the blurry figure slightly out of shot was a woman. Leo said he thought the photograph showed a woman on the ship, which wasn't unusual. Ship captains sometimes brought wives along, though it was mostly a North American tradition, not common amongst Dundee whalers. My mind turns to the crew roster that mentioned twenty people on board when there were twenty-one, and the logbook that mentioned a prostitute . . . These were all from 1901.

I stare at the photograph of the figure, halfway out of frame. The scratch at the back of my mind intensifies. Nicky

Duthie went missing in May 1901 and was still missing in October. The photograph on board the *Ormen* was taken in August 1901. It feels like a leap of imagination to even wonder if she's the figure in the photograph.

No. It's ridiculous. Why the hell would the shipmaster's daughter be on board as a prostitute?

It's midnight. My body clock is whacked, and I'm still tipsy, so I'm nowhere near ready for sleep. I pour some coffee from my flask and use a little of the solar charger to crank up the internet. No messages from the others, which makes my heart sink. Maybe I should stop looking.

Samara is still logged into the academic resource, so I search for info on the *Ormen* from the 1970s. Jens and I had been searching for information from 1973, but I decide to widen the dates until 1990. An article pings up from 1976, and I give a laugh of surprise. We'd made our search too narrow – that was where we were going wrong!

Letter delivered years late sheds light on crew's disappearance

Laura Finlayson (28), from Auburn, NSW, last saw her fiancé, Dennis Gordon, three years ago, when he boarded a research ship headed to the Arctic. Sadly, it was to be the last time the happy couple would set eyes on each other. Dennis sent letters home every week, and Laura began to worry when he failed to write.

'I knew as soon as the police pulled up outside my door,' she says sadly. 'I just had a feeling.'

In 1973, Laura was informed that the ship Dennis had been on – known as the *Ormen* – had been located by the Russian coastguard. None of the crew had been located, however, and while searches were continuing, it was highly unlikely that anyone would be found alive.

Laura moved to the Gold Coast several months later. 'I couldn't manage without Dennis,' she said. 'Our home became an excruciating place for me to live, so I needed to find a new place to make a fresh start.'

This seems to be part of the reason why Dennis' letter didn't reach Laura until August 1976. The new tenant at Laura's previous address in Brisbane finally managed to forward Laura's mail, and amongst the mail was a letter from Dennis.

'In the letter, Dennis mentions a guy on the research ship who had started to spend his days ranting and raving,' she says, visibly upset by the memory. 'He says this colleague was acting really out of sorts, not like himself at all, and that it was very upsetting and disruptive. He said that the chief [Dr Andrew Karsen] had locked the guy in his room for safety reasons. That strikes me as very coincidental, given that the ship went off-radar just a day or so afterwards.'

I ask her what she thinks happened.

'Obviously, I can't be sure,' she says. 'But Dennis would never have shared something like that with me if he wasn't really worried, or even scared,' she says. 'I feel like he was almost writing it in case something happened, and then I'd understand that this was the reason for it. His letters never went into much detail about his daily routine and the people on the ship, so this really stood out. I do think it has something to do with the crew vanishing.'

Interestingly, the inventory for the ship when it was located adrift on the Barents Sea was missing a key object – a rifle, normally held in a safety box on the top deck. When the coastguard located the ship, they found it had been damaged by storms, but most of the crew's personal effects remained on board.

While speculation may not bring any of the researchers back, Dennis's letter and Laura's knowledge of her fiancé bring her some closure on a mystery that has torn at hearts for years.

My mind turns to the microscope that Jens found. The one with the hole in the metal casing that he said was a bullet hole. I get up to try and find it, but it's nowhere to be seen.

The battery is running out on Samara's laptop, so I do a quick check on three different search engines to see if I can find Dennis Gordon and Diego Almeyda linked together, but I don't find anything. It strikes me that it's worth trying the academic resource; after all, the scientists on the research ship probably published their papers. I type the names into the box marked 'author' and a single research paper pops up from September 1970: 'Sea Ice Distribution in Franz Josef Land', D. Gordon and D. Almeyda.

My heart quickening, I read the paper, which has been scanned on to the website. I can't make sense of it – lots about sea ice dynamics and the distribution of mean ice drafts – but I see that Dennis Gordon was a PhD researcher at the University of New South Wales while Diego Almeyda was a geography lecturer at the University of Argentina.

The lead stalls after that, so I go out on to the top deck to search for the safety box mentioned in the article. The main cabin is really the only addition from the research era, but a rifle wouldn't have been stored in a safety box way back in the early 1900s. It might have been a box that was already there, but I figure I might find a modification of some kind, maybe an old lock that was from the 1970s.

Nothing.

But as I'm standing on the deck, finally a song comes into my head. The lilting melody that slid into my thoughts when I was in the captain's cabin, a tune that befits the words of the poem that Leo carved into the dining table.

> *these seas no more will cause thee strife*
> *if you'll become my selkie wife*

I think of the missing woman. Nicky Duthie, daughter of the *Ormen*'s owner. I feel the same scratch at the back of my mind start up again, the blurred face at the edge of the photograph flashing in my mind.

Samara's laptop battery is at 20 per cent; my own is dead. Jens and Leo's laptops are both password-protected. I kneel down to the internet terminal. Jens' solar charger has one bar left. Quickly I plug the internet terminal into it and log online, returning to Samara's laptop and logging back into the section of the academic resource where all the old newspapers are digitised. I search 'Nicky Abney' and find a mere four articles, two of which are about another woman entirely. But one from late October 1901 mentions that George Abney's daughter has not yet been found.

Hat found near dock suggests foul play; Abney & Co latest

A hat that George Abney's wife claims belonged to their missing daughter has been found near the docks of Dundee.

Mhairi Abney, wife of the owner of Abney & Co, identified the hat on Tuesday evening, following the disappearance of her oldest daughter, Nicky Duthie. Mrs Duthie's husband, Private Allan Duthie of the 1st Battalion Coldstream Guard, is said to have been killed shortly after Mrs Duthie went missing, having sustained injuries at Fort Prospect in September.

Chief Constable Richie of Dundee City Police says the discovery of the hat is a major step forward in the case, and has reiterated his invitation to the public to come forward with information. It is feared that Mrs Duthie boarded a ship and set off for a new life while her husband was overseas.

Mrs Abney is quoted as saying, 'I have no reason to believe that my daughter left these shores freely. I plead again for information, and assurance of her well-being.'

So she was a widow, and doubtless without realising it.

The battery is at 9 per cent. I scan quickly through the articles on George Abney. There are dozens, many of them focused on the business, and some photographs. He is a stout, proud-looking man. His obituary indicates that he died by his own hand; the wording is a plea to God to spare his soul.

I stare at the photograph of him smoking a cigar with the prime minister, Robert Gascoyne-Cecil, the scratch at the back of my mind growing worse.

What did you do to her, you bastard? I think. *What did you do?*

Nicky

I

September 1901
Banks Bay, Greenland

Nicky remembered the weeks after Morag's death. It had felt as though the world itself had been ripped apart, a strange reality in which she and Allan had to relearn their own lives, their own selves. A reality in which nothing had meaning, or sense. She had thought she might go mad.

It was two months after the funeral when she had woken to find Allan on the small balcony of Morag's bedroom. He was naked. It was early, still dark.

'Allan?'

He was standing, his back to her, looking down at the garden below. She reached out to touch him and he spun around with a roar. She reared back, and he charged at her, ranting. His face taut with fury, a stream of expletives and accusations that didn't make sense.

'How fucking dare you! Don't you ever touch me again, do you hear?'

She had fallen to the ground, and he had stood over her, a hand raised. A terrifying moment.

'Don't,' she had whimpered. 'Please.'

Her plea seemed to wake him up, his face softening, as

though he'd returned to his own mind. He dropped the hand that had raised to strike her and staggered backwards. Then he locked himself in the bathroom. She got up and moved tentatively to the door, pressing her ear to the wood.

She heard sobbing. Allan had never cried. She had never heard this sound. But she knew its nature. He was broken. He was a man without his daughter. He was expected not to mourn, but to carry on as though nothing had happened. He had worked the day after, as expected. She had witnessed the grind of it, but felt powerless to do anything.

'Allan, please let me in.'

'I'm sorry.'

She took a breath, steadying herself. 'I know you are. It's all right. Please let me in.'

Eventually, the door unlocked, and she stepped inside. She found him sitting on the toilet bowl, hands on his knees, his gaze on the floor.

'You frightened me earlier,' she said.

'I know.'

'I love you.'

He didn't answer. Then, after a few moments: 'I've enlisted to fight against the Boers.'

She thought she'd misheard him. 'What?'

'In the Transvaal,' he said, looking up. His jaw tight. 'My father was a soldier. It's my duty.'

She laughed, thinking he was joking.

'I resigned from the mill yesterday.'

'What?'

'I told them why.'

'Allan,' she said. 'You can't be serious.'

'I leave in two weeks.'

She was too stunned to answer. He was *leaving?* It felt like a punishment. She had blamed herself every single moment of every day for what happened to her daughter. If she had only listened to Allan and returned home earlier, if she had checked that the front door was locked behind them, if she had instructed Mrs Mackie to check on her . . . So many things she could have done to prevent this gaping hole in their lives.

He was right to punish her. He was right to leave her.

And so she had walked out of the room and gone back to bed, saying little to him throughout the mornings and nights that followed, until one afternoon, she saw a suitcase and an army uniform on the bed.

She realised that she knew him less now than when they first met. Her husband, transformed into a stranger.

Over time, their letters to each other became warmer, friendlier, and she missed him. She sensed he missed her. They had both been changed by Morag's death.

But love, she thought, was a constant. Perhaps it would help them return to each other, in their changed states. Maybe it would be enough.

II

She vomited for a week before it occurred to her that she might be pregnant.

She hadn't bled since boarding the ship, but had put it down to her usual irregularity, and the stress of the kidnapping. At first, she had thought it sea sickness. Or perhaps food poisoning. Her diet lately was seal entrails, dark, rubbery meat that she washed down with strong tea. She only ate when driven to it by ravenous hunger, and there was no telling if the meat was edible.

But she was still being sick, and now her breasts felt tender. A horrifying sign.

She climbed to the top deck in a daze. Should she throw herself overboard? The thought of giving birth to a child by any of the mariners brought bile into her mouth, hot and sharp. She hated every one of them, except now, a surprise even to herself, Daverley. Perhaps it was his kindness, his fatherliness towards her. Or their common grief.

How could she return to Dundee now? How could she ever face Allan? He would never shun her – of course not – but it would wound him, knowing that the child was not his. Knowing that it was conceived in such a horrific way. Would she give it up? How easy would it be to do this, given what they had suffered with Morag? To keep it, though . . . surely it was impossible. Whatever she did now would affect them forever.

She leaned over the side and vomited into the water below.

When she looked up, Daverley's gaze was fixed on her, contemplative. He was caulking a cask, glancing around to check that none of the other men were watching as he approached.

'Sea legs failing you?' he said.

She ran the sleeve of her dress across her mouth. 'Must be something I ate.'

'Maybe it's something you're carrying,' he said.

'And how would you know about that?'

'I had a wife. She carried four of our bairns. Each time she looked every bit as peely-wally as you do, now.'

She looked down again, wondering how long would it take to drown if she slipped overboard. Perhaps minutes? Or perhaps the cold water would rinse the child out of her. Her grip tightened on the edge of the hull, and he saw.

'You see something in the water?' Daverley said, glancing down. 'A mermaid, perhaps?'

She shook her head. 'Where are your children now?' she asked him.

'Two of them are with my wife,' he said. 'In God's arms.'

'I'm sorry,' she said. 'My husband and I lost a child. Our only child.'

Daverley tipped his hat with a free hand. 'My condolences.' He turned back to the water below. 'I've been watching for any sign of Thomas,' he said. 'That's why I asked.'

'Thomas?' she said. Did he mean his body? Surely not – the lad was laid to rest many miles ago, weighed down so he would not float. Even if the weights had shifted there was no way his body would have travelled so far north . . . It struck her that grief played with the mind.

'The old tales have it that a body rested at sea does not permit the soul to rest,' Daverley said, scanning the water.

'You've said that before. Why is that?'

'That, I know not. But the sea is where life began, and so the veil of death does not exist there.' He threw her a searching look. 'Surely you have heard these things, being the daughter of a shipmaster?'

'My father's a businessman, not a shipmaster,' she said. 'And he's certainly no storyteller.'

He turned, pressing his back against the edge of the hull. 'You've heard about selkies?'

'Too much about selkies,' she said drily. 'Selkie wives in particular.'

'I heard some of the men call you that,' he said. 'But it's incorrect, the way they've used it.'

She turned her gaze to him then, and he smiled.

'You want to hear the story?'

'Go on, then.'

'For a start, a selkie wife is simply a selkie female, whether married or no. And when a person is drowned or buried at sea, their soul arrives in the kingdom realm of selkie folk instead of heaven. A selkie changes form because it can possess the living, slip inside their skin like you or me putting on a coat, ye ken?'

She studied him. 'And you believe this?'

'I've seen it with my own eyes,' he whispered. 'Stout-hearted sailors possessed by a selkie, driven to throwing themselves into the depths, or steering the whole ship into rocks. It's no' a folktale about sacrifice. It's a tale about giving the sea more souls, more selkie folk to do the sea god's bidding.'

She tried to follow this. 'So the selkie wife in the original story drowned herself to join Lír's realm, but then possessed the souls of the living so they would drown, too?'

He nodded. 'It's a grim tale, indeed. But then, anyone who's ever spent time at sea will know that the ocean's a wild and savage place. And every time we take some of its fish for meat or whales for oil, old Lír sends his selkies out for revenge.'

'God.'

She found herself trying to explain the story away, her mind turning to other stories she'd heard over the years about the sea and its creatures. Sirens, mermaids, kraken . . . But then her foot twitched, and she remembered with a wrenching feeling the dark pelt that had formed over the wound. It had become infected, spreading all the way up her leg and transforming her foot into a flipper. She could barely bring herself to believe it, but each time she unwrapped the gauze, there it was, clear as day.

She had to get back to Dundee, to Allan. A doctor would help her. And the crew would be brought to justice for what they'd done to her.

'Can I ask you a question?' she said, lifting her eyes to Daverley.

'Aye.'

She bit her lip. 'Did you know? About Thomas' part in bringing me on the *Ormen*?'

He searched her face. 'No.'

'But you knew they were to kidnap me? You knew I was being brought on board?'

He shook his head without removing his gaze from her. 'Lovejoy asked Thomas to assist with moving livestock on board.'

'Livestock?'

'Yes. The day before we disembarked. We had to move the cows, the lambs, and the hens into the hold. He was gone for most of the day.'

She nodded, taking that in. 'That was the day I was attacked in Dawson Park.'

He frowned. 'By who? Thomas?'

'No. I've no idea who he was. An older man, late fifties, perhaps older. Stockily built, a dark beard. He was wearing a brown cap and a navy overcoat. Does he sound familiar?'

He shook his head. 'Thomas never mentioned it. But then, he was under orders from Lovejoy. I'd wager Lovejoy told him he'd be punished if he said anything. Especially to me.'

She searched his face, trying to work out if he was telling the truth. She supposed he had nothing to gain by lying.

He went to say more, but just then the watch started to shout. 'Ship ahoy!'

She looked up and saw Wolfarth pointing north. For a split second, it seemed that nothing was there, but then the light shifted and she saw it – a ship, its white sails glinting in the sun.

'It's the *Erik*,' Daverley said. 'Another whaler. We pass each other frequently on these voyages. Sometimes we take home letters and suchlike to the crew's families, others they do the same for us.'

'That's what Thomas told me,' she said, excitement growing in her. 'Do you think I could send a letter back to my husband?'

He hesitated. 'We'd have to be discreet. If Captain Willingham were to hear I'm passing on messages on your behalf . . .'

'You could say it's a letter from Thomas. He was writing letters back to his siblings.'

'What if they read the letters?'

'Do you think they would do that?'

'They might.'

'Well, hopefully by the time they do that, they'll be too far away to tell Captain Willingham.'

He shifted his feet. 'Why would Thomas write a letter to be passed on to your husband?'

She hesitated. 'My father, then. Maybe you can say it's his will? Instructions for his wages to be passed on in the event of his death?'

Daverley looked doubtful. She held him in a long, pleading look. At last, he sighed and looked away.

'I'll do my best,' he said.

Dominique

I

January 2024
Skúmaskot, Iceland

I think someone else is on board.

I'm in my bedroom, holding my breath. Shaking like a reed in high winds.

With the exception of my camera and the sensor, all the batteries are dead. The last couple of days have been completely without sun. It's the turn of the new year and the bleakest beginning I can imagine. No electricity for the kettle or the solar lanterns, no internet. And the singing is back. It's driving me mad. Always the same melody, a humming on the back of the wind.

I feel like I'm losing my mind.

I wake at four in the morning. There's a noise outside like someone is climbing the ladder, feet pressing into rungs and the metal grips at the top of the hull twanging with the weight. I sit up, excited; it must be one of the others. I race upstairs, expecting to find Samara or Leo or Jens there.

But as soon as I reach the main cabin, the noise stops. I hold my breath, listening. Picking up my torch, I head outside and shine a light down across the ladder.

There is no one there. I feel so confused. I heard it. I literally heard footsteps coming up the ladder.

I head back into the main cabin, locking the door behind me and heading back down to my own cabin. There, I climb inside my tent and zip it up.

But now I'm shaking because, as soon as I zip up my tent, the sounds of the ladder start up again. I sit, stunned, wondering why I can hear this. Nothing else makes that noise. I know what the ladder sounds like. I've heard it a million times now.

I wait for the footsteps to rise to the upper deck. Oh God. Someone is walking across the deck. No, not footsteps. One footstep, then a dragging of something across the wood.

And now I hear the same rhythm across the floor of the main cabin. It's so clear I can pinpoint exactly where the person is.

They're right next to the stairs, about to come down to the lower deck.

II

I have spent the last hour holding the handle to my cabin door with one hand and my knife with the other. Outside the wind is singing, singing. The darkness is a blindfold across the world.

The step-dragging has stopped. Still, I listen, waiting for it. Waiting for her to come.

III

I wait in the dark, my torch switched off, for the footsteps to continue down the hatch to the lower cabin. I am covered in sweat, my heart jackhammering wildly.

But the sound stops. I wait, shaking, until I feel like I'm going to claw my skin off from fear. I have to open the door. I have to *see* her.

My hand on the door handle, I open it slowly, slowly, holding my breath. The corridor is pitch-black, but I don't dare turn on my light. The wind outside is faintly singing. I'm so scared I think I might faint. I force my foot to lift and step forward, then another step, and another.

I take the stairs, super slow, my ears thrumming from my pounding heart.

The main cabin is empty, but I can feel her. She is here. Not in one place. She is the ship, every part of it.

My knife is sitting on the worktop in the kitchenette, glinting in the safety light. I know what she wants me to do. If I don't do it, she'll kill me.

I lift my shirt and stand in front of the fire for warmth. I need to be sure I cut in the right place – the shouting in my skin is so loud I feel I'm about to explode, my skin bursting with noise. Quickly I move the point of the blade to where the sound is loudest, which is across my ribs. I press it deeper than usual, a long, stinging incision that brings a moment of indescribable bliss.

Blood seeps down across my skin, but something feels different.

I can feel something literally moving under my skin, a stealthy squirm inside that makes me gasp and step back in surprise. It moves again, and I start to panic. Something is inside me.

All at once, a dark seam appears at the slit I've made in my abdomen, something protruding beneath the bloody film as though it wants to burst out. It seems to have a will of its own, pushing and writhing. I let out a scream, but the thing is insistent, the sharp sting rising as it begins to tear the slit wider. Oh God. A black snake, I think, crawling out of me.

An inky loop slips down, wet skin shining in the glow of the fire. With my finger and thumb I pinch the loop, then tug a little, my hand shaking. I want to be sick. My mouth opens and I want to scream but I'm too horrified to make a sound.

It's an eel.

It drops to the ground, coiling and thrashing for a few seconds before it falls still. I am trembling, my mouth wide, wide, and soundless.

An eel was inside me. Tears stream down my face and I struggle to breathe. An eel. An eel was inside me. I can't believe it. I daren't believe it.

I am howling now, crying *Help me! Help me!*

A slim black eel, about ten inches long, a fin along its back.

PART THREE

*attempt two hundred
and twelve*

Diego

October 1973
nr Svalbard, Norway

Diego Almeyda was in the High Arctic, and he was feeling relieved. He had plucked up the courage to tell Lorna, his colleague on a postdoctoral fellowship from Yale, about the figure he kept seeing on the stern. Always the same figure, holding the same stance – a woman, her back turned to him.

'How do you know it's a woman, then?' Lorna had said.

'She was closer, last time,' he said. 'I could tell she had a waist and hips.'

'If she was so close, why didn't you ask her who she was?'

'Because when I looked again, she was gone.'

Lorna had laughed and accused him of trying to freak her out. Diego's English was limited and so he wondered if it was a cultural thing, or if Lorna and the others pegged him as a nervous Latino who believed in ghosts. His grandmother had had the gift of sight, had spoken of ghosts like they were members of the family. Even so, he had never seen one. Until now.

It had been twelve hours since he last saw the woman. He had taken to staying in his cabin. Professor Joffre had knocked on his door last night, asking if he'd like a chat over a drink. Diego shook his head. He preferred to stay in his cabin.

'Research doesn't happen inside a cabin, mate,' Professor Joffre said. He was Australian and took no bullshit. 'You either get out of there or you leave the trip.'

They both knew there was no leaving the trip. They were docking at Svalbard in a week to collect ice samples from the Tunabreen glacier. Perhaps then he'd be able to muster the courage to go outside. He'd be able to leave the ship, then.

He woke when it was dark, a thick, pulsing blackness that told him he wasn't alone. He flicked on his table lamp and gave a gasp. In the corner of the room, facing the wall, was the woman he'd seen on the stern, the familiar shape of her head.

'*Por favor*,' he whispered. 'Please. Leave me alone.'

He wondered if he screamed, would anyone come? Would anyone believe him this time? And just then, he looked up again and saw she was gone. A sigh of relief. But something caught his eye. The woman was on the floor, elbows bent and her head tucked down, and behind her was a long, black tail. He whimpered, and she looked up with a craven look, the mouth stretched in a too-wide smile, revealing black gums and small sharp teeth.

He opened his mouth and screamed, a howl that stirred the other researchers from their sleep.

The nurse came again and sedated him, but when he woke, the woman was back. He knew what she wanted, now. He would be prepared, next time. In the lab, he found a scalpel, then locked himself inside his room.

A day later, Professor Joffre kicked the door down. Diego was on his bed, unconscious from blood loss.

'Oh, mate,' Professor Joffre said, rushing to Diego. But when he set eyes on what Diego had done to his feet, he fainted.

Svalbard sat on the horizon like a white stone when Diego went to the top deck. He had spent three weeks in the boat's first aid unit, and though they'd saved his life, they hadn't managed to repair the damage done to his feet. The deeper damage, though, was in his mind. He knew there were guns in the poop deck, protection against polar bears and pirates.

He took both shotguns and slotted the bullets into the chambers, then found a pistol.

'Hey, Diego,' a voice said. 'What the hell are you doing?'

It was Dr Karsen, a glaciologist from Montreal. Her eyes dropped to his feet, which were both bleeding from terrible wounds, the middle toes on both feet separated by a long gash.

'Diego, what *happened?*' she gasped.

But the woman appeared behind Dr Karsen, her long tail visible beneath her white dress. With a yell, he lifted the gun and pulled the trigger. He saw the glaciologist's head burst open, and it took a long moment for him to realise that his own bullet was the cause of it.

He saw a tail flick inside the main cabin, so he followed.

Inside, his colleagues were having coffee by the fire.

'Diego,' someone called. Diego lifted one of the shotguns and pumped a bullet at the woman, but she slithered out of sight. Behind her, Dr Jeong collapsed with a terrible scream. Blood splattered across the floor.

The girl Diego had liked, Dr Morton, was stooped over the body, yelling 'Leo!', and the professor was there, his arms up in surrender.

'Look, take it easy, mate,' he told Diego. His face shone with sweat, the whites of his eyes reminding Diego of the cows that lived behind his house. 'Come on, buddy. Don't do this. This isn't what you want, is it?'

Leo was screaming and Diego wanted it to stop. He went

downstairs through all the cabins, blasting the gun furiously until there were no bullets left, then lifted the other shotgun and did the same. And when he ran out, he was astonished to see that all was still.

A full moon shone down on the deck, a black, velvety ocean rocking the boat like a cradle. The galaxies were heavy overhead, a streak of green marking the awakening of the aurora borealis. Soon the green lights would fill the sky, dancing overhead in vivid rivers. Diego returned to his room, a sickening fear swelling in his solar plexus. He felt the boat groan with a new weight, the floorboards sounding out the presence of the woman. She was on board, and she was coming to him. And when he saw the shadow in the doorway, a spark of delight rested inside him – she was no longer monstrous, but beautiful, lowering above him on the bed to kiss his face. Even when blood plumed warm on the bedclothes around him, he couldn't bring himself to make her stop.

When the coastguard boarded the *Ormen* a month later, they found it empty. It had been lashed by tall waves, and the sails were damaged. The coffee machine was still running, and the generators. The laundry bags waited by the doors of the cabin, half-written letters were found under beds. Someone had left a record on the turntable.

They expected the *Ormen* to sink. But she drifted on, cradled by the waves, a piece of lint on the steely expanse of the Greenland Sea.

On the morning of the fifth of December, 1973, the ship swept into Skúmaskot, Iceland, coming to rest in the knobbly grip of volcanic rock.

And in the darkness, something climbed out of the water behind her, slinking into the shadows.

Dominique

I

January 2024
Skúmaskot, Iceland

I run out on to the deck, screaming at the thing I've just pulled out of my stomach. I lean over the side of the hull and vomit down the ladder.

A hand reaches up and touches me.

I scream. It touched me. She touched me.

I fall back on to the deck, shrieking at her to get away. I curl up into a ball, feeling the song of the wind wrap around me, enter me, clutching me.

'Dom?'

A man's voice. A familiar voice.

I uncurl slowly and look up. A shape appears at the hull, a watery shape. Jens. He's in a bad way, almost losing consciousness even as he struggles to climb over the top of the ladder. Quickly I move forward and grab the shoulder straps of his rucksack and stop him from falling, holding him there until he finds the rungs and clambers up.

I'm elated and terrified and angry all at once. He looks terrible, his knees weak and his hands visibly shaking as he staggers across the deck to the cabin. The wind is ferocious, too, and neither of us speaks until we're inside.

No sign of the eel. The seaweed frond is still on the floor, gleaming by the leg of the dining table. The cut in my abdomen has stopped bleeding, a dark clot forming already along the line that I made with the blade of my knife. I find a dressing while Jens removes his rucksack and coat, then sinks down on to the sofa.

'Is Leo here?' he pants. 'Samara?'

I manage to find my voice. 'Just me.'

He looks pained, but I'm relieved to have company again. I turn to the kitchenette and fill his water bottle with trembling hands.

'I thought you'd left,' I say, handing him the bottle.

He takes it and drinks deeply. 'We got separated in the storm.'

'You and Leo?' I ask.

He nods.

'Did you find Samara?' I ask.

He looks down, and I hold my breath. We sit in silence, because I'm too scared to ask if they're dead.

'Why did you come back?' I say finally.

'I wanted to make sure you were OK,' he says slowly, in between breaths.

I wonder if I heard correctly.

'You wanted to make sure I was OK?' I say.

He nods. 'I promised I would.'

'Who did you promise?'

He lifts his blue eyes to mine. 'You.'

I stare, trying to recall this promise.

'You don't remember?' he asks, and I shake my head.

'There's something I need to tell you,' he says. His eyes fall to my fingers, and I realise they're covered in blood. My blood.

'What happened?' he says.

I open my mouth to explain, but I can't. A sob swells in

my throat, and to my horror I start to cry. I can't help it. I can't remember ever crying in front of anyone, but suddenly I'm unravelling in front of him. He reaches out with his good arm and holds me to him, a feeling so alien and so comforting I can't let go.

Nicky

I

October 1901
Banks Bay, Greenland

The *Erik* was a whaler that set sail from Hull in the north of England, the crew every bit as leery and coarse as the *Ormen*'s shipmates. Lovejoy directed the men to sail the *Ormen* right up alongside the neighbouring ship, close enough for the men to jump from one ship to the other and greet each other. Morning sickness made the tight space of Nicky's cabin almost unbearable, a sudden aversion to the closeness of the walls around her, and so she stayed on the forecastle with a blanket, watching as the men exchanged kegs of beer and furs.

It was clear that the mariners intended to stay for a few days, Inuit tents growing on the bank running parallel to the ships. She watched row boats creaking back and forth between the tents and the ships, carrying female Inuit dressed in impressive fur coats and bringing food for the crew.

'Offerings,' Daverley told her, handing her a piece of dried caribou. 'The Inuit women bring gifts to entice our mariners to impregnate them.' He watched her expression change and smiled. 'Aye, not many folk from home would find it acceptable, either. But we're not at home, are we? We're in the Arctic, and the natives don't live in the kind of world we do. Their communities need births to survive. And they need foreign seed to prevent inbreeding.' He grinned at her expression. 'The native lassies see us Scots as fresh meat.'

She watched Lovejoy climbing on to the *Erik*, licking his palms to slick back his oily hair. 'I suppose one woman's poison is another woman's fresh meat.'

He followed her gaze. 'You could also say that the seed may be rotten, but the flower can be fine.'

'Every garden needs manure,' she said drily.

Daverley laughed.

She bit into the caribou and found it was delicious, the gaminess of the meat a welcome contrast to the diet of whales, seabirds, and seals that now turned her stomach. He passed her a parchment bag filled with ripe purple berries that burst on her tongue. She ate the lot without speaking.

'I'd best see if I can get you more,' Daverley said.

'Won't the Inuit women expect you to impregnate them?' she said, watching the women climb aboard the *Erik*. Wolfarth, Royle, and McKenzie all but fell over themselves in the attempt to reach the other ship.

Daverley grimaced. 'I'm sure one of my colleagues will happily take my place.'

She was puzzled at this. 'Why aren't you up for it? You were married to a woman, weren't you?' She asked it delicately. Her brother Harry was, as he had once whispered to her, Achillean, which she took to mean after the Greek hero Achilles, whose relationship with his battle mate Patroclus was romantic in nature. Harry told her that a surprising number of men and women were of a similar ilk, but of course to be outward about it was to put oneself in mortal peril. She had imagined her father's reaction, if he had cause to suspect Harry's inclination. A Dundee whaler, born and bred? He'd have disowned Harry without blinking.

'I'm still married,' Daverley said softly. 'I didn't stop being Thomas' uncle when he died. And I didn't stop being Eilidh's husband when she died.'

For two days, there was no hunting or whaling. Both the *Ormen* and the *Erik* were transformed into floating brothels, occupied by Inuit women who raced up and down the lower deck, naked, and Inuit men, who stood in their heavy caribou furs on the upper deck, smoking pipes, drinking Scottish ale, and playing cards with the crew.

Daverley promised to look after her, and he kept his word. He brought her food and fresh water from the land and traded his own tools for Inuit blankets to keep her warm.

The ship hummed with moans and squeaking beds, and it reeked of sex and caribou meat. Nicky found her vomiting began to subside. As long as the ship didn't move and she ate the sweet Inuit berries and the smoked caribou, the vomiting stopped. Her strength began to return, and the crew of the *Ormen* were preoccupied with naked Inuit women.

One night, she saw a flash of white weaving through the try-pots on the upper deck. It was the Arctic fox, though that single flash was as much as she saw. It had escaped the cage and was doubtless making its way back to land even as she marvelled at how it had broken free. Had the ship been at sea the fox would have been doomed, but the Inuit women had stalled the voyage, providing an opportunity.

And perhaps she could do the same.

II

'I need you to help me.'

Daverley looked around to check they weren't being watched. Harrow was caulking a cask with a cinching iron, his gaze hard and cold on them both. Above, Anderson sat on the rig, glancing at them. And on the bow, Royle and McKenzie were removing whale oil from a copper cooler. She caught them looking at her before whispering to each other.

'I'll collect your letters later,' Daverley said. 'We're setting sail tomorrow at dawn. I'll pass your letters on to the captain, all right?'

'I don't want to send letters home,' she said. 'I need to *go* home.'

He turned his eyes to her, realising what she was proposing.

'The *Erik* is returning to Dundee, is it not?'

He nodded.

'I could hide away on that ship. Three weeks, maybe less, until I'm home. I could manage it. But I need your help.'

Daverley lowered his eyes, and she feared he was going to refuse her.

'They killed your nephew,' she said, her voice a little louder. 'Surely you want your own revenge for that.'

He leaned forward angrily, pressing his face close to hers. 'What I want,' he said, 'is to get home to my sons in one piece. And if you think you're going to involve me in something that will prevent that, you've lost your mind.'

He looked over his shoulder, and she saw the men glancing over. She thought to remind him of his promise, but she had to tread carefully.

'Please,' she whispered. 'I just need you to signal when it's safe for me to go on board the other ship.'

He gave a small nod, and she kept her face turned from the men as she headed back to her cabin.

Later that night, she heard a knock at her door. She opened it to Daverley, a grim look on his face.

'Come in,' she said, and closed the door behind him.

'You risk your life going aboard the *Erik*,' he said. 'If those men find you on board, you'll not have the same protection as you've had here.'

She widened her eyes and gave a laugh. 'Protection? Are you joking?'

'I know they raped you,' he said carefully. 'But if you weren't George Abney's daughter they'd have thrown you overboard by now, I can promise you that.'

She gave an angry scoff. 'What, are my services no good? You think they'd rather me dead than prostituting myself day and night?'

He held out a hand to keep her voice down. 'It's still a three-week journey back to Dundee. You've not thought this through . . .'

'. . . I *have* thought this through.'

'How will you get food and water without being noticed?'

'That's the least of my concern.'

He scoffed. 'You nearly bit my arm off when I gave you a bag of berries and you think you can go three weeks without eating or drinking?'

'I'll find a way,' she said, folding her arms.

He sighed. 'Look, I know the crew on the *Erik*. I know what they're like. And if they find you on board their ship, they'll do much, much worse than what you've endured here.'

She turned away, stung with a sudden frustration. What option did she have? She couldn't endure another three months on the *Ormen*. And if she went home to Dundee, she could possibly recruit someone to help her with the matter of the pregnancy. Perhaps Allan would still be in the Transvaal. She would never have to tell him. Her mother had once whispered that Mrs Cross, the family housekeeper, had a sister who was a skilled abortionist.

If Nicky left it too long, she'd start to show. And perhaps she'd be beyond the point of help.

'As long as you know the risk,' he said after a long silence. 'If you come to the top deck at midnight, I'll help you aboard the *Erik*.'

'Thank you.' She leaned forward and kissed his cheek. He flinched, and she could tell he was embarrassed. With a nod, he turned on his heel and returned to his cabin.

III

At midnight, she slipped out of her cabin to meet Daverley. Fear crept up her spine and across her shoulders. A fresh mouthful of vomit raced up her throat, and she swallowed it back, stifling a cough as she made her way to the upper deck.

As soon as she raised her head through the hatch, she spotted Daverley, standing with a tankard of beer near the forecastle. He saw her and gave a loud shout.

'McKenzie! Have I ever told you about that time I swyved your ma?'

'Are you out of your wits, man?' another voice called.

Daverley appeared to be drunk, leaning his elbows on the side of the hull and taking a swig of beer. 'It was the time after I swyved *your* ma,' he shouted to Royle.

'What did you say?' McKenzie said, his voice closer. He had climbed down from the rig to challenge Daverley. 'Say it to my face, why don't you?'

'You heard me the first time,' Daverley said.

'I'll have your guts for garters if ye mention my ma again.'

'Leave him be,' Royle called out. 'He's off his head.'

Daverley spat in Harrow's face. With a shout, McKenzie swung his fist for Daverley, who ducked out of the way, the blow landing on Royle's jaw. Royle lifted his tankard and brought it crashing down on Harrow's head.

'What the devil's going on?' a voice shouted. Daverley glanced quickly at Nicky, and she saw her chance – the crew were distracted by the brawl that had sparked between Daverley, McKenzie, and Royle, more and more of the men drawn in. She looked up at the watch aboard the *Erik*. His gaze was on the swinging fists at the stern of the *Ormen*.

Under cover of darkness, she made for the starboard side of the *Ormen* and pulled herself on to the neighbouring ship.

The layout of the *Erik* was much the same as the *Ormen*. She had memorised the crawlspaces, those parts of the ship in which spare sails and coils of rope were kept. There would be enough space for her. The small storage room above the engine room was probably the safest and warmest. She planned to slip down into the engine room when possible to stretch her legs, and to eat. The hold would be best for that, though she would likely have to eat raw whale for the dura-tion of her stay . . . But these were small matters compared to the next stage of the plan.

The familiar cries and squeaking bedframes told her that the crew were busy saying goodbye to the Inuit women. Only a fire or murder would draw them out of their cabins.

She moved quickly towards the stairs that led to the hold, but when she lowered to the next level she found it was different than the *Ormen*.

For a start, the decks weren't as dark as the *Ormen*'s – wall sconces trickled warmth and light along the hallway, their small flames tilting as she moved quickly past. The cabin that was Dr O'Regan's surgery wasn't there, and instead she found herself staring through a crack in the door that led to the galley.

The galley was larger than the *Ormen*'s. Clean pots and pans hung from an overhead rack, and a cook stood at a table peeling potatoes. Her mouth watered – there hadn't been potatoes on the *Ormen* for months – but she had to tear herself away and find the crawlspace. The thought occurred to her that perhaps she should have found a reason to board the *Erik* as a guest in order to scope it out before escaping. But then, this was a last-minute plan, and so much hinged on it. Already she could hear the men returning to the rig and preparing the sails for their launch, and it was just enough to give her a boost of courage to keep moving along the deck.

And then, she found it – a barely perceptible brass hoop laid flat into the wood of the floor. She pulled it up and found the crawlspace beneath her feet. No sails, only a few dusty tar pots, a soothing warmth rising from the engine room below. A space about six feet by four, barely larger than a coffin. But the wood had gaps, and as she slid inside she felt a draught passing from the upper floor.

Outside, she could hear voices shouting, calling the men to their stations. She pulled the hatch door shut, tight, and lay down, a hand to her stomach. She thought of Daverley, starting a fray with his colleagues to draw attention away from her. Had he got into trouble?

She slept several hours before the sound of coal being shovelled in the room beneath woke her. She heard the whistle of the boiling water and the roar of the engine, more shouting. Feet pounded the wood above the crawlspace. Sweat gathered under her armpits and along her spine. They were moving.

Closing her eyes tightly, she took slow, deep breaths, images of home beginning to slip into her mind. The noise of the jute mill, the children's voices and the women singing. Her sister's dogs, the fluster of paws across the parquet each time she came home. Sunlight on the Tay. The photograph of Allan on her dresser.

Footsteps. She held her breath as they paced up and down the deck, praying hard that they'd keep away. There was nothing of any obvious value in the crawlspace, nothing anyone would be searching for, but that didn't mean they wouldn't check it. The footsteps moved away, and she allowed herself to breathe.

But then, light. The hatch lifted and a face looked in.

A grin.

'Hello, my lovely,' McKenzie said. 'So here you are.'

IV

She sat before Captain Willingham's desk in his office, Stroud and Cowie standing close by her side, as though she might burst out of the room and run for her life. Her arms and legs burned from where they seized her, bruises on her shins from where they dragged her roughly out of the crawlspace and took her, kicking and screaming, back to the *Ormen*.

She kept her eyes on the floor, fighting back tears of anger.

'Your father sent us a telegram via the *Erik*,' he said. 'That is why we searched for you and found you were not in your cabin.'

'My father?' she said. A burst of hope, vivid as fresh flowers. 'How does he know I'm here? What did he say?'

'It doesn't matter what he said,' Captain Willingham said tersely. He seemed irritated, bothered by something. 'What matters is you were found trying to escape.'

The mention of her father emboldened her. 'You don't own me, Captain. I have every right to leave if I choose.'

'We had an agreement,' Captain Willingham said, the matter closed.

'An agreement?' she said. 'Is that what you call it?'

'We had two telegrams from the *Erik* that you might wish to know about. The first was from your father, asking after you.'

She opened her mouth, astonished. 'But how does he know I'm here?' she repeated, her voice low and steely.

'We told him you were well,' the captain said, continuing to ignore her question.

'My father will have you in the courts,' she hissed, her voice quavering. 'He'll have you hung for what you've done to me.'

The captain held her in a flat stare. 'Oh, I don't think so.'

She lifted her jaw, tears wobbling in her eyes. 'I'll stake my life on it.'

Captain Willingham cocked his head, the edges of his mouth beginning to curl in a smile. 'I'm afraid that the second telegram was to inform us of an imminent change in the company ownership. Your father is dead.'

Her face dropped, all the hope that had risen in her sinking through the floor.

'Dead?' she said.

Captain Willingham nodded, his eyes cold. Then, taking pleasure in the telling: 'By his own hand.'

Her mind filled with metal shards. Grief, noxious and bitter, fell on her like a boulder. The tears that came were raw, guttural. And now that her father was dead, she feared what the men might do.

They had no reason to let her live.

Dominique

I

The singing stops.

I tell Jens what happened, and he spies the blood on my stomach. No sign of the eel, but he doesn't question me when I tell him. Despite his own exhaustion he cleans the cut on my stomach and applies a dressing. Then he presses a sleeping pill into my hand and insists that I go to my tent at once and sleep.

When the sun comes up, I start to feel better. The wound on my stomach doesn't hurt so much, and the light today is strong for the first time in weeks. Jens has made a pot of coffee and is sitting by the back window overlooking the beach. I pick up a solar charger and try to go online to check for any messages from Leo and Samara, but it won't connect. I try again and again, until the power runs out. Frustrated, I put the charger back by the window to power up the battery again for another try.

'What do you think has happened to them?' I ask Jens, sitting down opposite. 'Do you think they got lost?'

He nods. 'I got lost out there for a long while. I'm going out again, after this cup of coffee.'

'I'll come,' I say. I force a smile to show I'm well enough.

He holds me in a long look. 'I think it's time I told you something,' he says then.

'That sounds ominous.'

'I don't think it's ominous.'

'Bad, then. Anytime someone says they need to tell me something it's bad.'

He falls silent, and I crane my head up to see his expression. He looks down at me, a deep line of worry slicing his forehead. He opens his mouth, then closes it, before striding across the cabin to the wooden post with the column of cuts.

I watch, utterly confused, as he runs his fingers over the nicks in the wood.

'Two hundred and eleven times,' he says. Then, pulling a penknife from his pocket, he cuts a fresh line at the very top. 'Attempt two hundred and twelve,' he says with a sigh.

Have I missed something? 'Attempt at what?' I ask him.

He turns and holds me in a look of such despair that I wonder if he's lying about Leo and Samara. Are they dead?

A loud knocking breaks the silence. The chain beating against the hull.

'What *is* that?' Jens says.

'It's just the chain,' I say. 'The wind catches it . . .'

We hold our breaths and listen as the knocking shifts. Two knocks, now. Jens gets up, glances outside. Light rests on his face and I realise I have lost track of what time it is. It must be daytime, about noon.

'Where are you going?' I ask.

'I want to see what's causing that sound,' he says.

Outside, the deck has ripened with snow. An albatross the size of a chair is perched on the side of the hull, ruffling its feathers against the shining flakes that twirl in the air. The light is stronger today, hard on my eyes after days of darkness.

Jens climbs down the ladder and I follow, certain that he's avoiding me after what I said. Or what I didn't say. *I don't trust you.* I feel conflicted. What does he expect? We barely know each other.

'Jens,' I say, approaching him as he looks over the hull. 'Tell me.'

He stares down into my face. He hasn't forgotten our conversation. He was going to tell me something.

'We know each other,' he says then. 'From before.'

I frown at him, suddenly wary. 'That's what you wanted to tell me?'

He looks nervous and relieved, as though he'd been carrying around a secret that he had to get off his chest. 'Do you remember me?'

I run my eyes over him, confused. Memories swirl in my mind. The men's faces above me. The rapes.

I back away, feeling foolish. The urge to cut myself nudges at me. But when I glance up at him again, I feel it – recognition. A duality to the knowing of him. Dizzying déjà vu.

And as though he can read my mind, he steps forward.

'You do remember me, don't you?' he says, reaching out. I pull away, instinctive, and he looks shocked.

'Dom,' he says. Then, as though he's realised something, he turns and strides past me, right around the side of the wreck to the ocean. I watch, alarmed, as he wades into the tide, the waves thunderous.

'Jens!' I shout. 'Don't!'

He keeps walking until I can't see him, and I cup my hands to my mouth. Iceland's seas are treacherous, but suddenly I'm wading in after him, the shock of the cold as it seeps through my clothing making me shout out.

I'm up to my neck before I see him – he is swimming towards the back of the wreck, heading for the stern where a thick chain is clanging against the hull. The water is ice cold, snow drifts floating by like miniature islands. I pull off my coat, then close my eyes and push into the water. I start to swim, wheeling my arms and kicking hard, but waves slam into me, pushing me back. I can feel powerful currents pulling at me, insistent on taking me off course.

The illusion of the ship's closeness from land is laid bare by the length of the swim. But finally I'm there, panting with exhaustion and clinging on to the metal rivets with my fingertips, feeling the ship groan and swell against me with the force of the waves.

'What are you doing?' I shout over the noise of the waves crashing down on the beach.

Jens holds up the chain, its black loops filled with solid ice. 'There's something hooked on to this,' he shouts back. 'That's what's causing the knocking.'

'Great!' I shout back sarcastically. 'It doesn't matter! Come back to the ship!'

But then he dives under, and my heart stops. A moment later he surfaces, only to dive under again. What the hell is he doing?

The chain begins to move, stretching out towards the beach. I follow it, watching Jens' head bobbing up above the waves, waiting for the moment that he doesn't surface. I'm still so shaken by Samara's fall into the ice that I can't bear the thought of him going under, adrenalin flashing through me in case he doesn't come back up.

He has caught something, the thing the chain is hooked to. I swim quickly towards him, hard currents sapping my strength. I reach down to help him shift whatever he has found, my fingers finding a metal bar beneath the surface.

We drag it together on to the beach, then collapse on to the sand, utterly spent.

'Don't ever do that again,' I say, gasping between words. He turns to me, golden hair slicked across his forehead. The currents were frightening, and we both know we were lucky to make it back. Ironically, the thing we've dredged from the chain anchored us, helping us to shore.

After a moment he stands and shakes off his coat and shoes, then hefts the object at the other end of the chain out of the water.

'What the fuck?' I say.

Nicky

I

October 1901
Cape Raper, Greenland

They whipped Daverley first.

Twenty stripes with a strip of tarred ratline, each one lifting his skin in a livid welt. Nicky watched on from the forecastle as Lovejoy meted the stripes, putting all his muscle behind them. Her hatred boiled. Her father, dead. She was sure he was the reason she was on board the *Ormen*. How else would he have known she was here? She braced herself for what they would do to her. Throw her overboard, perhaps. Why would they spare her? They had nothing to gain from it.

Daverley sank to his knees, gasping, his back ablaze with bloody lines. The captain nodded grimly at Wolfarth, who pushed her towards the mast and tethered her wrists to it.

'Twenty lashes,' Captain Willingham called out. She fixed her eyes ahead, seeking out the faint bar of the horizon in the distance.

A shrill snap as the rope unleashed behind her, again and again and again. The sea singing, an invitation. A war cry.

After the beating, the mariners let her be. She stayed in her room for several days, no desire for food or water. She had stopped vomiting, and there had been blood, dark and arterial. When the men carried her back after the flogging, her bandage unravelled. Now, stretched out on the bed in front of her, she saw what had become of her foot. Dark as coke, a layer of fine fur, her toes bruise-dark and flattened at the end of a thin curve. Her ankle bone swallowed by sooty flesh, the whole foot sinuous and slick. Her right leg was still human, but the skin between her thighs had webbed, a darkness spreading at the seam.

The transformation of her foot was something appropriately selkie-like, horrifying and familiar at once. She had seen more seals in the last three months than she had ever thought possible, dozens of them. But so many of them were captured, hauled on to the ship, a mass of dead things. Walruses piled like sandbags, dolphins, polar bears.

She was becoming like them.

To the mariners, she was prey, the division between the ship and the rest of the world cut by species, and now, gender. The rape of the ocean was brokered by men like her father, like Lovejoy. Men who would take without impunity for their own gain, by whatever means necessary.

A noise outside her cabin door startled her as she lay there. She fixed the blanket across her legs and watched, stricken, as Lovejoy strode in. She could read his mood before she saw his face.

'Here she is,' he said. 'My selkie wife.' He had the same smile he had worn while lashing Daverley. The cruelty she had clocked in his eyes months ago had crystallised into something monstrous and consuming.

He lowered to his haunches, moving his face close to hers. 'What must you have done to be so worthless in the eyes of your own father?'

She kept her gaze on the ground. He wanted a fight. He wanted to provoke her.

'Your father offered you up, you know,' he said. 'I told him the men would walk without payment and he offered you.' A cruel smile. 'His own daughter.'

She closed her eyes, a tear spilling down her cheek. *He is lying*, she told herself, but her mind returned to the morning before she woke up in the hold. Her father telling her to keep out of sight, that he had done something that he regretted . . .

'You didn't know?' He reached down and gripped her cheeks, turning her face to him. 'Answer me.'

She moved her hand to the bedclothes, nervous in case he saw her tail. What then? Would he kill her?

'His company or his daughter, that's what it came down to,' Lovejoy continued, watching for her reaction. 'The crew wouldn't sail without a woman on board. Says he, "I have a daughter who I can offer as a selkie wife if the men will sail," and so we did.'

She shook her head. 'My father would do no such thing,' she whispered.

'Oh, but he did,' Lovejoy said, lowering his face to hers. 'Your own kin betrayed you. Your own *blood*.' He moved a hand to her face, and she didn't move. 'You think anyone's missing you back in Dundee, selkie? You may as well stay here on the ship. My selkie wife.'

He climbed on to the bed on top of her, lowering for a kiss. She kissed him, obedient, but she knew what was coming. He was unfastening his belt, and he would see her tail. Instinctively she moved a hand to the side of the bed to pull herself from under him, but her hand touched something familiar. The polar bear skull.

Lovejoy was reaching beneath, hauling up her skirts. Quickly she lifted the skull and raised it, a heavy upward swing that caught Lovejoy's jaw.

He fell backward against the door, his arms flung to the

sides, and she lunged again, swinging the skull across her body.

It connected with the side of his head, a long split across his eye spurting blood as he dropped to the floor.

Dominique

I

It's a cage.

About three-foot square, wrought of thick, sea-oxidised steel. Jens hefts it closer up the sand, and I lean my weight behind it, pushing it with him. Those couple of minutes in the freezing sea have left us wrung out. Even on the shore I can feel currents pulling at me, invisible hands snaking around my ankles, pulling me back, back.

Once the cage is free of the tide's reach, we sink into the sand and look over it in silence.

'It was hooked to the chain,' Jens says, as though that explains anything. As though it explains why he was so desperate to find it.

'So this was causing the knocking,' I say. We're both stunned, looking for answers.

I'm no expert, but it doesn't strike me as a standard fisherman's cage. For one, it's super heavy, and secondly, there are spikes on the inside, designed to wound whatever sits inside. Jens moves forward, tentatively, reaching out to check that the spikes are actually attached to the frame. And they are.

'Jesus,' he says.

Something moves in the corner of my eye, and I turn to see a figure moving in the mist, about a hundred feet to my right. The ghost woman. My heart thuds in my throat, acidic, noxious fear. I grab Jens' hand.

'Tell me you see her,' I urge.

'I see her,' he says, rising to his feet.

I start. 'You do?'

He squints. 'It's Samara.'

I turn, astonished. He's right – the figure stumbling towards us has morphed into Samara. Behind her, Leo emerges, his form hardening as he steps out of the fog. We both scramble across the sand towards them, laughing and shouting.

'Samara!' I call. 'Samara!'

It's a miracle, an actual goddamn miracle. She's alive! I pull her close to me, my arms around her, weeping into her neck. A moment later, Leo collapses. In my excitement, I haven't realised the state they're both in. Leo's gloves are missing, his fingernails caked with dirt. Samara has leaves sticking out of her dreadlocks and there's dried blood around her mouth.

Jens looks up at me. 'We need to get them indoors, quickly,' I tell him.

II

By the time we reach the cabin, the four of us are quaking and gasping from the cold. Jens and I are soaked through, the skin on my hands raw and split open from hauling the cage. I don't even go down into my cabin – I stand in front of the fire, stripping off my clothes until I'm naked, before slipping inside the sleeping bag. Jens watches me briefly before doing the same, stripping down.

I watch in horror. 'What are you doing?'

'We don't have much choice, do we?' he says, shaking off his trousers. He leaves on his boxers and climbs inside the sleeping bag with me. Jens feels like an older brother to me. The weirdness of it is only for a moment; soon, his skin against mine lowers my heart rate and helps me stop shaking.

Leo and Samara are curled up on the floor next to us, all of us trying to soak up the faint heat of the fire, huddled together desperately for warmth. Leo reaches for a piece of broken wood and, with a trembling hand, feeds it into the fire.

We must all fall asleep, because when I wake, Jens is sitting opposite, talking to Leo. He's dressed. I sit up, holding the sleeping bag to me. Samara is changed, too, holding a cup of something.

'Hello,' Jens says to me.

I smile back. 'Hi.'

It's dark outside. The mood is quiet, shellshocked. I can scarcely believe the events of today. Of the last few days. The dynamic between Jens and me has shifted entirely. And more importantly, Samara is here. I want to reach out and touch her to prove to myself that she's really here. That she's alive.

'Are you OK?' I ask, holding off my more existential questions until I find out where she's been.

Samara nods, though her eyes are haunted. She glances at Leo, and I follow her gaze, trying to read what they're not saying. 'We were so worried,' I tell Leo. 'Did you get lost?'

Another glance between Leo and Samara. 'I went after Samara,' Leo tells Jens. I notice he can't look me in the eye, though maybe it's just exhaustion. No – he's still angry with me.

'I saw footprints in the snow, just outside the caves,' he says. 'So I kept heading in that direction. Eventually, I found her. She'd lost her footing and rolled down a ravine, close to the river.'

Jens and I turn to Samara.

'But I don't understand,' I say gently. 'Samara, you were *dead*. I gave you CPR. I felt your pulse, and there was nothing. You were stiff, for God's sake.'

Samara looks uneasy. She shifts her eyes from me to Leo, who seems to nod, as though consenting to a shared decision.

'I thought . . . that I was free,' she says. 'I thought I'd made it out.' She presses her hands against her eyes.

'What?' I ask, astonished.

'You lost consciousness,' Jens says, and I'm grateful he's here, asking sensible questions. I'm reeling so hard that I can't think straight. 'That hasn't happened before.'

'I remember waking up here in the cabin,' Samara says

haltingly. 'Then . . . walking through the snow, feeling light-headed.'

'You just woke up?' I say, interrupting. I'm keen to under-stand how the hell she came back to life.

She nods. 'I kept walking,' she says. 'I wanted to get away from here.'

'We walked for days,' Leo says. 'Both of us. When I found Samara, I had already passed the *Ormen*. I figured I'd messed up the path and turned back on myself. But then it happened again.'

'*What* happened again?' I ask.

'Well, we kept going in circles, obviously,' Samara says, her voice filling with anger. 'No matter how hard we tried, we kept coming back here.'

'Seventeen times,' Leo says darkly. 'We passed the *Ormen* seventeen times.'

'We couldn't escape.'

The room sits in silence. None of us can process this. If they passed by seventeen times, how come I didn't see them? Why didn't they give up and come on board? Why did they not want to return?

'It's a labyrinth,' Leo tells me, as though explaining it has deepened his exhaustion. 'The wreck is in the middle of a vortex. We can't get out. Not you, not me, not any of us. We are stuck here.'

I give a small laugh, and instantly everyone turns to me.

'Sorry,' I say, swallowing back another laugh. 'I'm just . . . this is all crazy, isn't it? First you, Samara, looking like you'd died but then . . . not. And now you two getting lost.'

'The *Ormen* will be sunken tomorrow' Jens says, his voice raised.

'We'll wait for the coastguard,' I say. 'And if we can't get out, we'll ask them to take us back.'

341

It sounds like a reasonable plan to my ears, but I can tell that neither Leo nor Samara is paying me any attention.

Whatever they've gone through has been harrowing. Their minds are elsewhere.

Nicky

I

October 1901
Cape Hooper, Greenland

A gasp from the doorway made Nicky look up.

Daverley was there, his face like a broken window. Lovejoy lying face down in a pool of glossy claret, the side of his head bashed in. She dropped the skull with a clatter and keeled forward, gasping for air. Daverley lunged forward, catching her as she fell off the bed.

'Are you hurt?' he said, kneeling beside her, and she realised her hands and face were spattered with blood, the hem of her dress soaked red.

She broke into tears. She had killed Lovejoy. It had been a momentary reaction. She was glad and not glad. Relieved, terrified.

Daverley leaned his ear to Lovejoy's chest, listening for a heartbeat. He rolled back on his haunches, crossed himself. 'He's gone.'

'Lovejoy said my father arranged for me to be on the ship,' she said. 'As a selkie wife. Did you hear anything about this? Did you *know*?'

He hesitated. 'When you insisted you were no prostitute, I spoke to the men. To Reid.'

343

'Tell me,' she whispered.

'Your father didn't pay us last time,' he said quickly. 'He owed us all wages. He couldn't guarantee they'd be paid. Lovejoy told us he'd make a deal.'

'What deal?' she said.

'He said he'd ask for a woman for the men. Your sister.'

Her mouth fell open. 'Cat?'

'Your father offered you instead.'

The news knocked the wind out of her. She sank back against the bed, breathless.

'I shouldn't have told you,' Daverley said.

'Did you agree to it?' she said. 'The deal.'

Daverley lifted his eyes to hers. 'I didn't know you had been taken by force,' he said carefully.

He reached out to hold her hand. She let him.

'God's wounds!' a voice said. Wolfarth and Stroud stood in the doorway, looking in horror at the scene – Daverley with his hand in hers, both of them sitting by Lovejoy's battered body.

'Murder!' Wolfarth screamed. 'Murder aboard! Fetch the captain!'

The sentencing was swift, and without trial or record.

'In,' Captain Willingham said, pointing inside the brig.

They were standing on the upper deck, hard rain needling down. The whole crew watching on. The sight of Lovejoy's body had stunned them all. She'd gone mad, Wolfarth said. The selkie wife was a murderer.

It could have been any one of them.

Wolfarth gave her a shove. She stepped towards the brig, her hands still stained with Lovejoy's blood.

The clang of the cage door. Her knees to her chin, her spine pressed up against the metal. A spike brushing her scalp.

Stroud, Anderson, and McKenzie hefted the cage starboard, a heavy chain hooked to the top of the cage. She saw Daverley hauled in chains towards a barrel, his left arm held out as Royle brought down an axe. One clean, brutal blow taking off his hand. He let out a cry that sounded like no human she had ever heard. A roar like a bear.

The chain knocked against the side of the hull as the men lowered her down in the brig. She saw the blue sky and the sunlight reflecting off the metal rivets, the distant shape of Anderson in the crow's nest above. Then, her own reflection in the waters below.

The water received her like it had been waiting, patient. Fetching her home.

She held her breath for as long as she could, fighting against the heavy bars of the brig. The spikes cut into her arms, releasing long red feathers of blood. Her fingers reached through the cage, clawing at the hull.

Shadows in the depths. A face with whiskers, curious at the cage.

Her body fought. She jerked and convulsed, her lungs burning and her hands wringing the bars of the brig until her palms bled. The spikes pierced her scalp, her cheeks.

And then, a honeyed glow.

An awakening.

Dominique

I

January 2024
Skúmaskot, Iceland

Today, the *Ormen* is to be dragged beneath the waves, sunk to the depths.

The light today is sublime. A crisp blue sky, fat, picture-book clouds, a generous spread of gelatinous sunlight ruddying the hills. A night's sleep has been good for us all. Jens makes breakfast, cracking open double the amount of his expensive sachets and encouraging us all to dig in. He makes a pot of strong coffee, produces sugar and dried milk. I had no idea we had these. He must have been hiding them – his emergency stash. Small luxuries that make an otherwise ludicrous situation a little more palatable.

I want to find the right time to ask him what he meant before, when he asked if I remembered him. Everything feels so fragile. Samara is here, alive. The *Ormen* is about to be destroyed. We seem to be trapped here. If I don't stay focused on small things – the weather, food, the fire bucket – I'll go mad.

We take it in turns to keep watch for the breakers. We need to approach them to avoid them discovering that we've been living on board. If we present ourselves as hikers who have got lost, rather than urban explorers who have essentially been squatting on the wreck, we have a much higher chance of getting help. Jens says this is a better option than calling the coastguard for help. None of us want to be arrested, especially not in Iceland, and especially not in a part of the country where the nature reserves are protected. The penalties will be harsh. Better that we ask the breakers to take us back to civilisation.

At midday, Jens gives a shout from the upper deck. 'A ship!' he shouts, and we look outside. An orange coastguard vessel has appeared out to sea, moving swiftly towards us.

'They're going to tow it out,' Samara says.

'Maybe we should film this,' Leo suggests.

I fetch the solar chargers from the window. They have enough charge to allow the cameras to film this.

Jens comes inside. 'They're almost here,' he says. 'We need to go outside.'

Leo passes him his drone. 'Get some drone footage,' he says. 'I'll film from the rocks.'

'It's better if one of us approaches,' Samara says. It makes sense – she's the most charismatic of the four of us, the one most likely to persuade the breakers that we're hikers who got lost.

We plan it – Jens will climb the volcano to get drone footage while Leo and I get shots of the breakers arriving. We put on our backpacks and say goodbye to the cabin. I click on to the TikTok app on my phone, but the project account isn't there. I try again, closing down the app, then reopening it. Still not there, and neither is my own personal account.

'Something wrong?' Leo says.

'I can't find the account,' I tell him.

'Don't do a live,' he says. 'Upload it later.'

I follow Leo up the rocky outcrop once we've got our

footage, while Samara waits behind, waving her arms at the ship. It's growing closer, the insignia of the breaker company visible on the main mast. A mermaid.

Jens' drone buzzes overhead, and I scan the side of the volcano where he stands, controlling the drone. I hope he's right about the breakers. I hope they listen. Even if Leo and Samara are wrong about the path out of here, it's clear that neither of them have the strength to take on a fifteen-mile trek across lava fields.

I hold up my phone and film the ship, lifting my free hand to wave at them.

'Over here!' Samara shouts. 'Help us!'

Leo drops something beside me – his camera, I think – and I lower to help him find it amongst the shrubs. But as I stoop down, I feel my arms being pinned behind me. In the corner of my eye I see Samara, and it takes a moment to register what's happening – she's binding my hands together. I hear the zip of a cable tie, the friction of plastic against my wrists.

'Samara, what the fuck?' I shout, but she pushes me forward, tying my ankles together with another cable tie. I give a shout as she pulls the tie too tight, the plastic nipping my skin. Leo ties a leather belt across my mouth, fastening it at the nape of my neck. My eyes bulge as I stare at him, pleading for him to stop. But my cries are muffled, and he doesn't let go.

He looks past me at Samara.

'We don't have much time.'

II

Samara and Leo carry me down the outcrop, back to the *Ormen*. I squeal into the leather at my mouth but it isn't enough to rouse Jens, who has climbed high up the side of the volcano.

At the ladder, Leo throws me over his shoulder, then uses another cable tie to bind my wrists to my ankles, my arms thrown straight behind my head and my thighs bent until my feet are almost touching my head. I'm not flexible, and my shoulders feel like they're about to pop out of their sockets.

Inside the *Ormen*, they carry me down the lower deck. I'm bewildered and frightened – the breaker ship is right next to us, the thrum of the engine in the water making the *Ormen* sway. Through the window I catch a flash of a man in a luminous boiler suit leaning out to tether the *Ormen* to the orange vessel with hooks and chains.

Samara is meant to be approaching him, asking for help to get us out of here. What the fuck is going on?

'Inside,' Leo says, and they kick open the door to the captain's cabin. The ship sways violently as the tether to the breaker ship tightens, another roar of an engine as they pull us clear of the rocks.

They drop me roughly to the floor beside the toppled desk. Leo bends to me, anger etched into his face.

'This isn't just for me,' he growls. 'This is for all of them. Lorna, Dr Karsen, Professor Joffre . . . every one of those poor bastards Diego shot.'

'And Diego,' Samara says, and she kicks me, hard, in the gut. I jack-knife forward, gasping for air. She wipes her eyes, suddenly tearful. 'For all the people you've cursed.'

The door bangs behind them as they leave, the sound of footsteps moving quickly through the cabin. I hear the clank of the bow as the breaker pulls, again and again, the engine cutting out several times. I can't shift position, my legs bent behind and my arms stretched to the small of my back.

A dizzying bolt of panic – I can't get out. Jens is up the volcano. I'm going to drown like this. A couple of minutes and it's all over.

I roll over on one side, scanning the room for anything sharp that I might rub the cable ties against.

The ship sways heavily, the terrible whine of the bow deafening my screams as the breaker pulls the *Ormen* back.

And then, a deafening crash. It sounds like the bow has finally split, the whole floor tilting, flinging me hard against the far wall.

I can feel blood seeping through my hair, blood oozing quicky, the heat of it streaming down my face. The bookcase across the hole shifts, and it takes me a moment to figure out why my clothes are suddenly wet.

Black seawater is storming through the hole.

III

'Dom? Dominique?'

I hear my name from the upper cabin. Jens. Jens! I try to shout but the belt is too tight. Water laps up around my knees. A moment later, I see a set of shoes.

A knife, cutting me free. He pulls the belt from my mouth.

'Can you walk?' Jens says, and I nod.

'Good,' he says. 'But you'll need to swim.'

He pulls me through the lower deck and up the stairs to the main cabin. We're three hundred yards from the shore, the ship tipped forward as water floods through the hole of the captain's cabin.

'Jump,' Jens says when we reach the hull, and I do, I jump, down into the freezing water.

I panic in the depths, the shock of the cold and the stream of bubbles making me flail wildly for what seems like hours. The undertow of the *Ormen* almost pulls Jens back with it, a current that feels too strong to escape. I see him drift, his arms outstretched and his mouth open. Reaching out, I manage to grab his collar and pull up, up.

And then I haul him to the surface, holding him alongside me.

IV

Sand, then ice.

No sign of Samara and Leo.

We watch the orange ship move further and further away. Our chance of rescue disappearing.

The *Ormen* limps into the fog, the front tipped forward as though taking a bow.

The light is fading. Neither of us have our backpacks, our supplies. Our tents.

Jens gets to his feet, scanning the bay. His eyes settle on the turf houses, and I know what he's thinking. It's snowing again. We're drenched, freezing cold. We'll go indoors and spend the night there. Light a fire.

I stand up and link my arm through his as we head towards the nearest turf house.

'Do you know anything about that?' I say. 'Why Samara and Leo wanted to kill me?'

'They didn't want to kill you,' he says.

'You reckon they were just having a laugh by drowning me, then?'

He shakes his head. 'They can't drown you.'

I stop. 'What?'

He turns to face me. The look in his eyes is different, and I feel uneasy.

'Where did you buy your internet terminal, Dominique?'

'*What?*'

'Where?' he presses, shaking me. 'You can't remember, can you? You can't remember, because you never bought one. You didn't set up a TikTok account. You didn't google, you didn't film anything. It wasn't real.'

He's speaking so fast that the words are crashing into one another, his blue eyes wide and wild.

'Jens! Stop this!'

He claps his hands to my cheeks and pulls my face to his. 'That thing I was trying to tell you? You're dead, Dominique. We're all dead. All of us.'

I pull away from him. 'What are you talking about?' I say. Then, angry: 'Stop it. Stop saying this!'

'I know you remember,' he says.

'What?'

He says it again, and I step back. 'Why are you saying this?'

'You think you're still alive. But you're not. And neither am I.'

'Fuck you, Jens.'

I walk away, and when he reaches for my arm it might as well be a slap in the face. I pull away sharply, then spin around, my fists clenched. He sees.

'Nicky,' he says. 'You were born Dominique, but everyone called you Nicky. Your father was George Abney and your husband was—'

I hit him, then, a hard crack across the cheek. 'Don't you *dare* talk about my husband!' A sob steals away the rest. But, too late – it's as though the balloon has been pricked, and now the air seeps out, all the memories spilling from his words into my mind.

My husband. Allan.

The faces of the men.

Ellis. Lovejoy.

Daverley.

'Let me show you,' Jens is saying, his hand on my arm, and he is pulling me towards the pier overlooking the bay.

I'm asking him what he means by *let me show you*, until I realise that he has no interest in telling me. We are on the pier, the rotten wood making it difficult for my feet to find purchase. The force of the sea has ripped away most of the ice, carrying it in great chunks past the mermaid stone. If I slip, I'll fall in, and the memory of Samara seizes me.

'Let me go!' I scream, right into his face. For a moment, he looks at me with what seems to be tenderness. And then, in one sudden move, he shoves me in.

I feel my feet leave the ground, my body flying through the frigid air. I hit the water on my side, my feet catching a block of ice.

I'm under, the shock of it tearing through me. Freezing water gushes down my throat and up my nose, stinging my eyes. All I can think about is getting up, getting out, finding air, and warmth. My hands flail and I kick hard, but it's no use – the water is too cold, and soon my muscles won't work.

My lungs are screaming for oxygen, panic ripping through me, bright as a comet. I reach up but my hands find a block of ice instead of the surface.

And then, I stiffen. I can do nothing. Can't swim. I can only hope Jens sees sense and tries to pull me out.

But I don't drown.

Somehow, the water is no longer cold.

I look around, suspended in the dark. The panic softens. My lungs remember.

Shadows move in the depths, seaweed swaying there. I see a tail, long and black, flicking in the distance.

And I remember everything.

The Selkie Wife

October 1901
Cape Hooper, Greenland

Like all lies, the tale that Lovejoy told of Lír and the selkie wife was woven with threads of truth.

The sea was conscious.

This was the first thing she learned, once she left her body. Silvery strands of light radiated out from her like jute fibre, connecting her to the seals and whales and seaweed that drifted by, a vast web that spanned the planet in its past, present, and future dimensions.

Is this what you want?

A question posed by the sea.

Stay, and take revenge? Or go, and have peace?

There was no hesitation in her answer.

Stay.

A moment later, she felt something rest on her head, and when she reached up her fingers met the hard bone of the polar bear skull that Lovejoy had made her wear, the long fangs slender and sharp between her fingers. On her shoulders, two black guillemot wings, silken to the touch. The leg that had been human before joined the other, fusing, a muscular black tail. It was powerful enough to burst open the cage.

She swam out, relieved that her lungs were no longer straining for air. Bubbles drifted from her nose, and she saw clearly in the water. Her tail lengthened behind, twice the length of her former legs. Fish swam alongside as she moved into the blue depths. Above, the long shadow of the ship appeared, and she followed it, careful not to breach the surface.

Remember, the sea whispered, *that revenge is a stone tossed into water. You can't direct the ripples.*

The wind had heard her songs, and the dark wishes folded inside them. In the currents of the sea they materialised, a scrim, a wraith unleashed, craving retribution.

Now

I

I'm in one of the turf houses, curled up inside the cage. How did I get here? How am I dry?

I look out through the bars of the cage. It's the same one that Jens dragged from the sea. He is sitting next to me in a chair, and as my eyes adjust to the gloom, I see Leo and Samara there, too. I lurch. A moment ago I was underwater. Did I pass out? Surely they didn't rescue me?

'Jens?' I call out. My voice wavers, fearful. 'Will someone let me out?'

'We can't,' Jens says. 'The cage is in your head.'

I grip the bars and shake, the cold metal firm beneath my grip.

A moment ago I was underwater, my head bleeding. I reach up and touch it. There's a faint pain there, but no wound. No blood. I grab the bars and shake the door. Nobody reacts.

'Well, she's here now,' I hear Jens say. 'You still want your revenge?'

'Yes,' Leo says, right as Samara says, 'No.'

'What?' Leo says, turning to her. Samara clasps her hands together, and she looks tearful.

'Can someone tell me what's going on?' I ask.

'We're dead,' Jens says flatly. 'All four of us.'

'We're not dead, Jens,' I say, a sob in my voice. 'We're all very much alive.'

I just want him to let me out. I want to go back to the ship, and light a fire, and feel the safety of the cabin and the wood hold me close.

'Not in the real world,' he says in a low voice. 'Nice to see you're remembering things, though. Aren't you?'

I open my mouth to shout out, *I'm not dead!* but I remember the smell of Captain Willingham's cabin, teak and the earthy tang of pipe smoke, the amber glow of his oil lamp on the desk, my own reflection staring back at me from the window behind him. Beyond that, a strip of ocean, black as night, and the thump of the waves against the hull. The sway of the boat churning my stomach.

You must have stowed away.

And then they violated me, over and over again.

When I killed Lovejoy, they put me in the cage and threw it into the water.

The dreams I had. They were my own memories.

Everything was different. Something had switched inside me. I could see that now. I didn't feel time the way I used to. I would go to sleep and wake a week or even a year later. I would look out of a window and watch the seasons change, the trees turning from green to red to black naked branches, stripped of their leaves by wind and rain. The world around me moved on a different set of wheels. I didn't change, didn't grow old. *But I still felt like me.* I saw my face when I looked in a mirror. I got hungry, and tired, and happy, and angry, and I had dreams.

Sometimes I met people who spoke to me, and I knew they were in the river of time that I was in. They were like me, in the world and not in it, moving at a different speed. Unseen, invisible, but here.

Dead.

I remember.

I remember the man in the park, and waking in the hold of the ship. I remember the apologetic smiles of the men who appeared at my cabin door.

I remember what happened next.

I remember Daverley's hand being cut off. They thought he had helped me kill Lovejoy, but he didn't. All he had ever done was try to protect me. He died from blood loss, never returning home.

I remember taking revenge on the residents of Skúmaskot for burning down the whaling station, for preventing me from escaping when I might have had a chance to return home. To return to Allan. To live the life we promised each other.

'Let me out,' I say again, rattling the bars with my fists. 'Please. We can just leave, OK? The four of us. It doesn't matter that the coastguard have left. We can use the drone to help find our way . . .'

'We can't get out,' Leo snaps. 'Like, ever. Skúmaskot is a labyrinth.'

I stare at him. 'What do you mean, a *labyrinth*?'

'I mean, you walk and you walk and you walk and you'll come back to the ship. You go in any direction, you run as hard as you can, and you will always, always come back to the ship. Swim, walk, run, dig . . . always the same. Circles. Every cave, every current . . .' he stops, his face shining with tears of anger. 'It's because of you. You are doing it.'

I shake my head. 'I'm not. I'm promise you, I'm not doing anything . . .'

'I believe you,' Jens says.

'Oh fuck you, Jens,' Leo says, kicking the air in frustration.

'I do,' Jens tells me, ignoring Leo. 'I don't think you are consciously doing this.'

'So, what – it makes it OK that she's doing it *subconsciously*?' Leo asks Jens. 'We're all in her fucking self-created hell, her own personal Valhalla, and we literally *cannot leave* . . .'

'We're trapped in your nightmare,' Samara screams, her voice bouncing off the hard surfaces of the room. 'We're inside your fucking memories! The horses in the cave? They weren't real. They were your memories. The cameras, laptops . . . all in your head. And you possessed Leo. The poem on the table . . .' She starts to sob. 'I didn't know a ghost could possess another ghost. Jesus Christ.'

'She's not possessing anyone,' Jens says quietly. 'It's the legacy of what happened to her on the *Ormen*. Trauma is an element, remember?'

I listen, trying to make sense of it all. My heart is beating so fast, and I feel nauseous. How can any of this be real?

'I just want to go home,' Samara says after a thoughtful silence. 'Like, wherever we're meant to go. I want to move *on*.'

Samara tells me she was a field recordist working on a research project in Svalbard. Her parents were so proud. They'd grown up in Jim Crow, and here was their daughter, getting a doctorate, then a postdoc for a project in the Arctic.

'We were on a ship. The *Ormen*.' She squeezes her eyes shut. 'There was a guy from Argentina, Diego. Another postdoc, really sweet. I liked him a lot, and we really hit it off. And Leo . . .' She turns her eyes to him, and I realise he was there, too.

'I'd felt on edge the whole trip,' Samara says. 'I kept having nightmares. I put it down to being seasick, being away from home. Then I starting to hear Diego ranting. We all did.'

'What was he ranting about?' Jens asks.

'He said he kept seeing someone, or something,' Leo says.

'A woman, or a mermaid. He stopped coming out of his cabin. Then Professor Joffre found him in his room half-bleeding to death. He'd cut his feet apart. We thought he was having a psychotic episode. We called the station on Svalbard to see if we could arrange for him to go home,' Samara says. 'And then he had a gun. I remember him turning the gun on Leo.' Her voice drops to a whisper. 'Diego shot him.'

'I remember trying to tie my T-shirt around Leo's leg to stop the bleeding,' Samara says, her voice trembling. 'And then there were more gunshots, huge bangs, and everyone fell around me. Diego pointed his shotgun at me and I pleaded with him not to. I could see he was crying and mumbling that he was sorry. And he shot me.'

I feel like someone is pulling me backwards into an enormous hole, and then I'm falling and can't stop. I hear the gunshots, like the popping sounds of the ice through Samara's microphone. I remember Leo racing across the bay, leaping and ducking and diving, as though he's trying to dodge a bullet.

Eternally trying to dodge the thing that killed him.

'And then what do you remember?' Jens says.

Samara opens her mouth to speak, but the words don't come immediately.

My mind flickers with bright images, nauseating in their strength.

I haunted the horses, the prized horses of the men who owned the fishery, sending them to their deaths. I haunted the people who lived there, sending them running with fear, until not a single soul remained.

I hid in the wood, in the oil cans, in the hold of the ship, small as a knot. I changed form. I became.

I saw the explorers who stayed on the *Ormen*, heard their conversations. Picked up the shifting languages and turns of phrase, their technologies. Time moved in a staccato frenzy, whole years feeling like minutes. I was present and absent at the same time. I was a trace, a fragment. A haunted haunting.

Leo has calmed down, his arms folded and his chin to his chest like a scolded child. 'Let me ask you something: what's the definition of insanity?'

'What?'

'It's doing the same thing over and over and over again and expecting something to *change*.'

I blink. 'I don't understand.'

Leo throws his head back and laughs. It's a horrible sound, a forced laugh. The sound of torment.

'Do you even realise how many times we've tried to fix this?' he says. 'How many times we've tried to get you to know, I don't know, do whatever you need to do in order to let us leave?'

'No,' I say.

'Two hundred and twelve,' Samara says in a low voice. 'This is attempt two hundred and twelve.'

'You used to hang out in the turf houses,' Leo says. 'You would only come on to the ship at night.'

'You spent the longest time in the cage,' Samara says. 'You were this . . . creature. A selkie. Half human half fish half wolf, or fox.'

'That's three halves,' Leo says.

Jens looks up at me, tugging at his pink beanie. 'And then, you changed. The tail went. Your face became more human. You became like this.'

He runs his hands down in front of me. 'Human,' he adds.

Samara gives a loud, pained sigh. 'It gave us hope.'

'We hoped that the wreck being broken would change something,' Jens says sadly. 'And when you said something was "Lovecraftian", we thought that this time was different.'

'About twenty years ago,' Leo adds, 'I showed you a book on the ship by H.P. Lovecraft, and we talked about things that were in his style. You know, *Lovecraftian*. It was a sign you were starting to remember.'

Flashes of memory spool in my mind, erratic, a bombardment of smells and textures. Leo screaming at me to remember, to wake up. Samara on her knees by the pier, begging me to let her go. Countless times. I didn't know how to do what she asked.

I couldn't.

Finally, my thoughts turn to Morag, and it burns in me. The guilt of it. How can I ever make it right? The effects of guilt are stronger than any haunting.

It changed me, over and over and over again.

II

The cage melts away. In a moment, I'm sitting on one of the empty chairs with the others.

I look around, astonished.

'What happened?' I ask.

'The cage is only real in your mind,' Jens says. 'In this world. Or realm, whatever you want to call it. You must have done something.'

'I didn't,' I say.

'You did it without realising, then,' he says.

I look down at my hands, my knees. I still feel pain. I eat. I bleed.

I think of the woman I saw on the beach, at the bottom of the ladder, at the three rocks further down the coast. It was me, traces of who I'd been as a haunting. My memories eclipsing, superimpositions of the past and the present. Present absences, with all the ruptures in time and space that that creates. Like guilt.

'You killed me,' Leo tells me, the anger burning in his eyes. 'I fucking hate you. I've been stuck here for decades. I wanted to trap you in that fucking ship and sink you forever to the bottom of the ocean.'

'Easy, now,' Jens says.

Leo looks like he wants to kill me. He can't, I realise, but he can still hurt me. I don't know the rules here. In this realm.

'I'm sorry,' I say, glancing at Leo.

He scoffs. 'You're sorry? That's it?'

'Just . . . let us go home,' Samara says, holding up her hands. 'Whatever you're doing to keep us here . . . just stop, OK?'

I shake my head. 'I don't know what I'm doing.'

Leo lunges at me, but Jens reaches out to stop him, and his shirt falls away, revealing his stump. Osteosarcoma, he told me. Liar. He's Daverley. He risked his life on the *Ormen* for me. Jens Daverley. I hadn't realised that he had died, too, but I see it now, like a shared memory – he bled out when they cut off his hand. He never returned to Dundee.

I think of the way he spoke of his wife, Eilidh. I've kept him here. Maybe if he left, he could be with her.

Maybe it's too late.

'I'm sorry,' I tell him. Then, turning to Leo and Samara, 'I'm sorry about Diego. About everything.'

I'm pretty sure it's not enough for what I've done. I have died a thousand times over. The girl who was drowned on the *Ormen* was filled with revenge. Delirious with both trauma and guilt, she drove the living to their deaths out of revenge. Some part of her was me, despite how much it hurts to admit it.

But I don't want revenge anymore.

Something has changed. I just want to go home.

III

We're outside now, the four of us standing on the rocky outcrop facing the sea. The orange ship is a smudge in the distance. The *Ormen* bobs above the surface, a hard triangle of metal against the liquid dark of the ocean.

Samara gives a gasp, and I turn to see a shape on the tideline. A wet head, shoulders. A long grey dress. Her back turned to us.

Fear runs through me, sharp and swift as a javelin. But this time, I don't shrink. I force myself to move towards her, keeping my eyes fixed on her in case she disappears again. When my feet reach the sand I break into a run, screaming for her to turn around.

Turn around! Turn around!

She doesn't move. I get closer, all the terror I felt before turning to fury. I need to see her face.

She doesn't turn, her slender back to me. Her pale dress is worn and stained with blood. I move in front of her, my fear electric, a vivid current pulsing through me.

Her jaw is stretched open in a frozen scream, her dark eyes creased and bright with anger. Her eyes are white, no pupils, seeing nothing.

She is a trace, a quavering memory clutched by time. A haunting.

366

She is me, then. A version of myself. A trace.

I step forward, pressing my face to hers, and in a moment I seem to absorb her. All the hate and fury fusing with the hope and sadness and grief I didn't even realise was inside me.

The mists swirl, black sand snakes in a flurry around my ankles.

She's gone. I hear a dog bark. Behind me at the outcrop, Samara is on her knees, her arms around a black dog. I see Leo running past her towards another man. He leaps on him, his legs wrapping around his waist, his arms gripping his neck.

Jens approaches, and as I turn to him the light shifts.

The *Ormen* has disappeared beneath the surface. Jens keeps his eyes fixed on the land ahead, and right as I ask him what he's looking for, a figure appears.

A woman. She has soft eyes and a face that melts when she sees Jens. I see him raise a hand to his mouth, his eyes softening.

'Eilidh,' he whispers. He races towards her, glancing back just one last time, before disappearing into the mist.

I stand, watching the last of the sun liquefy into the hills. I'm glad for Jens, truly I am. And I'm glad that I had a chance to apologise to Samara and Leo.

But I'm alone. *That's* what's been different this time. This time I've felt alone. Felt *lonely*. Craved something that only someone else can give me.

The black sand stretches out at either side, the ocean like a toppled tombstone. I have been searching all this time for my home. But I could never imagine where that was.

It was never a place.

A shadow lengthens up the sand, a crestless wave. A head and shoulders.

And I recognise him, the lines of his strong form, the angles of his face.

It's Allan, heading towards me. Oh God.

The last of the light sweeps across his face. He smiles at me, and my heart leaps. I can tell he wants to go back to Dundee. To our home on Faulkner Street. Just for a while. To remember what it was like to be together in those early years of our marriage. To remember each other.

To remember our daughter.

Behind us, I hear the drumming of hooves. It is a low hum, growing louder as I strain my eyes to see into the fog. There they are: Icelandic ghost horses, untethered from the bodies that lie broken in the cave. I count two dozen of them, thundering their hooves against the sand, blonde and chestnut manes flying up as they race across the bay.

Thriving in the dark.

Author's Note

Memory and trauma pervade all my work, but I wanted to write about them more consciously, or intentionally, than I have in the past. I have always believed that ghost stories examine memory and trauma, how the past inhabits the present, how our experience of time can be erratic and non-linear, perhaps even a kind of disorienting spiral. Trauma disrupts our sense of the present even more drastically; in my own life, I've recognised patterns through the lens of generational trauma, repetitions that can be galling, flashbacks that can feel like a haunting – as though time is a prison.

I set myself a challenge to try and write about these ideas, or to write *through* them. As with my previous novels, the setting was important: place is how we forge meaning from time, the architecture of time chaptered by tide, stone, and wood. And of course, place can clutch memory; a site can haunt, tugging at the unconscious in uncanny ways.

A ship came to mind, both as a wreck and a moving vessel. I resisted this idea at first, knowing how much research it would take to write authentically about a whaling ship crossing the High Arctic in 1901. But then a link popped up on my Twitter feed, a news article from 1883 about a polar bear that escaped from a whaling ship after being captured during an Arctic hunt, prowling the streets of Dundee. It felt like a sign. And it felt like I should definitely use the newspaper article in my book.

I read 19th century newspaper articles and researched contemporary scholarship on the history of Arctic whaling and the Dundee whaling industry. I interviewed people with knowledge of ships and polar exploration. Although I had been to Reykjavik – for a few days in 2019 to teach at the university – I felt I needed to explore the Icelandic wilderness to solidify the fictional village of Skúmaskot (translating as 'dark corner') in my mind. Luckily, Creative Scotland awarded me a grant to carry out a short research trip, and in the spring of 2022, I drove to Iceland's south coast, visiting the famous (and dangerous) black sand beach of Reynisfjara, then up to the Snæfellsnes peninsula, where the glacier-topped strato-volcano Snæfellsjökull has sat for seven hundred thousand years.

From there, via ferry, I went to the Westfjords (where the road transformed to a gravel path for about sixty kilometres), where I visited the wreck of the *Garðar BA 64*, an old whaling ship grounded at Patreksfjörður. Though this vessel differs from the *Ormen*, which I imagined as a barque-rigged sail- and steam-hybrid built around 1880, visiting the wreck was a pivotal moment. There is something about visiting a setting in person that always seems to knit the scattered tendrils of a story together; maybe this is all the more powerful after the lockdowns of 2020-21, when so much of our lives shifted to virtual spaces – being *present* is something I still don't take for granted. Without giving away any spoilers, exploring the *Garðar BA 64* helped me push my story deeper, and the risks I knew I wanted to take with my ideas of memory and trauma felt a little more possible. I had the unlucky experience of losing a month's work on the novel to a glitch in my laptop (an experience which has taught me to triple back up everything!) – I'll admit that I cried for a good few days! But being in Iceland helped return many of the ideas I thought had been lost forever. And, when I returned to Reykjavik, I found myself standing on the word 'Skúmaskot', which someone had written across a pavement. It felt like a good omen.

The history of whaling is stridently masculine. Having researched the policing of female bodies for my previous novel, *The Ghost Woods,* and upon discovering the long-held superstition that a woman's presence – her body – on a whaler was a curse, I felt compelled to explore the feminine within that space, particularly in terms of the folkloric imaginings of femalehood. I find it intriguing that so much sea-faring lore reimagines sexual transgression and the female body; the water's edge figured as a liminal space, a site to imagine those human experiences outside the norm. In many oral traditions, the mythical figures of mermaids, sirens, and selkies evoke notions of illicit desire and sexual violation, often in terms of a woman who is captured by a man for his sexual pleasure. In the legend of the selkie wife, a man steals a selkie's skin to trap her ashore, whereby she is forced to marry him and bare his offspring. Later, her seal skin is returned by her children, allowing her to escape to the sea. Violence and vengeance figure brightly in these stories, too; just think of the sirens in Greek myth who lure sailors to their deaths. I love how these myths explore chimeras and monstrosity, the way they seem to disrupt binaries of gender and species, and how they force us to contemplate our relationship to place, and to the past.

I should say that the tale here of the mermaid stone and selkie wife, including Reid's shanty about Lír, are my own inventions. As I imagined Nicky's story, I found myself reflecting on how traumatic experiences can leave us feeling altered ourselves, right down to our identity, perhaps at a cellular level. Trauma can feel like a theft of one's skin, leaving

371

us vulnerable, uncannily *othered* from one's past self. At a time when language could not fully capture the effects of trauma, perhaps myth and metaphor served instead. Perhaps they still serve best.

C.J. Cooke, June 2023

Acknowledgements

I am so very grateful to everyone who helped me bring this novel into the world:

Alice Lutyens, my fabulous agent, for always being in my corner.

Lucy Stewart at HarperCollins UK and Jessica Wade at Berkley (US), and of course Katie Lumsden, for collaboration and encouragement and zingy ideas that set my brain alight, and for helping me find the best possible story in the quarry of possibilities.

Kimberley Young, Lynne Drew, and all at HarperCollins UK, the fabulous team at HarperCollins Canada, to Claire Zion and all at Penguin Random House US, to Deborah Schneider, my lovely US agent. Luke Speed (thank you for encouraging me to set this on a ship), and Anna Weguelin, Olivia Bignold, Caoimhe White, Samuel Joseph Loader, Liz Dennis, and all at Curtis Brown. Thank you all. I feel so unbelievably privileged to work with the absolute best in the business. Your talent and brilliance are both constantly inspiring.

Creative Scotland for funding a research trip to Iceland – finding the *Garðar BA 64* shipwreck in the Westfjords will forever be one of the best days of my life.

Carol Knott, fellow Moniack Mhor resident, who gave expert advice on the history of Dundee Whaling, and to Natasha Pulley for ship talk – all errors are mine.

Professor Willy Maley at the University of Glasgow for

sending fantastic scholarly articles on Iceland and Greenland whaling, and my colleagues in Creative Writing: Colin, Elizabeth, Zoë, Louise, Kerry, Jen, and Nicky. Thank you all for your support and friendship.

Angharad for the mermaid. She kept me going, you know.

My husband and children, for too much to mention here, but ultimately, for love.

Ralph and Winston, our darling dogs, for always being near (and often on top of me) while I wrote this book.

Booksellers, book bloggers/champions, and readers who have championed my books – my absolute love and thanks to you. There were times when your messages fished me out of dark places.

Hjörvar, my Icelandic brother-in-law, who sadly passed much, much too young, during the writing of this book. I hope this would have made you proud.